THE
SYREN'S
MUTINY

book one

JESSICA S. TAYLOR

To those who wanted a second chance at their dreams…
you can do this.

PLAYLIST

Black Sea - Natasha Blume
Blood On My Name - The Brothers Bright
Ship in a Bottle - fin
Run Boy Run - Woodkid
Dear Fellow Traveler - Sea Wolf
Human - Rag'n'Bone Man
Become the Beast - Karliene
Glitter & Gold - Barns Courtney
Sinners - Barns Courtney
Soldier - Tommee Profitt, Fleurie
Achilles Come Down - Gang of Youths
Master of Tides - Lindsey Stirling
Way Down We Go - Kaleo
Everybody Wants to Rule the World - Lorde
Bad Dream - Ruelle
Trouble - Valerie Broussard
Hoist the Colours - MALINDA
Hellfire - Barns Courtney
Take Me to Church - MILCK
I'm a Wanted Man - Royal Deluxe
Hell or High Water - The Rescues
Start a War - Klergy
Woke Up a Rebel - Reuben and the Dark

Pronunciation Guide

Characters:

Brigid (bridge-id)
Caelum (cae-luhm)
Sorcha (sor-sha)
Maira (my-ruh)
Cliodnha (klee-uh-nah)
Kellan (kehl-uhn)
Nehalennia (neh-ha-lin-ia)
Kyla (kye-luh ko-vahn)

Places:

Gaisin (go-shin)
Straits of Marbh (marv)
Seòltan Seas (shole-tuhn)
Bhodheas (vo-dees)
Tuathnach (too-ath-nack)
Caladhan (call-uh-han)
Neamh Na Mara (neve-nuh-mar-uh)
Faileas Seas (fay-lish)

FAIRPORT
CAELUM'S COTTAGE
TUATH
THE NEHALENNIA
WHITCAIRN
SEOLTAN SEA
STRAITS
SYREN'S CAVES
NEAMH NA MARA
DÀRNA COTHRO
TREÒIR COVE
CLIODHNA'S FORTRESS
CALADH

GAISIN
ACH
FINN'S COTTAGE
BRINEMOORE
BRINEMOORE HARBOR
FAILEAS SEA
MARBH
TEICH
BHODHEAS
PRÍOMH
N

Author's Note

This book contains mature themes and scenes and is not recommended for readers under 17.

Content includes scenes of violence, blood/gore, injury descriptions, dismemberment, death and murder, moderate sexual content, imprisonment, and other themes that may be triggering to some readers.
If any of these would be harmful to you, please protect your mental health.

For a full list of tropes, tags, and trigger warnings, including the level and the chapter/location of each potential trigger, please visit my website or scan the QR code.

A list of the triggers and their locations is also included at the back of this book, after the Acknowledgements page.

If you have any questions or concerns, or if there is a specific trigger not listed here that you'd like to know about, please email me at: jess@authorjessicastaylor.com

CHAPTER ONE

BRIGID

There was a certain satisfaction that came with the last breath of a dying man. Feeling it ghost across my lips, knowing I was the last thing that man would ever feel, was empowering. It was also time consuming. Men were slow to drown, slow to do anything except show anger.

The man I had in my grasp was desperately trying to free himself. His cheeks bulged as he pulled at my grip in a pathetic attempt to get back to the surface that was taunting him just out of reach. He managed to rip an arm away from me, but he only succeeded in tearing his own flesh open on my talons, tinging the water around us pink.

While he was able to get some space from me, it didn't last long. Using the strength of my tail, I surged forward and wrapped my talons back around his arm, pulling him close to me.

Bubbles escaped from his nose and mouth, and his body thrashed, still trying to escape. His obvious panic and suffering did nothing to me, and I only watched in utter indifference as he continued to try to break free of my grip. But I was a syren. And he was just a man.

His movements slowed, and he cast one last longing glance at the light fracturing down through the surface of the water. He tried to pull away again, but his strength was gone, and the attempt was pitiful. Watching him, I bared my pointed teeth at him, intent on making his last emotion be that of fear. Not of drowning, but of *me*.

The thrashing of the man in my arms finally ceased, lulling the water back into brief calmness once more, and I pulled back, supporting his body floating in the water. Blank, unseeing eyes stared back at me as I released his body into the cold depths. I watched him sink into the water, seeing his limbs float away from his body, reaching up toward the surface as if he could still escape his fate. His death stirred nothing in my chest. He was simply another face I would soon forget, another insignificant man who would never harm a woman again.

Beyond the faint ripples left by the man's sinking body, I observed Maira releasing her own corpses into the sea. My fellow syren was blonde, with an anger that rivaled the men we targeted. The wreckage of the ship our victims had inhabited now surrounded us, the splintered wood bobbing in the waves and shredded canvas blocking the sunlight from reaching the depths as it sank.

"Is that all of them?" Maira asked, her sharp voice bored

as she dodged the debris to move toward me in the water. A flutter of a sail fell in her path, and her talons ripped through it with ease. She moved through the gap in the fabric, sidling up beside me.

Searching through the waters before us, I saw only sinking bodies. There was no one left alive in these waters but us. "Yes."

"Let's get back." She dismissively turned away from the ship, swishing her lavender tail to power through the water, leaving a rippling of bubbles behind her.

Casting a last glance over my shoulder at the destruction we had caused, I turned and followed my companion back toward our home, *Neamh na Mara*. The heavens of the sea.

The sea caves I now resided in were beautiful, jutting up from the ocean floor and creating a sanctuary that protected us from anyone or anything that might stumble across our home. The caves' passageways, forged from years of the sea's relentless power, twined and burrowed through the cragged rock. Swimming through the arched main entry, Maira and I moved from the tunnels to a large open cavern.

The others had already gathered there, resting on the age-smoothed stalagmites rising from the sea floor. Kyla, with her dark ebony skin and darker hair, watched us closely as we entered, her bright gold tail swishing lazily. Next to her sat Iona and Nerina, who were not related, yet looked as if they could be twins with their light brown skin and caramel hair. Even turned into syrens, their tails were similarly colored with splashes of purple and blue.

"Brigid, Maira, report." Our queen's melodic voice was confident and proud, demanding respect in the same way the bold jut of her chin and set of her bare shoulders did. Her white hair lifted off her shoulders with a stray current flowing through the caves.

"One ship. No survivors," Maira said from beside me, her scales catching the low light as her tail moved restlessly. "There was no harm to us."

"Good, they deserved to be punished." Cliodhna glided toward us through the water, her silver tail lazily swaying back and forth, the light reflecting off her scales and bouncing onto her pale skin. My heart swelled at the pride in her voice. "My creations, you did well, as always."

Both Maira and I respectfully bowed our heads to the one who had saved us, rescued us from the cruelty of men, and breathed new life into our veins. Our queen raised her webbed fingers and laid them gently upon my head, trailing her sharp nails through my fiery red-orange locks, which undulated behind me in the ever-moving water.

"The wrath of men will never be as great as the wrath of the sea," I said, repeating the words she had said to us often. Taking in the flowing white hair that trailed behind her, her sharp cheekbones and piercing icy blue eyes, Cliodhna reminded me of a queen in every sense of the word. And she had chosen me. She had saved me when I had been thrown overboard many years ago. Unbidden, thoughts of my past returned. My stomach twisted at the memories, my heart racing. Remembering the icy chill of the water as I was thrown into the sea, my body shivered, my skin tightening. The cold of the water didn't affect me now, not in this form, but the ghost of icy needles lingered.

"That's right," Cliodhna said solemnly, moving her hand to my face. Her nails caught on my skin, the webbing scraping across the roundness of my cheeks as she stroked it. Even in the cold water that filled our caves, her fingers were frigid, and I shivered again. "You all are my greatest creations, my greatest pride."

My head bowed again, as did the heads of the others, as we honored our goddess. Our queen demanded respect, but we would all freely give it. I raised my head back up to look at Cliodhna. "You saved us all. We owe you our lives."

"That you do," she said, looking back at us with a smile that displayed her mouth full of pointed teeth. It wasn't a friendly smile. It didn't reach her eyes, but instead settled on her lips only, not disturbing her cheeks or wrinkling her forehead. "How many men today?"

Maira swam forward; she was always so eager to answer. Maira was bloodthirsty, and out of all of us here, she enjoyed inflicting pain upon men with her song and her touch more than the rest of us. "It was a small crew, ten or so. We drowned them all after they jumped into the water. The ship drifted and ran aground."

Cordelia, another redhead like me, watched us with interest, her blue eyes more focused on Maira than me. She smiled widely at the news.

Cliodhna raised her chin, baring her teeth in a semblance of a smile. "Good. There must be no one left to bear witness to our existence."

"As you command," Maira responded with another low bow of her head.

I was indifferent to the suffering of men, numb after all these years of killing the men who fell prey to our song. Their lives—and their deaths—held no interest to me, not anymore. I killed because I was told to, because that's what we did as syrens and servants of Cliodhna. It made me feel no sadness. It made me feel no happiness. It just…was.

"We have survived this long because no one knows we truly exist. Those who do witness us are called crazy and written off by their people. But as more and more people travel through my waters, the likelihood of someone believing them grows." Cliodhna's voice was firm and brokered no arguments, though none of us would ever argue with her.

"Are we in danger?" I asked. My stomach clenched, old feelings of anxiety threatening to bubble up again. Clenching my fists, I dug my talons into the palms of my hands, giving myself something else to focus on. I was not that girl any longer. *I* was the one to be feared now. *I* was the threat.

Cliodhna looked at me, her icy blue eyes softening almost imperceptibly. "Not at all, my child. We are safe down here. And men will never be a threat to us. I promised you that when I took you all in, and I will keep my word. I am growing in my powers and will continue to do so to keep you all safe. But we must be cautious, even still."

"We will be," Maira vowed.

We all nodded along with Maira, Kyla moving from her seat at the rocks to cross her arm over her chest and bow her head. "We will take care of each other."

"Men will never be a threat to us. Know that," Cliodhna repeated, jutting her chin out proudly and looking around at all of us. "I will protect you, of course, but more importantly, you have the power and the strength to protect yourselves now."

The room fell silent then, and I pondered the news Cliodhna had given. The depths of the seas were our home, and if we were discovered, they would attempt to control us as they attempted to control the sea's surface. Men roamed the seas, fishing and trading, and pretended that they alone held dominion over the sea. A delusional belief, but one that had permeated mankind as time drew on.

Being syrens made us powerful, but we all had troubling histories with men, and I knew it unnerved each of us to think about the possibility. Anger flared in Maira's eyes, and her fists clenched at her sides.

In the corner of the cavern, Kyla's face turned resolved, but I could see the fear shining in the amber of her eyes. Of us all, she had the most reason to be afraid of men, rather than just vengeful. Before she had been a syren, Kyla had been a wife and a mother. One day, she had angered her husband, and he threw her from a cliff in a fit of rage.

The oldest of us, Kyla, had been a guide to each of us as we entered the fold, and seeing her discomfort made my own body tense. I fought back the anxiety that had taken me years to overcome after my transformation. Men would not harm me again. I would rather die—no, I would rather *kill* than be afraid of being harmed by men.

"Go rest for the evening," Cliodhna said, raising her chin. Her fingers flicked dismissively, motioning for us to disperse. Without a second glance, she turned and left the cavern, heading toward her own chambers.

The others began to follow, moving toward their rooms within the caves. Kyla caught my gaze and nodded to the side, asking me to linger.

"You're clenching your shoulders again," she said, her soft voice full of concern. She reached out and grabbed my hand, her dark skin contrasting with my own pale flesh. "What happened?"

I shrugged, pulling my fingers away from hers gently. Her pity and concern was not what I needed right now. It would only make me give more attention to the emotions I sought to quell. "I'm fine, Kyla."

She raised an eyebrow, quirking up the corner of her lip in a sardonic smile. "No, you're not. But if you don't want to talk about it, I understand."

Kyla had always been able to see through me—see through all of us. And I knew she was concerned, but my anxiety was something I had to deal with on my own. Or rather, something I had to push down on my own. Regardless of what I did with my anxiety, I didn't need Kyla's help with it. "I'm fine."

She looked at me for a long moment, her dark amber eyes drilling holes in me, as if she could see into my very soul. "Okay. Goodnight, Brigid. May your dreams give you guidance."

"And yours," I replied, forcing a smile onto my face.

CHAPTER TWO
BRIGID

Life passed normally for the next few days. Our lives as syrens were routine; we patrolled the waters, searching for ships and men that our queen deemed marked for ruin. Despite how busy the waters were becoming, we didn't wreck every ship we came across. We had to be careful with how we attacked to keep from being seen.

There were eight of us, including Cliodhna, and even though we were powerful and deadly, we were no match for taking on multiple ships worth of men. When we found ships that fit our guidelines, Cliodhna would give us the final answer on if the ship and the crew would meet their end.

Today, Kyla and Nerina had just returned from their own patrol. They had been successful in wrecking a lone merchant vessel off the coast and killing the small crew. With any crew larger than fifteen, the rest of us would join the duo on patrol to ensure there were no survivors. Our song did most of the work, causing unbearable agony to any who heard it, driving them to madness and eventually ruin. But occasionally, if we weren't careful, some managed to get away before they drowned.

"You did well today, my daughters," Cliodhna praised, raising her chin and offering a small smile to Kyla. She had been with Cliodhna for the longest, and Cliodhna was softest toward her, though even that did not mean much.

Cliodhna was detached. Her emotions often bordered on cold, but then again, she was a queen. Her role in this relationship wasn't to be one of us, but to lead us.

"Thank you, my queen," Kyla said softly, returning the smile with a deep nod.

Cliodhna's head snapped up, looking up toward the surface beyond the cave walls that made up our home, her eyes glowing white as they peered far beyond the rock. "There is a woman in my waters."

I smiled at her words, showing off my equally pointed teeth in a less-than-friendly grin. A woman in the water likely meant that men had thrown her overboard. And it meant that we could seek revenge. While Cliodhna's previous words had brought back old feelings of anxiety and anger, this part was familiar. Rescuing a woman would give me something to hold on to, something tangible to focus on. A purpose. And more importantly, an outlet for my rage. "Let's go fetch her."

Together, my fellow syrens and I swam off, following our queen toward our destination. Our tails slashed through the water as we moved, shining and sparkling in the fractured light leaking through the surface. We weaved and dodged rocks and sea life, eager to get to the surface as we made our way to save a woman who had been undoubtedly shown the cruelty of men. We *would* save her.

As we moved closer and closer to the surface, bubbles formed around a figure sinking beneath the waves. She wore a flowing white dress, which wrapped around her body, making it even harder for her to kick and stay afloat. But she tried, her petite body thrashing and flailing through the water, trying to right herself. My chest tightened watching her. The familiarity of the situation stung as I surged toward her.

Maira and I reached her first, reaching up and wrapping our webbed fingers around her ankles and wrists. We pulled her down into the water more and adjusted her body to be upright. Maira waved her free hand, creating a bubble of breathable air around both of us and the woman. Her chest heaved as she glanced back and forth between us and the surface.

"Stay calm, we are here to help you," I said, holding onto her gently but firmly. Her eyes darted between Maira and me, but she finally stopped thrashing, likely realizing that she could breathe. I moved a hand to rest gently on her upper arm rather than holding her tightly. "We are here to save you."

"Who...what are you?" the younger girl gasped out, still trying to catch her breath. Her long, dark hair clung to her face and neck in heavy ropes, a stark contrast to her alabaster skin. She was thin, her sopping wet gown clinging to her bones inside the bubble.

"You are safe with us," Maira responded proudly, tugging

the woman gently toward her. She was careful with her talons, consciously flexing her fingers out to avoid digging the sharp points into the woman's skin. "My name is Maira, and this is Brigid. The others behind us will meet you when you are ready."

The woman's dark eyes, wide and frantic, darted up to the shadow of the ship that still lingered above us. The fear radiating off her was palpable, and I was overwhelmed with a desire to wrap this girl in my arms and shield her from the world. Despite that she only looked a few years younger than my own twenty-five, I felt protective already. My childhood had been cut short by my own misadventures with men, ending with me being thrown overboard in a similar fashion, and I didn't want this little one meeting the same fate.

Determined, I caught her gaze with my own and held it. "They will not hurt you again. We'll make sure of it."

"How?" she whispered, obviously afraid. My stomach hurt at the pain I was seeing in this young woman. It was like looking into a mirror and seeing myself all those years ago. Again, the feelings from my past bubbled up and threatened to break out of the chest I had locked them in. I would not be weak. This young woman in front of me needed strong and steady right now; breaking down could wait until I was alone.

I nodded over at the others swimming behind us at a distance, directing them to take care of the ship and the men above. They returned the nods to me, jetting toward the surface and the ship resting in the water. These men would not live, not after throwing this woman overboard. My attention turned back to her. "Those men will face the same fate they gave to you. They will have to sink or swim."

The young woman shuddered, her eyes closing tightly and her jaw clenching. She took a deep breath before opening her eyes wide. "You'll kill them?"

Surprised at the empathy still in her voice, I raised an eyebrow. I had not expected that reaction from her, not when she was so clearly impacted by what she had been through. "You want them to live? They just threw you into the sea."

She looked down, chewing on her lip. "They did. But they shouldn't have to die for that."

"They were ready to let you die for far less." I tilted my head as I studied her. The look of shame on her face was concerning, and I guessed there was more to her story than just her guilt over these men possibly dying. "Why did they throw you over?"

"Because I'm a woman. That was all the reason they needed, it seems." Her voice hardened, the soft and timid tone giving way to anger of her own.

"Sounds like men." Anger flooded through me, my fists clenched and my talons itched to tear through flesh, but I tamped it down. This young woman had seen enough anger for the day and did not need any more of it from me. She needed empathy and support. She reminded me of myself, of the girl who had died in these waters.

Maira's own face hardened at our conversation. Thankfully, she remained silent, simply holding the woman upright with me. I feared if Maira spoke, she would only make things worse and more overwhelming.

"I just wanted to be with my beau, Owen. My father forbade it, but I ran off anyway to meet him in the south, in Bhodheas;

we were to start our new life together," she explained, pain crossing her features as her brows pinched together. "I paid for passage on the merchant ship, but apparently, they just wanted my money. The crew members I had paid told the captain. And the captain didn't like a woman on his ship, even if she had legally paid. He said I would be bad luck, and that the trip through the Straits of Marbh would be hard enough without me aboard."

Understanding her story and her sadness, I nodded. "You'll not have to face the ire of superstitious men again, I promise. We'll take you to our home and help you."

"Where are we going?'" she asked curiously, looking down into the depths. She couldn't have been older than nineteen, her face still young. Her dark eyes were dull, almost as if she didn't want to get her hopes up that we were here to save her. That feeling was a familiar one too, and my protective instincts surged.

"We have a network of caves that protect us and give us privacy. We'll explain more there, but all you need to know now is that you're safe and no man will ever harm you again," I repeated, wanting to make sure she understood. Maira reached out, and we tugged the young woman through the water behind us, keeping her in the air bubble Maira had created. We led her behind the others back to *Neamh na Mara* and toward a fresh start.

CHAPTER THREE

BRIGID

It took us longer to get back to the caves than it did to leave them, as the air bubble caused some drag through the cold water. Eventually, we slipped through the rocky archway at the entrance and emerged into the large main cavern.

Another, larger air bubble encompassed the back of the cavern, where Cliodhna and the others were already waiting. The others remained in their syren forms, sitting on the craggy rocks jutting up from the floor of the caves with their tails draped over the edges. Cliodhna had shifted to her more human-like appearance and stood, naked, waiting for us to bring the girl into the bubble.

We released the girl as both Maira and I transformed into our human forms, tails shifting slowly into legs. I wanted to stay with the girl, to support her.

"Welcome to *Neamh na Mara*," Cliodhna said, her voice echoing off the rocks now that the water was not absorbing the sound. It was easy to hear the pride in her voice as she spoke of our home.

The young woman stood in awe, her gaze shifting back and forth between all of us, the cavern, and the water above. She twisted her hands into her dress, which still dripped cold seawater and clung to her waifish body. Her anxiety made me want to twist my own hands, a motion reminiscent of my childhood, but I flexed my fingers wide instead.

"What is your name?" Cliodhna asked gently, walking toward the young woman. Her pale blue eyes roved over the smaller woman.

"Sorcha," she whispered, looking down at the floor. She took a deep breath before raising her gaze bravely to Cliodhna and clearing her throat. "Who're *you?*"

"They call me Cliodhna these days," our queen answered with a regal nod, inviting Sorcha to continue.

"Okay..." she drawled, seeming to gain a little bit of courage in the face of Cliodhna. A dark eyebrow arched in challenge. "Then *what* are you?"

Cliodhna smiled widely, though I wouldn't quite call it a friendly smile. Sorcha was getting her spine back under her, rebuilding the fire that had surely been almost extinguished when she was thrown into the frigid waters. Warmth flowed through me, and my mouth twitched up in a ghost of a smile. This confidence would serve her well, if she could keep it.

"I'm a goddess, my child. Of the sea, of beauty, of many

things that have long been forgotten by man. These days, I'm a protector. Of the sea and of women like you. These are my syrens; they came to me the same way you have." Cliodhna jutted her chin out again, her voice loud and clear through the caves.

Sorcha peered around at the rest of us, taking us in, before settling her gray eyes on me. "You were all like me?"

"We were you, little one," I replied softly, trying to keep from overwhelming her. I recognized the signs of her anxiety, and it threw my own body back into the patterns I had fought to overcome. My fingers twitched at my sides, and my stomach twisted, muscles tensing across my entire body as the trauma resurfaced in my bones.

"Instead of letting us drown at the hands of hateful men, Cliodhna gave us a choice to stay with her," Maira said, her southern accent hanging off Cliodhna's name. *Klee-nah,* she pronounced it. "And now, we save girls like you and seek revenge on men like the ones who did this to you."

Sorcha's eyes snapped to Maira. "Revenge?"

Maira's gray eyes twinkled, as they always did when violence was mentioned. Her talons flexed, itching to tear into flesh. She was easily the most bloodthirsty among us, and it served us well, but now, it did little but frighten an already terrified girl. "Yes, girl, revenge."

"Don't overwhelm her," I scolded, seeing how Sorcha's hands trembled at her sides despite the resolved expression on her face. Maira scowled at me, but I ignored her, looking at Sorcha and remembering what it felt like to learn all of this for the first time. "If you choose to stay with us, you'll get your chance to avenge yourself."

"You do have options, Sorcha. If you do not wish to be part of this or to be one of us, we will take you to land and leave you in the care of someone safe. I will wipe your memories of us," Cliodhna explained, as she had to all of us before. "But if you wish to be one of us, you will be transformed. Part woman, part sea creature, all deadly. As a syren, you will become one of my children."

"Do I have to decide right now?" Sorcha asked, gripping her fingers together and twisting them roughly once again. Her index finger began picking at the skin of her thumb. My fingers twitched, wanting to reach out and pull her nails away from the torn skin.

Cliodhna smiled at her gently, more gently than I had seen from our queen in a long time. Her face typically displayed apathy or anger, but this look was soft and reflective. "Of course not. Take some time; think it over. Brigid will get you some dry clothes, and you can stay with her."

Sorcha looked around, her eyebrows wrinkling and forehead creasing. "Dry clothes? We're underwater."

I stepped over and put my hand on Sorcha's shoulder, which was still cold and damp from the seawater. The corners of my lips turned up in a teasing smile, trying to put her at ease. "We're blessed by a goddess, little one. We can do many things that may seem impossible."

Cliodhna nodded at me, jerking her head toward a passage at the back of the caves. "Take her to your room, Brigid."

I bowed my head respectfully. "Of course."

Taking Sorcha's hand in mine, I led her away from the rest

of the group and farther into the caverns. While Cliodhna had said "room," she'd meant chambers. There were no doors in the underwater caverns, but we respected each other's privacy and stayed out of the spaces we weren't invited to. We stepped into my chambers, and I led Sorcha to sit in the hammock that allowed me to sleep in my syren form. Waving a hand, I expanded the air bubble around her to encompass my entire room so she could move freely.

"You have the same accent as me," Sorcha said quietly, her eyes roaming my space. She tracked my movements as I walked over to a small chest of drawers and retrieved her a dry shirt and fitted pants.

I glanced over my shoulder at her before turning and pressing the clothing into her hands, which had finally stopped trembling. "Not quite, but close enough. I'm from northern Tuathnach, in Gaisin. I imagine you're from somewhere near there. Here, put these on."

"Yes." Sorcha looked down at me. Her cheeks turned pink, and she quickly raised her gaze back up to meet mine. "Why're you not wearing any clothes?"

I shrugged, amused at her embarrassment. My nakedness didn't bother me at all, having grown used to my body being exposed. It was just a body, and men would not sexualize my body without my permission lest they die at my hand. "I don't usually wear my legs anymore, and it's kind of difficult to put pants on a tail. And other clothes have too much drag in the water. Nakedness is purely functional."

"If you don't wear clothes, why do you even have any? And how are they dry?" she questioned, taking the clothes from me and inspecting them as if they were made of pure magic. But they were just clothes, and the awe in her eyes made me want to smile.

It was an odd feeling. I hadn't truly smiled in years, and yet this girl was bringing these emotions back in full force within minutes.

"We all have clothes we keep for moments like this. If you don't decide to stay with us, we'll wear them to take you somewhere safe. We'll give you supplies," I explained. I tilted my head, thinking through what other questions she would have. While Kyla and the others had been helpful to me, I wanted Sorcha to be different, to feel safe and protected. I didn't want her to feel like she had to grow up before her time. "But none of us wear clothes here. It's much easier to stay in syren form. And they stay dry because the drawers are enchanted by Cliodhna. I told you, she's a goddess. Her magic is nearly limitless in what it can do."

"And do you all...worship her?" she asked, her voice cautious, as if she were afraid I might be offended. Her unease set my teeth on edge, and all I wanted was to calm and reassure her. She had nothing to fear here, and certainly nothing to fear in me.

Tipping my head side to side again, I thought about how to answer her. The situation was more complex than she made it out to be. "Och, not really. We're more her helpers—I suppose would be the word. We honor her, but there's not a worship aspect involved. Only humans do that. And more and more humans are forgetting to do even that."

"Are there other gods and goddesses?" Her soft voice was

full of interest now.

I raised a shoulder slightly, unsure of exactly how to answer her. The questions of a child, despite her being nearly a woman, were always more complicated than they seemed. "Of course, there are. Most of them keep to themselves now since humans have taken over the world. Humans see them as abstract ideas, not real beings."

Her dark blue eyes opened wide. "Have you ever met any?"

My lips twitched up at her excitement, amused by how quickly her mind had moved from the trauma of the day to the excitement of the unknown. "No, little one. I've only met Cliodhna."

"So, Aine? The fae? They're real?" The interest was so clear in her voice, it was hard to keep from breaking into a full smile.

"I don't truly know," I admitted, letting myself smile at her. It felt freeing. And for the first time in a long time, I didn't feel like I needed to keep my smile hidden. The others were always so serious, so showing my emotions made me stand out from them. For the last ten years, all I had wanted was to fit in, to be accepted by my new family, no matter what it took. I had mirrored their behaviors, masking my emotions and shoving them down deep. "But I would imagine so. If we're real, I'm sure there are other stories that are real too."

"Do you think…I could meet another goddess?"

"Let's get you through this first," I said, reaching out to pat her shoulder. If anything, I admired her resiliency. "Then we'll talk about meeting other mythical creatures."

She blushed slightly, ducking her head. "So, what's your story…Brigid?"

I nodded, confirming my name for her. The thought of sharing my own story made my stomach clench. If I were alone, I would likely be curling in on myself. But Sorcha needed to see strength right now, so I shoved my anxiety and discomfort down into the depths of my mind. Rolling my shoulders back and holding my head up, I took a deep breath through my nose, calming my senses. "My story is one for another time. You don't want to hear it right now."

"Why not?" I wasn't sure why I had expected her question to be combative, but the genuine concern and curiosity in her voice threw me. She sounded like she truly wanted to know my story. Truly wanted to know *me*. It wasn't something I was used to.

"It's not a nice story, Sorcha," I said, my voice cracking slightly as my emotions threatened to burst through the dam I had built. Swallowing hard, I forced them back into their box and locked the lid. I couldn't talk about my past right now. I didn't want to remember what had happened that day on the ship. I didn't want to remember the boy who had suffered trying—and failing—to save me. I shook my head, trying to physically clear those thoughts from my head, before turning back to Sorcha. "And you just went through something traumatic. I'll not add to that right now. I'll tell you my story later."

She was silent, peering at me. Finally, she spoke again, her voice contemplative. "How long did it take for you to decide to stay?"

I shrugged, going along with the change of subject easily. While it was still talking about my past, the decisions I'd made after I was thrown off the ship weren't nearly as painful to remember as those that had come earlier. "I didn't need to think about it. I was angry when Cliodhna saved me. Saying no never crossed my mind."

"Are you still angry?" she asked, tilting her head again. Her dark blue eyes were wide and curious.

"No," I replied after thinking about it for a moment. It surprised me, but I hadn't considered my own emotions in a while. Indifference had been my only emotion. But thinking about what had happened to me as a child, I wasn't angry. "No, just tired. Men think they can just control anything and anyone they want to, especially those they think are smaller than them. And I'm tired of it. I could kill these men with one hand, and yet in my human form, they would dismiss me without a second thought."

"We are not beneath them." Her voice was quiet but firm, as if she were trying to convince herself. It made my temper flare; I wanted to crush any of the men who had made her question that statement before.

"No, Sorcha, we are not," I said firmly. My voice softened slightly; I didn't want my anger to overwhelm her. "Tell me your story. How did you end up here? What was your life like?"

"Like I said before, I was running away to be with my beau. His name is Owen, and he's wonderful. My father is a controlling man, and a violent one. He kept me isolated apart from my letters with Owen and our occasional meetings. I couldn't be around him anymore, couldn't take the abuse, so I took my fate into my own hands and tried to make my life better. It didn't work," she said, her voice going flat at the end.

She twisted her hands in her lap again. "And now I'm here, trying to wrap my head around the fact that I'm currently residing in a cave underwater with mermaids."

"It did work. It got you here," I pointed out, trying my best to reassure her. "You can either stay with us and start a new life, or we can take you somewhere safe where you can start a new life. Either way, you control your fate now. And we're syrens, little one, not mermaids. Mermaids are fairy tales; we are very real."

"Do you think I should stay?" She twisted her fingers together again, her voice uncertain and slightly shaky.

Dipping my head down to catch her gaze and force her to make eye contact with me, I put a hand on her shoulder. "I think you should do what is best for you. And you need to take the time to think about that and figure out what that is. Just because I gave in to my anger and became this doesn't mean that's the right answer for everyone. But if you do stay, we will be your family, and we will protect you with our lives."

"Will you tell me about the others?" she asked as she finally began changing into the clothes I had given her. She kept her eyes on me as she dressed.

"They've all got similar stories to us: men had wronged them, and they were rescued by Cliodhna and offered a new life. They've all been here longer than me. Some have been here for half a century. Maira is the newest before me; she was saved fifteen years ago. The others will introduce themselves," I explained. Telling the stories of the others was not my place, but I wanted her to understand that we were on her side and that we understood her pain and what she had gone through.

"But Kyla is the oldest, the first of us. She was thrown off a cliff by her betrothed when she said something to anger him. She's our leader when Cliodhna isn't here."

"You don't seem very close to them," she said."You didn't say anything to them when we left, not even a look or a nod at them."

Considering that, I sat in silence for a moment. She was right, we weren't close, not in the way some of the others were close to each other. "No, I suppose I'm not. Maira and Kyla mentored me when I was first changed, but I never really connected with the others."

"Why not?"

I sighed. This girl was going to pull my life's story and every emotion out of me if I wasn't careful. "Little one, this is a lot of information. You don't have to learn everything about us right now."

"How long have you been here?" she asked, only pausing for a moment before launching back into her questioning.

"Almost ten years now, I suppose," I replied, at least grateful she had moved to something less personal. Time wasn't something we often considered here, and while I had a general idea of how long it had been, it might have been longer.

"There haven't been any others before me?"

"There have," I explained, "but none of them wanted to stay with us as a syren. So, we took them to a woman in the south who helps them start a new life, finds them work and a place to stay, and gets them back on their feet. Their memories of us are erased by Cliodhna; all they know is that they were in the water and then they were rescued, waking up at their new home in the south."

"And the...revenge bit?" Her face was curious, if a little apprehensive. "What's all that about?"

I sat down on the hanging bed beside her, the netting dipping beneath my weight. "Aye, the revenge. You know those tales of the lovely women of the sea who lure the sailors into the water with just their voices? Well, that's not entirely accurate, but that's us. They call us mermaids, sea witches. But it's just us."

"But they haven't done anything to you personally? Why not just target the ones who actually wronged you?" she asked, still playing with her hands in her lap.

"All men have wronged us," I said fiercely. That was something Cliodhna had driven into our heads from the moment she saved us. And she was right. All men were bad, and all men were the reason for our fates. Men succumbed to our song quickly, showing the truth of how weak they were. And despite what Sorcha had said about her beau, I still believed Cliodhna's words. Men had never been kind to me, apart from one young boy a lifetime ago. My experiences with them had been those of violence or those of cold indifference to my suffering.

"There hasn't been a single man who was kind to you?" she asked, still playing with her hands.

"There was one. Once," I said quietly. It was more than I had wanted to admit, but I couldn't help myself. Thoughts of the boy from all those years ago, with his dark hair and bright green eyes, filled my mind. I could still see him reach his hand out to help me. I knew he'd been punished because of it—because of me.

"Is he not innocent?" Her voice was soft, as if she was afraid to jar me from my thoughts.

I thought of the boy often, picturing what he would look like now and wondering if he had survived. But I could not dwell on those fantasies and pushed them back into the chest in my mind. It didn't matter what I dreamed, I owed fealty to Cliodhna. "Likely not anymore. He's either dead or has turned into those men he was surrounded by. Innocence doesn't last long when surrounded by men like that."

"But what if he hasn't?" she pressed. "What if he's still the kind boy you knew, just grown up?"

"Then I pray to never see him on the seas," I said, meeting her gaze. I couldn't let her fill my mind with any more fantasies about that boy. Caelum. Even after all these years, I still remembered his name. Maybe if he had grown into a man, he would be different. But I knew better than to get my hopes up.

Sorcha stayed silent for a few moments, again wringing her hands in her lap. I wanted to reach out and soothe her anxiety, but I could see the motion brought her comfort. Her voice was quiet. "Will I have to do that?"

I placed one of her hands in mine, squeezing gently. "You will be able to if you decide to stay with us."

She looked over, our eyes locking. There was fire in hers, the kind that burned so hot it was blue rather than orange. Her voice did not waver as she replied, "I think I want to be one of you."

"You think?" I questioned, raising an eyebrow. "You need to be certain, lass. This isn't something you can change your mind about later. If you're with us, then you're with us forever. You need to be sure. Get some rest, take the night and sleep on it, and then we can talk about it more if you'd like."

She nodded and lay down, pulling a thin blanket over her as she turned on her side. I stretched out into the other hanging bed, pulling a blanket over myself as well. "Goodnight, Brigid."

"Goodnight, Sorcha. May your dreams give you guidance."

Chapter Four

BRIGID

The next morning, once Sorcha had cleaned up and dressed, we walked back out to the main cavern. There was now only an air bubble around Sorcha and me rather than in the cavern itself. The others, including Maira, who had transformed back into her syren form, swam around us, flitting impatiently back and forth. Kyla caught my eye, nodding at me with something akin to pride in her eyes. I furrowed my brow, wondering what she was proud of.

Cliodhna swam forward, stepping softly into the air bubble while she transformed as naturally as breathing. Her human form was just as regal as her syren form. She raised her head, jutting out her chin and peering down her nose at Sorcha. "Have you decided, my dear? Or do you need more time?"

Sorcha looked over at me, her dark blue eyes wide. Sensing her rising anxiety, I nodded my head and smiled in what I hoped was an encouraging look and not a grimace. Though we had talked at length about Sorcha's options, she hadn't outright told me what she had decided. She nodded back before taking a visibly deep breath. "I'm ready. I want to stay with you; I want to be fierce like you."

"Then you shall," Cliodhna said, her voice resonating with conviction. She looked at me, and her eyes hardened back to the expression I was familiar with. The queen may have put on her smile for Sorcha, but I knew better than to expect any sentimentality. "Brigid, please step out of the bubble."

Bowing my head, I stepped back into the water, letting the transformation take me back to my syren form. One moment I had legs, and the next, a silvery red tail took their place, moving me through the water with ease.

Once Cliodhna and Sorcha were the only ones in the bubble, Cliodhna placed her hands on either side of Sorcha's pale face. I couldn't see Sorcha's expression from behind her, but Cliodhna's eyebrows furrowed with concentration.

A strong current came swirling from behind me, rushing around my body and moving into the air bubble. The air around them filled with the cold water, swirling in thick ropes in a spiral around their bodies. The spirals danced and weaved around them, growing thicker and obscuring them from view. Suddenly, the spirals collapsed, and once the rush of bubbles dissipated, Sorcha and Cliodhna were no longer in an air bubble at all. They were out in the water with the rest of us.

Sorcha's borrowed clothes had ripped and fallen away

to reveal her pale skin covering new, powerful muscles. Her torso lengthened and transitioned into a shimmering indigo tail, lithe and muscular. The webbing between her fingers connected, and her nails grew sharp, as did her teeth. She truly was a syren now, deadly and powerful.

Cliodhna smiled, showing off her own sharp teeth, as Sorcha looked down over her new body, holding her hands out in front of her and swishing her tail experimentally. "Welcome, my child."

Sorcha finally tore her gaze from her hands and tail, looking up. Her mouth opened a few times as if she were getting used to not having to hold her breath beneath the waves. Her hand grabbed at her throat, and her eyes widened. Finally, she was able to speak. "So, what now?"

Maira grinned from across the cavern. "Now, we explore and show you your new home."

The others and I swam out of the cave, twisting and gliding through the icy waters. Sorcha was behind us, moving much more slowly, still getting used to having a tail instead of legs. She was catching on quickly, though, twirling and smiling as she swam between us.

We spun around, swimming between rocks and dodging sea life. The tall stalagmites on the ocean floor jutted up, creating pillars for us to swirl around.

"Look!" Iona said, pointing up toward the surface. There

was a shadow looming above. It was a ship, oblong and dark in the waters, its long hull slicing through the dark waves. The keel was jagged, and even from this distance, it was obvious the ship was old and unkempt. And it was alone.

Cliodhna nodded once at us, instructing us to deliver our wrath upon this ship. We all grinned and shot up again, swimming toward the shadow. Maira reached the hull first, running her claws across the wood and gouging deep gashes along it. When she reached the bow, she turned and did the same down the other side of the hull, marking the ship for doom as water spilled inside.

I turned to look at Sorcha as I explained what was happening. "Now, we sing. Our song will cause them to go mad and jump into the water to escape the agony. And then we will drown them."

"But you don't try to save them? Even if they're innocent?" she asked, still staring wide-eyed at the ship above us. She looked so much younger.

I swam over in front of her, blocking her view. "Sorcha, no man is innocent. They are the reason for all of our suffering."

"Some of them are innocent," she protested quietly, looking down at her tail. Rolling her shoulders back, she raised her head. "My beau was innocent. He never hurt me, never would have."

I didn't answer as the others jettied up, beginning to sing their song from below the surface. Even from beneath the water, I could see the men on deck holding their hands over their ears, trying to block out the agonizing noise. One man quickly succumbed, walking toward the railing with a frantic look on his face. Before the others could reach him, he jumped right over into the icy water.

Maira didn't hesitate, swimming up to him and circling him like a shark with an equally toothy grin on her face. Finally, he fell out from the madness our voices induced and began flailing in the water. But the current was too strong, or he was too weak a swimmer, and after a moment, he stopped flailing, sinking lifelessly into the darkness below. As Maira and the others began to sing louder, the ship veered off toward the jagged cliffs, crashing into the sharp rocks jutting up in all directions. The hull ripped open along Maira's gouges, and water began flooding into the large hole.

Sorcha swam beside me, her shoulders tense and her fists bunched at her sides. "How long will this take?"

"As long as it takes." I sighed, conflicted about how to address the uncertainty in her voice. I understood her conflict with what we did, but she needed to understand the choice she had made and come to terms with it. Again, her words before brought the boy who had tried to save me to mind, but I shoved down those thoughts and turned my attention to the scene before us. "This is what we do, Sorcha. We avenge ourselves on these men. Yes, there may be a few innocent men, but more likely than not, they're not. Especially not men who try to claim and control the ocean as their own and determine who can or cannot be on it."

Sorcha was quiet, her only movement her tail flicking back and forth. Her dark hair fanned out behind her in the current. After a few moments of watching the destruction behind me settle, she nodded. "I understand. You're right. My beau was not a sailor, and no sailor I ever met was kind to me."

Taking her hand in my own, I squeezed gently, pulling her from her visible anxiety. "This will take time to accept and acknowledge. You have all the time in the world now. Take it. You can watch us for as long as it takes to come to terms with your new life."

"Do we not age?" she asked, her eyebrows wrinkling, her attention finally focusing back on me. "What do you mean 'all the time in the world?'"

"We age, just slowly. Cliodhna says that we are her creations, and she enjoys our company, so her magic slows our natural aging process," I explained. Noticing the others finish with the ship and the crew, I watched the wreckage sink down into the darkness. "We can do many other things too. In our syren form, we're immune to the cold of the water and we can see in the darkness of the depths."

"But not in our human form?"

I nodded. Cliodhna's powers had grown over the past few years, and I had no doubt we would continue to find new things it allowed us to do. "Not unless we're in an air bubble created by one of us. Those hold the same syren magic."

She nodded, and I could see her mind trying to wrap around the new information. She looked over my shoulder. "We should go; they're leaving."

"Do you want to stay a moment longer?" I could see how this was affecting her; if she needed time to process what had happened, I would stay with her. When I had transformed, the others had thrust me into the life with no warning, explanation, or time to adjust. I wanted something different for Sorcha, and

I wanted her to take her time leaning into this new world.

Her gaze flicked back to the wreckage sinking into the darkness behind me. After watching for a moment, she shifted her focus back to me. "No, I think I've seen all I need to. It will just take me some time to understand my new reality, I think."

"And that's fine, Sorcha. You have a lifetime to understand. The others will understand as well. But just remember, there's no going back to being human. You're a syren now. Forever." My voice was stern, but I needed her to know that. Cliodhna had never taken back the transformation, and I feared what she would do if Sorcha requested it.

She nodded. "I understand."

Over the next few weeks, Sorcha and I grew close. She had elected to share rooms with me, and we spent many nights up later than we should have, talking. While I wasn't used to sharing my own space, something about Sorcha made it feel less imposing than sharing with someone else would have been.

We spoke of our lives before we transitioned, of our goals and dreams and how we both had wanted to explore the world. Sorcha spoke often of her beau she had left behind, wondering if he had moved on already or if he was still waiting for her.

My mind often drifted to Caelum, thinking of what my life could have been like if I had met him in a different place. Would we have been like Sorcha and Owen? But it was a fool's dream and a waste of my time to hope for things that could never happen. Men were our enemy, not something to be fantasized over.

Tonight, we had landed back on the topic of our revenge. It had been a rough day; the men we had targeted earlier did not die easily, but fought and thrashed every step of the way. I had seen it wear on her earlier; I'd known this talk would be coming.

In the semi-darkness of the sea caves, she spoke. "Why do we do this, Brigid? Why do we ruin these ships and these men?"

I sighed. I truly did not have an answer that would satisfy her, not after our conversations at the first ship she saw with us. "I suppose, mostly, because our queen declares it. We all have different reasons why we agreed to become syrens, but Cliodhna's word is rule here. Maira enjoys killing men—killing anything, really. I know this has been rough on you, Sorcha, but that's what we agreed to. What *you* agreed to."

She was silent for a moment before letting out her own sigh. "I know. And I'm not questioning her. She saved me, saved us. But I just can't help but think about how there might be another Owen out there, just stuck on a boat because he knows no better. And we might kill him."

My mind raced, unbidden, back to Caelum, who had fought to save me and been punished because of it. I would never be able to repay him for his kindness. "Aye, I know what you mean."

"You all are my family now, and I would never go against you. I just can't help but think that maybe some of the men don't deserve our ire."

"How are we to know, then?" I asked softly. "How can we tell which ones to punish and which ones to spare?"

She sighed again. "Maybe I'm too nice to be a syren."

I smiled at her, knowing she could see it in the little light cast through the cave. "You are too nice, but not too nice to be a syren. You're a great syren, little one. You have a kind heart."

"You do too," she said quietly, tentatively, as if she were afraid of my reaction.

My heart clenched. "Maybe once. Now? I'm not so sure about that."

"You do, Brigid. You're a good person with a good heart. Life just dealt you a bad hand."

"Yes," I said softly. "It did. But it ended up getting me here, so how bad can it really be?"

"True," she agreed. "Thank you for saving me that day. I'm glad to have met you."

"And I, you," I replied.

As we talked into the night about everything and nothing, I was glad I had found a friend, a true friend, at last. I had never had siblings, but this connection, this protective instinct to shield her from the troubles of the world, I imagined it was what I would feel toward a sister. Sorcha was a good person—much better than I could ever be—and kind. She had obviously been sheltered as a human, and I could see that she had potential. She was ready to become her own woman, and I couldn't wait to mold her and help her grow.

CHAPTER FIVE

BRIGID

We were out on a patrol, looking for anything amiss in the waters Cliodhna controlled. I was with Sorcha again, as she was still adjusting to her new reality as a syren. She had taken to it mostly with ease. Her tail was beautiful, and she knew how to use it well. She had practiced singing her song and creating air bubbles. The only thing she was still having issues with was accepting the destruction we would bring. But she was slowly coming around to Cliodhna's ways of thinking.

Swimming through the waters, we twirled and spun, having fun with each other as much as we were on a mission. Sorcha and I had only gone out once before, nearly a week ago. In the meantime, we had just been swimming around the caves with each other, getting her used to her new home.

She had been with us for nearly a fortnight and was adjusting quicker than I ever had. Though she still had many questions, they were endearing and almost comforting now.

"Do we do this often?" she asked, spinning around with some dolphins who had been following us for a while. When they had first shown up, she had been so shocked, I had laughed for the first time in what was likely years.

I had missed the feeling of joy.

Turning my head to face her, I explained our patrol schedule. "We're on a rotation, always in pairs. A pair goes out once every couple of days to patrol the waters. Kyla sets up the rotations, and we go out to see if there's anything that needs our attention. They kept us out of the last few as you got used to your new body."

Typically, I was paired with Maira. Being the only one who could put up with her harsh attitude for long periods of time, the others often used me as a buffer. Years of being a syren had only fueled Maira's anger, rather than tempered it like it had with some of the others. And while it often stung when directed at me, I had such practice shoving my emotions down that her words slid off my skin like water.

"How do you decide which ships to target?" she asked, weaving in and out of the craggy rocks. Her dexterity with her new tail was coming along nicely, as if she had never been without it.

"If we see any ships that are alone, we are to report back to Cliodhna. She decides their fate from there," I explained, moving through the water beside her. "Otherwise, if she senses a woman in the waters, we will all go then."

"And you never questioned how she chooses?" Sorcha asked, swimming closer beside me. She wrinkled her brow. "I mean, if all men are the target of our revenge, like she says, then why does she pick and choose?"

I tilted my head, halting for a moment. I had never thought of it that way before, never thought of questioning the choices my queen made. But perhaps Sorcha had a point. Why did Cliodhna pick and choose the ships for us to target? "I…I don't know. I never thought of it like that. We don't really question her."

Her eyes widened and her face became panicked. "I didn't mean to question her, really. I was simply curious."

I smiled softly. Sorcha was afraid of a cross word or a tense look. While she was comfortable enough to ask me questions, her apprehension still leaked through. It had taken me years to get over my own hesitations and anxiety, and even now I still tended to close down when someone became upset, bottling up my substantial anger to be unleashed in private later.

"Relax, little one. There's nothing wrong with asking questions. It's been a right minute since someone was around here to shake things up. And it's natural that you'd have these questions."

Her shoulders slumped, and the tension bled out of her face, erasing the soft crinkle between her eyebrows. We went back to playing with the ocean life as we circled the waters. We rounded a large rock sticking up high into the water column and stopped. There was a ship up ahead, a large one.

Sorcha looked over to me, her eyes wide again. "There's a

ship."

I almost laughed again at her tone of surprise. This girl was pulling me from my own shell as much as I was trying to pull her from hers. In the short time I'd known her, I had laughed and smiled more than I had in my entire life. It was odd, but welcomed. "Yes, we need to report back to Cliodhna and let her decide its fate."

"We have to go all the way back? What if they're gone by then?" Even in the water, she began twisting her hands.

"No, we just have to speak with our syren voices. It's similar to singing, but not quite the same. The magic carries our voices through the water. She'll hear us and be able to answer the same way," I explained. I held out my hand, and she slipped her taloned fingers in with mine. "Let me show you."

She nodded, her face resolved. She had sung before, but we hadn't talked about this part of it yet.

Straightening my spine, I began to speak, fusing the vocalizations with intent. We were far enough below the water that the humans on the ship would not be affected, and Cliodhna was able to hear us from wherever we were in the waters. "My queen, we've found a large ship. What are your orders?"

After a few moments, our queen's voice came echoing through the waters. "Wait there, my daughters. The others are on their way. This ship will face our vengeance."

I released Sorcha's hand and turned so my eyes were back on the ship again. "Now, we wait for the others. And we will keep watch and make sure the ship doesn't get away from us before they get here."

The ship did move, but not significantly, by the time the others swam up beside us. It didn't seem to be in a hurry, but rather was hugging the rocky coast as it continued through the water, the keel slicing through the waves. Through the water, I could see the name painted on the side.

The Nehalennia.

How fitting that this ship would be named after the lost goddess of seafarers. It was almost ironic, and my lip curled softly at my own humor.

I had not met other gods or goddesses, but I remembered them from my limited teachings as a child. Nehalennia had once been worshiped as widely as any of the gods but had disappeared as humans began to change. And unlike Cliodhna, no one had worshiped Nehalennia in years, her altars and temples lost to the new world.

Led by Kyla, the others circled around us, looking at us intently. Her eyebrow quirked as she looked at me, and I schooled my face back into indifference, erasing the hint of the smile that had lingered on my lips. Kyla glanced over her shoulder toward the ship. "What have you seen?"

"They're not fishing. There are no lines or nets. And they've not gone out into the deeper water. They're staying fairly close to the coast for some reason. It could be easy to get the ship to run into the rocks," I explained, nodding my head to the ship in the distance. It was odd that the ship was this close to the coast with no fishing lines, but who knows what they were doing. Maybe they were pirates, trolling for the vulnerable. "It's a wooden hull, and it looks old, but it's well taken care of. Either way, it should splinter if it runs into the peaks there."

Sorcha looked at me, an expression of shock on her face as her tail twitched. "I didn't know you were analyzing it like that."

I raised one side of my mouth in a half-smile, all the emotion I could risk showing around the others. "I'm always analyzing, little one. We need to be aware of what we're up against. The ships and the crews both suffer. Our focus is on the crew, of course, but the ships themselves face destruction just the same."

"If there are lines or nets, they could snag us in the water," Kyla explained patiently, "and then we'd be trapped at their mercy. Our claws are sharp, but it would still take us time to free ourselves."

"So, they could catch us?" she asked. "Have any syrens ever been caught before?"

"Not in my time," Kyla said, smiling reassuringly. "We're very careful to avoid them. If men discovered the reality of our existence beyond just legends, we would likely be hunted and captured to extinction. It's better to simply avoid any fishing vessels unless we can easily wreck and kill the crew."

Sorcha nodded her understanding. "But if they don't have lines or nets, what are they doing so close to shore?"

"It doesn't matter what they're doing," Maira interjected impatiently, flexing her talons. "They won't be doing it much longer."

At that, Maira and the others surged forward toward the ship. I tugged on Sorcha's hand, and we followed, tails slashing through the water as we neared the underbelly of the ship. We surrounded it on the side of the open water and began singing as one. Still holding Sorcha's hand, I squeezed her fingers as she joined our song. The power of her voice seemed to startle even her, but she adjusted to it quickly. Our song wasn't actual words, more of a melody filled with intent. And that intent was to drive these men to madness and ruin.

Abruptly, the ship diverted from its course, turning hard toward the rocky cliffs on the other side of it. Even in the water, there was a sickening crash and the sound of splitting wood as the nose of the ship rammed into the jagged peaks.

We kept singing.

The ship began to turn, its side now scraping along the rocks as well. Men, driven mad by our song, began jumping overboard as the ship started to take on water and dip lower beneath the waves. While still close to the shore, the water here wasn't exactly shallow, and the ship would sink in its entirety.

We circled, diving deep as bodies began tumbling in the water, the panic induced by our song preventing them from seeing reason and turning toward the cliffs for refuge. Sorcha looked over at me, her eyes wide as she processed the scene in front of her. She still seemed intimidated, yet interested.

I motioned for her to follow me. As we swam up closer to the surface, gleeful that these men would feel our wrath, a body crashed into the water in front of me. A man, based on the broadness of his shoulders and the general bulk of his frame. His body twisted, his limbs flailing as he sank through the water.

I stopped short, letting go of Sorcha, who continued swimming up toward the surface with the others. I swished my tail to hold myself steady as I stared at him. Instead of flailing, he was trying to steady himself. He righted his large, muscular body and finally turned in the water to face me. His eyes widened, but he didn't seem afraid of me.

Another man splashed into the water in between us, diverting my attention. This man, once the bubbles around his form dissipated, was terrified. His eyes widened, and he opened his mouth to scream, but only more bubbles came out. He furiously tried to kick to the surface, but Maira was faster. Swimming down between us from the surface, she lunged forward, grabbing his leg and pulling him down into the depths. He kicked, still releasing a stream of bubbles from his mouth as he flailed about furiously.

With Maira gone into the depths, I turned my attention back to the man from before. He was closer to the surface now, almost close enough to breach it. Flicking my tail, I used my power to surge up, wrapping my talons around his ankle just as his head surfaced.

I could not let him escape. This man seemed a powerful swimmer, and if I let him go, I had no doubt he would survive. And given how closely he had seen Maira and me, I couldn't let that happen. In the moment, I was grateful Sorcha had continued to the surface and wouldn't have to watch this. I wasn't sure she'd have the stomach to witness this death up close.

I yanked hard on his boot, pulling him back beneath the waves. Down, down, down we went before I released him. I wanted to see his face, this man who had not seemed afraid of us. Had he seen us before?

Tilting my head to the side, I looked at the man more

closely as he calmly treaded water, not trying to get back to the surface. His face was familiar to me...somehow. I swam slightly closer to him, whipping my tail in the water, impressed when he didn't back away. We stared at each other for a moment longer before it clicked in my head. The bright green eyes staring back at me, the dark hair floating in the water, the chiseled and strong face. While he had aged some, I knew that face, those eyes.

The boy from the ship.

Caelum.

My eyes widened, and my stomach twisted again, my heart in my throat. I never thought I would see him again after being thrown overboard. He had fought to try to save me, even knowing he would be punished by the captain for it. My mind was spinning, trying to process the man before me as I studied him.

He was still oddly calm, keeping himself upright but never trying to go back toward the surface. He studied me back, his eyes roving over my body and stuttering on my tail before traveling back up to my face. He seemed resigned to his fate. His gaze was intense, and I wondered if he recognized me as well. I doubted it, as he had only seen me for a brief moment. But I had remembered him.

His cheeks began to bulge, a sign he was running out of time under the water, and he finally cast a glance upwards to the surface before looking back to me. But still, he didn't make a move.

In an impulsive moment, I knew I couldn't let my only savior, the only redemption to men, drown because of us.

Because of *me*. Before I could stop myself and think about the betrayal my family would surely feel, I rushed toward him, grabbed him under the arms, and pulled his chest against mine as I propelled us toward the surface. He would not die on my watch. I would not be the cause of his ruin.

Not after he had suffered trying to save me on that ship.

Maybe Sorcha was right. Maybe he was still the innocent boy who had tried to save me all those years before.

CHAPTER SIX

BRIGID

We broke the surface, the man gasping for breath as water dripped off his dark hair and into his eyes. His chest heaved as I let him go, sure that he could at least tread water on his own. I put some space between us, still staring intently at him. Now above the surface of the water, I could see how clearly his face had changed since we had last seen each other. What used to be the face of a boy was now the face of a man, weathered, weary, and rough.

Despite the anxiety swirling through my mind, I schooled my face into blankness and calm. Hiding my emotions was not a new feat for me, and it was easier than I would have liked to put on the façade of indifference. Showing emotions would not benefit me here. The man—Caelum—was obviously a sailor, and had likely heard the legends. If he believed me to be anything but a bloodthirsty beast, I would be at a disadvantage.

"I thought you were going to kill me," he said cautiously, beginning to tread water to keep his head above the waves. "Like the other one did to Gordan."

My stomach was still clenching, and I didn't know why I was doing this. I was a rational person, and my logic was screaming at me that I was making a mistake by saving him. He was on the ship we had destroyed, and that meant he was likely one of the men we sought vengeance on. One of the men who sought to control those who would travel the ocean. But I couldn't stop myself from saving him.

In the near distance, the ship continued sinking. I could feel the others beneath the surface, but I was confident we were now far enough away that they would not shift their focus from the wreckage long enough to notice us.

I was betraying my family, the people who had saved me and given me purpose, for this man I barely knew. But he had saved me before, and I had thought I would never see him again. Faced with him again, I didn't know what to do, but I did know I couldn't have killed him or let him drown. No matter how much my gut was telling me this was wrong and that I should have just left him to drown, something else, something deeper, was telling me this was right and that saving him was the right thing to do.

Swishing my tail back and forth to keep my head out of the water, I peered at him, deciding to tell him why I had saved him from surely drowning of his own stubbornness. "You're the boy who tried to save me about ten years ago. I was thrown overboard from a merchant ship bound for Bhodheas."

The man seemed shocked that I had spoken to him. Finally, a glimmer of realization passed over his face like he had finally been able to place where he recognized me from. "Aye, that's right. You're the girl who stowed away in the hold."

"I am." I didn't know what else to say to that. I didn't know what else I even *could* say to that in this situation. He had tried to save me before, and I had been intent on drowning him today. I wanted to vomit, and I wanted to run back to my room and curl up with Sorcha and listen to her stories. But I had to face my actions, my choices.

The man looked behind his shoulder to the wreckage of his former ship. It was sinking below the waves now, more than halfway submerged. I could feel in the water that the others were still picking off survivors who had seen us, ensuring they drowned either on their own or with help.

He turned back to me, anger now prominent in his blazing green eyes. "Was that your doing?"

"Indirectly. Your wheel man is the one who drove it into the cliffs, not I," I replied, looking at the wreckage as well. My voice was confident and indifferent despite the warring emotions in my mind. It was what we did every day, and yet, I found myself feeling guilty about it now as I faced him. I didn't like the feeling. I hadn't let myself feel emotions this strongly since I was a child.

The anxiety and fear of the day I was thrown overboard had broken something in me, and I hadn't allowed myself to feel anything for a long time. Sorcha had brought it back some, and now being face to face with my past ripped the lid off the chest I had kept my emotions locked in. I fought to shove the feelings back down, to plaster my indifference across my face and be the deadly creature I knew I could be.

He opened his mouth to speak, but a wave crested and swelled around us, pulling his head under the water. With an inconvenienced sigh at the fragility of humans in the sea, I dipped beneath the water and pulled him back up. I held him wordlessly while he again caught his breath. Panting as he tried to wipe the water out of his eyes without going back beneath the surface, he asked, "Did any of my men survive?"

I shrugged, releasing him to hold himself up in the icy water. If I told him the truth, that my fellow syrens were picking off any survivors they thought had seen them, it would just make him angry. For some reason, I didn't want to make him angry.

"Why did you save me?" he asked, leveling his piercing gaze back at me. The accusation and anger there were almost tangible. "Why did you wreck my ship and then come back and save me?"

My eyes narrowed at his tone. I had just risked everything to save this man, including the anger of my goddess if she found out what I had done, and he was questioning me. I chose to ignore his question about me pulling him down and then saving him, because I simply did not have an answer. Anger bubbled up in my stomach, hot in my throat as I tamped it down. I smothered out the fire with practiced ease. "*I* did not do anything to your ship."

He went to respond, but seemed to think better of it, closing his mouth and nodding instead. "Thank you for saving me, whatever the reason."

"Let's get you to shore," I replied, tugging him along beside me as I began swimming toward the rocky coastline that I knew was just above the horizon. The cliffs the ship had wrecked into were completely inaccessible, and if I wanted to get him out of the water, I would have to take him a fair distance to the shore.

The water was cold, and while it wouldn't affect my body in this form, I only hoped I could get Caelum to shore before he became too cold and succumbed to the elements. Looking around, I searched for any wreckage that had bobbed to the surface, but none of the pieces this far away were big enough to hold his weight.

"What happened to you when you got thrown over before?" he asked after a few moments of swimming. He was trying to help hold his own weight, but the waves were making it difficult, and I still ended up bearing most of his weight as we moved forward.

I stayed silent for a few moments, pondering just how much detail to give him, before finally answering his question. "I turned into this. What happened to you?"

"But how? And what exactly are you? Are you a mermaid?" he pressed, shivers wracking his body as we continued swimming. "And I got punished, like I told you I would."

"Don't talk. We need to save our energy," I replied, staring straight ahead as we moved through the water and trying not to bristle at being called a mermaid. I also forced myself to ignore hearing that he'd been punished for trying to save me. I was repaying that debt with this action, and I didn't want to know the details, despite what I had pondered before with Sorcha's influence.

I didn't want to care what had happened to him when he was a child. And I didn't want to share my own story with him.

After swimming for several more minutes in silence, I looked down at the man, who had suddenly grown heavier in my arms. His eyes had closed, and as I shifted his weight, his head lolled forward into the water. Damn. I cursed, shifting more of his weight onto my own body to keep his head up. I needed to get him to shore, and fast.

The rocky beach seemed much farther than I remembered it being as I continued to swim through the water, propelling us forward with the power of my tail. While the coast itself was nearly right beside me, it was nothing but tall jutting cliffs; there was nowhere to pull the man out of the water. Finally, the rocky shore became clear, and I heaved one last push to get there. The water became shallower and slightly warmer.

Pulling us up onto the rocky shore as much as I could, I cursed the heaviness of my tail when it was out of the water. Not wanting the man I had just saved to drown in his suddenly unconscious state, I pushed him as far up onto the beach as possible, shoving against his back and thighs. I forced myself to ignore the feeling of the firm muscle beneath my hands. Eventually, his head was resting on the rocky beach, but his body was still mostly submerged.

Heaving a sigh, I transitioned quickly into my human form, shivering from the cold air. Working hastily, I bent down and dragged him out of the water and onto the beach. The air would still be frigid to him, but at least he would be out of the water.

Stepping back into the water, I sat down in the icy waves and transformed back—the shifting of my body as natural as breathing—before working my way back onto the shore and as close to the man as possible. I had to keep him from dying; and staying with him until he regained consciousness was the least I could do. I had gone against my own to save him, a fact they would find out about when Sorcha and the others realized I was no longer with them. My stomach churned. I wasn't sure how they would react, but I knew it wouldn't be good.

We lay there on the beach for what felt like an eternity but was likely only a few moments. The ship had almost completely sunk below the waves in the distance. Suddenly, there was a break in the water close to the shore.

A blonde head of hair.

Maira.

"What are you doing, Brigid?" she demanded, her head the only thing above water.

I looked down at Caelum, who was still lying unconscious across the rocks. I looked back up at Maira. "He's the one who tried to save me when I was a child. I had to return the favor, Maira. I had to save him."

"He's a man, Brigid. He is just like the rest of them. As soon as he wakes, he will destroy you. That's what they do," she said angrily, swimming closer to me. "They take and take and take and leave women for dead when they're done."

"I had to at least make sure he didn't drown," I said softly, trying to get her to understand. "I repay my debts."

"Your debts? What about your promises to us? What about

your vows to Cliodhna? What about those?" she asked, fury and hurt shining in her eyes. "He will tell others about us, and you will bring doom on us."

"I'll come back, Maira," I pleaded, trying to move closer to her without splashing water onto Caelum. I knew I'd vowed to be loyal to Cliodhna and the others. But I couldn't shake the debt I owed to this man either. "I'll come back. As soon as he wakes, I'll leave him and ensure he doesn't tell anyone about me. And then I'll come back and earn your forgiveness."

"Don't."

I reeled back as if she had struck me. "What are you saying?"

"I'm saying us or him. You come with us right now, or you stay with him and you don't come back at all," Maira said. The fire in her eyes that was usually directed at others felt intense and uncomfortable when directed at me. I couldn't believe she was doing this to me after all we had been through. I knew she was an angry person and despised men, but that she wasn't even giving me a chance to explain myself. "He does not deserve your help or your favor. He will turn on you as soon as he wakes."

"Do you speak for Cliodhna?" I demanded, jutting my chin up defiantly. Maira's anger was one thing, but I would not take her word as law.

"I speak for all of us," she said, pointedly not answering my question. "Don't come back."

"I am just making sure he does not drown in the surf," I snapped, growing irritated. I knew she didn't understand, couldn't understand. But I had to do this. "It's not like I'm running off to marry the man."

Maira shook her head, a look of disgust on her face. My stomach twisted at the thought of being so easily dismissed by my adopted family, but I couldn't bring myself to abandon the unconscious man in my lap.

"Let's not be so hasty," Kyla said calmly, swimming up in front of Maira. "Brigid, you've got to think this through. Is this truly what you want to leave us over?"

"So, you'd turn me away too?" I asked, hurt bubbling up. While Maira's dismissal had stung, it had also been expected. Kyla's, however, was like a gut punch.

"We don't save men," was all she replied, her voice apologetic but firm.

"Then I guess that's our answer," I replied, looking back down at Caelum. "I *will* save him."

"Sorcha will come back with us." Maira looked at me for a long moment, our eyes locking as she dared me to defy her, to give her an excuse to fight me.

"You won't let her decide for herself?" I demanded, pushing back the burning in my throat at the thought of having to choose between saving this man and staying with Sorcha. While Caelum deserved my penance, I did not want to abandon Sorcha. Not so soon after I had found her.

"No. She's a syren. She belongs to Cliodhna. Just like you were supposed to." Sadness and anger flashed in Maira's eyes, and she turned and disappeared, dragging a stunned Sorcha with her.

I was on my own with only the man I had saved for company. I hoped the fool didn't die now, or this would all have been for nothing.

CHAPTER SEVEN
CAELUM

What is that blasted noise? I asked myself as I drifted back into consciousness. There was someone singing, and it was annoying. Shivers wracked through my body, and I moved slightly, my damp clothes chafing against my skin. Rocks dug into my body as I tried to figure out where I was and what had happened. The pain in my chest, legs, and arms began to come back into focus. I groaned. The singing stopped.

"Are you awake?" the gravelly but feminine voice asked from above me. She was the one who had been singing, a folk song I vaguely recognized from my childhood.

Suddenly, the memories of what had happened flooded my mind. The shipwreck, my men being thrown into the water, *myself* being thrown into the water, the girl. My eyes opened and found her staring at me. I opened my mouth to reply, but all that came out was a string of wet coughs. My chest heaved as it tried to expel the seawater I had inhaled, and my body contorted as I leaned over, spitting water out onto the rocky beach.

She arched an eyebrow at me but leaned toward me and helped me sit up as I hacked and coughed, spluttering out water. Her voice was dry as she looked at me with barely disguised curiosity. "You gonna live, sailor?"

I looked at her once my coughing had passed. She was beautiful, with long, wavy red hair, pale skin, and blazing green eyes. And a bloody tail, of course. Couldn't forget that bit. She had changed some since I had seen her last, but she was still recognizable as that young girl I had tried desperately to save. "I'm fine. Just had a bit of water."

She rolled her eyes and huffed, adjusting her position by moving with her weight on her hands. "'A bit of water,' he says. More like the whole ocean."

"Why did you save me?" I asked again, still confused. My men were likely dead, yet she had deemed me important enough to save. Was she planning to kill me later? A more important question sprang to mind as I studied her. "And why did you stay?"

Her green eyes hardened at my questions. "Well, I could not very well let you drown, now, could I?"

"That's exactly what you did to the others," I pointed out, trying not to think about the men I had lost, about their families I would have to tell. Anger surged within me, but I tamped it down for the moment, preferring to get answers from this woman first. She had saved me, and despite my anger at what her kind had done to my crew, I was thankful for her actions. "Which is why I'm asking why I'm alive right now."

She was quiet for a moment, looking down at her lap. Her tail flicked in the water, sending flashes of silver across the rocks. She seemed hesitant, opening her mouth a few times before finally speaking. "I owed you a debt."

Now it was my turn to roll my eyes and scoff. This… woman was something, all right. She had saved me for a debt more than ten years old? It didn't make sense to me. "A debt? Are you daft?"

At my insult, her head snapped up and her eyes almost glowed with green fire. There was the spitfire I had seen beneath the surface, the one with death in her eyes. I wondered what it would be like to be consumed by that fire.

Wait, what? I shook my head to clear that surprising thought and focused back on the matters at hand.

"Yes, *boy*, a debt. You tried to save me when they threw me over years ago. You got punished because of it. Now, we're square." She nodded, and I wasn't sure if she was trying to convince me or herself. She fidgeted on the rocky beach, her tail flicking beneath the shallow water and splashing. As I watched her, she picked up a rock, rubbing it between her palms and tracing her sharp talons over it.

"So, you owe me a debt because I wasn't a superstitious old coot?" I asked, my eyebrows rising into my hairline. I shook my head, the cold suddenly shivering through me. That's also when my brain saw fit to remind me that the girl—nay, the woman—

before me was...naked. Or at least naked from the tail up. Her hair covered her curvy upper body mostly, but still, I had to know, "Aren't you cold?"

"Do not change the subject. My nakedness is none of your concern," she snapped, dropping the rock back into the water. It amused me how defensive she was being about the entire thing.

Her kind had just killed my men, one of them right in front of me, and she had the gall to say her saving me was because I had "saved her" before. Anger bubbled up in my throat, but I pushed it down. I had never struck a woman in my life, and I wasn't about to start now. Her words irked me, though. I had been a child, just like her. It didn't make sense to me that she'd saved me for something I had done over ten years ago. And something I had failed at, at that. Despite my anger, I needed to know the truth. "So, why did you stay? Honestly?"

"I was honest with you. I owed you a debt. Least I could do is make sure you didn't drown," she said, shrugging. She looked around, picking up another rock and digging it into the soft soil beneath. "I don't reckon you know where we are."

I looked around, taking in the hills and the rocky shore. Some of it was familiar. But I didn't miss that it was now her changing the subject. "Och, vaguely. Why?"

"You need to get dry before you catch ill," she said, looking at me like I was an idiot. I guess I *was* acting like one. Instead of getting away from the water and going to dry off like a normal person would, here I was, sitting inches away from ice-cold water and talking to a lady with a tail. In my defense, there was quite a bit going on that I had to wrap my head around, and my physical state was not one of the things I considered pressing.

"And you?" I asked. She had obviously been sitting with me for a while if the slowly setting sun in the distance was anything to go by. "You going back into the sea to kill some more of my men?"

She didn't respond, but her face hardened again and her hands stilled against the rock once more. "I don't know what I'll be doing after I leave you, but it'll not be that. The others told me not to come back after seeing me rescue you."

Well, then. Her casual statement caused a mass of thoughts and questions to pour down. There were others? Other mermaids? How many others? And why had they told her to not come back after rescuing me?

"Then why save me?" Her reasoning just didn't make sense, especially after hearing that she had been sent away by others like her. There couldn't have been that much of a sense of gratitude and debt for my kindness before. I had seen a girl hiding in the hold, and she had reminded me of myself, so I had tried, and failed, to save her. There was no reason she should be this adamant about keeping me alive.

She shrugged again, dragging her talons over the rocks under the water again. "Was the right thing to do, I suppose. I'll be fine. I'll go seek their forgiveness, and if they can't give it, I'll just have to find a new home. But you're the only man who's ever shown me kindness; I couldn't let them drown you."

I didn't like where my mind was going, but I never could ignore a damsel in distress—even one in mild distress. Even if this particular damsel looked as though she could easily kill me and had likely killed some of my men. My anger warred with my overwhelming desire to help her. The vein in my temple throbbed, and I reached up to rub at it.

She had obviously gone against her kind to save me from drowning, and even without knowing mermaid customs, it was clear that it was something the others would not approve of. My first meeting with the woman had been her running from something, and I hadn't been able to save her from being thrown overboard. Maybe now I could at least offer her some shelter until she was ready to decide where to go next. I needed to recover from my own near drowning before trying to find if any of my men had survived.

My stomach clenched. My men. My best friend and first mate, Duncan, entered my mind, and I desperately hoped he had somehow beaten the odds and survived.

"You wanna come with me? I know a place we can stay for a few days," I finally said, looking at her thoughtfully. She could at least rest and plan while I recovered enough to journey to find survivors and get back on track with my mission to stop my father. His evil plans wouldn't pause just because my ship had wrecked. I needed to get back to it before he got too far ahead.

She looked at me, her eyes piercing. "I don't know if that's a good idea."

Likely, she was right. But seeing the flash of sadness in her eyes when she had spoken about seeking forgiveness from the others still made me want to fix things for her. I never was one to push, though, so it would be her decision. "No, probably not. But the offer is there."

"Why would you even offer?" she asked, her eyebrows

furrowing. "You don't know me. My kind just tried to kill you."

I shrugged, struggling to keep my guilt and sadness over my crew's death tamped down, at least for now. I needed to deal with this first before I could mourn. "You need help."

Her face hardened, and I knew I had used the wrong words. She leaned in, her hands curling around the rocks beneath them. "I don't need anyone's help."

Unable to resist, I shrugged again. "Seems like you do. Unless you want to go back to those other mermaids who shunned you."

"We're not mermaids," she snarled. Leaning back, she crossed her arms over her chest and sniffed. "And I don't need your help."

"Fine," I conceded. If she didn't want my help, I wasn't going to force it on her. While I was grateful she had saved me from drowning, I had survivors to find and a mission to get back to, and neither could wait for me to convince the fiery-headed not-mermaid that she needed help. "I'll just be going, then."

"Wait," she gritted out after I had stood. I looked down at her expectantly, and she sighed heavily, letting her arms fall back to her sides. "I suppose I could stay with you for at least a night to make sure you don't have any lingering effects from the sea."

Sure, that was the reason. But I would let her think it for now. "Okay, then. Like I said before, I know a place not far from here."

"Which direction?" she asked, running her hands over her tail.

Bringing it back to my attention, I realized the tail would cause some issues with the travel to said place, though. "I'd have to get a big bucket for you to get there, though."

She laughed at that, a tinkling sound that I hadn't expected given the gravelly nature of her voice. From the look on her face, the laugh had surprised her as much as it had me. She recovered quickly, raising an eyebrow. "A bucket. I can just put my legs on. I'll just need some clothes."

My mind didn't know what to do with that bit of information either. I didn't exactly have any extra clothes for her just hanging around. I might have had some on the ship she had just caused to wreck, but not tucked away in my pocket of my now very wet trousers. And the house I was thinking of would be too far for me to carry a tailed lady. "You...can put... legs on?"

Now she let out a big laugh, throwing her head back, her hair shifting off her chest. Her fiery red-orange hair moved, uncovering her full breasts. I quickly averted my gaze, which seemed to make her only laugh harder. "You're such a gentleman. And yes, I can transform so I look just like a real girl. So, where's this place of yours?"

I swallowed, looking back at her but forcing my eyes to stay on her face and not her curvy torso and breasts. Every fiber of my being wanted to look at her, to drink in the curves I had glimpsed. But I reminded myself that she had killed my men, and, suddenly, she wasn't that tempting anymore. "If we're where I think, just a few miles over the hills in a little cove."

"Can you get to the cove from the sea here?" she asked, thankfully fixing her hair to cover herself again. Her nakedness obviously didn't bother her, but it did something to me. What, exactly, I wasn't quite sure of yet. "Since we don't have extra clothes or a bucket."

Going through the geography in my head, I nodded. While I could walk directly over the jutting land, she would have to swim around it. "Aye. It'd be longer than walking, but you can."

She looked over me, scanning my body from head to toe. While normally I would enjoy a pretty lady looking at me, her eyes were analytical as she scanned me, rather than appreciative. "Can you walk? Or if not, can you stand the water a bit longer?"

Taking inventory of my body—which was still very cold and sore, but not seriously damaged—I shrugged. "I can walk. What're you thinking?"

"You walk, and I'll swim and meet you over there," she explained, turning closer to the water. Finally looking up, she whirled quickly to glance at me over her bare shoulder. "Will there be clothes at this place? Or will you really need to get me a bucket?"

"I've not been there in a while, but there should be clothes for the both of us. Maybe not your size, but something," I responded. I hadn't been to the cottage in a while, but it should still be stocked with something to get us through the night. And if any of my men had survived, they would know I would try to get there at some point. If they were already there waiting for me, it could cause some issues, but I had confidence I could at least explain to the others before blood was spilled... by either side.

"What does it look like?" she asked. "Landmarks?"

"It's a stone cottage next to some big, mangled oak trees in a cove. There's a big rock arch at the mouth." The cottage was a ways from any large town, but close enough to the trade routes that I could easily get to port as I was needed. I was rarely there, preferring to stay on my ship, but now that it wasn't an option, the cottage would be seeing more use.

She was quiet for a moment, thoughtful, as she tilted her head to the side slightly. "I know where you're talking about. I'll meet you over there."

Using her hands, she pushed herself down the rocky beach into deeper water at the shore. "Are you sure you can walk that far? You were out for quite a bit."

My heart tugged at her concern. She had obviously given up something big to save me, and she was still concerned about my safety. While I was still reeling at the loss of my men and their uncertain fates, I was grateful for her mercy. I nodded at her in what I hoped was an encouraging manner. "Go. I'll meet you there. I'll beat you, so I'll have some clothes and a fire ready."

Slipping into deeper and deeper water until only her head remained above the water, she turned back to me, nodding once. "I'll meet you there."

As she disappeared into the waves, I turned and finally pulled myself to stand on the beach. Now that she was gone and I had only my thoughts to keep me company, I was cold. Very cold. I gritted my teeth as the brisk wind rushed across my skin and damp clothing. Great, just what I needed. Tensing my muscles, I geared myself up for the walk across the familiar rolling hills.

For some reason, I could only hope the girl actually met me at my cottage like she'd said she would. She had no reason to, and I already couldn't stop thinking about her. Much like when I was a boy, my thoughts raced over if she would be safe in the water. Despite knowing she was apparently more than capable of protecting herself, there were still things bigger than her in the seas.

I turned to the hills and started my trek. Nothing I could do about it now but walk.

CHAPTER EIGHT
BRIGID

Swimming toward the cove, my mind ran in circles. What was I even doing? I should be going back to the cave to grovel for the others' forgiveness and beg Cliodhna to take me back. To reassure Sorcha that I had not abandoned her. Goddess, Sorcha... What did she think of my actions? I had spent the past weeks convincing her that Cliodhna was right and that all men were evil, and then in the face of the one man I had admitted had redeeming qualities, I had left. Was she feeling vindicated? Or betrayed? I needed to get back to see her.

I should be going back to beg them to forgive my indiscretion and forgive my saving a man. And yet, here I was, swimming to go meet the boy again. No, he was a man now. A very handsome man. But still a man.

I was really doing this, saving this near stranger at the expense of my family. I knew Maira was upset, and maybe the others were too. They had every right to be, but I needed to make this right with the man. I needed to ensure he was safe and would be able to get back to wherever he had been going before we had wrecked him.

I had experienced little kindness in my life, and he had been the only man I ever knew to show me that. I valued my adopted family and my queen, and I knew no love for men, but there was something about this man that made me want to throw that conviction in the bin. Something about him that made me *need* to make sure he was safe.

He had been willing to risk punishment to hide me from his crew, and when we'd both been discovered, he still tried to fight to save me. No one before the syrens had ever done that before, and it had made a deeper mark in my heart than I even knew. I blamed Sorcha for dredging up these feelings and doubts in the last few weeks. But really, I knew the words she had said were true. Maybe not all men deserved our anger. And maybe this was my chance at proving that.

My heart was torn. The others, through the mouthpiece of Maira, had shunned me, and for understandable reasons. I wanted both their love and protection, but I also wanted to ensure the man's safety and earn his forgiveness for what I had done to his crew and his ship. I knew losing people was never easy, and we had likely wiped out his entire crew. I had never thought of our impact before, just followed my queen's orders without question.

But despite all of this, I was questioning myself. This man didn't know me. He didn't know how much importance I placed on his kindness. He wouldn't even question it if I left him. Likely, he would welcome it. Once the shock wore off, I was sure anger would be left in its place over his crew. And I could go back to the cave and beg for the forgiveness of Cliodhna and the others and hope they would take me back. But the thought of turning my back on one of the first people to show me kindness and care about what happened to me felt wrong, wrong down to my core. The sickening feeling when I thought about turning away from the cove where he was waiting made up my mind. I would go there, I would meet him, and I would stay until I was sure he was safe or until he turned me away.

As I approached the shore, there was something wrong with the sight before me. I was expecting to see one shape on the shore waiting for me, but instead, there were three. And that wasn't right. The man hadn't mentioned anything about the cottage being occupied or anyone meeting us, so I slowed down my approach, wary. Had he tricked me?

"Is that you?" I called out hesitantly. I was still far enough from shore that the figures were unclear, and far enough that if one of them wanted to reach me, they would have to swim a fair distance. "You all right?"

"No! Get out of here!" Caelum's voice came back, frantic. Ignoring his warning, I surged forward. His voice was enough of an indicator that he was in danger, and after the toll the water and the walk would have taken on his body, I wasn't optimistic he could defend himself against two attackers. After I'd risked everything to save him, I wouldn't let these men kill him now.

As I neared, the figures on the shore became clear. Two large men were holding him, and they were dragging him toward the water. Struggling, he still managed to shout at me. "Leave, lass!"

I had just saved the fool from drowning once, I wasn't going to let these brutes drown him again. The men had wrestled him down into knee-deep water as I approached. I smiled menacingly, baring my pointed teeth; that was plenty of depth for me to work with. Their eyes widened as they saw me moving toward them, but to their credit, they stayed true to their path, pulling Caelum into the water.

Snapping forward in a flash, I wrapped my webbed hands around one of the man's ankles, digging my talons in and yanking hard. It probably caught him off guard, because one rough pull was all it took for him to fall into the water. Using all my strength, I pulled him back into deeper water, dragging him by the ankle. My speed and strength prevented him from being able to pull his head above the water as I swam out to the deepest part of the cove. Finally, his body went limp and heavy in my grip, and I retracted my talons, letting his body sink down into the depths below. He had drowned quickly, and I was grateful.

Turning my attention back to the shore, I swam as close as I could before transitioning into my human form and surging out of the water, where Caelum was now fighting off the second man, and he was waning, his body sloppy and sluggish. The man he was fighting obviously had not expected me to come to his aid, as seeing me emerge from the waves made him stumble and lose his balance. That stumble was all the opening Caelum needed, and he swung a tired fist toward the man's face. It connected, and the man dropped onto the shore, unconscious.

Caelum looked at me, panting and shaking out his hand, his shoulders slumping. "I had him, *teine*."

"Obviously," I said, raising an eyebrow and again ignoring the name he called me. It was vaguely familiar, but his accent was from the south of Tuathnach, and it was a word I didn't know. I looked down at the man on the beach. "What did they want?"

He pushed his hand through his dark, messy hair, pulling it out of the tie that was barely holding it back any longer. It fell to brush his shoulders, wavy from the water that remained. His eyes roved over my body appreciatively before snapping back to my face, a blush spreading across his neck. "You. They wanted the 'mermaid,' they said."

My stomach dropped, and I cursed. Cliodhna had been right in her fears. My palms suddenly felt clammy, and my legs struggled to hold my weight as a flood of anxiety washed through me. I sucked in a deep breath through my nose, the cold air burning my throat. It gave me something to focus on as I shoved those feelings back down and steeled my spine. Anxiety would do me no good. I needed to find out more information and handle it. "Me? How do they even know I exist? Did they ask for me specifically?"

He held a hand out toward me, concern and suspicion shining equally in the green of his eyes. "Let's get you some clothes and we can talk more."

I looked away, trying to find something else to focus on.

Maybe I should have stayed in the water and taken my chances returning to *Neamh na Mara*. But I couldn't linger on that now. Jerking my head toward the unconscious man, I stopped. I could focus on disposing of this man. "What're you gonna do about him?"

He looked down at the man, still unconscious on the rocky beach. "Och, I had forgotten about him already. I suppose we can tie him up and leave him there."

"As soon as he gets free, he'll be gone in an instant. And he'd likely come back with company. We can't let him live," I bit out, frustrated at the situation I had found myself in. I couldn't risk him finding out more about me, about us, and endangering my family. I wouldn't say I enjoyed killing, but I had done it many times before and would be willing to do it again to protect what's mine—or what *had* been mine. "I will take him out and drown him like the other."

His eyes widened, but he had something akin to respect in them. After a moment of looking at me, he dropped his outstretched hand and nodded. "Yeah, that's probably for the best. It's quite lovely how bloodthirsty you are—when it's not me or my men that it's aimed toward, of course."

My eyes rolled. Of course, he would think me murdering people was attractive. The rest of his words registered, and guilt churned in my stomach before settling like a weight. "And I am sorry about your men."

"Whatever you say…" He trailed off. "What's your name again?"

"Brigid."

"Brigid," he drawled out, like he was tasting my name and

liked what he found. He smiled slightly, the corner of his lip turning upwards. It didn't quite reach his eyes as he nodded his head at me. "I'm Caelum, if you didn't remember. Go do your murderous fish-lady thing. I'll be here."

"I've got to get him into the water before I shift," I said, already reaching down to grab the unconscious man's arm. I had remembered Caelum's name, but hearing it aloud made things feel far more real.

Caelum pulled in a sharp breath behind me, and I realized belatedly that I had just bent over and showed him my entire arse. Before I could snap at him for his modesty again, he walked over and bent to grab the man's other arm. "Here, let me help."

Together, we pulled him out into deeper water. I was grateful he was still unconscious, as I did not want to deal with a thrashing man again. Once we got the man into deeper water where he could float off the bottom, I slipped into the water and laid back, my hair floating out behind me as I transformed. A tingling sensation started from my core, spreading down my legs as they merged and turned from human legs into a powerful tail. My fingernails lengthened into sharp talons, and my teeth pointed as well.

The transformation complete, I dug my claws into the floating man's arms, tugging him down into the water and out into the cove without a look back toward Caelum, who I could feel staring at me as I swam away. This man did not thrash as he drowned, thankfully. Once I was sure the man was dead, I let his body sink down into the depths of the cove before swimming back to the shore.

Transforming back into my human form, I entered shallow water and stepped out of the sea, my hair dripping icy water down my bare skin, which immediately pebbled as the equally icy wind whipped across me.

"I started a fire while you were out drowning that man." Caelum extended his hand again. "Let's go get you warmed up."

I nodded but didn't take his hand. I didn't need his help walking, and I didn't want to make this any more difficult on us when we eventually and inevitably parted ways. I was a syren, and once I ensured Caelum would be safe from any other immediate threats, I would be returning to my family to beg their forgiveness and do whatever it took to prove my worth to Cliodhna and ensure they were protected from the men who had been looking for me.

And Caelum would be grateful to be rid of the monster who had had a hand in killing his crew. But why was the idea of leaving him already making my stomach hurt?

When he realized I wouldn't be taking his hand, he let it drop once again and turned to lead me into the small stone cottage covered in soft green moss. He reached it before me, holding the sturdy wooden door open for me. I entered the cottage, immediately bathed in warmth from the fire going in the corner.

The small cottage was mostly bare, but it had a bed, a table and chairs, and most importantly, blankets. Shivers wracked through my human body once more as the cold spread through me.

By the time I noticed he had even walked toward the bed,

Caelum had returned with the heavy quilt that had been spread across it. He held it open and motioned for me to step in. "Here, *teine,* wrap up and dry off while I find you some clothes."

That word again. Deciding to continue ignoring it, I stepped into his arms, and he wrapped the quilt around me. I grabbed the corners from him and tucked myself into the large fabric, relishing its warmth and the weight around my shoulders. I didn't want to be reliant on him, but I knew when I was out of my element. And here? On land, in a strange house with a strange man? That was about as far out of my element as I could get.

My stubbornness to ensure Caelum would get back to wherever he had been going was overriding any sense I had. But despite being on land, I knew I was still able to take care of myself, whatever my anxiety might tell me. "Thanks."

Still holding me in his arms, he looked down at me. His eyes were intense as they locked with mine, and I was sucked into the swirling green there. No words were said, we just looked at each other as he held me in the quilt. My body was heating from his attention alone. The fierceness in his gaze wasn't aggressive, but I wasn't sure what it was. Determined, maybe. He blinked, and the moment was over.

He stepped back and motioned toward the bed as he turned toward a large trunk I hadn't noticed before. As I sat down on the scratchy sheets of the rickety wooden bed, he began rifling through the trunk. As he bent over, I took the time to study him without him knowing. His back was broad, and his still-damp shirt clung to the corded muscles there. As broad as his back was, he was extremely proportionate. Well-muscled all over and tall—very tall. His dark hair curled slightly where it brushed his shoulders. The sides of his hair near his temples and around his ears were shaved close to the skin. I wondered what it would feel like under my nails.

As he dug through the chest, his bare forearms flexed, showing off the muscle and power coiled under his sun-tanned skin. There was a thick, jagged scar around the wrist of his right arm, white with age, but puckered and extremely noticeable. I wondered where that came from.

Finally, he stood, then turned and walked over, handing me a bundle of clothing. "Here you go. They'll likely be quite big on you, but they should do."

Wordlessly, I took the clothes from him, standing and leaving the quilt behind on the bed. I heard his quick intake of breath before he whirled around, facing away from me. Shaking my head at his modesty, I quickly pulled on the clothes to ease his discomfort. The pants were scratchy and far too big, but the generous curve of my hips held them up…barely. Nothing could be done for the length, and I was sure I would trip over them embarrassingly often. The shirt swallowed me, the sleeves dangling past my fingertips where my talons had receded. I looked over at Caelum's back again. "I'm decent. You can turn around."

He spun around, his eyes sparkling with humor as he took me in, dragging his gaze slowly from my head to my toes. "You look like a little faery."

I rolled my eyes, ignoring his teasing statement. He was likely right. Even as a full human, I was much shorter than him, but that wasn't my fault. He was just extremely tall. "You need dry clothes too. Was there more in there for you?"

He shrugged, looking over his shoulder back to the open chest. "There was mainly blankets, but there's another pair of pants in there. I'll hang my shirt up to dry by the fire overnight and it should be fine. I'll set my boots out as well. They won't fit well at all, but there's another pair of boots in the trunk, too, if you need them."

Nodding, I sat back down on the bed, wrapping the quilt around me once more. It was warm, and despite its scratchy fabric, it reminded me of another time. "Do you have food?"

He shrugged again, turning his back to me and pulling the second set of britches out of the trunk. "We'll need to get some at some point, I suppose. Do you mind turning around?"

"Why? You shy?" I teased. I supposed I should have been more mindful of his apparent modesty issue, but over the past years with the other syrens, I had grown comfortable in my skin. Nakedness was normal to me now, and despite never seeing a man naked before, I doubted very highly it would make me feel different.

Snorting, he pulled his pants down over his hips, showing me his pasty white arse and legs, which were dusted with a dark smattering of hair. Keeping his back to me, he pulled on the dry pants quickly before straightening up and pulling his still-dripping shirt off over his head. Unlike his legs, his bare upper body was tanned by the sun, but it was still covered in the same dark hair. His back was mottled by deep and jagged scars, white with age like the one around his wrist. It looked like he had been whipped. Repeatedly.

While the scars turned my stomach at the thought

of someone inflicting them, they didn't detract from his appearance. He turned back around to face me, showing off his defined chest and stomach.

I was wrong. It had made me feel different to see him naked. Very different.

He tilted his head to the side as he studied me. "Wait. Do you even eat food?"

I blinked at him. I hadn't expected those to be the words out of his mouth. It took me another moment before I was able to respond. "Och, I do. I don't live off the seawater."

"Well, how exactly am I supposed to know what a fish lady eats? I didn't even really know your kind existed outside of fairy tales until today," he said, plopping his body down into one of the wooden chairs. It groaned under his weight as he shifted to get comfortable in the small seat. "I guess we'll have to find us some food, then."

CHAPTER NINE
CAELUM

"So, what is even around here for food?" she asked, still clutching the quilt around her frame. She really did look like a little faery, clad in too-big clothes and wrapped in a quilt. It was, in a word, adorable, but I doubted she would appreciate that thought being voiced aloud. In our brief interactions, it was clear there was a temper beneath the surface, burning as brightly as her hair. It was also obvious she tried to subdue that fire, to tamp it down and smother it. And something about that made me want to provoke her even more.

"I think there might be some dried meat in here somewhere," I replied, looking toward a cabinet in the corner. "And I can go into the next town over, Fairport, and get some things, depending on how long you want to stay here. That was where my ship was headed anyway, before it went down."

It would be a walk, but I was familiar with the town. There was lodging, food, and it would be close enough that if any of my men had survived, they would be heading there. Beyond wanting to get food, I desperately needed to see if anyone had lived through the wreck, if my best friend had lived or had fallen victim to the deadly women apparently prowling the seas. Trying to push my mind off my crew for the moment, I turned back to study Brigid. The conflict was clear on her face, as if she couldn't decide if she wanted me to leave or if she wanted to be the one to leave.

She was silent for a moment, looking out the small window toward the trees while chewing on her lip. "How long do we need to stay here?"

There was something in her voice that made me pause. It sounded almost like anxiety, and something in me wanted to fix it. "Just because those two were looking for you doesn't mean others will be. You'll be safe for as long as you're here. Until you decide what you're doing next."

Her brilliant green eyes snapped over to mine. Now her voice was firm and cold. "I do not need your protection. I was asking how long I needed to stay to make sure you don't die in your sleep."

A smile broke across my face. She was something, for sure, unlike any other woman I had ever met. Obviously, she didn't want me to worry about her and was disguising it by worrying about me instead. I didn't believe that the only reason she was staying was to make sure I stayed alive, but I'd let her hide behind it. For now.

"I won't die in my sleep. If you want to go, I'm not stopping you. But I would ask you to at least stay until I can get you some food." My anger was still simmering, but something about a woman—or anyone—in distress quelled it momentarily. It was a true failing of mine that had gotten me in trouble on more than one occasion, and I had little doubt it would again.

Despite wanting nothing more than to shake her and ask her why she believed all men were evil, I saw the hurt in her. It was the only thing that extinguished my anger.

"Fine," she huffed, pulling the quilt tighter. Her face pinched up, making her look even younger. Not for the first time, I wondered how old she really was. She had been young when I had found her aboard the ship, and although more than ten years had passed, she didn't look all that old. Not as old as I did, for sure.

After a few moments of silence and me just looking at her, she spoke again. "Why do you think they were after me? Do you think they really know for sure we exist?"

I heaved a sigh. I was wondering the same thing. Those men had jumped me as I was walking the last few meters to the cottage, ranting about a mermaid and asking where she was. They didn't mention any defining characteristics like Brigid's hair or the silvery red sheen to her tail, but I was still worried, same as she was. I walked over to sit down on the small bed next to her, my thigh brushing hers. "I don't know, but if you want, I can help you find out."

Her thigh was warm against mine, even through the quilt. I couldn't deny she was beautiful, and while she appeared to ponder over my statement, I let myself look at her more closely. She was stunning, of course, with a fire burning under the skin as bright as her hair. But there was obvious hurt there too, and I couldn't help wanting to ease that hurt however I could. It was a foolish notion, and one I should have been kicking myself for. Gods only knew that if my friends, my crew, could see me now, they would be furious.

She had been through a lot and was likely about to go through even more, if the day's happenings were anything to go by.

She still didn't speak, so after a moment, I added, "I can ask around in Fairport discreetly. You don't have to go if that's what you're worried about."

"I'm not worried about myself," she admitted, looking down at the quilt. She picked at the seams before stopping herself and flexing her fingers. She looked back up at me, determination shining bright. "If they know about us, my family is in danger, and I have no way to warn them."

"Why can't you warn them?" I asked. "I know they told you not to come back, but I'm sure they'd change their minds if you told them what happened."

She shook her head. Her fire was dulling, and her eyes were sad. I could see her chewing on the inside of her cheek. "They knew that it was always a possibility. But I don't know if I can go back. They might not let me in."

"Let you in…the ocean?" I asked, feeling like that wasn't what she meant but not knowing what else it could mean. I couldn't explain why, but in that moment, all I wanted to do was wrap my arm around her and pull her into my side, to comfort her, despite us both having better things we could be doing. More important things. I had my old crew's family to notify, a new ship to find, and a new crew to gather.

She snorted, and I couldn't help the smile that spread across my face. She was funny, and I was already connecting with her despite not knowing her that well. I felt guilty about that. She and the other syrens had killed my men. I shouldn't be connecting with her. But I couldn't seem to help it.

"Not in the ocean, you fool. Back where we live. Our queen has it spelled so only we or people we accompany can enter. After what I did, I imagine she's revoked my right to enter." As she spoke, her body visibly deflated, her shoulders slumping as she curled in on herself.

"But you don't know for sure?" I asked. I wasn't sure why I was encouraging her to return to her family—wasn't even sure why I was continuing to hold a conversation with her at all—but I was.

"No, I don't," she replied with a sigh, making an effort to sit back up straight and meet my gaze. "But what I did was a betrayal in their eyes. It wouldn't matter if I was trying to warn them, they wouldn't want to see me."

"Do you know that for fact?" I asked.

After a moment, she shook her head. "No, only one of them told me that. But the others didn't object. It's safe to assume that most of them feel that way, even if I've never done anything to have them doubt me."

"You saved me, *teine*," I said, the pet name slipping out of my mouth before I could stop it. Seeing her fire dull right in front of me had let the word slip right out, as if calling her "fire" could reignite that spark within her.

She raised an eyebrow at me, but thankfully didn't comment on the name.

Brigid had told me about what she and the other syrens did to men, but I still didn't quite understand what the big issue here was and why they had so quickly shunned her for interacting with me. It didn't seem like she was off saving every man she encountered, just me. They obviously hadn't saved any of the other men from my crew. Just thinking of them again brought my anger back to the surface, my fists clenching at my side. I took a deep breath to calm my rage, tamping it down for the moment. It would serve no purpose here other than pushing Brigid away. And I needed her to stay around a bit longer, at least until I understood if she could help us stop my father.

"You're a man. We syrens are all where we are, what we are, because men betrayed and hurt us. In the others' eyes, I chose you over them—I chose men over them—and that's apparently unforgivable. We made vows to our queen when we were turned, to be loyal to her, to follow her. And I broke those vows. It's just a matter of hearing the words straight from my queen."

Now it was my turn to snort. Lots of things were unforgivable, but saving my life was not one of those things—in my mind, at the very least. Perhaps the deaths of my crew could be unforgivable, but I had the feeling she was beating herself up about that enough. But we would get more into that later when she was more comfortable with me. "Well, that's just daft. Not all men were responsible for your pain."

"Not all men, no. But the people who caused our pain were all men," she pointed out, looking up at me. "That's how we all ended up together in the first place."

She had a point. I didn't know her story or what she had been through before or since meeting her on the ship that day. I certainly knew some men who should be punished. Maybe I would pass their names along to the other syrens, starting with my father. I bumped my shoulder into hers, trying to jar her out of her melancholy. "Well, thank you for saving my life. I do appreciate it."

"I told you before. You tried to save my life when I was a child, and I repay my debts."

"Well, now I'm in your debt," I pointed out. "I wasn't exactly successful at saving your life, not like you were with saving mine."

"We're even now," she argued. Debts were obviously important to her, and they were important to me too, but this situation wasn't as clear-cut as she was making it sound.

I waved a hand and stood up from the bed. I didn't want to argue technicalities with her. Now that I knew she needed food too, I needed to get us some. If it had just been me that was hungry, I could have stuck it out and waited, but again, my instinct to protect kicked me into action. Turning my back to her, I kept speaking as I looked through the cabinet by the wall. "Nay, you're stuck with me until we at least feed you. Plus, you don't really have anywhere to go unless you've changed your mind about going back to the other mermaids, and I happen to have this very cozy cottage."

"Not mermaids," she said exasperatedly. "Syrens."

I held my hands up apologetically. All right, good to know. "Syrens, then. Point still stands."

"This cottage barely has enough room for one of us, let alone both of us for any length of time," she said, the amusement in her voice coming through clearly. "But thank you."

"Still, it's something. We both need to get warm and rest before we start doing anything else," I said, finally successful in focusing long enough to find some dried meat in a cabinet. There was also what looked like some very stale bread on the shelf, but I wouldn't break into that unless it was a last resort. I turned back, handing her some of the meat. "Here, eat this while I stoke the fire."

She started chewing the tough meat, watching me as I bent over to tend to the fire in the small fireplace against the wall. I could feel her stare on me, and I liked it. For once, her gaze felt less analytical and more like she was enjoying what she saw. While I liked her attention, I tried to remind myself that she'd had a hand in the deaths of my crew, and I could not—would not—get involved with her.

Once the fire was going strong, I went back over to the bed and pulled the covers down next to her. I patted the mattress, grimacing when I felt how thin it was. I had gotten used to the hammocks on the ship, and going back to this hard and thin mattress would not be ideal. In a move I hoped seemed gentlemanly and not like I was passing it off to her, I motioned toward the bed. "Here, you can take the bed."

"Where will you sleep?" she asked, looking around the nearly bare cottage.

I rubbed the back of my neck, looking over at a spot on the

floor by the fireplace. It wasn't ideal, but with enough of the raggedy blankets in the trunk, I could at least sleep through the night without being in too much discomfort. "I'll take the floor."

"Why?"

I looked at her, confused. "Why what?"

She looked at me, exasperated. I had a feeling she would be looking at me like that a lot based on how our interactions had gone so far. "Why will you take the floor? The bed is big enough for both of us, isn't it?"

All the words in my mind escaped me. "But..."

Her lips quirked up into a small smile. "I appreciate your concern, Caelum. But we can share a bed for one night as long as it doesn't harm your delicate sensibilities. Besides, I need to make sure you don't die in your sleep."

I snorted. She still couldn't be seriously concerned about me dying; I was clearly in no danger of it anymore. I wasn't sure if she was being serious or using it as an excuse to not go back to her fellow syrens.

"I won't die sleeping on the floor. And I don't have delicate sensibilities, I'm trying to be a gentleman," I pointed out. Sleeping in the same bed as her was a bad idea, and even though I could see that she was goading me, I couldn't help my reactions.

A teasing smile lit up her face. "Are you scared to sleep next to a syren, Caelum?"

I sputtered, my cheeks and neck burning. "N-no. I'm just trying...trying to be respectful."

She full-on laughed at that point, and I could feel my

cheeks heating up. I wasn't used to being teased by a woman. *I don't think I like this.*

She turned her body, slipping under the blankets on the bed, which was big enough for both of us to lay comfortably, before spreading the quilt she was wrapped in out across her legs. She patted the space on the mattress beside her. "Come on. We both need rest. It's been years since I slept in a bed, anyway I might need someone to keep me from falling off it."

I should be jumping into the bed. She was a beautiful woman, and she wanted to share a bed with me. Just to sleep, of course, but the sentiment was still there. But she had been so young when she was thrown over, and I doubted there were male syrens around. My mind warred. On one hand, she was beautiful. On the other, she had just played a role, big or small, in the deaths of my men, and I couldn't just forget that.

"Not tonight, lass. I'll take the floor," I said, strengthening my resolve. I had to remember her actions, and I had to remember that if she hadn't recognized me, I would be dead along with my crew. It was a small distinction, but it built up the wall again in my mind. This woman would be trouble, I knew it.

She sighed heavily like she was yet again irritated with me, but she rolled over onto her side, her back facing me. "Goodnight, then. Get some rest."

I folded several blankets onto the floor by the fire, lying down on my back with an arm behind my head. Looking over at the long waves of fire and gold that spilled over the dingy pillow on the bed, I let myself smile at the sight. "Goodnight, *teine*."

As sunlight spilled in through the dirty windows, waking me, I became aware of someone watching me. I hoped it was only Brigid. If anyone else was looking at me, I was too tired to fight them. Peeking open an eye to avoid her noticing I was awake, I studied her. She lay on the bed on her side, an arm curled under her head as her eyes roamed over my body.

I studied her in return. She was gorgeous, and here, just waking up, she looked so peaceful and young. There was no tension in her face or her body for the first time since we'd met. She was at ease in my bed. Granted, it was a bed I never really used, but it was still one that I had slept in before. The thought that she was this relaxed around me sent my heart off at a run. I couldn't explain the reaction I was having to her, and I didn't want to stop to think about it at any length.

Suddenly, her body tensed beneath the quilt. "You're awake."

My smile widened, and I couldn't help but tease her. "Aye, lass. Been watching you watch me."

Her cheeks tinted pink. "I wasn't watching you."

"It's okay. I know I'm irresistible," I teased her.

She glared at me then, her embarrassment quickly forgotten, which had been my intent. "Well, are you going to get us some more food?"

I sat up, looking at her as she did the same to me. "Aye, I'll be leaving here in a moment once I wake up some."

"Is your shirt dry?" she asked, standing up from the bed quickly and walking over to where the shirt was hanging off a chair. She picked it up, scrunching the fabric between her hands.

"So eager for me to put my clothes back on?" I teased again. I couldn't seem to help myself; her lack of non-violent experiences with men was both alluring and a challenge.

I shook my head. No. I shouldn't be thinking that she was alluring. She killed my men, and I needed to remember that.

She rolled her eyes, oblivious to my internal argument, and tossed the shirt at me. "Here, go get us some food."

I caught the shirt, pulling it on over my head while I forced myself to laugh. For someone who had no problem with nudity, her lack of comfort at simple intimacy with another person was genuinely amusing. Though maybe she was genuinely just very hungry. "All right, all right, I'll be going. Let me just tend the fire."

"I can do that." She waved a hand, nodding her head at the door to the cottage. "You go on so you can get back while there's still daylight."

"I'll be off, then. There should be enough wood here to make it for another day. If we end up staying here longer, I can go chop some more," I said, motioning toward the crackling fire. I looked out the window to see the sun rising up over the horizon. "I should be back from the town by dark, but if I'm not, I'll be back first thing in the morning."

"I can take care of myself, Caelum," she replied, smiling.

My heart took off at a dead run again when she said my name. She hadn't said it since she'd pulled me from the water, and I very much enjoyed hearing it come from her mouth.

Again, I shook myself at the thoughts. Why couldn't my body keep in line with my brain when it said to not get attached to this girl, this creature who had killed my crew?

I went back over to sit next to her on the bed once more. I took her hand in between my own. They were still cold, but hopefully she would warm up more now that she was moving around. "I know you can. And I hope you'll still be here when I get back."

She tilted her head, and her gaze locked with my own. "Why?"

"We still have much to talk about, including why you chose my ship to wreck," I said, only lightly teasing her this time. I really did need to find a new ship and see if any of my crew had washed up alive in the town. My plans to stop my father would be really set back if I had to start from scratch again.

Hopefully, going into Fairport to get food would be a twofold mission. I could get food, yes, but I could also see if my crew was alive and find any survivors.

"I did not know it was your ship. Why would I intentionally wreck your ship just to go against my queen to save you?" she pointed out, still holding my gaze. It was getting warm in here again, and I wasn't sure if it was from the freshly stoked fire or from her eyes.

"We'll discuss that when I get back. You stay here, stay inside. I'll be back with food and supplies, and we can go from there," I said, releasing my hold on her hands and patting her knee. I stood up, slipping on my boots. They were finally dry after sitting out by the fire all night. "I'll be back soon."

She smiled at me. "Be safe as well."

With a smile of my own, I turned and walked out of the cabin before I did something really stupid—like kiss her.

CHAPTER TEN

CAELUM

After several hours of walking, I finally made it into the small village of Fairport. It was barely a village, but it would be the closest place any of my crew would have found if they had survived the wreck. And I desperately hoped they had. Fairport would also have food and clothing for Brigid and me. I could only hope again that she would keep her word and still be there and be safe.

But first, I needed to see if any of my men had survived. I turned my path toward the first place they would go if they had lived through the wreck. The pub. With food, a fire, and a place to sleep, it would be the perfect place for them to post up and recover.

Hustling down the dirt path, I pushed open the door to the

pub, stepping in out of the brisk air. I held my breath, trying not to get my hopes up.

"Caelum! You made it!" a loud voice sounded off to the right. My first mate, Duncan. I let out a heavy breath, tension bleeding out of my body. We had been friends for so long, I was grateful that I didn't have to learn to live without him. I had been doing my best to not think about him as I walked, and a wave of relief washed over me, nearly buckling my knees.

I walked over to his table, where he was sitting with two more from our crew, Cameron and Maddock. I stopped, speechless for a second as gratitude over their survival clogged my throat.

Cameron had a cut on his forehead, slightly covered by his brown curls, but it did nothing to detract from the relief in his dark eyes. Maddock looked visibly uninjured, his own dark hair pulled back neatly from his light brown skin. He studied me, his eyes likely scanning me for injuries as I did the same for him.

It didn't surprise me that of all my crew, these three were the ones that made it. A breathless laugh left my lips. "Duncan, I'm so glad to see your ugly face!"

Duncan stood up, towering over me, and yanked me into a crushing hug before pushing me back to look me over. We shared a smile that I felt down to my bones before I stepped over to give equal hugs to both Cameron and Maddock.

Duncan quickly reclaimed my attention, putting his hands on my shoulders and looking at me intently. I could see the worry and fear in his bright blue eyes. It was similar to the fear I had been trying my best to ignore since being rescued by

Brigid. He smiled sadly. "Are you okay, Caelum?"

I didn't want to tell them about Brigid yet, for some reason. I wouldn't risk that until I was back to protect her, not that she needed it. But my loyalty to Duncan, Cam, and Maddock weighed heavily. They should know. Sidestepping the questions, I turned and studied them. They were relatively unscathed, and I was almost giddy with the knowledge that they had lived. I wanted to ask them how they had survived, but I was overwhelmed by the relief washing through me; all I could do was smile like a fool.

Duncan leaned in, his eyes hardening as he reflected on the ordeal and the question I hadn't been able to verbalize. "When Archer steered us into the cliff to get away from whatever was making that horrible noise, we all jumped over on the cliff side instead of into open water. We figured the beasts would be waiting on the water side to pick us off."

"Did you see them?" I asked, knowing he was talking about Brigid and the syrens. I swallowed hard and forced the next words out. Brigid was not a beast, but I knew they would be expecting me to call the syrens the same thing they did. "The beasts?"

Duncan shook his head. "Not clearly, but what else could it have been? I know they're a myth, but come on. It was obviously mermaids. Did you see them?"

I exhaled sharply, about to answer honestly and tell them everything, but I stopped myself. Those men had found my cottage, a cottage only my crew knew about. And they had known about Brigid and what she was. Obviously, someone had let information slip, and I needed to be more careful about what we spoke about in public.

I knew in my gut that the men in front of me had not been the ones to tell those men where to find Brigid and me, but someone had obviously told them. And it had been someone who had heard the myths of mermaids. While that didn't help narrow down my suspicion, it guided me toward someone familiar with the stories of the seas. I rubbed at my forehead, my mind flickering back to the rest of my crew. "Did anyone else survive?"

"We're the only ones who have washed up here so far. We've been watching for others," Duncan said, sitting back down and motioning for me to do the same. He looked me over again, questions in his eyes. "Where did you wash up?"

"South of here, near the cottage. I stopped there last night to rest," I explained. Then something hit me. "How did you all get out of the water? There's no accessible coast by the cliffs."

"You swam all the way to your cottage? You blasted fish!" Duncan exclaimed, his eyes wide and suspicious. "How did you get that far?"

Shit, I shouldn't have said that. He was right, there was no way I could have reached the cottage on my own from where the ship went down. I wiped a hand over my face before pushing my hair back. Gods, how I wanted to just tell them the truth. But my protective instincts soared. If I told them, Duncan especially would never let me return to the cottage. "I walked from the coast over the hills to the cottage. I only swam to the shore on the other side of the cove."

"Still, that's a long way in cold water," Duncan said. He motioned to the others. "We climbed up the cliffs a bit to a ledge and waited until another boat, some fishermen, came by. They brought us back here."

Fishermen. My mind churned with possibilities, none of them good. If my men had told them what they had seen, that we had been attacked by what could have been mermaids, would they come after us? Mermaids were a myth in my world, but if anyone thought they were real, it would turn into a hunt to prove it. I turned to Cameron and Maddock. "Did either of you see anything in the water?"

Cameron nodded, crossing his arms over his narrow chest. "Just some vague shapes in the depths. Looked like long fish, but I swear one of them had hair. Blonde hair."

Maddock nodded as well, leaning forward to rest his forearms on the table. "Same as Cam. Nothing for sure, but it wasn't like any sea creature I'd ever seen before. We've all heard the stories, it had to be the mermaids. Why?"

Ignoring his question, I continued my own line of thoughts. "Did you tell the fishermen what you saw?"

"Caelum, what's going on?" Duncan asked, putting his big hand on my arm. He was concerned. I knew it. We had basically grown up together, and he knew me better than I knew myself sometimes. "Did something happen?"

I sighed heavily, rubbing my free hand over my face. I was either going to have to quickly become a better liar to my oldest friend, or trust that he and the others would at least listen to what I had to say. I decided to take a chance, mainly because I knew Duncan would see right through any lie I told. "Two men met me at the cottage and attacked me. They were asking about a mermaid."

Duncan took a sharp inhale of breath, immediately looking around suspiciously. "At your cottage?"

I nodded. "Aye. That's why I need to know if you saw anything and if you said anything. Only the crew knows of my cottage."

"Are you okay, Captain?" Cam asked, worry in his eyes as they scanned over my body again. "Did they hurt you?"

"No, I'm fine. I took care of them. But did you all tell anyone—anyone at all—about the cottage or about anything you saw in the water?" I pressed. If they had told someone, even if it hadn't been maliciously, there could be others on the way to the cottage now. And Brigid was there alone.

"We didn't say anything, Caelum. We know the cottage is supposed to be a secret," Duncan said, leaning in closer to me. He lowered his voice. "But what's this really about? I can tell there's more to it."

I hated that I hesitated. Brigid's safety was important to me for some reason that I didn't want to stop to think about yet, but these were my most trusted men and my best friend. If I couldn't trust them, I couldn't trust anyone. I took a deep breath, steeling my nerves. "You all need to come back to the cottage with me. There's a situation. And I'll not explain it here, so don't ask me."

"What do you need from us, Captain?" Maddock asked, leaning in as well. "You know we'll do whatever you need us to."

"Okay, then we need food and clothes. Clothes for me, and clothes for a woman." Brigid would likely be furious at me for bringing others back with me without telling her, but I needed their help. And I needed her help.

Duncan's eyebrows shot up into his sandy blond hair. His voice was loud. "A woman? When did you have time to meet a woman while you were swimming to shore?"

"Duncan, what part of 'don't ask' was unclear?" I hissed, lowering my voice and looking around. If I gave any more details here, Duncan would likely figure it out. And if he could, anyone listening could. The jump from naked woman in the water to mermaid wasn't a large one for someone with any intelligence, unfortunately. And Duncan was anything but stupid. "Help me get clothes, help me get food, come back to the cottage with me, and I will explain everything then."

"Sure. Whatever you need." Suspicion was still clear in his eyes, and I could see the wheels churning in his head, but I hoped that he would remain ignorant for a bit longer. Thankfully, our legends about mermaids—no, syrens—seemed to be somewhat false, given that we hadn't known they could transform into human forms.

"Captain, I know you said no questions," Cameron started tentatively. "But what about the mission we were on when the ship was wrecked? We have to keep going to stop your father, or he's going to get too far ahead of us."

"We'll get back to that once we can find a crew and a ship," I explained. That mission was important to me and to the men. We wouldn't forget about it or the children we were working to save from my father. "We'll need to notify families of those we lost as well."

"Who are we sure is dead?" I asked, sighing heavily. I didn't want to go through this, but if we had any chance of getting back to stopping my father's nefarious plans, we needed to know our numbers. If any of our crew had survived, I needed to find them.

"Archer and Gordan for sure," Duncan said immediately. "And I saw Alastair go down as well."

"Bain and Connor as well," Maddock added. "Grady, Curran, and Liam also never resurfaced."

Cameron cleared his throat. "I only saw Sloane and Whelan go under."

"So, we don't know what happened to over half of our crew?" I asked, counting the names as they spoke. I tried hard to ignore the knot forming in the center of my chest as they named those we had lost. They had all been good men, ready to fight to stop my father.

My fists clenched, anger bubbling up. I spread my fingers out across the table, focusing on the feel of the wood beneath my fingertips to calm down. Anger would do me no good right now.

"We can keep searching for the rest of them," Duncan offered softly.

"With what ship, Duncan?" I asked, my anger seeping into my voice. Why had we been chosen for ruin by the syrens when men like my father were free to sail the seas spreading their evil wherever they chose? It hardly seemed fair. I took a deep breath to calm myself. My anger was of no use pointed at my own crew. They knew how despicable my father was. "Sorry. I'm just frustrated."

"Aye, we know, Captain," Cameron said quietly. "But it's not your fault. We all knew the risks of sailing. If it wasn't...

whatever it was, it could have been a number of different things that did us all in."

"We need to notify their families," I repeated, as if saying it again would take care of the task for me. Most of the crew had come from Brinemoor, and I was not anxious to get back there and inform the families of the losses. But I knew I'd have to travel there eventually, as that was my father's home base, and he would likely be returning there soon.

"Aye, we'll handle it as soon as we can," Duncan said, standing from the table and clapping a hand on my shoulder. "Now, let's get back to the supplies you need. When did you have time to find a girl in the middle of all this?"

Despite the sadness of the situation, Duncan's words brought a smile to my face. But I couldn't tell him the truth. Not yet. "You'd be surprised."

"Well, since you know what your girl looks like," Maddock outlined, standing as well, "you and Cam can get clothes. He has some coin we managed to grab before jumping off the ship. Duncan and I will get food, and we'll meet back here when we're done."

"First," I said, stopping them from moving away from the table. I reached over and picked up a mug of ale and raised it. "A toast to those we lost."

We all stood, clanking our mugs together and sloshing some of the golden liquid onto the table. Duncan nodded his head solemnly. "To those we lost."

Emptying our glasses, we set them back onto the table. Maddock smiled sadly at me. "We'll get through this, Captain. We've gotten through worse before."

I nodded, grateful that he was giving out instructions for once. Maddock always was a planner, which made him an invaluable asset to my crew. I picked at a stray seam on my shirt, peering out the window of the tavern. "I want to be back to the cottage before dark, if possible."

The boys all nodded back to me. Duncan clapped his hands. "We better get moving, then."

A short time later, Cameron and I had walked back to the pub, bundles of clothing in sacks slung over our shoulders. I had gotten several days' worth of sturdy, casual clothing for both of us, and some thick socks and rugged boots for Brigid. The boots were likely too big for her, but they would fit her better than the ones of mine at the cottage. And if she was going to be in her human form for any length of time, she'd need them.

As we walked up to the entrance, Duncan and Maddock came around the corner with their own bags. Duncan held his up. "Got it, Cae."

I smiled at his enthusiasm. "Then let's start walking. We should be able to make it back to the cottage before it gets too dark."

"Uh, hey, Caelum," Maddock started tenuously, "That cottage only has one bed, and it's fairly small. And if you've got a girl there, how are all of us supposed to fit to sleep?"

My smile dropped. I hadn't thought of that. Well, damn. Tight quarters were usual for us, but sharing tight quarters with a woman was definitely not the norm.

Maddock laughed at my expression. "It's okay, Captain. You've had a lot on your mind, apparently. We can meet you in the morning with the clothes if that's okay to you, so you don't have to carry both bags all that way. Or we can all bunk on the floor together."

I ran a hand through my hair, which reminded me that I needed to replace my band that I used to hold it back. "If you can all keep your traps shut tonight, you can meet us in the morning at the cottage."

"Steel trap, Captain," Duncan said. He handed me the heavy bag of food and took my bag of clothes. "We'll leave here at first light."

I nodded at them, grateful they were alive but still mourning those we had lost. "Stay safe. I'll see you in the morning."

"You as well, Captain," Cameron said, stepping over to stand next to Duncan and Maddock.

I turned and began walking away before I remembered something important. Stopping and turning around, I walked back up to them, leaning in conspiratorially. "Oh, and if you see a girl at the cottage with red hair and I'm not with her for whatever reason, assume she's dangerous, eh? I'd hate to have her kill you when I just found you alive."

"What the hell kind of girl have you found, Captain?" Duncan asked, narrowing his eyes.

"Don't worry, boy. It'll be fine." Smiling at them, I waved as I hefted the sack of food onto my back and began my journey back to the cottage, and back to Brigid…hopefully.

CHAPTER ELEVEN

BRIGID

As soon as Caelum left the cottage, I jumped from the bed. I watched from the window until he was out of sight. I needed to get into the water and back to the caves. I needed to at least *try* to warn the others.

Stepping out of the cottage, I made my way down to the shoreline, pulling off my clothes as I went. Bending down, I folded them into a pile, leaving them on the beach for my return. I stiffened at the thought. Would I be returning? Did I even *want* to return?

That thought stopped me in my tracks. I had never imagined a life away from the syrens; I had never wanted to. But less than a day with Caelum had me questioning my choices.

Warning the others was the most important thing to me

right now, but I couldn't help feeling like I still owed Caelum a debt. The one I owed for him trying to save me may have been paid, but he had lost his entire crew at the hands of my kind.

Shaking my head, I decided to deal with that later. I stepped into the icy water and waded out into the deep. Letting my transformation take over, I quickly began swimming toward the caves.

As I neared them, my chest tightened. Would I even be able to get in?

Thankfully, I was able to swim to the entrance and make my way inside the large cavern. As I rounded the rocky walls, I heard the others talking, though I couldn't make out their words.

Steeling my spine, I swam forward, revealing myself. The conversation stopped.

"What are you doing here?" Maira hissed, swimming up to me in an instant and leaving her seat next to Sorcha behind. "I told you to not come back."

"I know, but—"

"No, there is no reason for you to be here. You left us for that man." She bared her teeth at me, her talons flexing at her side.

Cliodhna swam forward, a frown marring her otherwise perfect face. "Maira told us what you did, Brigid."

I nodded, lowering my gaze respectfully. "Aye, I saved him. But he tried to save me from the violence of man when I was a child."

"He didn't succeed." Cliodhna's voice was harsh, harsher than I had ever heard before. She swam closer to me, stopping directly in front of me. "So, why did you feel like it was worth using my gifts to you, *my power,* to save him?"

Shame swirled in my stomach, but I pushed it down. I had spent years shoving down my emotions, and I needed to do it once more. "He is innocent."

"That does not mean he deserves your kindness now," Cliodhna bit out, grimacing. Her jaw clenched, and her forehead furrowed. "You are squandering my gifts to you for this man."

Again, her words were like a knife, stabbing through my stomach. I couldn't reply. I knew there was nothing I could say that would make this better for them.

"Maira spoke the truth. You are no longer welcome in our home. You have disgraced me and your fellow syrens by siding with this man." She raised her chin high before turning away dismissively.

I looked up at her, my throat burning as I fought back tears. I wanted desperately to search out Sorcha and talk to her, but I knew if I gave Cliodhna anything less than my full attention, I would regret it. "I understand your ire, my queen. But I will repay this debt to this man. And then I will earn your forgiveness."

"Why did you return?" Maira asked, her eyes narrowing. "You knew you would not be welcomed."

"There are men on the surface," I explained. "They were looking for mermaids. I wanted to come warn you."

"And you think that would earn our forgiveness?" Maira spat, disgust clear in her face.

"No," I admitted. I knew there would be much more that I

would have to do to earn their forgiveness, if I even could. "But I still had to tell you. I couldn't bear it if something happened to you all."

"No one will find these caves. We are protected here," Cliodhna said, her eyes narrowing at me. "And for you to imply that I cannot protect my creations is…unwise."

"That's not what I was implying," I said, raising an eyebrow. My protectiveness would not be dismissed or looked down on. "You all matter to me, and I want to make sure you are safe."

"Don't pretend you care about us now. You abandoned us on a whim."

"And now you're abandoning me as well," I replied softly, knowing my words would cause even more anger. But they needed to be said. Yes, in their eyes, I had betrayed them,but they had decided to denounce me after more than a decade together for one decision I had made.

Maira shook her head, a look of disgust on her face. She didn't say anything else before turning and disappearing deeper into the caverns.

Cliodhna looked at me for a long moment. "You will leave here and not return. Once you leave, the caves will be closed to you. And once you leave, you will lose your song."

"You're taking my powers?" I asked, the breath rushing out of me. No, she couldn't. She'd never taken anything back before. Would she make me forget them as well?

"I am taking back *my* powers, girl," she said, her voice as icy as her eyes. "They were never yours to begin with. Some of them I cannot remove; I don't have enough power to do so currently. You will still be able to transform, but I am stripping the magic that makes it painless. It will be excruciating for you now. You will no longer be able to communicate with us in the seas. And you will not be welcomed in my waters any longer."

Without another word, she turned and disappeared into the caverns as well. The others, except for Sorcha, followed, although much slower. Kyla lingered the longest, casting me a sorrowful glance before she too turned and left. Sorcha remained, just watching me, an unreadable expression on her face. My stomach twisted at the thought of being so easily dismissed by my adopted family, but I hadn't been able to bring myself to abandon Caelum on the beach, and I couldn't now.

Sorcha swam closer, almost hesitantly. She looked hurt, betrayed, but also confused. "Why are you doing this? You left me, Brigid."

I shook my head, trying to get her to understand my choices. "I have no love for men, Sorcha, you know that. But this man, when he was just a child, tried to save me, and he was punished for it. I have to repay that debt. I couldn't let him drown. You were right, maybe some of them are innocent. Or at least innocent enough to deserve a second chance."

She looked at me for a long moment, her eyes betraying nothing. Her face was conflicted, her brows pinching together as she studied me. As quickly as it had come, that expression vanished, replaced with blankness that I feared she had learned from me. Maybe the others had already gotten to her, turning her against me. She sighed heavily. "I hope he's worth it, Brigid. And I hope he truly is innocent."

I offered her a small smile before jerking my head toward the exit of the cavern. "Go on. I'll be fine, lass, and so will you. I am sorry."

Once they had all left, I took one last look at the caves I had called home before I turned and departed. Swimming back to the surface, I lingered near the beach, not wanting to leave the water. I wasn't ready to give up my tail and my song, the form I had known for ten years, and the power that came along with it. I just wanted to sit here for a while before it was taken from me.

CHAPTER TWELVE
BRIGID

The sun was just beginning to set, blazing streaks of red and orange over the waves, when I finally left the water. I let the transformation take over me, relishing the feelings and sensations moving through my body, painless one last time. Sadness filled me and burned at my throat once the change was complete. I was human again. Mostly.

With a heavy heart, I pulled the clothes from the beach onto my body, ignoring how they clung to my wet skin uncomfortably. I deserved the discomfort. I deserved the hatred from my family, and I deserved the angry looks from Caelum whenever he thought about his crew. This was all my fault, and at the end of the day, when Caelum was ready to leave, I would be alone again.

I trudged back up the beach to the cottage, taking out my frustrations on the heavy wooden door as I flung it open and entered. The inside of the cabin was cold again, reminding me that I had been gone nearly all day. Caelum would be back soon, if he returned at all. I still wasn't convinced he wouldn't cut his losses and leave me behind.

Sighing, I bent and tended to the almost extinguished fire before settling in at the table to wait.

The sun had nearly set when Caelum appeared through the window, walking toward the door. I stood from the table, unsure if I should go out to meet him or not. I hated that I was excited to see him. I shouldn't be, and the knowledge that I was tasted sour on my tongue. I was hurting those I had been closest to; I shouldn't be happy about it.

In the time I took to question my actions, Caelum had opened the door and stepped in, a huge smile spreading across his face. His eyes lit up before narrowing and turning suspicious, like he wasn't sure why I was still in the cottage. "You're still here."

"I am," I replied hesitantly. Did he not want me to stay? I took a deep breath to calm the anxiety coursing through me. If he wanted me to leave, he should have told me so. "You brought a bag?"

He held up the canvas sack in his hand, the grin returning easily to his face. "Yes, I brought food."

At the mention of food, my stomach grumbled loudly. Before I had gone to the sea, I had eaten the remaining dried meat from the cabinet, but that had been hours ago. The sensations of my empty stomach clenching around nothing brought back memories from my childhood that I would rather have stayed forgotten. With a twist of my jaw to unclench it, I took a deep breath and shoved the memories down. As a syren, I hadn't really had to worry about food, as Cliodhna had always provided for us. But those days were over. My stomach grumbled again, and my cheeks heated at Caelum's grin.

"So, what did you bring?" I asked, trying to take the attention off my demanding body.

"I'm not actually sure. A friend got it for me," he said, opening the bag and peering down inside.

My stomach clenched, but not from hunger this time. He had met someone in town? He hadn't mentioned that when he left. My mind wondered what else he hadn't told me. "Friend? Did you tell someone we were here?"

He nodded but held a hand up quickly, palm out as if I were a wild animal. "I found some of my crew that survived. They'll be coming here in the morning to meet with us. To help. They're not going to hurt you. I didn't tell them what you are."

Glaring at him, I grabbed the sack out of his hand and stomped over to the table. I couldn't believe it. One man was hard enough for me to deal with, but others? I didn't think I could do it. The feelings of shame and betrayal were enough when I was just with Caelum, but now, with more men coming to the cottage, I was sinking further and further into the feeling that maybe Maira was right, and I had made a mistake saving him.

Dumping the contents out of the bag, I tried to smother my fiery anger. I concentrated my attention on the food sprawled across the table: cheese, crusty bread, meat, and fruit. My stomach grumbled again. I was furious. We had already been attacked by two men, and now Caelum was inviting more here. My emotions warred again between staying and leaving. But if I left, where would I go? I had nowhere and no one to go to. Maybe, if I could get to the syrens' contact in the south in Bhodheas, I could use her help. I'd never met her myself, but I knew she was willing to help those in need.

I heard him walk up behind me, his body heat encroaching onto my skin. His voice was soft. "Hey, it's okay. They will not hurt you."

My jaw clenched tightly, and the muscles in my cheeks protested. His soft tone irritated me for some reason. It was like I was a rabid animal he was trying to calm, and maybe I was to him, but it still grated my nerves. "I don't need your protection. From you, your men, or anyone."

He put his hand on my upper arm, gently tugging me to look at him. Somehow, I was able to keep from ripping out of his grip and grabbing his throat for touching me. I wanted to be angry. Goddess, I wanted to be angry. But the softness I found in his green eyes tempered it down against my will. "You may not need it, but you have it. They're going to help us. Help you find a way back to your family and help me find a way to continue my mission."

This was the third or fourth time he had mentioned a mission. I was curious, but also hesitant. I didn't want to get involved in whatever he was involved in; I knew it would only make it harder to leave. And I would leave. I would leave and return to my home, I promised myself. Though, a tingling sensation of doubt began to form in my stomach. *I am returning to them,* I vowed. I remained silent, looking deep into his eyes.

After a few heartbeats, he released my arm and stepped around me to pick up a piece of bread. He pressed it into my hand. "Here, you need to eat. We'll talk more about my men while you do."

Eat. I could do that. I nodded at him, moving around the small wooden table to sit down. I tore off pieces of the bread, eating it while watching him do the same. I swallowed hard, pushing my anxiety back down as far as I could get it. I needed to be strong. "What are their names? How many survived?"

He looked at me, and for a moment, I didn't think he would answer. His eyes were sad, and I realized he was likely thinking of the men he had lost. I opened my mouth to tell him that he didn't have to tell me. He didn't have to share that with me if it hurt too much.

But finally, he spoke. "Duncan is my first mate. He's smart, sharp, keeps my head on straight. Then there's Cameron and Maddock; I've known them both for years. Cam is a fun guy; he's my quartermaster and strong as an ox for being so skinny. And Mad is too smart for his own good, always analyzing everything and everyone. A bit like you, actually, always observing. They're good men. They won't hurt you."

I wasn't sure what to say to that, so I just shoved more bread in my mouth. After chewing slowly, I was finally able to respond. "How did they survive?"

"Fishermen found them, rescued them from some cliffs."

"Did they question how you survived?" I was sure they had, and yet I had to know all I could. Understanding the entirety of the situation would ease my anxiety and make it easier to manage my expectations when I met these others.

"Aye. And I imagine they'll have even more questions once they meet you."

That set my spine on edge once again, my jaw tensing so hard my teeth groaned at the pressure. Consciously, I unclenched my jaw and flexed it from side to side. "Did you tell them about me? About what I am?"

He looked at me from the corner of his eyes, hurt flashing in the depths. "Of course not. You asked me not to. They know I'm with a girl, and that's what they'd be asking about."

I felt foolish, but how was I to know? I was a mythical sea creature who had killed the friends of these men. I wouldn't even blame Caelum if he'd told them or if they showed up here with pitchforks and nets, ready to kill me in revenge. More surprising was that he had not told them, to be honest. "Will you tell them about me?"

I debated telling Caelum about the shift in my powers and the new limitations thrust upon me. But I didn't know anything about him, and to tell him my vulnerabilities when I knew he blamed me for the death of his crew was…unwise. He seemed willing to forgive me, but I was not ready to forgive myself. Or ready to trust anyone else yet.

He turned his body to face me, grabbing one of my hands in both of his. His hands swallowed mine, the skin rough and calloused against my own, and deeply tanned against my pale flesh. "That is entirely up to you. You can tell them if you want. And if you don't want to, then all they need to know is that you helped save me. That's all that will matter to them."

"That's not all that would matter to them," I whispered, afraid that if I raised my voice, it would break the moment. Our eyes locked, and I hoped he could see the guilt in mine, the apology. "My kind killed your crew. They would be right to hate me if they knew what I am."

He didn't reply, instead just looking at me. I wanted to crawl inside his mind, to see what he was thinking. After a moment, he pulled his hands away, and the moment was lost. "Maybe I should tell them. They'll be upset if they find out on their own."

"Would they…tell anyone?" I couldn't put the others at any more risk. If these men told anyone about my existence, I could bring doom upon myself and the other syrens. Despite their anger at me, I couldn't knowingly lead someone to hurt my family. If Caelum's men hated me, wanted to kill me, I could live with that. But I could not abide them seeking out the others.

He shook his head, looking at me curiously. "No, they wouldn't, not if I told them to keep it quiet. But you should know, they did see something in the water. They know the myths, same as I did."

I nodded, leaving it at that. I would have to wait to meet these men to make my own determination. If I felt they were a threat to the others in any way, I would leave. I had stowed away before, and I could do it again.

A lump formed in my throat at the thought of leaving Caelum. I wasn't sure what had changed since I drug him out of the water, but something had. I was growing to enjoy his company, despite knowing that I shouldn't.

We sat in silence, eating our fill of the fresh food he had brought. I wasn't sure what else to say to him, what I even could say after that. Eventually, my stomach was full, and the sun had fully dipped below the horizon. I looked over at the fire. "Should we chop more wood tonight?"

Caelum turned to look at the fire and the few logs left beside it. "Probably, but I think we'll make it through the night. We won't be staying here tomorrow, anyway. It's too small for us and the men."

I started at that. That was new information. He spoke like he was planning on me coming with them, and I had not been expecting that. "Where will we go?"

"Once they get here in the morning, we're going to set out toward a town a bit farther away but closer to the bay," he said, putting the leftover food back into the sack. "Will you stay with us? Or return to your syrens?"

Swallowing hard, I weighed my options on how much I should reveal to Caelum about what I had done while he was gone. "I don't think the syrens would take me back. Not now. I don't think returning is an option anymore."

"But you don't know that for sure," he said. If he was trying to be reassuring, it didn't work. He didn't know that I had gone back and had been stripped of everything I had known for the past decade.

"I do know," I said softly, deciding to tell him the truth. "I went back while you were gone. To warn them. They banished me instead."

"Oh." He seemed torn, his brows furrowing. "Were you planning on coming back if they hadn't banished you?"

"I…" I swallowed hard again. "I don't know."

He nodded, his jaw tensing. His voice was gruff when he spoke again. "Then why did you send me out for food? If you weren't planning on coming back, what was the point? I could have stayed in Fairport and kept looking for more survivors."

On instinct, I ducked my head at the anger in his voice and the tense hold of his body. Pressing my lips together, I quelled my anxiety and reminded myself that I could easily take on Caelum if I had to. "I needed to warn them. They are still my family, as your crew is yours."

"So, staying with me is your second choice?"

"We just met, Caelum," I reminded him, my own anger building in response. I took a deep breath through my nose, using it to put out the fire building in my chest as I flexed my fingers. "What possible reason would I have to prioritize you over them? Yes, I wanted to help you in repayment for us wrecking your ship. But their survival trumps your need for a ship and a crew of men who likely deserved to die."

"They didn't deserve to die," he said, his voice icy. "And if you ever say that again, I will throw you out of this cabin so fast your head will spin."

We locked gazes for a moment, the fire building in both of our eyes. It was obvious we were both intense individuals. I did want to help him, even after all of this, but I wouldn't let him dismiss my need to protect my fellow syrens. "Fine."

"Fine."

"So, where will you go from here?" I asked again, hoping to get the conversation back on track.

"To Whitcairn," he replied. When I looked at him,

confused, he waved a hand. "It's a small town south of here. We'll be able to find a new ship and hopefully build a new crew to get back to our home port."

I officially couldn't wait anymore, and my curiosity damned me once again. Likely, he wouldn't tell me, but I had to ask. "Why do you need a new ship so badly?"

He was quiet for a moment, his eyes flitting about as if he were thinking of what to say. "We were on an important mission to stop someone who actually *would* have deserved to die at your hands. I'd like to get back on track with that as soon as possible."

"What's your mission?" I asked. Logically, I shouldn't be trying to connect with Caelum any more, but I wanted to know as much as I could. Caelum intrigued me, despite my better judgment. He didn't seem the type to be a pirate, plundering innocent merchant ships, but I was used to living my life beneath the waves, not atop it. Ships were ships to us. We didn't differentiate what we chose to wreck based on the goods they were hauling.

He raised an eyebrow at me, challenging me. "Tell me your story, and I'll tell you mine."

I hesitated. While I did want to hear his story, I wasn't quite sure if I was ready to tell him mine. I hadn't even told Sorcha my whole story, and Caelum and I barely knew each other. Despite our shared history, my story largely involved the others, and I couldn't put them in any more danger than I already had.

Caelum seemed to sense my hesitation and offered a small smile, his earlier anger already gone. "I can go first if that makes it better for you."

I exhaled slowly and nodded. "Yeah, you go first. I promise I'll keep your story to myself."

He reached over the table and grabbed my hand, squeezing it gently while looking into my eyes. "And when you're ready to tell yours, I will keep it to myself as well."

Smiling at him, I tugged at his hand until he stood with me. I motioned toward the bed. The idea of telling my story to Caelum while he looked at me made my stomach turn, and I needed at least a ruse of solitude to be able to push down my anxiety. "Let's go lie down."

His eyes widened in equal parts curiosity and suspicion. "Lay down?"

I dropped his hand and stretched out on the bed myself, getting as comfortable as I could on the lumpy mattress. I may not have laid in a bed these past years, but my hanging canvas bed in *Neamh na Mara* had seen and heard many a story. "Stories are always better when you're lying down with your eyes closed. But you don't have to if you're uncomfortable. I can lay on the floor."

He looked at me for a moment, an unfamiliar look in his eyes. He walked over and put the last of the logs onto the fire. Finally, he kicked his boots off and stretched out on the bed next to me, folding an arm behind his head. "Aye. But I'm not sure where to start."

I rolled over onto my side, propping my head up on my hand and putting my weight on my elbow as I looked at him. "Start from the day we met ten years ago. What were you doing on that ship?"

"My father had sent me away to learn how to be a sailor. He always had high hopes for me to work with his crew. But I never wanted to be like him, my father or that captain. After they threw you over, I lost the little bit of respect I had for the captain and started revolting more than I had been. Ignoring directions, doing my own thing. I was whipped badly for the disobedience, but that captain eventually got tired of my attitude and sent me back to my father."

"I saw the scars on your back." I was beyond furious, my anger bubbling beneath the surface of my skin, begging to be unleashed. My fingers twitched, claws aching to extend and punish someone, punish whoever had given him those scars. "They did that to a child?"

He grimaced. "Aye, they did. It took months to heal."

"They won't touch you again." The protectiveness I felt over Caelum shocked me, but it also felt natural. I wanted to tear apart that captain and Caelum's father both, piece by piece. Drowning would not be enough for them, for anyone who would do what they had done to a child. "Is that captain still alive? Does he still sail?"

He smirked at me, delight twinkling behind the pain in his eyes. "Why? Are you going to avenge me?"

I raised an eyebrow. "I was planning to, yes."

"The captain is dead, so there's no one left to punish for that," he said with a sad smile. "But I appreciate the sentiment. I can take care of myself now."

Unbidden, I reached out to place my hand on his cheek. The desire to comfort him had come out of nowhere, but I didn't stop myself. His eyes closed and he leaned into the touch, but as quickly as he'd melted, he stiffened and opened his eyes. The wall he constructed between us was visible in his eyes. Slowly, I lowered my hand, pulling back into myself. I shouldn't have touched him. Obviously, he would not welcome the touch of a killer—of a monster. "I apologize. Please, go on."

"He wasn't pleased that I had…disobeyed him, so he punished me. At first it was mental, just belittling me, giving me shit work to do. Then it turned physical as I got older and bigger. He would beat me, but it didn't affect me the way he wanted it to. I could turn off the pain and ignore it. So, he turned to other physical abuse. The final straw for me was when he tied me up and dangled me upside down over the water. My arms were completely in the water, my head just barely out of it. Some lovely fish decided to gnaw on my hand while I was hanging there, but I was too exhausted to try to keep myself out of the water. When the blood attracted more sharks than anything, he finally pulled me back in, laughing the whole time. That's where this scar came from," he explained, holding his right hand up so I could see the jagged and puckered skin circling his wrist. I wanted to reach out and touch it, but his reaction to my touch earlier made me curl my fingers in, digging my nails into my palm instead. "I almost lost my hand. Had even debated what kind of hook I would get to replace it. But it survived. And so did I."

He shrugged. "I knew my father wasn't a good man, but that solidified it for me. When I was finally better and able to use my hand again, I started learning more about what my father actually did; what he used his ship for, where he made his money. And I made it my life's mission to stop him at whatever he's doing."

There was more to it, that much was obvious. But I could tell it pained him to talk about it. Despite his reservations at my touch, I placed a hand on his arm, wanting nothing more than to erase the pure anger in his eyes. It was an anger I recognized in myself, one I knew would consume him if he didn't unleash it at some point. "What was he doing?"

He hesitated, opening and closing his mouth a few times. The conflict was clear to see on his face. He didn't want to tell me, and I understood his apprehension. I was wary of sharing my own story with him.

"It's okay, you don't have to tell me," I said slowly, understanding the struggle he was going through. We had barely met, and I knew I was not eager to share my story with Caelum, so how could I expect him to be open with me? But his words rang in my ears and settled deeply in my stomach, running together with Sorcha's words from our last night together. She was right, maybe we *were* punishing innocents. The thought made me sick to my stomach. How many men had we killed who had not deserved it?

"Aye, thank you," he said, looking over at me, pulling me from my spiraling thoughts. He placed his other hand over mine, still resting on his arm, and brought it over onto his chest. His gaze turned back to the ceiling, and he squeezed my hand. "Would you be open to joining us? Now that I don't have a full crew, I could use all the help I can get to stop him. He's one man I would actually encourage you to kill."

I didn't know what to say to that. My heart went out for him, and maybe under different circumstances, I would have jumped at helping him. But I couldn't forget that my kind had just killed his crew. *I* had just killed his crew. That would surely lead to some less-than-positive feelings. While I could handle myself, I wasn't in the habit of putting myself in situations where I knew I would be vulnerable. "I don't know, Caelum. I don't even know what your mission truly is."

His forehead furrowed, and his voice was cold. "Do you think we would truly be trying to harm people? Helping us is really the least you could do."

"What?" I asked, confused. He had been soft as he told his story, but now his voice was hard, and anger was seeping into his eyes, blazing like fire.

"You and the others are the reason I'm having to basically start over on this mission. My father is an evil man, and we were so close to catching up to him and finally being able to stop him. The least you could do is help me get it back on track. What's there to not know?" He seemed frustrated, his body tight against mine.

I was speechless. He was right, but at the same time, I despised being told what I should and should not do. Caelum seemed like the type who was accustomed to being listened to, not being questioned. And maybe in another life, I would have cowered and folded to his harsh words, but not anymore. However right he was, however true his statement, I would never do what men told me to do just because they told me to do it. Not anymore.

Stubbornly, I raised my head to meet his gaze, my back straight and eyes steady. "I don't know what you want me to say to that. I don't know you, Caelum. I don't know your mission. I'm not going to blindly jump into something I have no understanding of."

He sighed before motioning at me with his hand. "Go on, then, tell me your story. Fair's fair."

I took a deep breath, flexing my fingers against my legs. Caelum had trusted me with his story, I could do the same. Despite his anger, I felt safe with him, and confident that he wouldn't harm me like other men had. At least, not physically.

"I grew up on a farm with my father. My mother died when I was born, and he's resented me ever since. But I worked, pulling my weight on the farm while my father gambled all of our money away. I didn't have any siblings, no other family I knew of, and no friends.

"Eventually, when I turned fifteen, my father tried to marry me off to a man nearly three times my age. He wanted to cover his gambling debts. The man was awful, and I wanted more than that. I wanted a life of my own choosing. I wanted to make a name for myself the right way. So, when I heard that your ship was going to Bhodheas, I just needed to get away from Tuathnach and start over for myself. But I didn't have any money, so I had to stow away. There were no other ships leaving, not for several days, and I wouldn't have made it walking. I considered hiding in a supply carriage, but I couldn't have stayed hidden long enough."

"He was basically going to sell you?" Caelum asked, his voice angry but controlled. His anger surprised me. He was upset for me, and I wasn't used to having someone care about my well-being. Sure, Kyla had been kind to me when I first joined the syrens, but largely, they were indifferent to me unless

I was needed for something.

I looked over to find him staring at me with an intensity in his eyes that stirred something in my stomach. I unclenched my jaw again before continuing. "He said at least I would be good for something that way. But regardless, I was found by your crew, thrown over, and then I was rescued by a sea goddess and the others. She offered me a choice, to seek my revenge on men or to be taken to a women's shelter in Bhodheas. At the time, I was so angry. So, I decided to become a syren.

"I worked with my fellow syrens, learning the seas, the creatures, and what it meant to be part of a people that cared about each other. We looked out for each other, sought comfort and companionship in each other, and we sought revenge on those who had wronged us, and on all men. Men had never brought us anything but suffering, so we repaid the favor," I explained. My fingers, still resting on his chest, twitched, bunching up his shirt slightly. Slowly, I relaxed my fingers one by one, smoothing out the fabric. "But maybe there are some good men out there."

He grinned, but it was slightly forced, and squeezed my fingers again before dropping his hand to his side. "Well, I'm glad you're coming around to that thought."

I smiled back before laying my head down on the pillow. He was still upset; I could feel it radiating off him. But he tried to hide it from me, to mask it beneath that forced smile. He turned his gaze away from me and up to the ceiling. For a moment, we just laid there in each other's company and warmth. We stayed like that until the light in the room began to dim and the fire began to sputter. A breeze moved through the cottage, sending shivers through my body. "We should put more wood on."

He sighed and sat up, moving me off his chest. Looking toward the fireplace, he cursed, running his hand through his hair. "There's no more wood. I just put the last of it on before we laid down."

"How cold will it get?" I asked, sitting up in the bed as well. I wasn't used to the cold in my human form yet, and I was not looking forward to trying to sleep while shivering. "We have other blankets. Will that be enough?"

"We're pretty far north, so it will get fairly cold tonight. But the blankets should be enough, as long as you don't mind having to huddle under the same blankets as me for warmth." His voice was hesitant. "We don't have enough to each have our own."

My cheeks flushed at the thought of feeling his body pressed against mine all night. But I also couldn't help but think of how adamant he had been the night before about not sharing the bed with me. I knew we needed to stay warm, but I also didn't want to be curled up next to someone who didn't want to be there. "I don't mind. If you're sure you're okay with sharing."

He stood, walking over to the trunk to collect the last of the blankets. He brought them back over to the bed and was silent as he spread them out over me. Just as he was finishing, the fire sputtered out, the room darkening even more until only the glow of embers remained. Wind fluttered through the cottage. He pulled back a corner of the blankets, jerking his head at me. "Move over, *teine*. I'm coming in."

I bit my tongue to keep from asking what that word meant. He had said it several times now, and it seemed endearing, but I wasn't sure. The language was familiar, but I couldn't place it. Once we were both under the blankets, we lay there, side by side. I could already feel a chill starting and couldn't help the shiver that racked through me. My fingers twisted into the rough fabric of the blankets covering us as I tried to control my body's reactions. I could feel the warmth seeping off Caelum's skin, and I wanted nothing more than to press back into it. But he was still angry.

I debated moving to lay on the floor so that my shivering wouldn't wake him. I didn't like the cold, but I also did not want to rely on this man who obviously was angered by my actions, no matter how much he tried to hide it. I understood his anger, so it made it easier to accept the reality.

Before I could move to leave the bed, another shiver racked through my body. Caelum cursed again, wrapping an arm around my shoulders and pulling me into his side, my head resting on his chest. He pulled the blankets higher over us both and interlocked his fingers behind me, holding me to him tightly. "Get some sleep."

"Goodnight, Caelum," I whispered, holding my body deathly still. If I moved, it would ruin the moment, and I wanted it to last just a little while longer, to relish the feel of him next to me.

As I drifted off to sleep, I swore there was a soft press of lips to my temple. But I couldn't be sure, as I was already succumbing to the body-heat-induced sleep.

CHAPTER THIRTEEN

BRIGID

The morning came way too soon. Light filtered in, shining into my eyes as an arm tightened around my midsection. Caelum. The feeling of his weight on my stomach was comforting. Rather than uncomfortable, like I'd thought it would be, spending the night next to Caelum had been relaxing. Comforting. I shifted around, grumbling sleepily to confirm if it was truly him still holding me. "Caelum?"

He smoothed his hand over my hair and pushed it out of his face, his own voice rough from sleep. It sent chills down my spine, and that, more than the light, woke me up instantly. "Good morning, *teine*. Sleep well?"

"What does that word mean?" I asked, rubbing my eyes as I sat up. I needed to get away from him, from my body's reactions to him. Our paths were not destined to stay together long, and trying to pretend otherwise was foolish. Other than making up for the sins of syrens, the only thing I could offer Caelum was my body. And I doubted very much that he would want that after the deaths of his crew.

He didn't reply, just looked up at me with a sleepy expression on his face. It made him look younger, the tension gone from between his eyebrows.

Smoothing a hand over my wild curls, I sighed. I shouldn't have asked, and I feared now I would never find out what the pet name meant. "I slept well. Did you?"

"Aye, better than I have in a while," he admitted, smiling at me and jarring me from my thoughts. "You're a much better sleeping partner than a bunk room full of snoring sailors."

I smiled at that, trying to convince him that nothing was wrong. So many things were wrong. The smile slipped off my face and my jaw tightened, my teeth grinding together. "When will your friends be here?"

Caelum looked over through the window at the sun rising softly through the hills. "If they left Fairport at first light, they should be here fairly soon."

"Where will we be going from here? I don't think five of us could fit in this little space," I said, waving my hand around the cottage. I was used to having more space to live in, and this would be confining even if I were the only inhabitant. Sharing the cave rooms with Sorcha had been less cramped than this. Standing, I righted my clothes that had rumpled from sleep. Picking at the frayed seams, I looked around the cabin, doing anything possible to keep my mind from racing and my attention off Caelum.

Thinking about sharing the room with other men brought my mind back to Sorcha. What would she think if she could see me now? Would she be pleased I was coming around to her views of men, or had the others gotten to her? In the same breath, my mind switched to worrying about Caelum's friends and how they would treat me. Despite what I told myself, I wasn't sure if I could keep my confidence in the face of four men.

"Whitcairn is just a day's walk south of here. We'll be headed there to try to find a new ship and build back up a crew," he explained, clearing the sleep from his eyes and voice. "I hope you would consider coming with us. Help us stop my father."

I hesitated, unsure how to answer. I would be useless to them without my powers to help them with anything, let alone a mission as important as this one seemed to be. Without my song, I was just a fish with arms. I could see in the dark and live in the cold water, but I doubted that would be useful to them. If Caelum discovered I had no more powers and had no use to him, maybe his mind would change. But his words the night before had resonated with me, and really, I had nothing left to lose. Maybe dying to stop a truly evil man would atone for my sins against the innocent ones. I let my gaze rise back to his. "I'll help you. You're right, it really is the least I can do after what happened."

He paused, studying me for a long moment. I could almost see the wheels turning in his head, thoughts racing about what my motivations were. It was clear he didn't completely trust me yet. That was fine. I wasn't sure if I entirely trusted him yet either. Being cautious was healthy, and given what we both had faced, I didn't blame him.

"Do you want some breakfast?" he eventually asked, getting out of the bed and walking toward the sack of food still sitting on the table. He pulled out some bread and handed it to me. "The others will be bringing some fresh clothes for us, and hopefully some more food for the journey."

We ate in silence, and as we were finishing up our food, voices drifted in from outside. Male voices. I tensed up, looking to the window. My heart raced, though I knew it was likely only Caelum's surviving crew. Still, anxiety raced through me; sweat slicked my palms and a trickle slid down my spine. Would they immediately know what I was? Would they immediately want to kill me? My jaw popped from how tightly I was clenching it, and I opened my mouth to flex it from side to side, forcing it to relax.

Caelum stood, walking over to the window and peering out. His shoulders relaxed, and he turned back to me with an easy smile. "It's just my men. Nothing to worry about."

I couldn't bring myself to respond, thoughts of what was about to happen kept me still and terrified. I had faced many things in my life, but facing them without the backing of my powers was disconcerting. It threw me back to when I had first met Caelum and how helpless I had been then. I never wanted to feel that again, and yet, here I was. Caelum cast a curious glance back at me before walking over to the door and opening it.

"Caelum! Morning," a large blond man greeted, stepping

through the door and clapping a hand on Caelum's shoulder so loud that I couldn't help but wince.

But all Caelum did was smile at the man. "Morning, Duncan. Come on, you oaf, let's get inside."

They all moved inside the cottage, Caelum, the large blond man, and two other men. The dark-haired one was well-kempt and stiff, assessing everything in the cottage with a focus that unnerved me. The curly-haired one smiled carelessly, but I felt his gaze on me as well, curious. I tried not to fidget beneath it despite every muscle in my body screaming in protest to move, to leave. Flexing my fingers against my leg, I bent and straightened them one by one, focusing on the feel of the fabric beneath them. I wondered if they noticed I was still wearing Caelum's clothes.

"Brigid, this is Duncan, Cameron, and Maddock. Men, this is Brigid," Caelum introduced, motioning to each of them in turn.

Duncan, the large blond, walked right up to me and stuck his hand out. I didn't miss the suspicion in his eyes as he studied me, though. "Duncan. Nice to meet you."

I stared at him, shoving down my fear and crafting a practiced look of blankness on my face. Despite how enthusiastic he was with Caelum, this man was much larger than me. Without a second thought, he could kill me in my human form. Maybe he would once he found out about what I had done. Maybe I deserved it. I tensed my body, trying to clear my mind and keep my emotions off my face. Swallowing, I extended my hand to meet Duncan's. "You as well."

"So, how'd you meet Caelum?" Cameron, the sandy-haired man, asked, sitting down at the other chair. He was smaller than Duncan, but seemed more open and relaxed with me. His eyes roved over me, but not in a way that made me feel uncomfortable.

My gaze flicked to Caelum briefly, but I forced myself to look back at the man in front of me. Caelum was *their* friend in this situation. He could do nothing to protect me from them. I could do this. I could tell them this story without giving away my secrets. I needed more time to prepare for how they would react and how I would react. "I helped pull him out of the water. He was almost to shore, and I saw him from the beach. His head dipped under, so I swam out and helped pull him out. I stayed with him to make sure he didn't drown."

Cameron reached over and squeezed my fingers. It took every muscle in my body to keep still and not jerk my hand away from him. The touch of a man was jarring, but his face was serene and genuine. "Thank you for saving him. I don't know if the fool has thanked you himself, but I will."

I forced myself to return the squeeze and offered him a small smile. While I likely deserved more anger and disgust from them, I would take their kindness for the moment. Until I could figure out exactly how they would react when they found out the truth, this façade was the safest for me. Even if it meant deceiving those Caelum obviously cared about. "He has. But the gratitude is appreciated."

"I'm glad you saved our captain here as well," Duncan added.

"Someone had to," I said lightly, trying to keep the tension out of my voice. My jaw clicked as I clenched it tightly. "He didn't seem to be succeeding at doing it himself."

All three of them roared with laughter. Caelum crossed his arms over his chest, but the large grin stretched across his face told a different story. I almost wanted to smile with him, but I kept my face carefully neutral.

"Yeah, yeah, laugh it up."

"So, tell us about the men who attacked," Duncan said, suddenly serious. He looked back at Caelum briefly before focusing his attention on me. "Did they hurt you?"

I shook my head, afraid that this conversation would turn in an ugly direction. I had to be careful with what I divulged. Deciding to keep it safe, I replied, "No, I'm not hurt. Caelum handled one, I got the other."

His eyebrows shot up. "You did?"

"Is that so hard to believe?" I asked, arching an eyebrow at him. My discomfort waned for a moment, replaced by indignance that this man would so easily dismiss me. Taking a slow breath through my nose, I calmed myself before my temper got the better of me and I let something slip that revealed more than I intended.

Duncan backtracked quickly, his eyes widening slightly. "No, not at all. Just a bit surprising given how…small you are."

"I have a few tricks up my sleeve," I said, leaning back in the chair and crossing my arms. Maybe I was antagonizing them, leading them on. But I would never be dismissed by a man again, whether I had my syren powers or not.

He laughed at that, reaching over to pat my shoulder. I was proud of myself for not flinching under his touch. Oblivious, he continued to smile at me. "Aye, I'm sure you do. I'm glad you're both okay."

"Did any of the rest of your crew survive?" I needed to know. If these men had survived, maybe more of them had as well. It wouldn't erase my guilt or my obligation to help them, but perhaps it could ease my conscience. It would also help me gauge the anger they would feel when they discovered the truth.

The dark-haired one named Maddock answered this time. "Not that we know of. We were waiting for any who washed up when Caelum found us. You can call me Mad, by the way."

I looked down at the table, fighting the sudden urge to twist my fingers like Sorcha had. Instead, I picked at my nails, cursing the sharp talons beneath them. I wondered what it would feel like now when they extended. I took a deep breath, unclenching my jaw that had unconsciously tightened again, and raised my gaze. "I'm sorry for your losses. Caelum told me what happened in the water."

Caelum stepped up behind me and squeezed my shoulder, surprising me. He at least knew the truth, and he should not be comforting me. But I supposed that if his men didn't know the truth, it wouldn't make sense for him to shun me in this moment. "It's all right."

As if he'd read my thoughts, he pulled his hand back. Perhaps he had realized exactly what he had said. Nothing about this was all right, and it was important that both of us remembered that.

"Aye," Cameron chimed in, "it's not like you drowned them."

I couldn't help but flinch at his words. My body tensed,

and I bit down on the inside of my cheek hard enough to taste blood.

Caelum straightened. "All right, let's—"

"Tell me about them," I demanded, interrupting Caelum's dismissal. I wanted to know. To know the men who had died at the hands of my kind. "Tell me about your crew."

"Are you sure you want to hear about this?" Caelum asked, eyeing me suspiciously. Perhaps he didn't want me to know about them. Did he think me unworthy enough to know their memories? "We don't have to talk about them."

I gazed at him, hoping my determination shone through. "No, I want to hear about them. If you're willing to share."

"Wait, are you sure we can trust her?" Duncan asked, his voice loud in the quiet room despite him trying to whisper to Caelum. In any other instance, I would have smiled. But this was serious. They likely shouldn't trust me, but in reality, who would I tell?

"Can we trust you not to go telling anyone about this? Some of the men have families still at home, and I don't want anything happening to them if it's discovered they were part of my crew," Caelum asked. His tone was teasing, but the glint in his eyes told me exactly how serious his question was.

Nodding at him, I raised an eyebrow. Who else would I tell? "You can trust me. I won't tell another soul."

I have no one left to tell, were the words left unspoken.

Caelum jerked his chin to the others before dragging over the trunk filled with blankets to sit on the lid.

Caelum began, "All right. We'll tell you about them. Our crew was thirty-three men. Not quite enough for a full crew on the barque we sailed, but it worked well for our purposes. They all came from different walks of life. Some had been sailors their whole lives. Some were there for other reasons. They all knew why we were sailing. They were all good men."

I wanted to throw up at his words. It must have shown on my face because he stopped talking and looked at me with concern. How could he be concerned about my feelings after this? He should be furious with me, telling me to get out of his cottage and never come back.

"Why were you sailing?" There was more to the story than he had told me, a more specific purpose. I clenched my jaw again to keep the burning in the back of my throat down. I took shallow breaths through my nose to stay focused on the men in front of me and not my own emotions.

Duncan looked at me, his hazel eyes wary, before turning to look at Caelum. They seemed to have a conversation without words. Caelum nodded at him before continuing the story. "Aye, I told you last night, my father was a bad man. He had taken something dear to us, to all of us, and we were sailing to figure out a way to find him and get it back."

Cameron looked at Caelum for a moment and then turned his gaze to me and continued the story. "I don't know how much Caelum told you, but a lot of the men were there hoping to find the…thing that was taken. But when we get back, at least we can tell their families that the ship went down, and they can get that closure."

"Aye, it's better than not knowing," Duncan said solemnly. The overwhelming urge to vomit came over me once again, and I unclenched my jaw to draw in breaths through my mouth instead.

"Good men," I repeated. Maybe if I said it enough, it would take back the actions. But I knew that was a foolish hope. Almost as foolish as the hope that I would be able to stay with Caelum. "You all seem like good men."

Maddock grinned at me, oblivious to the numbness I was feeling. "We like to think so."

My jaw clenched painfully. They should want to kill me. Why Caelum hadn't that first night, I would never understand. I deserved it. I opened my mouth, unsure of what to say but needing to say something.

"All right, that's enough. They were good men, and we lost them. But we owe it to them to get to Whitcairn and figure out our next moves." Caelum stood from his seat on the trunk, interrupting what I had been about to say.

Cameron pulled a map out of his bag and spread it across the table before diving into the best route to get to Whitcairn, a town further south of here, and the supplies we would need. While the change in subject was nice, my thoughts continued to race about what the future would hold and what would happen once they discovered the truth. They may be good men, but I had little doubt they would want my head once they knew.

CHAPTER FOURTEEN
BRIGID

After a full day of walking, a town finally appeared just over the hill. I could have cried out in relief. For the past ten years, I had almost exclusively lived in my syren form. My feet were not used to this much movement and this much work. To add to that, the boots Caelum managed to get me in Fairport didn't exactly fit properly, rubbing painful blisters on my heels and toes.

"Hey, are you okay?" Caelum asked quietly, slowing down to walk beside me.

"Yeah, I'm fine," I replied, taking care to not wince as I stepped over some rocks. My ankle twisted, rubbing one of the blisters harder, and I couldn't hide the wince at that. I was beyond ready to rest, though I wouldn't be the first one to ask for a stop. I knew if I said anything, we would stop immediately, and I didn't want to show these men any weakness.

"You've been wincing like that for the past three hours, lass," he said dryly, raising an eyebrow. "You're not okay."

Shit. I shook my head, not wanting him to be concerned about me. I was fine, or I would be. These men, however good they may be, would only see me as a weakness. And I was not a weakness, not anymore. "Just not used to walking so much. I'm fine."

Grabbing my upper arm, Caelum pulled me to a stop and moved to face me. "Why didn't you say anything? We could have stopped to rest."

That was the last thing I wanted. I couldn't give them any reason to think me even weaker. I was of no use to them—more of a hindrance, really—and as soon as they realized that, I would be gone. But I needed to get closer to Bhodheas, closer to my chance at potential freedom. And if that meant holding in my winces, then I would. I had shoved down my emotions for years, a few more days was nothing. "I didn't need to stop. And we're almost there, so there's no point in stopping now."

Thankfully, Caelum let us start walking again after staring at me for a long moment, and we caught up to the others. He reached down to squeeze my fingers. "We're talking about this later. And I'm going to look at your feet."

I rolled my eyes but didn't say anything. He would *not* be looking at my feet, but it would take too much energy to argue with him now. When we got to the inn we had planned to stay at and I could sit down, I would argue with him then.

We finished our trek into the town, and my mouth fell

open in awe as we stopped on a hill overlooking everything. I had only seen a few towns in my childhood, and nearly none as a syren, so I didn't have much to go on, but this town was large. There were dirt paths twining over the ground and in between thatch-roofed structures. A stream ran along one side of the town, snaking into the forest in the distance. There were people out, walking between the buildings, carrying baskets and bags. Children were playing somewhere; I could hear the tinkling laughter. On the other side of the town, the harbor and coastline carved into the sea, the smell of fish and sea salt permeating the air. Off to the right of the town, a large field was being worked in the distance. My eyes couldn't stop roving over the scene, taking in all the details I could.

Caelum turned to peer at me where I had stopped to take in the view. "You coming, *teine?*"

I nodded, shaking myself from my haze and walking behind him again. We reached the first dirt path, and Maddock led us through the maze of buildings and pathways until we reached a small building set off to the side. Its white stone was partially covered in soft green moss, accenting the rickety wooden shutters and the brown thatched roof.

Entering the small inn, Caelum took the lead, walking up to the man at the counter. "Got a couple of rooms?"

The older man looked over his glasses at Caelum and then over at Duncan, Maddock, Cam, and me, still standing by the door. Beside me, Maddock chuckled at the innkeeper's face.

"He's offended," Maddock whispered, leaning in close to my ear.

The innkeeper's eyes narrowed in suspicion as he looked at

us before he looked back at Caelum, likely questioning why one woman was with three men. "How many rooms do you need?"

"Two, if you have them." Caelum's voice was confident and sturdy. Either he was oblivious to the offense of the innkeeper, or he didn't care.

After an uncomfortable silence where the man just stared at Caelum, he eventually reached under the counter and reluctantly brought two keys out. Caelum paid the man with coins from a pouch at his belt and then walked back over to us. He handed one key to Duncan and kept the other for himself.

"So, what are the arrangements?" I asked. I had never stayed in an inn when I was a child. Would I get my own room, or would I have to share? My heart sped up as my thoughts raced. Would Caelum make me share with the others?

"Duncan, Mad, and Cam in one room, and then you and I in the other," Caelum explained. He looked at me. "I'd feel a lot better if you were within eyesight and not out in a room by yourself."

Despite relaxing slightly, my cheeks burned at his casual tone when he announced we would be sharing a room. Logically, I knew the other men must know Caelum and I had likely shared a bed in the small cottage, and I wasn't known for my modesty, but still. The society I had grown up in as a child had frowned upon it, and I was sure this one still did. "I can stay alone. I don't need to be supervised, Caelum."

"I know you can take care of yourself," he said, his tone obviously trying to placate me. He lowered his voice so that only I could hear him. "But just three days ago, we had men trying to find you and capture you, and we still don't know who they were, who told them about you, or how they found us."

I crossed my arms over my chest, irritated that he made a great point. I just wanted a night to myself to regroup and gather my thoughts, which were quickly going down paths I had never dreamed possible since becoming a syren. There was so much happening, and I just wanted to take it all in and not have to hide my emotions from everyone around me. But Caelum was right. "All right, I suppose that would be fine. Someone obviously needs to keep an eye on you to make sure you don't die."

He smiled like I had just given him the biggest compliment of his life. He shouldn't be smiling at me like I had given him anything. Crossing his arms proudly, he inclined his head toward me. "Thank you. Your cooperation is noted and appreciated."

Off to the side, Maddock snickered. It was cut off by a grunt when Cam elbowed him in the side. I snapped my gaze over to them, irritated by their amusement. "What are you boys giggling about over there?"

They all quickly schooled their features back into seriousness. "Nothing."

"Let's go get settled. We'll meet back up in an hour or so and go hunt down some food and figure out our plan," Caelum said, his face suddenly serious and concerned again. He jerked his head at the others, and Duncan returned his nod.

Message received. Caelum did not like me making friendly with his crew. I suppose it made sense, given the reality of our situation. I tamped down the feelings of unease in my stomach. These were his men, and if he didn't want me being friends with them, I would respect that. Crossing my arms over my chest, I tried to hold myself together, at least until I was alone again. Years of practiced indifference with the others made my emotions easy to hide. But my time with Sorcha, and now with Caelum, was making it more difficult than it had ever been in the past.

"Take two hours. I'm going to go ask around about a ship, and hopefully I'll have something by dinner," Duncan said, clapping Caelum on the back.

"Aye, good plan," Caelum replied. Turning to me, he tugged at my hand once before letting it drop and leading me up the stairs.

We walked into a room at the top of the stairs, small and dark, and I looked around. There was a desk and a wardrobe against one wall, and a small wooden bed on the other. The large bay window was framed by gauzy cream curtains. I quickly moved over and sat down on the bed, sighing in relief as the weight was finally off my sore feet.

Caelum looked over at me out of the corner of his eye. He grabbed the chair from the desk and dragged it over in front of me. He motioned to my foot, leaning down toward it. "Here, let me look at that."

I rolled my eyes, not moving an inch. "You don't need to inspect my feet like I'm a child, Caelum."

"If you're injured, I need to know about it," he said, his voice cool. He motioned for my foot again. "Stop being stubborn. Let me see it."

Sighing, I lifted my leg, plopping my booted foot into his lap. His irritation at my stubbornness was palpable, and I didn't want to waste any more energy on this discussion. My feet did hurt, after all. "Fine, take a peek."

More gently than I was expecting, given his mood, he pulled the boot off. We both grimaced when we saw my bare foot. It was torn up, bloody, and my heel had a giant blister on it. "*Teine,* you should have said something a lot sooner."

"Can we bandage it?" I asked, twisting my ankle to get a better look at the damage. I really had messed it up. And without being in the caves with Cliodhna, or at the very least, in the sea, I wouldn't be able to heal quickly like I normally could. A sour taste filled my mouth as I thought about the healing powers I used to have access to. I wondered if Cliodhna had taken those from me too, but I wasn't keen on trying to slip away from Caelum to find out, not in a strange place like this.

Looking over his shoulder at the basin in the corner, he glanced back to me, gently lowering my foot to the floor. "Aye, we can clean it up and bandage it. But we really need to get you some better-fitting boots and some socks."

"Can we find those here? How can I afford them?" I didn't have any money, and I was already irritated about using Caelum's money. For some reason, Cliodhna providing for us with her magic did not feel like depending on Caelum for his money. I supposed it had to do with being in the sea versus being in the world of humans.

"We can find you some. And I can get you boots and socks. It's the least I can do for you saving my life," he said, not looking up as he gently touched my feet. He winked at me playfully.

My mouth turned sour. Even though I had saved his life, it had cost him the life of much of his crew. I had begun to forget that fact as he had inspected my feet. Intent on keeping my vow to return to Cliodhna and the others eventually, I added a new one that I would make amends with Caelum for the death of his crew. I would do what I could to help him get back what his father had taken, and only then would I set off on my own.

"How do you have money?" I asked, trying to change the subject from his helping me.

He raised his head to look at me. "Why do you want to know?"

"Are you a pirate?" I asked, raising my eyebrow. It seemed unlikely, but if they were so intent on stopping his father, I doubted they had time for legitimate merchant business.

He laughed. "No, *teine*. We're not pirates. Though some people might call us that."

"Then what are you?" I pressed, curiosity burning. "What do you do?"

"We're smugglers," he said matter-of-factly. "But the good kind."

Both eyebrows shot up my forehead. That had not been the occupation I was expecting. "There's a good kind of smuggler?"

He grinned, pride and amusement flashing equally in his eyes. Rubbing a hand over his beard, he tapped my foot, letting me move it back to the floor. "Aye, we smuggle people looking to escape from something or those needing help. And we smuggle goods to places where they're needed but can't be gotten."

"That's…very noble," I replied, still processing his words. It was similar to what the syrens did with those we rescued. Again, my stomach churned as I thought that I had almost killed this man in front of me. This man who helped people escape horrible things and fought to stop evil men.

"I'm sure to some. To others, we're a nuisance at best." Laughing quietly, he stood and walked over to the basin in the corner, wetting down some rags there. He returned to sit in front of me, pulling one of my feet back into his hands. "Let's get you cleaned up some before we try to bandage it."

"I don't need your charity. If you buy me boots and socks, I'll pay you back. Somehow," I replied softly, watching him run the cloth gently over my torn skin. I appreciated his help and the sentiment, but I had survived for this long and would continue to do so. "And I am sorry about your crew and your ship, again."

He paused in cleaning my foot and looked at me so intensely that I had to force myself to keep from squirming under it. "Brigid, let me help you. It's a pair of boots, nothing more. You don't have to pay me back. And do I miss my crew? Yes, of course. Do I mourn them? Yes. I'm allowed to be upset about the situation without being upset at you."

I bit the inside of my cheek, keeping silent. He was right, and he had every right to be as upset with the situation, with me, as he wanted to be.

I turned my mind to the original conversation. I really didn't want to have my feet torn up like this every time I had to be on my feet. Nor did I want to be the reason we slowed down, and I would be now that Caelum knew about my feet. "Fine, we can get me some new boots that fit. But only because I don't want to be a burden to the group."

"You wouldn't burden the group, but I'll take what I can

get," he said, continuing to wipe the blood away from my torn feet. He was silent as he finished cleaning one foot, then pulled the other one into his lap and did the same. His body was warm and firm beneath my feet, and some part of me wanted to stay like this, with him. Patting my ankle, he ceased his movements. "So, want to tell me more about your syrens?"

"Not really," I admitted, shrugging. "Want to tell me more about your past?"

Caelum stood, pointedly not answering my question as he walked over to one of the bags he had brought in, pulling out some white bandages. Still ignoring my statement, he sat back down in front of me and pulled one foot into his lap again, resting it against his inner thigh as he unwound the bandage. Not wanting to watch him bandage my feet, I tilted my head back to stare at the ceiling, letting myself feel instead. If he didn't want to talk, that was fine. But I wouldn't be the only one speaking.

His body was warm against the sole of my foot, and I couldn't help myself from wiggling my toes into his leg. It had been so long since I had felt the warmth of another person. The last time had been when I shared a bed with Nerina nearly a year ago, both of us seeking the comfort of another person just for a night.

His rough hand grasped my foot, holding it firmly but gently in place. His voice was gruff, "Don't do that, *teine*."

My eyebrows scrunched as I brought my head down to search his face. I didn't think I had wiggled my toes that hard. "Did I hurt you?"

"Not exactly." He looked down at his lap pointedly, then

back at me. "Not at all, actually."

Following his gaze to his lap, my cheeks blazed at the tenting in the front of his pants. I hadn't realized my foot was that close to his manhood. While I had been relatively young when I became a syren, I was not sexually inexperienced. A woman did have needs, after all. But still, I ducked my head, warmth spreading down my neck, and looked down at my own lap instead of his. "I'm sorry, I didn't mean to. You were just warm."

He tucked a finger under my chin, pulling my gaze up to meet his. His eyes were soft and warm, and I wanted to get lost in them. If he kept looking at me like that, I might. "Don't apologize. I'm sorry if I made you uncomfortable with my reaction."

I shook my head quickly. Uncomfortable was the wrong word for what I was feeling. Overwhelmed, maybe, but Caelum didn't make me uncomfortable. "You didn't. I just didn't realize what I was doing."

"Well, you are a beautiful woman," he pointed out. His face was calm, and again, I felt like a skittish animal he was trying to avoid being bitten by. He smiled slightly. "It was bound to happen sooner or later."

"Oh yes," I muttered dryly, "I'm sure my bloody feet are absolutely what's doing it for you."

He stopped his movements and looked up at me, his gaze heated and direct. "No, *teine*. You are doing it for me."

He went back to wrapping clean bandages around my feet. "We don't have to go down that road right now, or ever, if you don't want to. I know we've both been through a lot in the past few days. This doesn't have to mean anything. Let me finish wrapping your feet, and we can go get boots now instead of after dinner and then meet the others."

I nodded, grateful he had given me direction. That was a good plan. Anything to get out of this room and push down the heat that was building between us. It was purely physical attraction, I told myself, echoing Caelum's sentiments earlier. That was all. There could be nothing between us emotionally. There were too many bodies—thirty of them, to be precise—that barred that path.

Caelum continued to wrap my feet in silence. His hands were calloused and rough, but his touch was gentle as he wound the fabric around my bare feet. His skin was warm, and I found myself silently protesting when he put my foot down. Then, he picked the other one up and began to do the same.

As he wrapped, my mind wandered, thinking about what else his hands were capable of and how they would feel on other parts of me. I shivered at the image of him running his hands down my back, over my stomach. He set my other foot down and patted my knee, pulling me from my thoughts. "All done, *teine*."

"What does that mean?" I asked again. He was calling me that with increased frequency, and with a familiarity that I knew meant something to him.

He blushed, running his hand through his hair. "It's just an endearment in my mother's tongue. It doesn't mean anything."

I swallowed hard. Of course, it didn't mean anything. What had I been thinking?

Staying with him was one thing, but laying with him

intimately? The syrens would never take me back if they knew the thoughts running through my head about the handsome man in front of me. And Caelum didn't think of me the same way, despite the physical reaction he'd had to my touch earlier. I had to get a hold of myself and face my reality. This was not a time for fantasy. "Thank you, Caelum."

He looked at me, his eyebrows raised and his mouth curved in a crooked grin. "Are you okay? You've never thanked me before."

I scowled. Of course, he would open his mouth and ruin it. The teasing was too familiar, too casual, to make distancing myself easy. I quirked a brow up, smirking at him. "I've never had anything to thank you for before now."

Grinning, he pulled me to my feet. "There she is. Come on, put those old boots back on. You just have to wear them long enough to get to the shop next door. They should have something in your size."

CHAPTER FIFTEEN
BRIGID

Boots purchased and now snugly on my feet over thick, wool socks, we walked back to the inn. Duncan, Cameron, and Maddock were already sitting at a table over by the fireplace. Striding over, Caelum led us to take a seat with the others.

"We already ordered stew and bread. It should be here soon," Duncan said, looking over at me as I sat. "You doing okay with all this traveling?"

I nodded. It was unlikely he actually cared for the details, but I couldn't help but give them. "Got me some new boots, so I'll be able to keep up better now."

His eyes widened as he looked down at my feet. "You walked that far today in boots that didn't fit?"

Caelum snorted, making me want to retreat in on myself. I knew I shouldn't feel shame, and yet I couldn't help it in the face of his laughter. "She did that, the stubborn thing. Her feet were all bloody. Didn't say a peep."

Instead of curling in on myself like I wanted to, I crossed my arms over my chest and frowned. They were my feet, why did these men care what I did to them? "I didn't want to slow us down. I know you were all already going slower than you normally would because of me."

"Aye, because you got short little legs, Brigid. Not because you're a woman. If you had legs as long as Caelum's, we'd have gone at a regular pace. You'll do us no good if you keel over because we walked you to death's door on the first day," Duncan teased me, oblivious to my true emotions. For the better, I supposed, given that Caelum did not seem to want us being friendly.

I felt myself beginning to shut down, wanting to wrap my arms around myself. My heart pounded and my jaw was clenched so tightly my teeth might crack. Badly, I wished Sorcha were here. She made me feel balanced. These other men threw me of, and I wasn't sure how to behave. I had spent years mirroring the behavior of the syrens, but these men were all over the place and hard to read.

"Relax, Brigid. I did the same thing when I first joined this lot," Cameron said, bumping his shoulder into mine with a smile. His easy grin was supposed to be reassuring, but it just made my palms sweat and my jaw clench tighter. He continued, nodding his head at the others. "They don't care any about appearances. Just be yourself and do what you can."

I tried to smile at him, unsure if it came across as genuine or not. Likely, it came across more as a grimace than anything else. Be myself? Myself was a murderous sea creature who apparently killed innocent men. But even that wasn't really accurate anymore, given that I was no longer welcome with the other syrens. And while I would not apologize for becoming a syren, I was beginning to regret my actions as one and the blindness with which I had destroyed those ships. Caelum's disposition despite his losses was eye-opening, to say the least.

"So, I found us a ship—a pinnace, to be precise." Duncan got back to business, plopping his burly forearms down on the table and leaning in. His expression let it be clearly known that there was more to this finding than he was saying. He looked around, lowering his voice. "But it's not *exactly* for sale."

Caelum crossed his arms over his chest as he leaned back in his chair, his eyebrow raising. "What exactly is the situation, then?"

"Well, we'd have to borrow it, technically. The owner doesn't use it, he admitted that, but he also said he wasn't willing to let anyone else use her." Duncan's face twisted into an expression somewhere between a grin and a grimace.

Caelum sighed, leaning forward and pinching the bridge of his nose. "Borrow, you say?"

"Aye," Duncan said, his voice still low.

"Borrow?" I couldn't help but interject. My curiosity would likely be the death of me, I was sure. "You mean steal?"

"Keep your voice down. We don't want to tell the whole town our plans," Duncan hissed, leaning in close.

I fought to keep myself from shrinking in at his tone,

instead digging my fingers into my thighs and tensing the muscles of my back to stay upright. I was no longer the wilting flower I had been as a child. No, I was a syren now, and even without my song, I was powerful. "Have you stolen many things before?"

Duncan raised an eyebrow at me. "And if we have?"

I returned the expression. "I suppose that depends on what you steal, and from whom."

"And would you judge us if we told you the truth?"

"I'd judge you if you didn't."

His lips curled slightly. "All right. Yes, we do steal. Gotta live somehow."

"So, you *are* pirates?" I asked, leaning back and crossing my arms over my chest. Had Caelum lied to me earlier?

Caelum scoffed. "No. I told you before, we're not pirates. We just…need a little financial help now and then."

"We don't steal from those less fortunate," Maddock said quietly. He cleared his throat. "We only take from those who won't miss it."

"Honorable pirates, then," I said, smiling. I supposed that did fit with the good man persona.

Caelum rolled his eyes and looked around at the busy tavern before leaning in and lowering his voice even more. "How exactly would we borrow this ship, Duncan? Would we be able to do it with just the five of us?"

"We might be able to, but it would be difficult. I'd feel more comfortable if we could get a few more souls to help. It would go a lot smoother if there were at least a dozen of us to crew her." Duncan leaned back in his chair and crossed his arms, spreading his large body casually over the small chair.

"Me too. Do you think we can find any here?" Caelum asked, rubbing his chin and the faint stubble that covered it. I could see his mind turning behind his eyes, calculating what the next step should be.

Duncan shrugged and looked over at Cameron and Maddock. "I think we could. You two go ahead and see if you can feel out anyone. Caelum and I will come by tomorrow tonight and make a final push."

Cameron nodded. "Good plan. How many are we aiming for? Six or seven others?"

"At least five more would be doable in addition to us, but I'd like to get more. It would get us out of the town and would let us bring it into Brinemoor, where Kellan's likely at. We don't need her to be a warship." Maddock went through the scenario quickly, his eyebrows furrowing as he fiddled with the handle of his mug.

"Wait, Kellan?" I interrupted, leaning in. They hadn't mentioned that name before.

"Kellan is my father," Caelum explained, a pinched expression on his face. It was obvious he did not like talking about the man.

"So, how far away is Brinemoor?" I asked, changing the subject and tucking a loose strand of hair behind my ear. The idea of sailing made my stomach twist. As a child, I had not traveled off my father's farm often; I wasn't familiar with the town they spoke of or with being on top of the seas. The one and only time I had attempted to travel by ship had ended with my turning into a syren.

"Too far to walk," Caelum replied, grimacing slightly. "It's on the other side of the mountains, and it would be far faster and easier to sail through the Straits of Marbh to get there."

"The Straits are dangerous," I said instantly, looking at him. As syrens, we had often roamed the Straits of the Dead, looking for ships to target. The rocks beneath the water there meant few survivors, if any, ever made it out of the wrecks. If we sailed through there, I had little doubt the others would come for us.

"How do you know that?" Duncan asked curiously. His voice was light, but I could see the suspicion in his eyes as he studied me.

Duncan's suspicions aside, I kept my eyes on Caelum, trying to convey the true meaning behind my words. He needed to be prepared in case they tried to wreck him again. If he had been upset at starting over before, having to do so again would likely ruin the little progress I was making in my redemption.

He smiled at me, but it was obviously forced and didn't reach his eyes. My message seemed to have gotten through, at least. "We'll be careful."

I nodded hesitantly and reminded myself to warn him more explicitly later. My presence on the seas could anger the syrens even more, and the last thing I wanted was for Caelum to be faced with their ire again.

Caelum rubbed his hands together, leaning forward. His eyes were bright with genuine excitement. "Mad, you and Cam go tonight, get a feel for any men we might be able to get onboard. See if we can pull this off."

"If we can get the boat and the crew, when would we be

doing this?" I asked, leaning across the table to get closer. Having as many details as possible helped calm my anxiety. If I knew what to expect, I could prepare for it.

"We get the crew on board tomorrow. And then, depending on the type of men they are, we could maybe pull it off tomorrow night and be out of here before the sun rises," Duncan explained.

"Type of men?" My voice was colder than ice. I had little patience for the dismissal of women, even from these men. My entire life had been one long dismissal until I became a syren, and I would no longer stand for it from anyone. My anger overrode my anxiety of the situation. "Would you turn away women who wanted to join your crew?"

"Women are bad luck on the seas," Duncan said, his words an echo of those I had heard right before I was thrown overboard. It made my stomach churn. "Just because we're willing to let you sail with us doesn't mean we're going to risk it further than that."

"The only bad luck on the seas is the luck we earn," Caelum said, scoffing. "Superstitious oaf."

"You're not bad luck, Brigid, ignore him," Maddock said with a smile. "He's just traditional like that."

My jaw clenched almost painfully, and I bit my tongue to keep from saying something I would regret. Duncan's sentiment was common, and until I could prove them otherwise, arguing would do nothing but make him more suspicious of me. Leaning back, I spread my arms out wide. "So, where do we start?"

Staring up at the swinging wooden sign, I took a deep breath. My nerves were as worn as the sign advertising The Silver Serpent tavern. This was where we were to meet the men Cameron and Maddock had found. At Duncan's insistence, both Caelum and I were dressed for the part as well.

'You've got to dress as a captain if you want them to take you seriously, Caelum. And the girl can't keep wearing your clothes either,' he had said to us. Caelum had resisted initially, as had I, but the large man had gotten his way in the end. Duncan was right, I supposed. Us showing up in casual clothes that didn't fit properly likely would not make a good impression on the men we were asking to help us.

We had spent all day rounding up an appropriate outfit for the both of us. It had been a true pain in the arse, but we had finally found everything we needed. Caelum was dressed in a lace-up white shirt that cut low to show off his tanned chest. The shirt was tucked into dark breeches, which were then tucked into high leather boots, laced up tight. He had also tied his hair back into a low knot at the nape of his neck, showing off the freshly shaved sides of his scalp. A silver chain around his neck, a scrap of black fabric around his wrist to cover his scar, and a couple of silver rings rounded out the ensemble. He looked devastatingly handsome.

While Caelum looked every bit the harsh captain he needed to be tonight, I felt like a child playing dress up. Cameron had offered to braid my hair, much to the surprise of everyone. He wove into intricate sections, forming a crown around my head and leaving the rest spilling in wild curls down my back. If nothing else, my hair was truly beautiful.

I wore a similar outfit to Caelum, a white blouse covered by a dark leather corset that sat beneath my bust and laced up the back, displaying my figure more than I necessarily wanted. My pants were tight and tucked into boots with thick silver buckles, like Caelum's. Despite the discomfort at the attention I knew I would receive from men tonight, I did feel beautiful and powerful.

We stopped just inside the door, looking for where Maddock and Cameron were. I spotted them over in the corner, at a table with a small group of six men. Cam waved his hand over his head in acknowledgement. Caelum nodded his head back, and we made our way over to them.

"Men, this is Caelum, our captain, Duncan, the first mate, and Brigid," Cam introduced us. He stumbled over my name, likely unsure how to best introduce me. I hoped the men sitting before us had not noticed. They seemed more focused on Caelum than me, which I was eternally grateful for.

One of the men stood, extending his hand to Caelum. His hair was dark and messy, and his clothes disheveled, as if he couldn't care less about his appearance. "I'm Alan. We hear you're looking for a crew."

"Aye." Caelum sat down in the empty chair, leaving me to stand behind him. I tensed my body, ready for anything. "Are you looking for a captain?"

Alan grinned at Caelum, delight playing in his dark eyes. "Aye, sir. Me and my men here."

"Do you have any experience as a crew?" Duncan asked, taking the last empty chair beside Caelum.

I stayed behind them, observing the situation. My mind was good at taking note of things other people missed, and I was watching everyone in the room. This tavern had every nerve in my body on edge, surrounded by men and people I did not know. But I would take in every detail as if I were analyzing a ship the syrens were about to ruin. I crossed my arms and schooled my face into blankness.

"Aye, sir," one of the other men added. "We worked on a merchant vessel up until recently. The captain retired, and we haven't been able to find work since."

"Are you opposed to less-than-legal work?" Caelum asked, his voice quiet.

Alan grinned even wider. "Nah, we're open to any work, legal or otherwise."

Merchant vessel...sure. From the grin on Alan's face, I assumed they were former pirates. I raised an eyebrow, continuing to study them.

Caelum looked at Alan for a long moment and then moved his attention to the rest of the men sitting there. "And you all? Any problems following orders?"

"No, sir," they all responded, echoing each other.

Caelum looked over at Cameron and Maddock, who had apparently spent most of the night before and the afternoon with these men. Maddock nodded his approval. After a moment, Caelum clasped his hands together, leaning forward. "All right, let's do this. Can you start right now?"

One of the other men across the table leaned forward on

his forearms. "What's the plan?"

I could hear the grin in Caelum's voice as he launched into a discussion of payment, followed by the plan he and Duncan had devised to get control of the boat and out of the harbor with minimum fuss and involvement. Once everyone was on the same page, we stood, following Duncan out of the pub.

As we left, Caelum grabbed my arm, pulling me off to the side as we all walked toward the harbor. "Hey, *teine,* are you okay? You've been quiet tonight."

Shrugging, I met his gaze, trying to keep my anxiety out of my eyes and maintain my façade of indifference. "Had nothing to contribute to the conversation."

His own eyes narrowed and pulled me to a stop, turning me to face him. "What's going on?"

I couldn't meet his gaze. Couldn't tell him that the thought of being on a ship with these men terrified me and being out on the water my sisters patrolled terrified me even more. I couldn't tell him any of that. He seemed to think me useful, and if he knew just how wrong he was, I would be an afterthought in a moment. "Caelum…I'm fine."

He gripped my chin in his hand, forcing me to look at him. I fought my instinct to pull away from his grip. His skin was warm against mine and sent chills down my spine. "You are valuable to this, Brigid. I need your help, and they will not hurt you."

How he managed to land on every single insecurity in one sentence, I didn't know. But he had. I swallowed hard, flexing my fingers at my side and forcing my jaw to unclench. "I know that."

"You are in control here," he said, leaning his head down. I could feel the warmth of his skin radiating into my face. "They. Will. Not. Hurt. You."

I looked at him for a moment. He could make no such guarantees, especially not once the others found out the truth of my involvement in the shipwreck and what I truly was. But I would let him feel as though he could for now. I nodded at him, looking up into his eyes. "They won't hurt me. Now, let's go get this ship."

He smiled at me, dropping my chin and instead twining our fingers together. I should have, but I didn't pull my hand away. His smile grew slightly before he masked his face into blankness. The captain was back. "Let's go get us a ship."

CHAPTER SIXTEEN

BRIGID

On the trailing ends of the sunset, we approached the harbor carefully, spotting the ship we would be taking. The three-masted pinnace had its sails tied up, but it was clear it would take all of us to crew. The small ship was old, the wood weathered and flaking in some places, but according to Caelum, it would make it to where we needed to go. Duncan corralled the men, explaining what each of their roles were. One by one, they slipped through the harbor rows before climbing aboard the ship.

Finally, Caelum and I joined, strolling hand in hand through the rows as the harbor master made his rounds. My steps were wooden, and I was relying all too much on the grounding of Caelum's hand against mine. I forced myself to focus on the heat of his skin, the roughness of his palm, the tingles that spread up my arm and down my spine at the contact. It kept my mind from spiraling down into anxiety. We didn't have time for that, and I needed to get my emotions back under control.

We walked together, passing the ship we would be taking. *The Voyager*, it read. Once the harbor master was out of sight, we changed our course, climbing up the rungs to board the ship.

"Hey, you lot! Stop there!" a voice yelled from the harbor docks.

"Shit," Caelum cursed aloud, turning from his position at the stern to see the harbor master and an older man I assumed was the ship's owner running down the docks toward us. He turned to Duncan, his eyes frantic and his forehead furrowed. "Are we ready to go?"

I looked at Duncan too, who grimaced. "Not quite. We're still tied on by one of the cleats on the dock. We were gonna climb down and loose it before we left."

"Can we cut it from up here?" I asked, leaning over the railing to look down at the rope keeping us attached to the dock. If we could cut it, we would be on our way easily. But I did not pretend to know anything about ships, and would gladly defer to those more experienced than myself.

Caelum shook his head, grimacing. "No, we'll need it when we get to Brinemoor. One of us will have to climb down and unwind it."

I looked back over my shoulder at the rest of the crew, an idea forming in my mind. While the others would likely not want to risk it, I had no such illusions of my own importance. "Other than that line there, are we ready to leave?"

"Aye," Duncan said, his attention already back on the rest of the ship and crew.

Caelum narrowed his eyes at me. "What're you thinking, lass?"

"Get ready to go," was all I said before jumping up onto the narrow railing and proceeding to climb down the line. I could get it untied faster than any of them could, and I could climb the lines faster than any of them too. Behind me, I heard Caelum curse.

"Aye, move, men!" Duncan roared, catching on to my plan.

I reached the dock, and with one hand holding on to the line still attached to the ship, I began unwinding the figure eight securing it to the cleat. The harbor master noticed me and started running. I needed to pick up my pace. My hair was still in the intricate braids Cameron had woven, but a strand of hair fell into my face, irritating me. I puffed a breath, moving it out of the way, and continued working.

We needed to get out of here, and I needed to prove I was useful beyond my powers.

Just as the harbor master was about to reach me, the line came free and I swung, the tips of my boots glancing off the water. I slammed into the side of the boat with a groan and then the rope began to move, pulling me closer to the deck rails. Finally, we were out into deeper water where no one from the dock could reach us, and I pulled myself the last few inches to reach the railing, digging my fingers in. That had been a rush, one I hadn't felt since seeing Caelum's ship in the waves above me. As I climbed up to the railing, Caelum grabbed me under my arms and hauled me over, both of us landing on our arses on the deck.

I couldn't help but grin at him, the excitement of the moment overtaking the previous nerves I had felt about this journey. "Got the line."

He laughed. "Aye, that you did."

"Good work, Brigid!" Duncan boomed, walking over to us. He pulled me up and into a bear hug. "You'll be a sailor yet!"

"You'll pay for this!" The harbormaster was yelling from the dock, shaking his fist at us as we sailed away. The owner of the ship next to him was running his hands over his face, resting them on top of his head as he watched us, distraught.

"They'd have to catch us first," Caelum muttered, rolling his eyes.

"Thanks, Duncan," I replied, my smile still etched on my face. The praise was wonderful, and I would relish it while I could.

Caelum stood from the deck too and tucked me under his arm, pulling me into his side. "Aye, lass. Fine job."

"I told you I'd keep up."

"That you did," he said again, letting go of my shoulders and twining our fingers together. Once again, I didn't pull away from him, relishing the contact instead.

After several heart-pounding moments of movement I was sure would be heard, the ship was finally ready to leave. The darkness surrounding us made this much harder, but we couldn't risk lighting any lanterns, as that would surely set off warning bells to the harbor master. Finally, with Maddock at the wheel, the ship began its departure.

But we weren't in the clear yet. We still had to get out of the harbor, and we wouldn't be safe until we were out of sight and in the open water off the coast. My palms were slippery with anticipation. Once we were on open water, all bets were off. The syrens could, and likely would, come for us.

"Let's go get you settled in," Caelum said, squeezing my fingers.

He led me down below deck to the captain's quarters. This was an older ship, and there wasn't a proper bed in the quarters. But there was a netted hammock and a trunk full of blankets. It would do. I had slept in a similar hammock as a syren, and it would be comfortable enough.

"We need to talk about the journey," Caelum said, leaning his hip against the table in the room, his voice suddenly serious again. "Will the other syrens come for this ship too?"

I rubbed at my face. "I don't know, not for sure. There's a marking I can put on the hull so they would know I'm onboard, but I'm not sure if that would stop them from wrecking it. It might make them want to wreck it more."

"What happens if they do anyway?" he asked, his brows pinching.

We would all likely die, was what I wanted to reply. But that would do none of us any good.

"I don't want to risk everyone's lives again, but we need to get back on track before my father gets any further in his plans." His face was conflicted, and I could tell just how important this mission was that he was willing to risk the lives of these men. But maybe it helped him that they were strangers still.

"I can take the wheel," I said instead, shrugging slightly. If I could help get us all through this alive, I would do whatever it took. "I can at least keep us from crashing. But I don't know if I can do anything against their song if they decide to sing it."

"Would plugging our ears work?" he asked, motioning at his head. "I've heard of that in the myths before."

"Potentially. I've never seen it done, but I don't think our myth is as widely told as it once was," I admitted. Cliodhna often spoke of how man was forgetting her and the ways of the old gods, more intent on pretending this world was their creation.

"I'll see if we have any wax aboard. Will their song affect you?"

I hesitated, flexing my jaw and snapping my mouth shut. Would their song affect me now as well now that I didn't have one of my own? Cliodhna had not said, and I was not sure I was keen to find out in such a dire situation.

Caelum must have sensed my hesitation, raising an eyebrow at me. "What aren't you telling me?"

"I don't have to tell you everything, Caelum." I knew my voice was cold, but I couldn't bring myself to care. This was my burden to bear.

"No, but if it could impact our journey, I need to know it," he said, his anger rising.

He was right, of course; he did need to know. I rubbed my forehead, sighing heavily as the motivation drained out of my body. I would have to tell him. "Fine. I don't have my song anymore. When they banished me, our queen took it from me.

So, I'm not sure if I'm even immune to the song of the others now or if I would be just as vulnerable as you."

"She stole your song?" he asked. His eyes swirled with curiosity and what looked almost like worry. "What else did she take? Are you even still a syren?"

The urgency in his voice gave me pause, and hurt washed through me. He had been hoping to use my syren powers for something. My stomach dropped and my throat burned. "Is that all I am to you? Is that the only value I hold?"

"No, of course not. But like I said, I need to know if it will affect our journey." He was quick to recover, but the thoughts were already there, worming their way into my mind. He only valued me for the abilities I had once possessed. Now, I truly did have no purpose in his eyes. How long would it take for him to ask me to leave? I had been expecting it, but the idea that it would be coming soon created a pit in my stomach that I did not appreciate.

"I can still transform into a syren, if that's what you're asking," I said slowly, answering his questions. If he needed me to be a syren, that was fine. I technically still was one. And if that was the only value I showed, I needed to exploit it until we could get closer to the Bhodheas so I'd be better off when they asked me to leave.

Caelum was silent for a long time, rubbing at the stubble on his chin as he stared at me, likely wondering if I was worth the trouble anymore.

"What will it take to mark the hull?" he asked finally.

"I just need to get in the water, then I can mark it with my talons. If the other syrens see it, they'll know I'm onboard,"

I explained. I had not transformed since Cliodhna had taken away her magic that made it painless. I had no idea what it would feel like to transform again. "But like I said before, that might not be enough to stop them, especially if they're still angry. Or if our queen commands them to wreck the ship."

"Does she wreck every ship that goes in the water?"

"No, she tells us which ones to target. It's more likely to be wrecked if it's alone, though. We avoid witnesses."

He nodded, the resolve clear in his face. "We'll take the chance, then. Let's go get you into the water to mark the hull."

"I don't want the others to see me," I said firmly. I really didn't want Caelum to see me either, but I doubted he would trust me enough to leave me alone and not observe. My pain was private, and not something I liked sharing. "I don't know the new men, and I don't want to risk them turning back because of the danger."

"Agreed. We'll make sure they don't see you," he said, nodding solemnly. I held back my sigh.

Leaving the quarters, we walked to the lower deck, avoiding the men gathered there. In the darkness, the water was pitch black and likely freezing. While the water wouldn't affect me once I transformed, it would still shock my human body. Already, the ship was moving out of the harbor, the strong winds picking up the sails.

Looking at me, Caelum motioned down to the water. "How are we going to do this?"

I looked around, glancing at the crew on the other side of the deck. Determined as I might be, this was going to be tough. I had no idea how much pain I would be in or if I would even be able to get myself back out of the water. "I'm going to jump over. Once I'm in the water, I'll transform and mark the hull, but I'll need you to help me back out of the water. And I'll need clothes once I get out."

Caelum sighed again, sensing my hesitation. "What is it? I need you to be honest with me, *teine*."

"The transformation may be painful for me. That was another condition of my banishment. I'm not sure what shape I'll be in after I transform back," I finally admitted after a few moments of consideration. I didn't want to tell him, but if I needed help getting back on the ship, he was my only option. Admitting weakness went against every fiber of my being, but for whatever reason, I trusted Caelum would not betray me. As much as I figured he wanted to, he wouldn't leave me to the mercy of the other syrens.

"Painful?" he asked, something akin to concern flashing in his eyes. It was gone in a moment, though, the calculating captain's look back once again. He raised his chin, his forehead creasing. "What do I need to do?"

"I might not be able to get myself back up the ladder," I warned, wanting him to understand the gravity of the situation. "I might need your help. And I might need your help getting back into the clothes. But I won't know until I transform back."

"Aye, understood. Should we tether you to the ship somehow?" he asked, his eyes flicking down to the line on the deck.

I shook my head. "No, it might hinder my transformation."

"What do we do if you can't get back to the ladder?"

"Throw a rope down. If I need your help, I'll tug on it." It was the only solution that came to mind.

"Okay, let me go get some things ready." With a quick step, he went over to the supplies we had brought, coming back with a bundle of fabric and a blanket. He nodded back toward the men, who had not looked over from their place across the deck. "I'll make sure they don't see you come back as well. Keeping them busy should do the trick. And if you're in pain after, we'll take care of that when we get there."

I tried to look reassuring as I peered down over the railing into the water and then back at Caelum. "Be right back."

And then, before I could overthink it, I swung a leg over the railing and plunged into the black sea below. The cold water shocked my system, my muscles clenching up painfully. As I sank deeper in the dark water, I prayed that Cliodhna would not notice I was in her waters. Bracing my core, I willed the transformation to begin.

Pure agony rolled through my body as it began, the muscles of my legs tearing and reforming together. Bones snapped, and bile surged up my throat. I fought it back, gritting my teeth so hard I was surprised they did not crack. As my leg muscles continued to tear and reform, my talons began to emerge, slicing through the skin of my nail beds. The pain was searing hot, and I saw the blood dispersing into the water from them. I loosened my jaw, my teeth slicing their way through my gums now as well. Copper flooded my tongue, and I fought the urge to gag.

This was a miserable experience. I fought against the blackness outlining my vision, willing myself to stay conscious through the pain. Clenching my jaw to keep from crying out, my entire body ached and screamed in protest.

Finally, after what felt like an eternity, the transformation was complete. The ship had moved ahead while I had been busy being broken and remade. I swam toward it, the muscles of my tail and core aching in protest.

I reached the hull, raising my hand to the old wood. Ignoring the pain searing through my nailbeds as I carved, I drew Cliodhna's symbol, a small trident with waves beneath it, into the ship, marking it for the others to know there was a syren aboard. The only thing left to do was hope that they would not wreck the ship purely because of the symbol.

Marking it with my talons meant that some of the residual magic, whatever I had left, would be imbued into the wood. The others would sense it. We hadn't used the symbol or the practice often, but the ships used by our contact in the south were all marked to protect them. Cliodhna had marked other ships and even buildings from what she had told us, but she hasn't shared the reasoning behind those marks.

While I wanted to remain in the water and relish being back in my syren form, my body was aching. Besides that, I didn't want to risk staying in the water longer than necessary. That was asking for the others to come investigate, and that could only bring ruin upon Caelum and his men. The blood could also attract other sea creatures, but I was hoping to be well out of the water by the time they noticed the possibility of food.

Reaching a hand up to the ladder on the side of the ship, I gripped it as tightly as I could as the transformation took over once again. The pain was slightly more bearable this time, but I could still feel the muscles of my legs ripping beneath the skin. White-hot fire spread through my limbs as they split once more. It was a struggle to maintain my grip on the ladder, but I knew I needed to. Without my tail, I wouldn't be able to catch up with the ship if it left me. Finally, the transformation back to human was complete, and I began the daunting task of climbing up the ladder.

I knew Caelum was there if I needed him, but I wanted to prove to myself that this curse from Cliodhna was something I could overcome on my own. Arms and legs shaking, I panted as I climbed, stopping at nearly every rung to rest. As I neared the top, Caelum's head peeked over. His face shone with relief, and he reached down to grab my hand, hauling me up and onto the deck, where he immediately wrapped me in a blanket.

Thankfully, the others hadn't looked up from their game and their work. I let out a sigh of relief that I wouldn't have to explain myself immediately.

My legs were screaming in protest, but I fought to remain upright as I dressed. Once clothed, I pulled the blanket back up around me, relishing the warmth. I looked at Caelum, answering the question shining clearly in his eyes. Even speaking was exhausting, but I needed to tell him I had succeeded at what he asked of me. "I've marked it. Hopefully, it works."

He pulled me into his arms and pressed a kiss to my wet hair. I closed my eyes and let myself lean into him. "Thank you."

"Don't get your hopes up, though," I warned, my voice muffled against his chest. I looked up at him but made no move to pull away. I could barely hold my own weight, and despite not wanting to rely on Caelum, this moment of weakness was acceptable. "This might not work, Caelum."

"Aye, maybe not." He shrugged and pulled me closer, taking on more of my weight. He didn't comment on my condition, which I was grateful for. "But you tried, and that's what counts to me."

I let out a yawn that made my jaw ache, and Caelum led me down to the captain's quarters without another word. Climbing into the hammock, I immediately curled up on my side, tucking my sore legs up against my stomach. The position provided some relief.

"Get some rest, *teine*. We're going to sail through the night, and I'll wake you when we get to Brinemoor," he said, brushing a loose strand of hair off my forehead as he looked down at me. For a moment, I could have sworn there was caring behind his eyes. But I knew better; exhaustion was making me foolish. "You need sleep."

I looked up at him, suddenly unable to keep my eyes open. "G'night, Caelum. Wake me if you need me, please. If you hear the syrens, don't try to play a hero."

As I stretched out in the hammock, he pulled the blanket up over me. In an instant, I was asleep.

Chapter Seventeen
CAELUM

With Brigid fast asleep nearly immediately, I turned to head back up to the deck. Brigid may have helped us get out of the harbor, but I still needed to discuss some things with the crew without her listening in.

"Caelum, you disappeared on us," Duncan greeted, his brow quirking suspiciously. He moved away from the others, and we walked over to the other side of the deck, leaning against the mast.

"Had to talk to Brigid about what to expect on the Straits," I replied, keeping my voice casual. Despite itching to tell the others what Brigid was and her attempts to keep us safe, while we were on the seas was probably not the best moment. The crew, especially Duncan, would be angry, both at me for hiding the truth and Brigid for her involvement in our wreck. Maddock would likely want to ask Brigid a hundred questions about what it was like being a syren, and Cam would try like hell to keep the peace.

"And what can she offer that we haven't already learned for ourselves?" Duncan demanded. "We've sailed the Straits of Marbh at least a dozen times over the years."

"I was telling *her* what to expect," I lied, the words burning like ash in my mouth. It was a white lie, but it was still a lie. Before he could question me and cause me to lie further, I changed the subject. "We need to discuss some things about the mission."

"You don't trust her." His statement wasn't a question, but it still deserved an answer.

"I don't know her well enough yet to trust her or not." This, at least, I could be honest about. Brigid may have saved my life, but she was still a syren. And she had likely killed far more men than she had saved. She was dangerous, and until I was certain she was completely on our side, there would be things I would not tell her about our mission.

"Your father is getting ahead of us," he grumbled, crossing his arms over his chest. "And we're running out of money."

I pushed a hand through my hair with a sigh. "Yeah, I know. He's going to take those children and do god knows what with them."

My father had been kidnapping orphaned children, mostly boys. We'd known about it for *months*, but every time we had gotten close to figuring out what exactly he was doing with them, either my father got away, or something else happened to keep us from getting the information we desperately needed. As a child, my father's ship had engaged in piracy mostly, but he'd also dabbled in smuggling. And unlike us, he wasn't discerning in what he smuggled.

We smuggled people who needed passage away from something horrific. Often, our customers were women. Maybe my desire to engage in this type of smuggling stemmed from the failure to save Brigid as a child. But either way, I helped those who needed it start a new life.

"We need to get to Brinemoor. He's probably going back there," Duncan said, heaving a sigh as well. "He always ends up back in Brinemoor."

Shouts rose from the railing, and ice ran down my spine. Something was wrong. Duncan and I shared a look of concern before running over to the crew. I reached them first. "What is it?"

"Rocks ahead," Maddock said, his face serious. "And the darkness doesn't help. We can't see them until we're right up on them."

"We just need to all be on watch, then," I replied, leaning over the railing to peer down into the water. "Stay as close to the middle as possible; that should keep us away from the worst of it."

"The weather's on our side, at least," Cameron commented, tilting his head back to look at the sky.

The moon was full, which gave us more light than we normally would have, and thankfully, the clouds were sparse. The wind was strong enough to keep us moving, but steady. Hopefully, the weather would remain good until we passed through the worst of the Straits.

They weren't called the Straits of the Dead for nothing, after all.

We needed assignments. Alan and his men seemed capable of following orders and knew their way around a ship. I turned to Duncan. "Take the wheel. Cameron, you watch the sails and the weather. Maddock, you're with me."

"What do you want us to do, Captain?" Alan asked, motioning toward his men.

"Watch for rocks, and do whatever Cameron tells you to."

"Aye, aye, sir."

"Don't call me sir," I said firmly, pointing at him. "Captain" I could live with, but I was no better than any of my men, and I wouldn't have them calling me sir. I had too many bad memories associated with that word and my father.

"What did you say, boy?" my father barked out, stepping up close to my face. His hot breath stank.

"I...I said...said that I would...said I would do it," I stuttered out, cowering under his hard gaze.

"Would do it, what?" he growled. He reached down to grab my shirt by the neck, yanking me even closer to him.

"Sir," I gritted out, somehow managing to keep eye contact with him. If I looked away, it would have only made it worse.

"Ten lashes," my father said loudly, releasing me and shoving me toward Iain, his first mate. Iain grinned at me, holding up the whip in his hands.

I swallowed hard, bracing myself for the pain.

"Get to work," I said, shaking my head to clear the memories. This was *my* ship, and *my* crew. And I would not be like my father.

"Captain," Maddock called me over, waving his hand at me. I stepped up next to him and he lowered his voice, keeping the conversation between us. "We need to keep an eye out for whatever wrecked *The Nehalennia* too. Should we tell Alan and his men about them?"

"We don't even know what they were. Not for sure," I said, swallowing the taste of the lie once again. The safety of my crew was a priority for me, but we needed Alan and his men. And telling them that we suspected the legends of murderous half women, half sea creatures could very well scare them off. "Better to keep it to ourselves. You and I will watch for them."

"Should we get Brigid up here to help?" he asked, raising an eyebrow.

I shook my head. "No, she's sleeping. Let her rest."

Maddock nodded, turning back to the railing. "I like her. She seems like she'd be good for you."

"Not happening, Mad," I replied, going to stand next to him at the railing. "It's not like that."

He turned, raising his eyebrow even more dramatically than before. "Okay, Captain. Whatever you say."

"Go keep watch," I grumbled, focusing my attention back to the water.

The smirk on his face as he walked away was visible from my peripheral vision. I shook my head at his antics. Brigid may have been attractive, and we may have bonded, but I needed to be careful. Getting involved with her romantically, or even just physically, could lead to repercussions with my friends that I didn't want to think about.

And for now, I wouldn't think about it. For now, I needed to get us through the night, watching for rocks and calling them out to keep us from wrecking. That would require all my attention, and hopefully keep my thoughts off a certain red-haired syren sleeping below.

Chapter Eighteen
BRIGID

I woke to sunlight hitting my face through the dirty porthole in the captain's quarters. It was morning, which hopefully meant that we were almost to Brinemoor. My body was sore, but it had thankfully turned from the sharp pain into a dull ache. A dull ache I could ignore if I tried hard enough.

Climbing out of the netted bed, I made my way to the upper decks to look for Caelum. On deck, I was surprised to see a town in the distance, just above the horizon. Still looking out over the water, I walked over to where Caelum was standing with Maddock, looking over the maps.

"Any issues last night?" I asked carefully. If we had almost made it into the town, I hoped that meant we had avoided the others through the night. It was a miracle we hadn't wrecked even without their influence, but if they had come for us, we should not have been alive right now.

He smiled at me, broad and genuinely happy. "None at all, *teine;* clear weather and the sea was on our side. We're about to pull into Brinemoor now, actually."

I let out a sigh of relief. We had avoided the other syrens, by some miracle. I didn't want to stop to question our good fortune. "Good. That's good. What can I do to help?"

"Once we get to the harbor, we might need you, but we're all right for now," he replied, still smiling at me.

Hesitantly returning his smile, I nodded. While I was grateful we had made it through the Straits unharmed, Caelum should not be smiling at me like he was. "Aye, all right. I'll let you get back to your maps. I'll just be watching for a bit, then."

After a while, Alan and Duncan began to guide the ship into the harbor, pulling it into a slip at the end. I stayed seated on my perch by the mast, watching the crew bustle around, securing the sails and tying off lines to the dock cleats.

I wasn't used to so many people—so many men—around me, and I was slightly overwhelmed along with still being physically exhausted. I knew I could help prepare the ship, but I found myself unable to do anything but sit there and watch, my legs tucked up under my chin.

Instead, I watched as the men scurried around the ship, preparing the ship to dock. Despite the new men on the crew, it was a well-oiled machine. Everyone knew their role, and I wasn't sure where to even start with offering to help. Perhaps I could haul the lines, securing down everything on the deck, but Alan and his men were already doing it so efficiently.

Logically, I knew I should be helping them somehow, but my body was frozen. I hated what I had become and how anxious I was. I was a syren, for goddess' sake. I could kill every man aboard this ship if I wanted to, and it was time I started remembering that. Rolling my shoulders, I flexed my neck and loosened my jaw, pulling up all the feelings of anger and fire I had been subduing.

Caelum stopped in his path across the deck and turned to come over to me. He put a hand on my shoulder. "Hey, *teine*. You okay?"

I looked up at him, raising a brow at his concern. "I'm fine. I'm not used to being around so many men. And I'm still sore."

"Do you need to go rest?" He sat down on the mast banister next to me, concern in his eyes. I wasn't sure what had changed after my excursion the previous night, but it was obvious that something had. "You have been with only women for the past few years. I can understand that. How can I help?"

"I'll be fine," I said, uncrossing my arms and lowering my legs. I appreciated his concern for me, but I needed to get over myself. I was already starting to rely on Caelum, and I couldn't go any further down that line of thinking. It wouldn't happen again. It *couldn't* happen again.

He tilted his head at me, a strand of his dark hair flopping down into his face. "You don't have to be. It's okay if you're not."

Standing, I straightened my back and looked at him, smiling with what I hoped was a reassuring expression. "I'm fine, Caelum. Now, how can I help?"

"You can grab that line there and follow me."

I stood, grabbing the line he pointed at. I would be useful, even as a human. My value did not lie in my syren abilities. Fire in my belly, I turned it inwards, fueling my determination. At whatever cost, I would stop Caelum's father and I would redeem myself, and then I would make a new life for myself, whatever that looked like.

After successfully securing the ship into the slip at the harbor, it was well into the afternoon. While Duncan was sent to deal with this harbormaster to pay our mooring fee, the rest of us inventoried the supplies that were on the ship, getting things ready for our evening adventure and finding what money we could.

One of Alan's men would be staying on the ship to keep guard, a decision that had been made while I was sleeping, apparently, and the rest of us would be spending the night at the inn attached to a tavern in town.

I almost would have preferred to sleep on the ship, but according to Caelum, the inn was closer to where we needed to be.

Once we were all ready, the rest of us left the ship and walked into the pub Duncan had said would be our first starting point. Maddock and Cam went off in one direction, leaving Duncan and Caelum on either side of me. I turned to them, already over-stimulated by the crowd and the noise. Clenching my fists, I took deep breaths through my nose, pasting on my façade of indifference. "What's the plan?"

"Cam and Maddock are going to see what they can discover. We are going to blend in and observe the crowd and see if anyone sticks out or if we can overhear anything," Duncan explained as we followed Caelum over to a table.

"How are we going to blend in?" I asked, looking around. There were people drinking, dancing, bumping into each other. I really hoped that was not Duncan's idea of blending in. Sitting and looking angry and unapproachable, that was what I could accomplish right now. But if someone asked me to dance, I would likely murder them, consequences be damned.

"Relax." Caelum laughed as we sat down at a small table in the corner. "We'll just be sitting here and pretending to have a good time."

Duncan remained standing and clapped Caelum on the shoulder. "I'll go get us some ale."

"Get Brigid a pint too. She can pretend to drink it," Caelum said before Duncan walked off toward the bar.

"Pretend?" I asked, offended. Granted, I had never drunk ale before, but I wasn't liking the assumption that I couldn't drink it. I didn't enjoy the embarrassment washing down my spine. It was not an emotion I was used to, and I didn't like how it felt, slimy and coiling in my stomach and heating my cheeks.

"Fair enough," he replied, nodding agreeably. "Then, let's get you a drink."

Duncan walked back over shortly after, three mugs in his large hands. He sat them down on the table, sliding one toward me and one toward Caelum. He and Caelum picked theirs up, holding them together toward mine. Picking up the pint, I lifted my own mug, touching it to theirs. I took a drink and promptly grimaced as the wheat taste flooded my tongue. "Goddess, that's vile."

Caelum roared laughing. Duncan sputtered, wiping the golden liquid off his mouth where some had escaped during his own laughter. "It's not supposed to taste good."

"Then what's the point of drinking it?" I asked, wrinkling my nose at the mug before me. They really did this for fun? No wonder men were so easy to kill.

"To get drunk, of course."

That could be nice. Goddess knew I wanted to forget about what had happened lately. Between being banished by my sisters, hunted by strangers, and now this, a night to forget sounded perfect. I picked up the mug again and, without another word, emptied it into my mouth, swallowing hard. I slammed the empty mug down onto the table as my head swam. Maybe that was not a smart decision.

"*Teine...*" Caelum trailed off, looking at me wide-eyed. Duncan cast him a confused side glance, likely at the nickname.

I somehow wasn't embarrassed anymore. I felt almost free. All my life, I had never been one to enjoy myself; I had never been able to. But tonight, here with Caelum, it seemed like I could. Yes, I wanted to prove myself. But more than that, I wanted to live. And live I would.

Duncan nodded his head, pursing his lips and appraising me. He slid his still full mug over to me. "Have at it, Brigid."

I lifted the mug to my lips, but hesitated slightly, turning to Caelum. "This isn't smart. What if we need to move?"

Caelum's face softened. "I've got it, Brigid. Enjoy yourself for a night. A mug of ale won't have any effect on Duncan or me. We can handle things if needed."

Likely, I should be setting the mug down and pushing it away, making sure I could still be useful if anything did happen tonight. But the temptation of experiencing something for the first time, of being so free, was too much to pass up. I pressed the worn mug to my lips and let the liquid slide down my throat.

Over the next hour or so, I downed three or four more mugs of ale, abhorring the taste each time. But the more I drank, the lighter I felt. And the warmer I felt, the freer I felt. It was a nice change from being constantly on edge and waiting for something to go wrong. I looked over at Caelum, who was talking with Cameron. They had their heads leaned together, whispering.

Caelum was attractive—seriously attractive. His dark hair was shaved close to the skin on either side of his temples, fading into long waves that he had tied back in a bun at the crown of his head with a strip of leather. The short beard covering his strong jaw was enticing. I wanted to see how it felt under my fingertips. His fingers flexed around his mug as he spoke to Cam, drawing my attention to his rough skin there, the scar around his wrist, and the dark smattering of hair covering his muscular forearms.

I wanted to run my fingers over his arms, to feel the muscle under the skin. From his arms, my gaze drew up to his shoulders, broad and powerful. They were tense, likely from whatever he and Cam were talking about. His face was just as attractive as the rest of him, weathered and tanned from the sun, with a smattering of freckles over the bridge of his nose that made the green of his eyes stand out.

A throat cleared, and I was able to refocus my gaze after some effort. Caelum was grinning at me. "Can I help you, Brigid?"

Shit. He had caught me staring at him. Cheeks flushing, I pushed a strand of hair off my sweaty forehead. I had thought I was being discreet, but apparently not. "No, I'm just looking at you."

His eyebrows rose. Damn, I hadn't meant to admit that out loud.

He laughed loudly before turning to Duncan and Cam, who were watching us with undisguised amusement. "Men, go have a night. I'll stay here with her."

Without another word, they left, leaving Caelum and I sitting alone at the table. I dropped my head into my hands, embarrassment washing over me once again. I was making a fool of myself, and already regretted my attempts to be free. "Sorry. I didn't mean to say that out loud."

He chuckled, softer this time, as he moved his chair closer to me. He bumped my shoulder with his own. "Don't apologize. A pretty girl is staring at me, I'm fine with that."

"I was not staring!" I protested. He raised an eyebrow at me. I looked down at my lap, tucking a loose strand of hair behind my ear. "Okay, fine, maybe I was staring a little. Have you seen yourself?"

Cheeks turning pink, he ducked his head slightly, rubbing

the back of his neck. "Thanks. You're a pretty sight yourself."

My cheeks got even hotter. My whole face felt like it was on fire now. He thought I was beautiful? My brain was screaming at me that I was being foolish, but my stomach fluttered at the compliment. "I…uh…"

"Not used to being called beautiful, *teine*?" he asked, the sides of his mouth quirking up. "Those syrens of yours never told you?"

I rolled my eyes. Teasing was good; I knew how to respond to teasing. "We had other things on our mind, Caelum."

He leaned in closer, tugging gently on the strand of hair that kept falling into my face. His breath puffed against my face as he whispered, "That's too bad. Someone as pretty as you should be told more often."

"Are you flirting with me, Captain?" I asked, leaning in just as close. The ale had made me braver than I would ever have been. I shouldn't be doing this, but I was being free tonight, and I wasn't thinking about how hurt my family would be if they found out. How much *more* hurt they would be.

No. They had shunned me. Banishing me without a second thought had lost them any right they had to be angry over how I chose to live my life.

"Are you flirting back, syren?" he asked, bumping his shoulder into mine again.

I didn't even try to stop myself as I reached out and looped my arm through his, pressing myself to his side and resting my head on his shoulder. He was warm and sturdy, smelled like sandalwood and rain, and I fit a little too well into his side. "Did you know you're attractive, Caelum? Real handsome."

He laughed softly, tilting his head down to rest against mine. "Aye, you mentioned that already, *teine*. You're real pretty too."

I laughed with him, tilting my head back and full-on laughing. I wasn't sure if it was the drink or him that made my body light up like a crackling fire. I hadn't laughed like this in a long time, and it felt good surging through my body. "I bet you say that to all the girls."

He shrugged, his fingers going back to playing with the strand of my hair that seemed to fascinate him. He tucked it back behind my ear, letting his rough fingertips slide across my cheek, where he rubbed his thumb over the swell. "Only if it's true."

I sat up straighter, tugging at the tight corset around my waist. I needed it off. I needed to breathe. "It's too hot."

His hands quickly covered mine, stilling them. "Let's not take that off here. Do you want to leave? The others can stay and keep gathering information."

I stopped moving, my eyes locking on his. He wanted to leave with me? Unbidden, thoughts of us lying together, of me running my hands over his chest and tracing the scars on his back, entered my mind. And I wanted it. Badly, I wanted it. "Leave?"

"You've got a dirty mind, *teine*," he said with an easy grin. He dropped his hands away from my waist. "Not for that, but so you can go change and cool down a bit."

My stomach dropped in disappointment. He didn't want me, not really. But who could blame him? I was a sea monster who had killed all his friends, and he was a handsome captain, on a mission to stop a truly evil man. There was no hope for us, no matter how much I might want there to be. "Oh, okay."

Suddenly, my face was engulfed in his warm hands and our faces were so close our noses almost touched. His eyes locked with mine, and I felt like I might be lost in the intensity of the green flames there. "Brigid, you are beautiful, don't doubt that. But you are also completely steaming drunk for the first time in your life. So, let's go back to the room and get you some rest, okay?"

My brain was really not working, because all I heard was that he said I was beautiful. "You think I'm beautiful?"

He smiled, still holding my face. "Aye, I do."

I smiled back at him, staring into his eyes that were like shining jade. His lips quirked, drawing my attention there. He even had freckles on his lips. Leaning in, I wet my suddenly dry lips. His eyes shot down to my mouth. I leaned in closer, intent on seeing what his lips felt like against mine. My lips parted as I whispered his name.

Suddenly, he blinked, and his gaze cleared of lust. He leaned back away from me, dropping his hands from my face. "We can't do this."

Stomach dropping, I swallowed back the tears burning in my throat. Of course, we couldn't. What had I been thinking? I leaned back in my chair, squeezing my hands tight into fists and letting my nails bite into the skin at my palms. I clenched my jaw tight, biting into the soft skin of my cheek until my mouth flooded with copper. The pain was a welcome distraction from my foolish idea that had been fueled by alcohol I shouldn't have been drinking.

I was a fool to think I had any kind of chance at a normal life, even for a night. I had given that up when I said yes to Cliodhna, and I would give it up again when I decided whether I should go back to her or live my life as a human in Bhodheas. And I was even more of a fool to think that any sense of normalcy would come with Caelum, given the fate of his crew at my hands.

I managed a nod, somehow keeping the tears from spilling. "Yeah, yeah. I should go back to the room."

I stood quickly, ready to leave, but the room spun on its side, my vision blurring. I slammed a hand out on the table to steady myself, and Caelum quickly stood and grabbed my elbow. "Steady there, *teine.*"

I pulled my elbow from his grip, forcing my muscles to tense up and allow myself to stand on my own. Speaking took entirely too much concentration, but I managed. "I'm fine. I can get back by myself. You can stay."

He sighed heavily, wrapping his arm around my waist and holding my elbow in his other hand. "No, Brigid. You're drunk, that's all I meant. But let's get you back to the room."

After more stumbling than I cared to admit, we entered the room we shared at the old inn a few doors down from the pub. Caelum let go of me, letting me stumble further into the room as he lit the lamp sitting on the table by the bed. I slumped down onto the bed, suddenly exhausted. But I knew I needed to get out of this corset and these pants. I reached behind my back and began tugging on the strings.

Gentle hands pushed mine away. "Let me, *teine.*"

I somehow managed to keep from asking why he kept

calling me that as Caelum began unlacing my corset, freeing my ribs from the compression. He pulled me up to standing before kneeling at my feet and doing the same to my boots and pulling them off one by one. He guided me to sit back down on the bed and pressed a kiss to my head. "What do you want to sleep in?"

"I'll just sleep in this," I said, running a hand over the tight pants that covered my thighs. It would be uncomfortable in the morning, but I was drunk right now and didn't care about my comfort. All I cared about now was the embarrassment still churning at Caelum's rejection.

"No, let me help you change," he said. He motioned for me to stand up, which I thankfully managed to do on my own. "Or do you want to do it yourself?"

Still unable to bring myself to speak and make this situation any worse, I shook my head. I knew I would need his help, at least with the pants. There was no way I was getting myself out of them in this state, no matter how much I wanted to.

He nodded, pulling me into his arms and looking down at me. "Let's get you ready for bed."

CHAPTER NINETEEN
CAELUM

Brigid was absolutely smashed.

I held her gently in my arms as I pulled her slightly away from the bed. It was a pure exercise in self-control as I unlaced her pants and pulled them down over her full hips. She held onto my shoulders as I bent down to my knees, helping her step out of the tight pants. Her legs were beautiful, and up close it was almost too much to take. All I wanted was to press my mouth against her legs and feel the soft skin there against my face. But she was drunk, and I would not become one of the men she feared. We would do this her way, when she decided it was time, if ever.

Once she was out of her pants, I rose from my knees and helped her back to sit down on the bed. She was adorable, her hair mussed, her cheeks flushed, and her lips pouty. I motioned vaguely. "Arms up."

She lifted her arms immediately before putting them back down just as fast and narrowing her eyes at me. "But then I'll be naked."

I raised an eyebrow, amused at her pouting statement. "Suddenly, you're modest? You had no problems showing off when we first met."

She spluttered, her cheeks turning even pinker and the blush spreading down her neck and disappearing beneath her shirt. "That was before I made a fool of myself. Now, you don't get to see my body."

"You didn't make a fool out of yourself," I said with a sigh, sitting down on the bed next to her. Taking her hands in mine, I twined our fingers together. Why I felt the need to comfort her, I didn't understand. I shouldn't be wanting this, wanting *her*. She had a large hand in killing my crew, whether it had been her idea or not. I couldn't forgive that yet, and I certainly couldn't forget that—no matter how much I wanted to. But something about her drew me in like a moth to a flame, and I was curious to see what getting burned would feel like.

She was silent for a long time, and if I wasn't looking at her eyes, darting back and forth, I would think she had fallen asleep standing up. Finally, she spoke. "I shouldn't want to kiss you. I shouldn't be wanting to do any of this."

Her words hit me like a sucker punch to the gut. Hearing her admit out loud that she wanted more than just existing in the same space as me was surreal. Hearing that she was also struggling with the notion that we shouldn't be doing this was validating, but somehow even more frustrating. I wanted to make a move, to be with her in some way, but I couldn't forget what had happened. And I couldn't forget about what *would* happen once the others found out her involvement.

"What exactly is 'any of this,' *teine?*"

Even keeping that secret still made my stomach hurt. I didn't like lying to my men, even if it was just by omission. They deserved to know the truth about the wreck, but I still found myself protecting Brigid. If we were both denying ourselves, would anything ever happen? I doubted it. But I still needed to know what she was specifically talking about.

She waved a hand vaguely around the room. "All of this. I want to live, I want to experience life with you. I want to kiss you, and to hug you, to feel your skin on mine and to wake up next to you. I want to see what all I've been missing. But I shouldn't. I shouldn't want any of that. I should be leaving, groveling to my queen to take me back. And you shouldn't want me either. I was part of causing your wreck; you should hate me. You probably do hate me."

I pulled her into my arms, pressing a kiss to the top of her head. I should hate her, but the more time I spent with her, the harder that was becoming. Instead, the more I learned about how she had been no more free from her queen than I had from my father, it made me feel closer to her. "Brigid, you were faced with an impossible choice to make when you were too young to know any better."

"But I still made that decision," she said, her voice uncharacteristically small. I wasn't used to hearing her so meek or seeing her wrap her arms around herself as if she would fall apart. Her jaw worked, and my fingers itched to massage at the joint, but I kept them to myself. "And now I'm torn between wanting to run back to them and beg for their forgiveness and wanting to stay here with you. I like you, Caelum. But I shouldn't."

"Forget about shouldn't. Let's talk about what you want for yourself. You wanted to make a life for yourself when you stowed away on that ship. What would that life have looked like?" I asked. Even drunk, she needed to face her decisions and really see what it was she wanted out of life. And if that was me, then great, I returned the sentiment. But if it was going back to the others, I would accept that too. Ignoring the part about the wreck seemed smart for now, until I could get a grasp on my own emotions on the subject.

"I don't know. I've never thought about it," she said, looking down at her hands still in her lap. "I didn't know what I was going to do when I got to the Bhodheas, and then I never even got that far."

"You can do whatever you want now. What were your dreams when you were a child?" I asked, sitting down next to her. She had to have something she'd aspired toward when she was younger.

She shrugged, her body slumping in on itself even more. "To be free. To have my own life and make my own decisions. I was never really allowed to be a child, not with my father. I always had to be strong, dependable."

"So, you wanted freedom and ended up just serving a different master," I pointed out. She had run from her father only to end up with this queen she talked about. Anger burned in my chest for her. The more she spoke, the more difficult it was for me to stay angry at her alone for the shipwreck. She had been nothing more than a soldier, following orders. "Why?"

"I was angry when the syrens found me. I guess I never stopped to consider the consequences," she said, her voice wobbly. I studied her; her chin was quivering, but her jaw was tense. This side of her, this vulnerable and emotional side, was new to me, and new to her as well, I believed.

The past few days, she had tried to hide her vulnerabilities, masking them with confidence and snark. Even when she was in such pain from her transformation that she trusted me to hold her upright, she had still been reserved, hiding away the extent of the pain I could see in her eyes. I highly doubted she would appreciate being seen as vulnerable now, especially while she was drunk. Making the decision that we didn't need to talk any more about this heavy subject, I tugged at her hands, making her look at me. "We can talk about it later. Let's get you changed and get some rest."

She nodded, her eyes cast down at the floor. "Okay."

Note to self, Brigid is a sad drunk. I stood again with a sigh, turning to face her. "Now, arms up this time. You can wear my shirt to sleep in. I promise I won't look."

This time, she didn't hesitate, just pulled her shirt right over head, leaving her upper body completely bare. My mouth dried out, but I forced myself to stay focused on her face as promised. I pulled my own shirt off quickly before turning it around and slipping it over her head and pulling it down. It engulfed her, and my heartbeat quickened seeing her in my shirt.

Pulling her hair out from beneath the collar, I sat down beside her, taking out the pins and ties holding her braids back. Without speaking, I unraveled her long hair from the braids, running my fingers through it until the biggest of the tangles were gone. "Are you ready for bed?"

"Thank you, Caelum," she said softly, leaning into my side. "I'm sorry for all of this."

I turned, cupping her face. The way she looked up at me, her green eyes so fucking soft, it almost melted me. "I know you are. This is an impossible situation that has no easy resolution. I'm still angry about what happened, I won't deny that. But I see the guilt you hold too. And honestly, it makes me feel quite proud that you think about all these things with me. You've been against men for years, and look at you, trusting me enough to be attracted. It's an honor."

Her cheeks turned pink under my touch. "I still shouldn't have said anything. We can't ever have a future. Not between the syrens and your mission to stop your father, and my involvement in the wreck. The others would never accept me, not if they knew the truth."

I bent forward and kissed the top of her head. Giving credence to her thoughts, telling her she was right, wouldn't be a useful conversation right now. Not when she was drunk. Against her hair, I mumbled, "We'll figure that out when we get to it. But we've still got a mission to fulfill. So, let's table this discussion for later."

She giggled, and the noise shot right through me, turning my blood to fire. "Yeah, good idea."

We separated, and she turned, stretching out in the bed.

The shirt rode up on her thighs, revealing the pale skin there. She truly was gorgeous, and I would make sure she knew it. Tomorrow.

I pulled the blankets up around her, tucking them around her. "Goodnight, *teine*."

"Wait, you need rest too. We can share the bed," she said, reaching her hand out to grab my own.

I swallowed hard. I could do this. I could sleep next to this beauty and behave myself for the night. "All right, then, scoot over."

Deciding to keep my pants on, tight as they may be, I unlaced my boots and tugged them off. I walked over and extinguished the lamp on the table before sliding into the bed next to her. Almost immediately, she turned on her side and curled up next to me, slinging an arm over my stomach and resting her head on my chest. It felt nice. It felt right. But I had to keep my hopes from getting too high. I clenched my jaw, trying to ignore how warm she felt against me. Then, she twined her bare leg in between mine. Fuck.

Looking up at the ceiling, I huffed out a breath as I tried to keep from pulling her even closer. I had to behave. She wasn't aware of what she was doing right now.

"Caelum?" she whispered into the darkness.

I turned my head to look at her. "Yeah, *teine?*"

"Thank you for being worth saving," she whispered, and then her small hand was on my cheek and her soft lips were on mine.

All thoughts left my brain at that point. I tangled my hand in her hair and deepened the kiss, pulling her tight to my body. This was really happening, and my heart was pounding in my chest so hard I feared it might explode. After enjoying the feel of her against my lips, the taste of sea salt and citrus and of her, I pulled away, leaning my forehead against hers and panting more than I'd like to admit. I wanted to continue, to take this as far as she would let me, but I had to remember she was still drunk. We would have time for this later, if I had my way.

I pressed another gentle kiss to her lips before tucking her under my chin and wrapping my arms around her. "Get some rest, *mo teine.*"

"G'night, Captain," she whispered, snuggling down further into my chest and thankfully ignoring my small addition to her pet name that would have made all the difference in the world.

I pulled the blanket up around us both and sighed contentedly. This was going fast, and I knew the only reason she had kissed me was because of the ale, but I didn't regret it. I just hoped she wouldn't also regret it in the morning. I wanted to get to know her more, to protect her, and to help her experience the life she talked about wanting. But I couldn't help but think about the losses I had suffered.

They might not be directly because of her, but they came from her kind. I doubted my ability to be able to separate those things in my mind, and more importantly, I doubted the others would even want to try to separate them. Despite my turmoil, feeling her in my arms was good. If I turned off my mind, I could truly be happy for a moment.

Taking one last look down at Brigid, who was already breathing deeply into my chest, I smiled into the darkness. I only hoped I could keep her.

CHAPTER TWENTY

BRIGID

The morning came in like a blasting drum. My eyes burned, my head pounded, and my stomach churned, revolting against all that I had consumed the night before. Slowly, awareness came back to me, and I did a quick scan of my body. I was in a bed, once again pressed up to the warmth and hardness of Caelum's body. He didn't have a shirt on, and he had his arms wrapped around my waist as I lay across his chest.

My memories of the previous night came rushing back, and my cheeks burned at the embarrassment. I had kissed him. Cursing to myself, I ran through the blurry memories in my head, searching for anything else I had foolishly done. I had kissed him and basically threw myself at him, and he had rejected me. What had I done?

I must have moved slightly, because Caelum grunted, opening his eyes to look at me sleepily. When he saw I was awake, his eyes became alert and filled with laughter. "Good morning. How are you feeling?"

I groaned and dropped my head to his chest, hiding away from his knowing gaze. "What have I done?"

He chuckled before tucking a finger under my chin and pulling my face back up to look at him. "You had a fun night, that's all that matters. No harm done."

"I kissed you," I pointed out, trying to bury my face in his chest again to hide my embarrassment. I had kissed him, but he had kissed me back. Did that mean he actually did want me?

He dropped a kiss on my hair, suddenly more comfortable with me than we had been the previous day. Had the kiss truly changed that much about our relationship? Was it possible his attraction to me could overcome his hatred?

"That you did. Please feel free to do it again now that you're not plastered." The teasing smile on his face made me question whether he was serious or teasing me. And even more, I wasn't sure which one I wanted it to be.

I needed to change the subject before I did something foolish, like kiss him again. We couldn't do this. I pushed myself up to sitting, looking down at him. For a moment, I lost my words. He really was a sight to see, with his broad and muscled torso lightly dusted in dark hair. He was all power. As if sensing me staring, his stomach flexed. My mouth dried, and I'm certain it even dropped open a bit.

"Like what you see?" he teased.

Mentally shaking myself, I finished pushing myself up to put my feet on the floor and my back to him. "What are we doing today?"

He sat up behind me, movement shifting the bed slightly. "We'll have to meet the men and see what they're planning to do. My father always returns to Brinemoor. It's his base. But since he won't be back until tomorrow, we need to take the day to prepare. We lost our weapons in the shipwreck."

"Sounds like we have a busy day planned," I replied, getting out of bed and turning away from Caelum. I needed to get my head on straight. Every time he mentioned the shipwreck, it brought things back into focus. *Syrens* had caused that wreck, and I would always be a syren, forever associated with that.

Caelum rose too, moving to stand in front of me. He brushed a strand of hair away from my face before tugging on one of the laces of the shirt I was wearing. His face moved close to mine as he whispered, "I'll be needing this back, *teine.*"

My cheeks burned again, something they had been doing quite a bit since Caelum had come back into my life. Ignoring the voice in my head screaming that this was a bad idea, I turned my face closer to his until our cheeks were almost touching. I couldn't resist feeling the heat of his skin radiating against mine. "Aye, you likely do."

Locking gazes, we stood there for a heartbeat. The heat in the room was building at the same time the heat inside my own body grew. His eyes dipped down to my lips, and all the air left the room. His voice was rough as he looked down at me, his eyes darkening. "Brigid..."

"Kiss me," I whispered, tilting my face up toward him. Consequences be damned, I wanted to feel this man against me, and I wanted it now.

In an instant, one large hand threaded through my unbound hair to cup the back of my head, and his lips crashed down on mine. His other hand grabbed onto the swell of my hip and pulled me closer to him as our mouths moved together, his days-old stubble rubbing against my face roughly. My own hands reached up to grab at his chest, his shoulders, at anything, and he groaned into my mouth. His fingers explored and squeezed at my curves as he nipped at my lips and tugged at my hair. It was breathtaking, overwhelming, and like no kiss I had ever experienced before. He pulled back, as breathless as I was, and tilted his forehead down to rest against mine. Our breath intermingled as our chests heaved in unison.

"Now that's a kiss," he said hoarsely, rubbing a thumb over my swollen lips.

Somehow, I was able to find my voice. "Aye, that was definitely a kiss."

"Good morning to me." he smiled. He pulled back away from me and tugged on the laces of his shirt again playfully. "We really should meet up with the others, though."

He was right, of course. My brain was already going at high speed, and some space and food would do me well. I nodded before stepping back away from him and pulling the shirt over my head. "Aye, you're right. Here's your shirt."

Looking up to the ceiling, he let out a pained groan. "*Teine,* you cannot just do that."

My neck and chest flushed. Caelum's kisses had left my

mind swimming, and I had just pulled his shirt off to return it, not giving any mind to the fact that I was now standing naked before him. I probably should have moved to cover myself up, but my body was one of the few things I was not ashamed of. Raising an eyebrow, I held his shirt out higher, shaking it at him. "You said you needed your shirt back."

He looked back at me before grabbing my face with both hands and pressing a quick and rough kiss to my lips that left my entire body tingling and wanting more. Pulling back, he looked like he wanted to do a great deal more, but restrained himself. He took the shirt from my hands finally, but made no move to put it on. "You really have no idea the effect you have. Now, put your clothes on before we're really late to breakfast."

I did know the effect I had on him, but it was almost endearing to see him think me innocent and inexperienced. Caelum's reaction to my body burned through my blood, lighting my whole body ablaze. I knew from my childhood that I should have felt ashamed, but I didn't. Knowing the effect I had on this gorgeous man made me feel powerful in an entirely different way than being a syren felt powerful. And I was beginning to like it. Quirking up the corner of my mouth, I couldn't resist teasing him. "Maybe next time, then."

He laughed, reaching over to hand me my own shirt from last night and then pulling his own on. "Aye, next time."

We dressed in pleasant silence. I decided to forgo the tight corset I had worn last night, dressing only in the loose, white blouse and leather pants. Caelum and I both laced up our boots before facing each other. He smiled at me, reaching over to squeeze my fingers before leading me out of the room.

When we got down to the dining area, Duncan was the only one there. We sat down at the table with him, and he grinned knowingly at me. "How you feeling?"

I rolled my eyes, knowing his question was more teasing and less genuine. "I'm fine, big man. Thanks for your concern."

"How was the rest of your night, then?" he asked, looking at Caelum now. The smile had dropped from Duncan's face, and the two of them looked at each other, no doubt having a conversation with only their eyes in the way only longtime friends can. I wondered if Duncan could tell we had kissed. More than that, I wondered if he approved or not.

While I only slightly regretted kissing Caelum last night, I did not regret kissing him again this morning. But I was nervous about him telling anyone else. I was still coming to terms with my own feelings and questions related to my family and to Caelum. I didn't want to be figuring out those feelings under the scrutiny of others. And I didn't want Caelum to feel the judgment of his friends more harshly if—when—they found out my role in their wreck. I was under no illusions, it would be discovered. My only surprise was that Caelum had not immediately told them.

Finally, Caelum ended their secret conversation and shrugged a shoulder. "Entertaining. And yours? Was it as informative as we hoped?"

Duncan nodded, the smile back on his face. "Aye, it was. Let's wait for Cam and Mad to join us before I fill you in. They got most of the information."

As if they were waiting for their names to be said, the other men walked down the stairs, plopping down at the table with us. Cameron reached over and fingered a strand of my loose hair. "Want me to braid it again, B?"

I smiled at him, a genuine feeling of friendship building. It scared me, thinking about how quickly it would change when he discovered the truth, but I would cherish it for now. "Yes, please. After we eat."

"I meant to ask last night," Duncan said, leaning in, "but where'd you learn to do a girl's hair like that, Cam?"

He shrugged nonchalantly, picking at the splinters in the table in front of him. "Three younger sisters. When my ma died, someone had to tame their hair. And it sure as hell weren't my da."

"That's nice," I said, smiling at him, thinking how different my life may have been if I had had a brother like Cameron, like any of them. These were good men. It still sickened my stomach to think that myself and the others had almost been the cause of their ruin. I couldn't help but feel myself growing closer to them, and I shuddered to think of what their reactions would be when they eventually found out the truth about me. My heart broke at the thought of being shunned again. But I had endured far worse before, and I would continue to do so until my last breath.

"Okay, down to business," Caelum said, running his hand through his own unbound hair. "What did you learn about my father's plans?"

Duncan looked over at me from the corner of his eyes, not bothering to hide his suspicion. "Should we be talking about this here?"

Caelum met Duncan's eyes, and they had another unspoken

conversation for several moments. At the end of it, Duncan sighed and nodded, waving a hand loosely at Caelum. Caelum's shoulders dropped, the tension bleeding out of him slightly, and he turned to me. "If we tell you this, you're in this until the end, Brigid. If you don't think you want to help, it's time to tell me now."

I rolled my shoulders back, steeling my spine. Caelum was right before, I did owe him this. And I would do whatever it took to earn his forgiveness and the forgiveness of the syrens. One at a time. "I told you I would help, and I will. I won't tell a soul what I hear."

Caelum looked at me, an assessing gaze that I had not felt from him before. After a moment, he nodded, a strand of hair falling onto his forehead. "All right, then. My father has been stealing children."

My mouth fell open. Of all the things I had been expecting him to say, that was nowhere near anything I had dreamed. Only a monster would target children. My temper boiled under my skin, my hands clenching into fists at my side at the thought of these innocent children being harmed. "Children?"

"Keep your voice down," Maddock said softly, looking around the room to ensure no one had heard us.

"We don't know who my father has on his payroll. If they find out we're going after him, he'll move again," Caelum added.

Nodding, I took a deep breath to temper my anger and lowered my voice to a whisper. "Children? Really?"

Caelum nodded, his eyes sad. "Aye, children. That's why we're trying so hard to stop him."

My mind raced, churning through thoughts of what all Caelum had told me. The other syrens and I had wrecked a ship on a mission to save children. Perhaps we truly were the monsters men thought us to be. How many men had we killed before that had been on journeys like this? How many men had we doomed to death that did not deserve it? Sorcha's words about some men being innocent rushed back at me, and guilt flooded my mouth, sour on my tongue. I swallowed harshly, trying to erase the taste of death from my mouth.

Peering at me curiously, Caelum watched a moment before turning back to his men. "Go on, Cam."

Cameron sighed heavily, and I knew whatever he was about to say wouldn't be good. "Well, we're in the right place. We have reliable information that he's been holding the children somewhere in this town. Last night, we finally found out what he's doing with them. He's selling them."

"To whom?" Caelum gritted out, his forearms corded and tensed as he clenched and unclenched his hands into fists. His anger was palpable, rolling off his hunched shoulders in waves. It only served to feed my own anger that was building again beneath the surface of my skin. It was clear he had not known this part of his father's plans.

"Our sources didn't know that bit. They suspected it was a woman, but reports were too mixed to say one way or another."

"So, what are we going to do?" I asked, sick at the thought of these young children being sold, much like I had almost been. If I still had any reservations about helping Caelum, they had disappeared with Maddock's words. I would do everything in my power to save these children. After we saved them, which we would, I would make sure they were safe and cared for too. The syrens' contact in the south would be willing to take them in, I was sure.

"We're going to go get them," Caelum said angrily, standing abruptly and leaning with his fists on the table. "Now that we know what he's doing and where he is, we can't keep waiting around."

Maddock put a hand on his arm, pulling him back down. "They're not there."

Caelum returned to his seat with a heavy and irritated sigh. He waved a hand at his friend. "Explain."

"They're not in town right now, and our sources say they won't be back with new…children." Maddock swallowed hard before continuing. "They won't be back with new children for at least another day."

"So, we have to wait?" Caelum asked, his irritation and impatience nearly palpable. "We can't go find where he's holding them and wait?"

"Aye, Captain," Maddock confirmed with a grimace. "We'll have to wait."

Caelum ran a hand over his face before sighing again and leaning back in his chair, crossing his arms over his chest. "We didn't find out anything else except that he's selling them to someone who may or may not be a woman."

"We also found out for sure that he's only taking orphans. Mostly boys, but it seems any orphan will do," Cameron said slowly. "People here in town are reporting that it's only street children that are disappearing. Children with no one to miss them. Which is why it's taken so long to notice."

My brow furrowed. What could anyone possibly want with only orphaned children? I couldn't fathom a reason, but I also couldn't fathom harming children in the first place. Yet it was obvious Caelum's father had no such reservations, given what he had done to his own child. Maybe the others knew more about the motivations. "Why?"

Cameron looked at me, and the corner of his mouth twitched. "Lass, if we knew that, we'd have been running around celebrating that we finally found something out."

My cheeks flushed. Obviously. They had been searching for information for who knew how long, and I had just come into this mission. I had questions, sure, but I doubted they wanted to sit here and answer them for me right now.

"So, the plan," Duncan said, leaning forward. "We need a plan."

"Aye," Caelum said. "Do we know exactly where he's holding them?"

"A building on the outskirts of town was the most consistent information," Cameron said, crossing his arms over his chest. "But they won't be back for at least another day."

"Aye, I got that bit. But we can scope it out and know when they get back." Caelum rubbed his forehead. "Do we know where my father is coming from?"

"Up from Bhodheas. Along the coast, according to the townsfolk," Cameron explained.

"Not through the Straits, though?"

Cameron shook his head. "Old man said they avoid the Straits and stick to the east."

"We can have Alan and his men rotate a patrol around the

building. Your father won't recognize them like he would us or Duncan. When they bring in the children and return, we can go in and rescue the children," Maddock proposed. "Some of us can go in and get them and send them out to the others, who can get them far away quickly in case something goes ass over teakettle."

"Set it up," Caelum said before casting a glance at me. "And then we need to get prepared."

"We need new weapons," Cam said, crossing his arms. "All of ours went down with the ship."

"Do you know how to handle a sword, Brigid?" Duncan asked, looking over at me.

"I can learn," I shot back, not wanting to advertise that I had absolutely zero experience with weapons of any kind. I had grown up using farm equipment, and anything beyond a utility knife was foreign to me. But that didn't mean I wasn't still dangerous. I knew how to kill a man with my bare hands and with my talons.

"Maybe we'll start with a dagger," Maddock suggested, tilting his head to look at me.

CHAPTER TWENTY-ONE
CAELUM

"Will people notice if we just walk around here with swords and knives?" Brigid asked as we walked into the blacksmith's shop, her eyebrow raised once again.

I chuckled at the incredulous look on her face. "We're in a port, *teine*. No one will give us a second glance."

"There's a lot of pirates here, then?" She stopped walking, turning around fully to face me, curiosity clear on her face.

"Yes and no," I said, opening my arm wide to allow her to walk through the door first. The town *was* a haven for pirates and other illegal services, but it was also a legitimate port for merchant vessels. And it was getting harder and harder to tell the difference. "Let's get weapons first, then we can have a history lesson."

She looked like she wanted to ask more questions, but hesitated and nodded, moving to enter the shop fully.

The heat inside was overwhelming even though the shop was separated from the forge. Bells tinkled as the door swung shut behind Duncan, and Brigid moved to run her fingers over the blades displayed on the wooden counter.

"I'll be right there," a loud voice shouted from the forge. Moments later, a large man with a leather apron came out of the door to the forge, pulling off his heavy leather gloves and tucking them under his arm. When he saw me, his weathered face broke out into a wide grin. "Caelum! Welcome back, my boy. What can I do you for?"

"Looking for some blades, Galen. Broadswords, cutlasses, daggers, whatever you've got," I replied, raising my chin slightly as I returned the smile. I knew this smithy wouldn't question why we needed such weapons. He had long been the go-to smith for those in less-than-legal businesses. And even more, Galen had known me since I was a child, and I trusted he wouldn't tell my father I was here.

"Well, you've come to the right place," he said, beaming at me. His eyes fluttered over to Brigid before landing back on me with a mischievous grin. "Let's get you geared up."

"Don't skimp on me, Galen," I said, raising my eyebrow teasingly. I knew the older man would only give me the best, but I still had to poke at him a bit. Kept him on his toes.

He threw a glove at me, laughing. "Should send you in there to make your own bloody sword."

"You know how to smith?" Brigid asked, looking over at

me. The admiration in her eyes was alluring, and I felt myself preening under her attention.

"Aye, I do. Galen here taught me whenever I wasn't with my father," I explained with a smile. Out of the memories of my childhood here in Brinemoor, my time with Galen was a reprieve from the constant violence of my father. It hadn't been an easy reprieve by any means, but it had given me a reason to be away from my father and a chance to heal from whatever injuries he had inflicted upon me. "Speaking of, have you heard anything about him lately?"

Galen shook his head. "Naw, son. Can't say I have. He don't come in here much anymore. Prefers to get his steel from Bhodheas now, I hear."

"He still staying in the old house when he is here?" I asked. Galen was an unlikely source of reliable information, as the old man rarely left his forge, but I knew I could trust whatever information he did have.

"Suppose so," he said with a shrug. "Haven't heard of him staying anywhere else."

I nodded, content with the information. At least I had trusted outside verification that my father was at his old home in Brinemoor. Though I hadn't been there in years, I knew where it was and the basic layout. It would give us an advantage, albeit a small one, in our raid of the house. "Thanks, Galen."

Galen studied me for a moment. "You're going after him, aren't you?"

I gritted my teeth, keeping silent. I might trust Galen, but the more people who figured out I was finally able to take on my father, the greater the likelihood my father himself would discover our plans. I had been waiting years to be in a position to stop him. I wasn't going to give it up now just to catch up with Galen. "The blades, Galen."

He raised an eyebrow at my tone, but shrugged. "All right, your business, boy. Let me see what we've got ready for you. How many of what do you need?"

"Just bring out whatever you've got made."

He nodded, turning to head to the storeroom in the back. I let out a harsh sigh, turning to Duncan. "Maybe you should have done this on your own. He knows me too well."

"He won't tell Kellan," Duncan said confidently. "He dislikes the bastard as much as you do."

"He saved you as a child," Brigid commented quietly. She was far too observant for her own good.

"Aye, he did," I finally replied. I didn't want to talk more about my childhood. Not while I was trying to mentally prepare myself for the possibility of fighting my father directly. I needed to be ready, and remembering the balm Galen had been as a child would not help me channel my anger.

Thankfully, Galen returned from the back, a bundle of swords in his arms. He spread them out on the wooden display counter with a clatter. "All right, Caelum. Here's what I've got made. Let me know what you want and I'll get them all sharpened and polished for you."

I glanced down briefly at the weapons along the counter. Given that my father's men had an arsenal of weapons at their disposal, anything we could get to rebuild our own arsenal would be needed. "We'll take it all."

"All of it?" Galen asked with an eyebrow raised. He paused

for a moment and then sighed, shaking his head. "All right, I'll go get it ready."

"Oh, and we'll need some daggers for Brigid here," I said, jerking my head at her. She had been quiet but bold in her stance, watching Galen's movements with equal parts curiosity and suspicion.

Galen nodded, reaching under the counter to pull out a box. He set it on the counter and motioned toward the display of daggers already set up. "This is all I've got. While I go sharpen these swords, you see which ones fit you best, girly."

He left to the back, and I turned to face Brigid, leaning my forearm against the counter. "All right, then. Let's get you a knife."

Quickly, it was clear that Brigid was a natural with a dagger. The smile on her face as she tested the weight and grip of each one was almost dreamy. I should have expected it, but even then, it still brought a smile to my face.

After going through the box of knives Galen had brought, two daggers stood out as favorites. The way she held them, with her fingers fitting snugly around the handle and hefting it in her palm, they were obviously the ones for her. The sparkle in her eyes was amusing, and even Duncan let out a chuckle watching her.

"So, you like daggers, huh?" Duncan said, leaning onto the counter as he watched her twirl one of the daggers in her fingers.

Brigid seemed to come back to herself and realize we were both watching her. Her cheeks flushed pink, and she set the dagger down roughly on the counter, clearing her throat. "I suppose I do."

"Good. I would hate to have you unable to defend yourself," Duncan said with a smile. "Shame we don't have time to teach you to use a sword."

She smirked. "I can defend myself without a blade, but I appreciate your concern."

"Swordplay will come later," I said with a nod. Brigid may be feeling fiery with her new blades, but we didn't have time to afford Duncan's questions. A woman being able to defend herself wasn't unheard of, especially here, but Duncan was too curious for his own good.

Thankfully, Galen came back out of the forge with the bundle of a dozen swords. He spread them carefully out on the counter. "Sharp as can be, Caelum. Now, do we need sheaths as well?"

"We need it all, Galen," I replied. My eyes flicked to Brigid before returning to the older man. "We lost all our weapons and supplies."

"I'll get you fitted up," Galen said with a grin. He nodded his head at Brigid. "You like those two, girly?"

She nodded, pushing them across the counter to him. "I do."

"You're gonna let Caelum there teach you how to use it?" he asked, raising an eyebrow.

Returning the gesture, she smirked at him. "If he behaves."

Now, it was my turn to raise an eyebrow. Brigid normally wasn't this forward with strangers, but I liked it. The fire I had seen was coming more to the surface. But she was wrong. I would teach her how to use the dagger no matter what. "Sure thing, *teine*. Whatever you say."

CHAPTER TWENTY-TWO
BRIGID

Weapons gathered, we met back up with Cameron and Maddock at the inn. The blacksmith had been intriguing to me, and Caelum had been different around him, more childlike.

But beyond that, the feel of the daggers in my hands felt… right. For years, I had relied on my talons, my strength beneath the waves, and my syren powers to defend myself. The idea of using an external blade felt strange at first, but feeling the weight of the handle was natural. Now I just needed to learn how to wield it effectively.

"Get everything we need?" Cameron asked, walking up to meet us and taking the canvas bag of swords from Caelum.

"Aye. Swords with scabbards, some daggers for Brigid, and

all have been sharpened." Caelum tilted his head toward the innkeeper, who was looking over at us with narrowed eyes. "Best take those up to your room there, Cam."

Cam nodded before turning and heading up the stairs.

Maddock crossed his arms over his chest. "We need to do some recon, don't we?"

"I'm familiar with the house, but we need to see what my father is doing in terms of patrols and security," Caelum said, shrugging. He looked at me, and I could almost see the thoughts churning in his head. "We should split up. Someone needs to teach Brigid how to handle those new daggers of hers. And the rest of us can go observe the house for a bit and see if my father has security already set up at the house."

"Who's going to teach me?" I asked, raising my eyebrow. While I was comfortable enough around the others, I felt much more relaxed with Caelum and would greatly prefer him to teach me than the others. Not that I would ever admit that out loud.

"Caelum is the real knife hand," Maddock replied, smirking slightly. "But I'm a good second."

Cameron walked back down the stairs, joining us by the windows once again. "So, what's the plan?"

"Cae and I are going to teach Brigid how to use a knife," Maddock explained. He clapped Cameron on the shoulder. "And you and Duncan are going to go scope out the house. Maybe take Alan with you."

"We need to go over plans again tonight," Caelum added. "With everyone present, including Alan's men. I want everyone to understand what's going to happen and what needs to happen if something goes wrong."

"Aye, aye, Captain," Cameron said with a lazy salute that made me smile. "We'll have everyone back here at sunset. We'll meet in your room; it should be big enough."

My smile only grew wider when Caelum waved off Cameron's honorific, giving him a rude hand gesture in the process. These men were truly a family, and it made me both warm with joy and cold with envy. I had never experienced a family like that, not with the syrens and certainly not with my father.

Caelum had his own grin on his face as he jerked his head at me. "Let's go, *teine*. Got a lot to teach you."

"Going to your room, Cae?" Maddock asked, also smiling at Cam and Duncan as they laughed and walked out of the inn.

"Probably smart," Caelum agreed with a shrug. "We'll be in close quarters, most likely."

We walked up to Caelum's room, and Cam shut the door behind him. Caelum nodded to Maddock, and they began moving all of the furniture against the walls to clear the middle of the floor.

"Have you ever fought before, *teine?*" Caelum asked, walking back to stand in front of me.

"Not quite like this," I replied, raising my eyebrow.

"Then let's see what you can do and go from there," he said, grinning. He reached over and grabbed the two daggers, handing one to me and keeping the other for himself. Opening his arms, he motioned for me to come to him. "Try to stab me."

"I will not," I said, aghast. I may not know how to use a dagger, but if I got near him, I wouldn't want to hurt him, even accidentally.

Maddock laughed, a bellowing sound. "Brigid, don't worry. I doubt you'll get anywhere near him."

"Come on, *teine*," he said, grinning even wider now. "Try to stab me."

With a sigh, I tightened my grip on the handle and charged at him, slashing the dagger toward his midsection. He reached down with his arm and blocked me easily, sweeping my legs out from under me in the same movement and pressing his own knife to my throat.

If he grinned any wider, his face would split. Quickly, he stood and held a hand out to me, pulling me to my feet. "Don't advertise your moves. Again."

Well, this was going to take longer than I'd thought. With a sigh, I picked up my dagger and moved toward him once more.

Sore, irritated, and slightly bloody, a knock on the door halted our training sessions, finally. It was time to meet with everyone and go over the final plans for tomorrow. I let out a sigh of relief, letting my muscles relax and tucking the dagger into the sheath on my hip.

As the others filed in, they claimed seats where they could. Taking a seat between Duncan and Cameron at the small table and chairs by the door, I smiled in what I hoped was a reassuring way and not an I-almost-accidentally-stabbed-your-captain-earlier way.

I settled down into the hard wooden chair with a sigh, shifting around in a feeble attempt to get comfortable as my sore muscles protested.

"Training go well?" Cameron asked with a sardonic smile.

I narrowed my eyes at him. "I have a feeling you know exactly how it went."

He shrugged, mirth sparkling in his eyes. "Might have an idea."

Caelum came over to us, sitting down across the table from me and pushing a plate of food he had conjured from somewhere in front of me. "Eat. You need the energy."

I wanted to raise my hand in a mock salute, but my arms were too sore to follow through. I did narrow my eyes at him, though, which only made him grin. "Aye, aye."

"Don't you start that too." He rolled his eyes before turning to address the rest of the room. "All right, let's get started, everyone."

The low chatter of the room stopped, and we all turned our attention to Caelum. Seeing him in his element, being the captain, was certainly attractive. It made heat build in my stomach. His jaw, now dusted in a thicker coating of dark hair, was tense as he spoke.

"Cameron, Duncan, what did you all discover about the house today?"

"Looked like they set up guards. Only one at each door, but we saw about five others moving around inside," Cameron started, leaning forward to rest his elbows on his knees, lacing his fingers together. "We could likely get inside easily, but there's no way to tell where the guards are stationed on the inside."

"Do you think they'll bring more guards when Kellan returns with the children?" Caelum asked, his eyebrows furrowing together.

Cameron shrugged. "Unlikely. Unfortunately, a guard at each door seems plenty. It's a fairly quiet street."

"How are we going to get inside, then?" Alan asked from his place sitting cross-legged on the floor.

"I had a thought on that," Duncan said slowly, looking at Caelum. "But you won't like it."

Caelum raised an eyebrow at his friend. "Tell me anyway."

"We send Brigid in as a maid delivering groceries. We saw several delivery people going in and out of the house, so it should be easy enough to get her to the house without attracting notice."

"No," came Caelum's immediate response. He barely spared a glance at me as he continued. "I'm not putting her at risk for this."

My blood burned. "I can help, Caelum. I'm not a child."

His eyes snapped to mine, and I saw the fire burning there for the first time. "Not happening."

I took a deep breath through my nose to keep from snapping at him and saying something I would regret. I turned to Duncan instead, moving my whole body to show Caelum my back. "Why does it have to be me?"

A small smirk crossed Duncan's lips before he schooled his features. "Well, it could be one of Alan's men, since Kellan doesn't know what they look like. But a woman would be much more likely to be able to approach the house without raising suspicion. And I doubt very much we would want to risk asking a local for help."

I nodded at him, satisfied with his answer. I *would* be doing this whether Caelum approved or not. Shifting my body around to face Caelum again, I raised an eyebrow. "Do you disagree with that assessment?"

He leaned back in his chair, crossing his arms over his chest. "And how will you get the guard to leave his post to let us into the house? You won't be able to get all those children out by yourself. We'll need to join you somehow."

I opened my mouth to speak but caught myself before I could say what I wanted to. Admitting that I had killed many men before would likely raise questions I couldn't answer right now. "You did just teach me how to use a dagger. I can handle it."

"We're not killing anyone," he said, his jaw flexing. "I am not my father. We will not kill anyone unless absolutely necessary and in self-defense."

"Fine, no killing." I shrugged easily. I could still easily incapacitate a man. Granted, I wouldn't have my syren strength or the advantage I had in the water, but I still knew how to handle myself.

Caelum just looked at me for a long moment, our eyes locked. I could tell he didn't want me to do this, but I just stared back at him, trying to convey that I *could* do this. Maybe saving these children could redeem me for the lives of potentially innocent men that I had taken. And more, I wanted to help Caelum stop his father. I saw how much it meant to him, and something deep in my soul that I didn't want to acknowledge yet made me want to do anything to see a smile on his face.

I was scared of what that might mean for my plans afterwards, but that was a problem for the future. For now, I needed to focus on convincing him to let me help him.

"Cae, it's a good plan," Maddock added quietly.

Caelum's eyes reluctantly left mine to look at Maddock. "I'll not put anyone else in danger for this, especially not her. I can easily sneak up and knock the guard out."

"They'd see you coming from a mile away," Duncan said immediately. "You really think your da hasn't told them to be on the lookout for you by now? He's got to know we've been asking around about him."

With a heavy sigh, Caelum slouched back into his chair, rubbing between his eyebrows. After a moment, he straightened up, his face resolved. "Fine, she can do it."

I nodded at him, smiling slightly. "Thank you. I'll be fine. I'll incapacitate the guards and make sure the hall is clear before letting you all in."

"And once we're in," Caelum continued, going into full captain mode now, "we'll *incapacitate* any other guards we run into. Cameron, you, Alan, and three of Alan's men need to wait outside the house. When we find the children, we'll send them out to you. You don't wait for us. You get them out of there immediately."

Cameron nodded. "Aye, where should we take them?"

"I have an arrangement with the orphanage. The matron there agreed to house them once we're able to rescue them. Take them there and tell her I sent you," Caelum explained. It made me wonder just how long they had been planning this.

"What if things go south?" Maddock asked, raising an eyebrow. "We need a backup plan."

"Aye," Caelum said, leaning forward. "If we don't come out in fifteen minutes, Cameron, you are to leave and go back to the ship."

"No, absolutely not," Cam started.

I leaned forward, intent on arguing as well. Caelum would not be dying. No one would, if I could help it. Even out of the water, I was able to transform my talons and teeth, and despite the pain, I would be more than willing to use them, even if it meant revealing myself. The only men who would die tomorrow would be Kellan's.

Caelum held a hand up to stop us both. "Let me finish. If we can't get out, then someone needs to keep this mission going and still be alive enough to try again."

"I don't like it," Cam grumbled, crossing his arms over his chest.

"Aye, and I don't like the idea of Brigid being the first one to approach the house," Caelum said. "But here we are. I'm the captain, this is the plan. Is everyone on board?"

"Aye," came the responses from everyone in the room. Cameron's was more reluctant, but eventually joined the chorus.

"Good, then take your weapons and go get some rest. We start at dawn," Caelum said, standing up.

CHAPTER TWENTY-THREE
CAELUM

Watching the house my father was staying at was a test of patience. I wanted nothing more than to barge through the doors and confront him. But I knew I couldn't, not without risking the children he held. I had no doubt that if my father thought he was in danger, he would use the children as shields. And I wouldn't risk that.

We would have to do it according to the plan. The plan I was very much not on board with and very much still angry about. I knew that Brigid could handle herself, but the idea of sending her inside that house with only a dagger she had just recently learned to use, was disconcerting. The others were on board, electing to trust Brigid's words when she said she could handle it, so I supposed I would have to as well.

Brigid, disguised as a maid delivering groceries from the local market, would enter the house's side door. Once the guards were incapacitated, she would let us in. From there, we would find where the children were being held. Brigid and Maddock would lead them out, while the rest of us covered the retreat and faced off against any guards inside the house.

I took a deep breath as I sat beside Duncan and Cameron, watching the house from a safe distance away. I blew the breath out through my nose as Brigid rounded the corner of the alley, walking toward the side door with confidence, as if she belonged there. Turning the handle, she looked to where she knew we were hiding in the nearby bushes and smiled slightly before pushing the door open and entering the house.

That was our cue.

Standing, we swiftly but cautiously walked toward the side of the house, trying not to draw attention to ourselves from anyone passing by. While I doubted anyone passing would notice us, I couldn't risk someone stopping to ask us what we were doing, potentially drawing the guards' attention to us. We had to be patient now, without getting caught out in the open. All we needed now was for Brigid to open the door again and let us in. We stood along the side of the house, waiting.

In a flash, the door swung open, and a red braid flung out over a shoulder. Brigid. She smiled. "It's clear. Come on in."

We rushed in through the door, turning right down a long, stone hallway. Continuing through the large estate house I had grown up despising, we opened every door, checking inside before moving on. Thankfully, the house was only one story tall, but it was large and sprawling. We would have a lot of rooms to check. As we continued down the hall, I became eerily aware of how empty the house was. We had not run into a single soul yet, and in a house this big, I knew there had to be workers and servants. My gut churned with unease, but we continued our search.

At the end of the next hallway, there was a large metal door, with several unlocked padlocks on the outside, ready to be locked. This had to be it. I motioned to the others, and we continued toward the room. Brigid was beside me, her dagger now drawn, with Duncan and Cameron next, then Maddock, Finn, Aiden, and Blaine, with some of Alan's men bringing up the rear. We entered the room, and I stopped dead in my tracks. My heart sank into my stomach, and my legs felt like steel weights. No. It couldn't be.

Before me, leaning against the wall all too casually, was my father. And filling the rest of the room were about six of his men. It had been a trap, and we had walked right into it.

"We should run," Maddock whispered under his breath, keeping his eyes locked on my father straight ahead.

I looked over my shoulder to see more guards coming down the hallway behind us, swords drawn and boxing us in. I cursed lightly; their numbers were greater than we had been expecting. "Not an option."

Brigid stood behind me, her own tension radiating out from her body. I doubted she recognized my father, but I was certain she would know it was him from my reaction alone. My biggest fear, that someone else would get hurt by my father's hands, was staring me in the face. I wanted to rage, to run at him with my sword swinging and cut him down. But his men outnumbered us twelve to seven, and I wouldn't risk the lives of those with me.

"Ah, boy," my father boomed, grinning at us as he pushed off the wall and drew himself up to his full height. "Glad you could join us."

I gritted my teeth. "Can't say I was expecting to run into you here, sir."

My hatred couldn't overcome the years of respect my father had drilled into me through violence and pain, and so I still called him by the honorific he had insisted upon. I stared at him, waiting to see what he had planned, because I knew he had something planned.

Looking over at the man in front of me, I was disgusted. I got my looks from my father, almost certainly, and I wished I hadn't. We looked like mirror images, just a few years apart. He, too, wore his hair longer, but he left it down, hanging over his shoulders and down his back. Our faces were similar, with sharp angles and bright green eyes.

"I imagine not," he finally replied, studying us. His eyes flicked over to Brigid, interest sparking. "Interesting company you're keeping, my son."

I shrugged, not wanting to draw any more attention to her. If my father knew what she was, or even just how important she was becoming to me, there was no telling what he would do. "I accept help wherever it comes from."

My father didn't reply, simply fixed his gaze on me. After what felt like forever, he turned and nodded to one of the men on his right. The men in the room moved swiftly, circling behind us and boxing us in. Alan and some of the others had been waiting outside to help get the children to safety, so we were very outnumbered. One of the men moved forward, and before I could blink, he had a hold of Brigid's arms and had dragged her over to my father. She struggled, trying to get out of his grip, but another man moved to help, holding her so she could get no leverage to escape. The one on the left pinched her wrist, causing her fingers to open and drop her dagger to the floor. The man kicked it away.

I lunged forward, my hand tightening on the sword in my hand, but Duncan grabbed my wrist, squeezing hard. Fighting my instincts to reach out and protect Brigid, I stayed. If my father knew how important she was to me, he would find a way to kill her. Maddock tensed beside me as well, no doubt also ready to move to save Brigid. He looked at me and shook his head minutely, telling me to wait.

"Why are you here, Caelum?" my father asked, his gaze roving over Brigid even as he spoke to me. The curiosity in his gaze as he stared at her made my stomach churn and my head pound with anger. If he touched her, I doubted I could guarantee I would not kill him, despite my words the previous night.

"To rescue the children you've stolen," I said bluntly. There was no doubt in my mind that he knew exactly why we were here, but if he wanted to play this game, we would.

"And if I told you there were no children here?" he asked, walking in a circle around Brigid, still studying her intently, looking her over from head to toe.

"Then we'll just kill you and find where you've taken them," I said with a shrug. Although the thought of killing my father made me sick, I would be able to make the tough decision if needed. It was putting my nerves on edge how closely he was looking at Brigid, and I feared he may already know her secret somehow.

My father paused in his pacing, looking at me before throwing his head back in a loud laugh. "Oh, my boy, you do amuse me."

"I'm glad you find it funny." I found nothing about this situation funny.

"You could never kill me. You don't have the stones." His face turned serious, and he grabbed Brigid, pulling her to him so her back was pressed against his front. He had her chin in a grip so hard that I could see where his fingers dug into her skin. She looked irritated, and I could see her fingers flexing at her side. Quietly, I willed her to keep her talons to herself, lest he discover what she was. Fire surged in my veins, but I took a deep breath through my nose to calm it. How dare he touch her? My father smiled. "Son, there's only one way you and your men are going to live to see another day."

I swallowed hard, fearing the answer to my next question. "Aye? And how's that?"

He squeezed Brigid's face tighter. I saw her wince slightly as she tried to pull away, but her eyes were full of bright fire and anger. "You leave the syren with me."

My stomach dropped, and the room went silent. He knew. Shit.

Chapter Twenty-Four

BRIGID

"The *what?*" Duncan's voice was outraged as his eyes flashed to mine, glaring. He shifted his sword in his hand, schooling his features and turning his focus back to the men surrounding us. They hadn't restrained any of our men yet, but they still could easily overpower us if they decided to.

Kellan laughed loudly. The sound was grating in my ear, but it distracted from the vice-like grip he had on my face. No doubt, I would have bruises in the shapes of his fingers. "Oh, ho, this is perfect. Your men didn't even know the creature you had in your midst? Keeping secrets from your crew, son?"

Caelum didn't answer right away, his eyes locking with mine. I saw the panic there, the anger. I knew without a doubt that this would cause a rift between Caelum and Duncan, and guilt swirled knowing it would be because of me. Caelum swallowed, moving his gaze to his father. "She's not going anywhere with you."

His father clucked his tongue. "It wasn't really an option. She's coming with me, regardless. I have someone who's very eager to…*meet* her."

Bile rose in my throat. Someone wanted me? What did that mean? I swallowed back the sour taste in my mouth, not wanting to think about the reality I could soon face. From the way Caelum spoke of his father, there was no one Kellan could give me to that would end pleasantly for me.

Rolling my shoulders back as much as I could in Kellan's grip, I made a decision. I would not go with Kellan—not alive, at least.

"You're not taking her fucking anywhere," Caelum growled, his voice low and more angry than I'd ever heard.

"And you think you can stop me?" Kellan's voice was amused as he raised his voice to address the others with us. "You think you and your little friends can stop *me?*"

Maddock's eyes met mine, and I saw the betrayal there. It hurt more than any bruising grip from Kellan ever could. He smiled sadly at me before drawing his sword from the scabbard at his side. "Aye, we do."

"Then you're as delusional as my son," Kellan sneered. He gripped my chin tighter, bending down to put his cheek against mine. "The little syren is…coming…with…me."

"I am not property that you can just take," I gritted out around his tight grip, struggling to pull my face from his grasp.

"And neither are those children."

"Ah, she speaks!" his father crooned. He let go of my chin, only to grab my upper arm in his tight grip and spin me around to face him. He lowered his face closer to mine, sneering. "And you *are* property. My property."

I glared at him, my fingers itching to unleash my talons and drag them across his throat. Rearing back slightly, I spat at his face, relishing his grimace as my saliva slid down his cheek. "I will never be the property of men, especially not men like you."

He laughed, shaking his head as he wiped his cheek on his sleeve. "Child, there are no men like me."

"There's always men like you. And I've killed many before. You'll be no different," I snapped, vowing that I would kill this man if it was the last thing I did. I might have to fight Caelum for the privilege, but it would be worth it. Men like this, who believed they were superior to everyone else in the world, were a danger to everyone. And they were everything that syrens were *supposed* to fight against. But this time, I would fight against it. And I would win.

"Sure, darling," he said dismissively. He still held onto me but shifted his focus to Caelum, ignoring me as I continued to struggle. For a man so comparative to size, his grip was strong and unyielding. "Now, run along before you get hurt, son."

"Like you ever cared about hurting me," Caelum snarled, taking a step toward us.

The men on either side of Kellan, one an absolute giant, met Caelum's steps, moving in front of Kellan and me with warning hands raising their own swords up. Wordlessly, I tried to get Caelum to stand down with my eyes. If I could just get free from Kellan's grip, I could do at least *some* damage to him.

"You're right." His father sighed dramatically. "Then I guess we shall have to see who the better man is."

Without another word, his father's men jumped into action, barreling toward Caelum and the others. Metal clanged and flashed as swords met, and a cacophony of grunts and metal meeting metal filled the room. I pulled away from Kellan again, managing to get one of my arms free enough to push against his chest. Beginning the transformation, I willed my talons to extend; flesh began tearing, and blood pooled down my hands as they protruded from my nailbeds.

"Now, now, none of that," he said, looking down at my hands and pulling my arms back down to my sides.

As the others fought, my eyes darted among our men, tracking their movements. Maddock was fighting two men, his sword a blur as he moved back and forth between each of them. Caelum was engaged with another two men, as was Duncan. Alan's men were fighting their own combatants. So far, the fights seemed even, but I feared the numbers game would overpower them soon.

Watching the scene in front of me unfold, worry and nausea swirled in my stomach. His father was going to make me do goddess knows what. Flashbacks to my father telling me he was marrying me off flooded through my mind. I would never be the property of men again. And if I died trying to get away, then that was fine. My life was my own now, and I wouldn't give it to anyone else. I took a deep breath in through my nose, reminding myself that I didn't need to depend on

Caelum to keep me safe. I was a syren, after all.

And now that Kellan had let my secret out, it was time to show what I could do.

Pulling my body as hard as I could to yank us to a stop, I tensed the muscles of my neck and flung my head forward toward Kellan's face, grinning at the sickening crunch that resulted. His hand loosened around my arm, and I whirled, yanking my arm the rest of the way out of his grip. I took a step back before raising my leg and kicking at his knee, raking my talons across his face at the same time. Blood spurted out, warm and sticky as it covered my nails and ran down my fingers.

Kellan dropped to one knee, groaning in pain as his hand clapped to his bleeding face. I reared back, readying a punch, when strong arms wrapped around my middle, pinning my arms to my sides and pulling me off my feet. The other man held me there, roughly squeezing me as Kellan rose to his feet, grimacing. He gripped my chin in his hands again, smearing his blood across my face.

"I like that spirit, lass. I cannot wait to break it," he said with a wicked grin. He released my face and looked up at the larger man holding me. "Take her to the ship."

I struggled, but the man was so much larger than me, larger than even Duncan, and I knew I stood no chance. But still, I kicked at his legs and clawed at his arms, attempting to get out of his hold. His flesh shredded under my talons, but he paid no mind. Out of the corner of my eye, I could see Caelum still fighting off other men. Maddock had downed one of his and was now assisting Caelum. Back-to-back, they moved elegantly as they fended off three of Kellan's men with swordsmanship that would have been mesmerizing to watch under any other circumstance.

If they took me, there was no telling what my fate would be. The man lifted me effortlessly, walking behind Caelum's father as he led us to a door at the back of the room I had not seen before.

"Caelum!" a man's voice roared. It was Duncan, I realized after a moment. "They're taking her."

Twisting my neck, I strained to see where Caelum and Duncan were now. I managed to get a brief glimpse over my captor's broad shoulder, seeing both Caelum and Duncan trying to make their way toward me, cutting down anyone in their way. I knew that Caelum didn't want to kill anyone, and I could see he was aiming for non-deadly attacks. Maddock and Finn, one of Alan's men, were still fighting the others.

My captor attempted to walk faster, but I began flailing more strongly than ever. Caelum was right there; I just had to hold out long enough for him to reach me. I had to get away. Whatever happened, I couldn't let this man take me.

"Stop that," the giant brute muttered, tightening his hold on me so much that my fingers began to tingle. "Captain, they're gaining. What do we do?"

"Stop them," Kellan gritted out next to us, holding his hand to his face, trying to staunch the blood. "Give me the girl. You keep them at bay until we're out."

I was roughly set back on my feet, only to be grabbed again by Kellan's bloody hand. The bastard would surely leave even more bruises across my arms, smearing blood where he touched. He pulled me harshly, yanking me off balance, but

I continued fighting and struggling against him. I was more evenly matched in strength with him, at least, than I had been with the giant. He cursed under his breath, pulling me even more roughly to him to bend his face toward mine. "This will only end badly for you, girl. Stop struggling."

"Never," I breathed, continuing to pull away from him. I managed to get out of his grip, and I turned to move back into the room just in time to see the giant raise his sword and swing it down toward Caelum. My heart stopped, and I froze. Blood rushed in my ears and my vision tunneled into only seeing that glinting steel arcing down toward the man who was worming his way beneath my skin.

"Captain!" I heard Maddock roar, and I watched Maddock move in what felt like slow motion.

Maddock flung himself in front of the sword just in time. Instead of ripping through Caelum's neck as his father's man intended, it slashed across Maddock's chest, ripping his shirt and his skin open. Blood began to weep from the cut almost instantly, and Maddock swayed for a moment, looking down at his chest before falling to the ground with a loud thump.

Chapter Twenty-Five

BRIGID

The sound of his body hitting the ground echoed in my ears, and I stood motionless, watching the blood pool on his chest. My ears rang. I could hear nothing of the room around me as I stared at Maddock on the dingy floor.

My shock was all the opening Kellan needed, however, and he took advantage of it and yanked hard. He pulled me off balance and, despite my stumbling, we were moving toward the exit once again. I was forced to tear my gaze from Maddock and turn forward, lest I fall flat on my face.

There was another loud thump behind me, no doubt another body hitting the floor, but I could not turn around to see who it was. I couldn't bear to see who it was. The sight of Mad falling to the floor, his shirt stained crimson, would be burned into my mind forever. I had killed men before, but never like this. And never men that I had *known*. Tears stung my throat and clouded my vision, but I shoved it down, trying to keep from falling as Kellan dragged me down the hall.

Kellan had me by the upper arm, his arm extending backward as he dragged me along. Suddenly, a metallic flash filled my eyes, and a sword was coming down. It connected with the hand holding my arm, severing it at the wrist. I turned my head and saw Caelum, chest heaving and eyes red, holding a bloodied sword. My eyes found their way to the floor, where a severed hand was lying in a quickly forming pool of blood.

Caelum had cut off his father's hand. The hand that had been holding me captive.

Hands found their way to my shoulders again. For a moment, I flinched, ready to fight, but these were familiar hands accompanied by a familiar, if less-than-friendly, voice. "Come on, *syren*, we've got to go."

Duncan. And as grateful as I was to hear his voice, I knew I was not out of the woods with the whole syren thing.

Caelum moved in between me and his father, who was clutching his now handless arm and wailing in pain. Duncan turned me completely around, pushing me gently toward the door. They had dispatched Kellan's men that hadn't rushed to his side, and only we remained. Finn had picked up Maddock, and Duncan moved to help him carry him out as another of Alan's men guided me out of the room. I was numb, unable to form any thoughts or do anything other than let them lead me.

"Is he alive?" I heard Duncan ask behind me, his voice hoarse.

"Aye, for now," came Finn's quiet response. "We need to get him help. Fast."

"Caelum," I managed to croak out after we had taken a few steps, my mind finally catching up with the reality in front of me. I looked around wildly, not seeing him next to us. "We have to help Caelum."

Duncan jerked his head around to look at me, his eyes hard. "He's coming, syren. He's right behind us. But we need to move."

In my haze, the others had led me outside. The sun shone down on my face, but it felt wrong. My face felt cool in some places and warm in others. I raised a hand to my cheek, pulling it away. My fingers were smeared red, and all I could do was stare at the blood on my hand. It meant I had blood on my face, but I knew it was not mine. My heart pounded in my chest, and panic crawled up my throat. I needed to get if off. Get it off. *Get it off.*

I took a deep breath through my mouth, trying to avoid the metallic smell of blood surrounding me. There were more important things to focus on right now, like Maddock bleeding out.

I needed to pull myself together. Now was not the time for my anxiety to resurface. I had seen death before, and I needed to get over it. Shaking my head to clear it, I pulled myself out of Cameron's grasp, holding myself upright and steady. My jaw clenched, and I let it, relishing the feel of my muscles tightening and my teeth grinding together. It gave me something to focus on.

Cameron, Alan, and the rest of his men rushed toward

us from an alley around the corner. They stopped short when they saw the scene that awaited them: Maddock's body slung between Finn and Duncan, and the others standing next to a blood-covered woman. Someone brushed up behind me. Caelum.

I turned then, seeking out his face. His eyes were dark and pinched, and his shirt was covered in fine sprays of blood as well. I reached down to grip his fingers, relishing the connection for a moment. "Are you hurt?"

He shook his head, his eyes glassy and far away, before turning to the others, his eyes focusing on Maddock. "We need to get him help. Now."

"There was an apothecary shop down the alley," I croaked out. I cleared my throat. "They should have medical supplies."

Caelum nodded, turning to search the alley. "Move. Now."

In a wordless rush, Maddock was gathered up and we moved as one down the alley. Taking the lead, I burst through the apothecary shop doors, causing the young woman at the counter to jump. "We need help."

Her eyes widened as the rest of them came in through the door behind me. She motioned toward a cushioned couch sitting against the wall. "Yes, lay him there. There's bandages under the counter."

"Alan, Finn, watch the doors," Caelum barked out, pointing as he moved around her, going directly to the counter. The young woman, a petite blonde with her hair pulled back in braids, rushed over to Maddock, who had been set down on the couch.

Without hesitation, she ripped open his shirt, pulling it

away from his wound. I winced as the fabric tore away from the dried blood on his stomach.

"Bandages," the woman called out, holding her hand out. Caelum pressed them into her hand in an instant, and she moved to push them onto Maddock's chest, causing him to emit a low groan. "I need water. There's a bucket in the back room. Get it and some cloths."

I stepped back to go fetch it, but Duncan held his hand up, stopping me. His hand was covered in blood. "No, you've done enough, *syren*."

"Now is not the time for this," Caelum snapped, handing the woman more bandages.

Duncan glared at me before moving out of the way to let me fetch the bucket and bring it back. I handed it to the young woman and stepped back, letting her and Caelum work.

Cameron stepped up between Duncan and I and lowered his voice as he raised an eyebrow. "Syren?"

"Apparently, Brigid here is a syren, like the legends say," Duncan muttered angrily, crossing his arms over his chest. "And Caelum knew about it. *We* had to find out from Kellan."

I rolled my eyes, irritated by the larger man's words. "Get over yourself. You're just mad you didn't figure it out yourself."

Caelum stood and spun around on his heel to face us, his eyes blazing mad. "You two fucking stop it, right now. This is not the fucking time. Maddock is *dying*."

Duncan glared at me as Caelum turned his attention back to Maddock, stepping away from me to hand the apothecary woman bandages and clean rags. I ducked my head, cheeks burning at Caelum's admonishment. He was right, this wasn't the time to argue with Duncan.

Cameron looked down at me. "You're covered in blood."

I raised my hand to inspect it, realizing my talons were also still out. "I managed to get a swipe in at Kellan."

He raised an eyebrow. "Those are new."

"We're losing him," the young girl's urgent voice jarred us from our conversation, then Cameron was moving toward his friend.

I took a step forward, intent on joining them, but Duncan spun around and pinned me with a glare, stopping me in my tracks at the pure fury there. His lip snarled. "You stay there."

Normally, I would have ignored him and pushed past him with an eye roll, but Maddock was their friend first, and he was injured because of me. I swallowed hard, stepping back and willing my talons to retract. Wincing as they slid back beneath my skin, I crossed my arms over my chest, holding myself together.

More muffled curses filled the room, and bloody bandages and rags fell to the floor with wet plops. Slowly, fewer and fewer movements came from the couch. After a long moment, Caelum stood from his kneeling position and turned to face the rest of us. His eyes were rimmed with red, and blood covered his arms and shirt.

"He's gone." His voice was flat and empty, and it broke my heart.

"I'm sorry I could not save your friend," the young woman said quietly. "He lost too much blood."

Caelum shook his head, turning to look at her. "Thank you for your help. We'll leave you money for the mess."

The woman put her hand on Caelum's forearm, her own arms covered in blood to her elbows. "You won't."

"We need to regroup now, Captain," Duncan said softly, still looking down at Maddock lying on the couch. From the gap between him and Cameron, I could see Maddock's lifeless eyes staring up at the ceiling. I forced myself to look away, focusing back on Duncan. "And we need to bury Mad."

Bile rose, mixing with the tears in my throat. He was dead. *Maddock was dead.*

Caelum nodded, sniffing harshly before wiping at his eyes with his shoulder. It was the only clean part of his shirt. "Aye. Aye, we do."

"Where will we bury him?" I asked, keeping my voice as soft as possible.

Duncan whirled around, stomping toward me. "There is no we. You need to leave. Now."

I didn't say anything, but I also didn't back away from the hulking man looming over me. He was angry, and rightfully so. But I wouldn't cower to any man.

"Duncan, stop it," Cameron muttered.

"So, you don't care that she's been lying to us since the minute we met?"

"I care that Maddock just died and we need to find somewhere to bury him," Caelum snapped. "We can have this argument later."

Duncan glared at me again, but fell silent.

"What about your old house, Cae?" Cameron asked softly. "In the garden?"

Caelum nodded. "Aye, let's do that."

Carefully, Duncan picked up Maddock from the couch, and we wrapped him in a sheet the young woman provided. In somber silence, I lingered behind the others as we walked through the maze of alleys toward a derelict estate, with vines overgrowing the wooden structure. This was Caelum's house? It must have been where he had grown up. I itched to ask more about it and the history of why it wasn't where he still lived.

Caelum led us to the back of the house, where an overgrown garden sprawled over the estate. He nodded toward a patch of wildflowers. "Set him down there. There should be a shovel in the shed somewhere."

Wordlessly, Cameron went over to the small shed and returned with a shovel, handing it to Caelum. "Do you want us to help?"

"No, I need to do this," Caelum said, his voice watery.

My fingers flexed, itching to reach out to comfort him, but I held back. I had a strong feeling that my touch would not be welcomed by either Caelum or Duncan.

We were all silent as Caelum dug the hole for Maddock to rest. His shoulders heaved with effort, and I watched the blood on his forearms dry to a dark brown and begin flaking against his tan skin. But he never stopped digging and never let anyone take the shovel from him.

After several wordless hours, Maddock was buried among the wildflowers.

"He'd like it here," Cameron said quietly.

Duncan nodded his agreement. "Aye, he would."

Caelum cleared his throat, wiping the sweat from his forehead with his forearm. "We need to find a new place to stay. If my father knew about our plan, he likely knows where we're staying."

Duncan cast a suspicious glance at me. "We need to figure out how he knew we were coming."

"It wasn't me, if that's what you're thinking," I snapped, growing immediately defensive. Did he really think that I was working with *Kellan?* Rage simmered beneath my skin, and I flexed my fingers. As if I would ever work with a man like that. It was a miracle I was choosing to work with men at all.

"My family has a house about an hour's walk from here," Finn volunteered softly, interrupting our glaring session. "It's empty, so we can all stay there. There's no way anyone else will know where it is."

Duncan looked at Caelum, his blue eyes filled with concern. When Caelum didn't answer and kept staring at Maddock's grave, Duncan did. "Aye, let's do that."

CHAPTER TWENTY-SIX
BRIGID

After burying Maddock, we all changed out of our bloodstained clothes, bundling them up into a bag and burning them in the fire pit behind the house, and began the trek to Finn's family house. Everyone was quiet and reserved. My own heart was heavy, realizing again that this was likely what they had all been feeling since the wreck. Nausea built in my stomach, wondering how Caelum could even stand to look at me after the deaths of his crew.

Losing people close to me was not something I had experience in. And witnessing this first-hand made my guilt rise even more.

I hadn't spoken to Caelum since we left the house. But then again, Caelum hadn't spoken to anyone, not even Duncan, since we had buried Maddock. Though Duncan and Cameron had continued tossing me glances throughout the walk, I had not spoken to anyone either.

I had a feeling Caelum's silence was guilt and that he was destroying himself over Maddock's death. It was doubtful anything any of us said would convince him it wasn't his fault, but I still did not want him to wallow in misplaced guilt. Maddock's death was the fault of Caelum's father and his men. And me.

All of this was ultimately the fault of syrens. The wreck was our fault. And Maddock's death was partly due to Kellan wanting me. All of it led back to the syrens—back to me.

After about an hour of silent walking, we finally made it to the large but modest cottage sitting in the rolling hills. It was situated on a high plateau overlooking the coast, and the stone of the cottage was covered in a soft green moss. The building was inviting, and I hoped it would be safe for us to regroup. I wanted desperately to sit and rest and check on Caelum.

We entered the house, which was as welcoming on the inside as it was on the outside. It was warm, decorated well, and I could tell it had been lived in and well-loved. There was a large kitchen along one wall, and a massive round wooden table with eight chairs surrounding it. The fireplace in the corner looked cozy. There was a separate living area with another fireplace and two large cushioned chairs.

Everyone gathered in the kitchen, taking seats at the table. I stayed leaning against the wall, watching them. My anxiety was too high to sit, my body wired with energy.

"So, what are we going to do?" Cameron asked quietly from

his seat at the table. "How did they know we were coming?"

"And how did they know about Brigid?" Duncan added, glaring at me. At that single look, I knew without a doubt that Duncan blamed me for Maddock's death now too. "*We* didn't even know about Brigid."

"Are we really going to do this now?" Caelum asked, sighing as he sat down. He waved a hand. "Let's go, then. Get it all out there now so we can move on."

The vein in Duncan's forehead throbbed, and he acted on Caelum's permission, stabbing a finger at me. "She is a fucking syren. And if that's true, then we know exactly what we saw when *The Nehalennia* wrecked, don't we?"

"And I saved Caelum from drowning to what? Trick him?" I asked, crossing my arms. I knew my own anger was feeding off Duncan's, but I couldn't help it. He wanted to intimidate me, and I was no longer a scared little girl who could be frightened by men. He might be able to physically overpower me, but I could take care of myself in a fight. "If I had wanted to do that, I would have killed him in the water."

"I'm missing something here," Alan piped up slowly, looking back and forth between us. From the table, I watched as Caelum rolled his eyes.

"Brigid is a syren," Cameron explained patiently as Duncan and I continued glaring at each other. "You might have heard them called mermaids in old legends."

"They're real?" he asked, his voice going high. "And they really wreck ships like the legends say?"

"Yes, they're very real," Duncan snapped. "She and her ilk wrecked our ship and drowned our crew."

"Then why are *you* still breathing?" I retorted, raising an eyebrow.

"Okay, enough," Caelum said, sighing and pinching his forehead. "That's enough."

"And you," Duncan continued to rage, turning on Caelum, "I'm your best fucking friend. And you couldn't tell me what she was?"

"Would it have mattered?" he asked, his voice defeated. His shoulders slumped and he rubbed at his red eyes. "No matter when you found out, you would have been angry."

"Aye, I would have. Because she *killed* our crew." Spittle flew from Duncan's lips as he spoke. In the corner, Alan and his men watched with rapt interest. Duncan crossed his arms over his broad chest, glaring at Caelum. "Or have you forgotten that?"

Caelum jumped up from the table, his chair screeching across the floor and tipping over. He stepped up chest to chest with Duncan, his eyes hard. "Shut your fucking mouth, Duncan. I've forgotten *nothing*."

"Okay, that's enough," Cameron snapped, standing up from the table to move between them, putting a hand on each of their chests. "Tensions are running high. We all need to calm down. Brigid is a syren, yes, but she's been helping us. So, we need to move past this for now. We can revisit it once we avenge Maddock and save those damn children. Or did you both forget what we're doing here?"

After glaring at Duncan a moment longer, Caelum broke away first, bending down to pick up his chair and sitting back down heavily. He rubbed his forehead. "I'm sorry I didn't tell you all."

"It's not your fault," I said, my voice steadier than I was expecting it to be. "I asked you not to tell anyone."

Cameron sighed as Duncan snapped his attention to me. Duncan advanced toward the table, and I craned my neck to look up at him as he loomed over me. "All of this is your fault, syren."

I shrugged a shoulder, pushing my anxiety at his anger down. If he tried to hurt me, I would defend myself. My talons in my human form could still easily rip through his flesh. But I had a feeling that Duncan just needed to get his anger out of his system. And if I killed his best friend, I very much doubted Caelum would let me live. "That's one way to look at things, I suppose."

"As if there's another way?" he scoffed.

"Okay, we're done," Caelum said, slapping his palm on the table. "I'm the captain, and it was ultimately my decision to keep this information from you all. Now, it's time to get over that, move on, and figure out what our next move will be. Knowing she's a syren before wouldn't have changed what happened in that house. He still would have gone after her to get at me."

"If we'd known, she never would have been with us in the first place," Duncan muttered, stalking over to lean against the wall.

Ignoring Duncan's comment, Caelum spoke again, turning in his chair to face the rest of the room. "Obviously, someone told my father we were planning to go after him in Brinemoor and had us fed false information. It would be a waste of our time trying to figure out who it was."

"Why?" Alan asked, tilting his head. From his spot sitting cross-legged on the floor, added with the head tilt, he looked like a puppy.

"No one would ever give up my father. They're too scared of him," Caelum explained, sighing heavily as he rubbed at his forehead. "We need to find out where he's actually holding the children, and if he even really is selling them, or if that was a lie too."

There was silence. Today had been rough for all of us, and no one knew what to say just yet. These children were important to all of us, and yet we were no closer to stopping his father than we had been before. I was frustrated, and I had only been involved in this mission for a few days. I couldn't imagine how angry the others were.

"We can ask the syrens for help," I offered quietly. If they knew that Caelum's father was aware of our existence, it might be the push needed to get them to help us. I had no idea how I would get back to them or talk to them once I got there, but I would figure it out if it meant stopping his father. As women, and especially as women who had never been associated with Caelum before, we might be less suspicious when we gathered information. "It would give us the element of surprise."

At first, I was unsure if anyone heard me, as the silence only continued. Then Caelum spoke, his voice firm and unyielding. "No."

"But—" I started to protest. They could help us if they were willing. And if Kellan tried to escape via ship, they could help stop him. I just needed to talk to them and try to convince them they were in danger if Kellan continued to live. If children weren't enough to sway their minds, at the very least, their own survival might be.

"No, Brigid. We'll not be going to the others for help," Caelum said firmly. His words drove a dagger deep into my heart. The little progress we had made toward forming a relationship had been ruined with Maddock's death. "And I'll not hear any more discussion of it."

Before I could respond, Caelum turned to Cameron and Duncan, who had somewhat calmed down and joined us at the table, and began talking. Hurt washed through me. It seemed that Caelum had finally discovered that the losses I'd caused outweighed any interest he might have had. Maybe it was for the best. We had only just gotten over the initial hurt to begin exploring our feelings toward each other, and now, it seemed we would never get to continue that. Caelum was done with me.

Out of the corner of my eye, I saw Duncan smirk at Caelum's dismissal of me, quickly hiding it behind his hand. At least someone seemed pleased at the turn of events. But I supposed it would please Duncan for Caelum to rebuke me so publicly.

Caelum's dismissal hurt, but I wouldn't continue speaking where it was obvious my contributions were not wanted. Quickly, all the other men joined in, none of them casting me a second, or even a first, glance. Slowly, it felt like I wasn't even there at all. Standing up from the table, again without anyone so much as looking at me, I moved over to the cushioned chair by the large window that overlooked the hills and ocean down below.

My only course of action was to prove to Caelum that I could help. I understood his pain, I understood his anger, and I would do what I could to rectify the situation, even if he did not want to be around me anymore.

My stomach hurt. Perhaps I should have just ignored Caelum's words and gone with his father. At least then, Maddock would be alive. Duncan likely would have offered the trade himself, given his reactions toward the discovery.

Sitting in the chair, I watched the men talk for what felt like hours. They went through several ideas for how to get back at Caelum's father, then managed to dismiss every single one of them. There just wasn't enough information on his father's operation to be able to make good plans, and Caelum's input seemed intent on avoiding the deaths of any of the rest of his men.

I had to go to my family and at least ask for help. If they could help us, it would provide a way to attack that I doubted Caelum's father would expect. I was on land, something that the legends of syrens often said was impossible. It was likely he assumed I was alone, especially since he hadn't seen any other women with us. If we could get the other syrens to help and keep them under Kellan's radar, it could be an advantage for us.

Day turned into night, and I watched the sun set over the water as the men continued poring over alternatives at the table. Eventually, Cameron stood up and began gathering ingredients to make a pot of stew. Debating for a moment, I rose to help him, moving to wordlessly chop vegetables and passing them to Cameron. He smiled sadly at me as he took them. At least this was something I could do.

As he cooked, I watched the tension in his shoulders and the furrow of his brow. He was hurting; they all were. Once the stew was done, he walked over and handed me a bowl, sympathy in his eyes. I bristled. I wanted him to see me as part of their team, as someone who had good ideas. I wanted him to convince Caelum to listen to my plan. But I knew I couldn't ask that of Cameron. We had grown close, but Cameron had been Caelum's friend first, and we had only known each other for a few days.

Cameron smiled at me sadly, reaching out and tugging on a lock of my hair. "You still have blood in your hair."

I shrugged. "Adds to the aura."

His smile grew slightly wider, his eyes sparkling. "Wash it tonight, and I'll braid it for you in the morning. Now, eat up."

Nodding, I turned to my bowl of stew and ate it, alternating between watching the water through the window and listening in on the continued conversations surrounding Kellan. It had been established that he would have to seek attention for his hand, which would buy us some time, thankfully. But we still didn't have time to dawdle with our plans.

Night fell, and the conversations began to dwindle. The scuffing of chairs brought my attention away from the window and back to the room before me. All the men had stood and were leaving toward the bedrooms.

Caelum walked over to me and stopped, standing above me, an unreadable look on his face. "We won't be sharing a room tonight, lass."

I nodded, having mostly been expecting that due to his

anger at the situation I had brought about *and* that we would be sharing space with more people. Even though I had been expecting it, it still brought on some unpleasant emotions that I didn't want to process right now. Just previously, I had been saying that I didn't need to share a room with him, and now I found myself wanting nothing more than that. But maybe it was for the best if we put some distance between us. Maddock's death had brought up emotions that Caelum had likely been shoving down. Losing most of his crew was one thing, but one of his closest friends was a much different matter.

I glanced over at the fireplace and the warm chairs in front of it. Sharing a room with a stranger, or even by myself, was not appealing. I turned back to Caelum. "I'll sleep out here. Give my room to the men."

He stood there a moment longer, as if he wanted to say something further, but he simply nodded and retreated to the room that Cameron and Duncan had previously entered.

Standing briefly, I moved over to the basket sitting next to the fireplace and pulled out a thick wool blanket. I spread it over me and settled back into the cushioned chair to continue watching the water from the window, longing to feel the waves on my skin and smell the salt in the air. I only needed to stay awake long enough that everyone else would be asleep. And then, I would enact my own plan.

Find the syrens and convince them to help.

CHAPTER TWENTY-SEVEN
BRIGID

Stepping up to the beach, I took a deep breath, steadying myself. I could only hope that asking them for help would work. If they chose not to help, I wasn't sure what I would do next. Caelum was still angry, mourning, and shooting down every idea that was brought to him, so I needed to make sure my plan was solid before taking it to him. But first, I needed the help of the syrens. We needed the ruthlessness of Maira, the cunning and insightfulness of Kyla. Together, we could stop Kellan, I had no doubt.

I removed my clothing, folding it by the driftwood log before stepping out into the cold water. It washed over my feet, and a shiver moved through my body, but I continued out until the water reached my waist and the ends of my hair floated in the sea. Taking another deep breath, I dipped beneath the water and began my transformation. The magic swept over me, ripping my muscles apart and then merging my legs together and lengthening them into my powerful tail. My fingernails and teeth pushed through my flesh and lengthened to sharp points. My body no longer felt cold, but rather, I was filled with power. The pain washed over me, but I pushed it down, ignoring it. There was no time for my pain.

I needed to help Caelum. I needed to avenge Maddock, save the children, and kill Kellan. Despite what Caelum had said before, I was willing to kill. And I would if needed.

Swimming more into the sea, I swished my tail, stretching and flexing in an attempt to ease the soreness. It had been mere days since I had transformed before our journey to Brinemoor, but after more than ten years of living primarily in my syren form, these past days in my human form had me missing the sea, despite the pain transforming brought me. Flicking my tail again, I swam out into deeper water. The water was dark, light barely filtering down, but I had no trouble seeing.

Without my song, I couldn't call to my family. Cliodhna could sense me in the water, but I was unsure if she would send the others after me or simply ignore my presence. Not wanting to rely on Cliodhna sending the others to me, I swam toward the caves I knew I could not enter. For hours, I waited. The waters were all familiar to me, the rock formations all similar, but not being able to enter this one system marked it as my former home. As time passed, light slowly began to filter down through the surface, a sign that the sun was beginning to rise. Hopefully, they would come soon. Otherwise, I feared for

Caelum's reaction when he woke and I was not there.

Or maybe I feared for his lack of reaction.

Thankfully, I didn't have to wait much longer after the sun rose. Within moments, I felt the power of the others nearing. One by one, I could make out their shapes as they exited the caves, swimming toward the surface. First, Kyla appeared, then Maira, Sorcha, and the rest of them. Sorcha swam by, her head turning to take in the water. Her eyes landed on me floating near the outcropping of rocks by the cave. Her eyes widened and she opened her mouth to speak, but I couldn't hear what she said. My heart shattered in my chest. *I couldn't hear her.*

She guided the others toward me until all of them were there, swimming in front of me. Maira's face pinched and her mouth opened. I could tell her words were angry, but I still couldn't hear them. I shook my head at them, pointing to my ears, trying to convey that I could not hear them.

Maira rolled her eyes and fisted her hands at her sides in frustration. If she had legs, I'm sure she would have stomped her foot. She pointed roughly to the surface and then took off, blasting through the water and leaving a trail of bubbles behind.

Kyla looked at me, her gaze kind but closed off, before she too took to the surface. One by one, they followed. Sorcha pulled me into a quick hug before leaving as well. I closed my eyes briefly to center myself. I needed to be my best when I faced them again; I needed them to understand me. My hurt would need to wait, so I pushed it down, down, down as I swam up toward the surface.

Breaching the waves, the cold air stung against my wet

face and hair. The others were waiting for me.

"Can you hear us now?" Maira snapped.

I nodded, keeping my face neutral. "Aye, yes. I can hear now."

I couldn't help but notice that Cliodhna wasn't among them. While I hadn't expected her to be, I had been hopeful. I wanted our queen's approval and forgiveness. If she was sympathetic, maybe the others would be as well. With Cliodhna's power, we would have the best chance possible to stop Caelum's father.

Maira spoke again before I could. "What do you want, then?"

"I need your help," I admitted. "And I know you owe me nothing, not after what I did. But there is a man using the seas and his power to steal children and sell them. I am working to try to stop him, and I need your help."

"Why should *we* help you?" she demanded, her eyebrows furrowing. "You abandoned us for that man you saved on the beach. Go seek help from the other humans."

A pang of guilt pierced through my heart, my anger building in contradiction. While I wanted nothing more than to give them all a verbal lashing for being so quick to dismiss me as a traitor, I needed their help. And making them angry would only succeed in getting them to say no even faster. "Aye, I know. I needed to save him for my own reasons, and I understand that my actions hurt you. I apologize for that."

"So, you think you can come back and offer an apology and we will just jump to help you with your new priorities?" Maira asked.

"No, I don't think that," I replied. And it was the truth.

I didn't expect them to help me, but I did hope they would. I hoped they would remember what it was like to feel human, to want to protect those less fortunate. We had all been victims, and I hoped they would understand the plight of these children. "I do hope that you will help. I hope that you will show the world that you are good and kind, as I know you are. I will respect your choice, though; I know this is my fight, not yours."

"And these children, tell me, are they girls? Or are they boys?" Her lip curled up on the last word. After years of violence at the hand of men, and even more years under Cliodhna's rule, Maira truly distrusted and vilified men in any form. At one time, I would have agreed with her. But Caelum, Duncan, Maddock, and Cameron had begun to change my mind.

"Mostly boys, but the man taking them isn't entirely discerning," I said quietly. I knew that could very well change their minds, but I would give them all the information and then accept their decision, whatever it was. I could only hope the past decade we had spent together meant *something* to them, like it had for me.

"We will not help you rescue children who will one day grow up to be the very men we punish," Maira spat. "And I cannot believe that you would be willing to do this. You've changed. And you've betrayed everything that our queen has done for us."

A pang of hurt went through my heart. I'd known they would label me as a traitor, yet hearing it aloud was another thing entirely. I didn't feel like a traitor. I felt like a woman fighting for what was right and trying to make up for the mistakes I had made. Was I a traitor? If so many people—

the syrens, even Duncan—thought I was one, did that make it true?

"I am not betraying you," I said, my voice quiet but firm. "I am doing what is right."

"According to whom?" she snarled, moving closer to me. "Because according to our queen, the right thing to do would have been to kill that man when you saw him in the water."

"I've told you why I wouldn't, and I'll not keep explaining that decision," I said, just as angry now. "But I've come to you all for help to save children, and you're using my decisions as an excuse to not act."

"Now, wait," Maira started, raising her hand.

Kyla swam between us, holding a calming hand out toward each of us. "Calm, sisters. Maira, we will hear her out. Brigid, you say this man is stealing children? And selling them?"

I swallowed my anger, looking into the calming amber eyes of Kyla. "Aye, he's stealing orphans and children who have no one to miss them. We don't know why he's selling them or to whom, but we tried to stop him ourselves. It…didn't go well."

Kyla tilted her head, studying me. "The children remind you of yourself."

A lump formed in my throat, hot and leaden. She was right. I knew what it felt like to be treated as property, to be taken and sold to further someone else's agenda. To be forgotten. "Aye."

"What happened when you tried to stop him?" she questioned. I noticed that Maira's own anger had softened slightly as well, and she simply floated behind Kyla, watching me.

"One of the men was lost. And the man we were trying to

stop knew I was a syren. He tried to trade me for their safety."

"He knew you were a syren?" Kyla seemed shocked. "But how?"

I shook my head. "I couldn't find out. There was too much violence, and we were trying to escape. But I cannot let children be punished for the sins of adults. I must help them. And I can't do it alone."

"We'll not help you, Brigid," Kyla said softly after a long silence. "We sympathize, me especially, and wish you well, but we won't get involved in the troubles of men. And we can protect ourselves down here. *Neamh na Mara* is a safe place for us."

I nodded my head, sad but understanding. I wouldn't push them further; I had my answer. If any of them would have agreed to help, apart from Sorcha, it would have been Kyla. She had a soft spot for children, and her motherly instinct had survived her transformation to deadly syren. "Thank you for listening to me. And I am truly sorry for leaving before."

Kyla simply nodded back before they all turned and swam away as one, disappearing beneath the waves.

Dejected, I turned to leave. Caelum had been right, my family was not an option. Maybe they never had been. Pushing my fingers through the plants rising from the ocean floor, I swished my tail, watching the bubbles it created.

"I'll help you, Brigid," a soft voice came from behind me.

I whirled around. Sorcha floated there in front of me, a small smile on her face. Tentatively, I raised a questioning brow. I had considered asking her directly, but didn't want to draw attention to her in front of Maira. "Why did you stay behind?"

She looked over her shoulder at where the others had retreated, no doubt heading back to the caves. "You're right. The minute we let children suffer for the sins of adults, we've lost. I told you before you left that I thought some men were innocent. You working with your man and the others proves my point. I want to help you."

My heart squeezed. After our long nights of conversations and her adamant defense of innocent men, I had hoped Sorcha would want to help. Her friendship filled me with gratitude. I swam up to her, looking at her for a long moment before I surged forward and wrapped my arms tightly around her neck.

"Thank you," I whispered into her hair, breathing in the briny scent that saturated her hair. "Truly."

"Now, stop weeping. Tell me what's going on," she said, hugging me back just as tightly. "Take me to where you're staying."

I released her and then we swam back up toward the shore by the cottage. As we neared the shallow water, our heads broke the surface. Reaching out through the cold water, I found her hand, squeezing it. "I have clothes for us if you want to transform. Have you done that yet?"

"Aye." She nodded. "Once before. I'm glad you brought clothes. I hadn't even thought about bringing some with me."

I smiled. "I figured as much. It's hard to remember to bring them after being without them for so long. Let's change and put some clothes on. I don't want you to be alarmed, but my transformation will be painful."

"Is it...bad?" she asked, worry playing across her features.

Placing a hand on her arm, I tried to reassure her. "I'll be all right. It's nothing I can't handle. I just didn't want it to surprise you."

We both transformed there in the shallows, tails morphing and splitting into equally strong legs. Stepping out of the icy water, we both shivered as the wind whipped across our skin. I reached for the bag of clothing sitting by the driftwood log on the shore. Taking out black pants and a cream sweater for me, I handed her the bag. Dressing quickly to get out of the wind, I sat down on the wood and watched as Sorcha dressed in something similar, her sweater about five sizes too big for her.

She sat down next to me. "So, are we going back to wherever you're staying?"

I looked over my shoulder at the cottage and let out a sigh. Caelum was still angry with me, and until I could talk to him and apologize for getting Maddock killed, I couldn't face him, let alone face him with another syren. I looked back at Sorcha. "No, we can stay here for a bit if you're okay with that. We can just talk, like we used to. The sun just rose, we have a few hours before anyone will come looking for me—if they do at all."

Her head tilted to the side, and her eyes drilled into me. "What's happened?"

I pushed my hair behind my ears, shivering slightly as the water from the strands ran down my back. "I...it's my fault one of their men, Maddock, died. Add in the wreck as well... and I think the reality that I was the cause for so much of their pain has finally sunk in with the man I saved. I expect he's still angry with me."

"Was it your fault?" she asked. "Did you deliver the blow that killed him?"

"No, of course not." I shook my head vigorously. "He was killed by one of Kellan's men. That's Caelum's father."

"Then how is it your fault?" Her voice was quiet.

Looking down at my lap, I twisted my fingers together, a habit I had picked up from the girl in front of me, a girl who was wise beyond her young age. "The ship wrecked because of us, and with no one else to blame, they blame me. Caelum's father wanted me. That's what started the fight that killed Maddock. How could they not blame me?"

"They cannot blame you for the actions of another," she said, twining our fingers together. She squeezed them gently. "And if they do, since when do you cower to the anger of men?"

I couldn't help but laugh, a loud noise that startled even me. "You're right, little one. You're right."

She smiled reassuringly at me as if she was seeing why I didn't want to go back to the cottage. She reached out and squeezed my hand briefly before letting it go. "Aye, I know I am. Now, tell me everything that's happened since you pulled him up on that beach. Don't leave out a single thing."

CHAPTER TWENTY-EIGHT
CAELUM

I woke up to the sound of Duncan snoring like a bear. Why had I decided to punish myself and share a room with him and Cameron? *Oh, that's right, because another one of your friends died yesterday and you wanted to be near the remaining ones.*

The image of Maddock being sliced down by a sword meant for me would haunt my nightmares forever, I was sure. His death had been my fault, and I wasn't sure if I could ever forgive myself. The deaths of the crew, that had been bad enough, but I knew now that we hadn't been targeted specifically, just attacked at the whims of an ocean queen. But Maddock's death? That had been my fault. It had been my idea to go after my father, to go into that house, and now my friend was dead.

Sighing heavily, I ran my hands over my face before pushing my hair back out of my eyes. I needed to get up and go check on Brigid. I had wanted to give her space last night, space from me and my sour mood. Likely, she was furious with me for leaving her alone, but I didn't want her around my negativity. I only hoped she was okay and willing to forgive me.

I stood, dressing quickly before I walked across the hall into the room that we had decided would be hers. It was empty. No, it didn't even look like it had been slept in at all. My heart began racing.

Had she left? Had she abandoned our mission and left us? Where had she gone? Was Duncan right? My thoughts swirled, and I tried to catch my breath as I searched the room for any sign that she had been there.

When I had gone to bed last night, she had been wrapped in a blanket, sitting in the chair by the window. Maybe she had fallen asleep there. Trying not to panic, I walked quickly into the main living area, my eyes scanning the room. Apart from Alan, putting a kettle on the stove, it was empty. The chair was empty, the blanket Brigid had been curled up in last night flung across the back. I rushed over and picked it up. It was cold; she had been gone a while. Where was she?

I turned to Alan. "Was Brigid out here when you woke up?"

"No; I think I heard her moving around in the middle of the night, though. Thought I heard a door shut. Maybe she went outside?" he asked, shrugging as if it was no bother to him where she had gone. The man had no sense of urgency in anything he did.

"And you didn't think to wake one of us up and tell us she had gone?" I asked, my anger rising. My father wanted her. She shouldn't be alone. Again, I cursed myself for not sharing a room with her. I should have been there to protect her. I had failed. *Again.*

He shrugged again, and my blood began to boil. He turned, taking the kettle off the fire and pouring the boiling water into a cup. "I just figured she wanted some fresh air. Plus, I didn't want to go after her. I'm still wrapping my head around the whole syren thing."

I bit my cheek to keep from saying something that I would regret later. Instead, I turned on my heel and stalked back to the room. I slapped Duncan roughly on the shoulder before doing the same to Cameron a bit more gently. "Wake up."

They grumbled but opened their eyes. Duncan spoke first, "Wha'dya want, Caelum?"

"Brigid is gone." Just saying it out loud made my heart pound in my chest. I ran a hand through my hair, anxiety skyrocketing.

Cameron sat up, his eyes wide and no longer holding sleep. He at least had come to care for Brigid and her safety. "Where'd she go?"

"If I knew that, I would have her back here," I retorted. I took a deep breath. Cameron had not taken her; my anger at him was unwarranted. "Alan says he heard her leave in the middle of the night."

Duncan eyed me, the suspicion clear. "Do you think she just left?"

I sat down forcefully on the bed, my mind racing with a hundred different possibilities. Irritation bubbled, lodging beneath my ribs, right next to the tight ball of worry. "I don't know why she would have. After yesterday, I'm more certain than ever that she wasn't working with my father, like you suggested. But I don't know what happened, and she's not in the house."

"Maybe she just needed some space," Cameron suggested, rubbing at his eyes.

"Space from what?" Duncan asked, scoffing. "She's a bloody syren, what could she possibly need space from?"

"Space from you being a giant arsehole?" Cameron asked angrily. "Since you found out what she was, you've been nothing but mean. She saved Caelum. She's been helping us. That has to count for something. She told us why she did what she did. I know she had a hand in our friend's deaths, but can you blame her? If any of us had gone through what she had, we likely would have lashed out at those responsible just the same. Since she's joined us, she's done everything she can to help us. Do not keep punishing her for the choices she made to stay alive."

Duncan looked ashamed, and rightfully so. Cameron had put into words what I had been thinking since the day we had lost Maddock. We were allowed to be angry and grieve those we had lost, but Brigid, right or not, had been trying to make amends for her actions and the actions of her fellow syrens.

Cameron turned his eyes back to me. "But Caelum, what if she really did just need some space from all this? She watched a man die yesterday, and watched you cut off a hand that was holding her. That's got to have rattled her at least a little bit."

"We need to find her," I said, ignoring their suggestion. If she needed space, she should have just bloody stayed in the living area and not gone wandering outside. "My father wants her for some reason. We can't let him get her."

They both nodded before dressing and following me out back into the main living space. Alan and Finn were both out there, eating their breakfast.

Alan looked at me, finally seeming at least slightly concerned. "You lot still going on about Brigid? I'm sure she's fine."

"We need to find her," I gritted out, still angry at the man. "My father just tried to kidnap her, so we can't have her just wandering off on her own."

"Let's split up. We can just look around the property," Duncan suggested, despite his body language being obviously unconcerned. I wasn't sure what angered me more, Duncan's intentional lack of concern, or Alan's lack of attention.

I nodded, not trusting myself to say something that wouldn't be angry, then turned and walked out of the house. I was furious with her, and when I found her, I would be letting her know. I had just lost one friend to my father; I couldn't lose her as well.

Knowing Brigid, she had likely headed down to the shore if she truly had wanted space. I turned my footsteps down the hill and toward the water. Trudging down the grassy bank, I tried to settle my anger. As I neared the shore, I saw her. My breath left my chest in a heavy, relieved sigh. She was okay.

The closer I got, I saw that she was sitting on a driftwood log, and she wasn't alone. A smaller figure sat next to her, with long dark hair cascading over her back and shoulders. Their hands were clasped together in Brigid's lap. Who was she? Was she a syren?

My vision turned red. She had gone back to the syrens despite my instructions. Why couldn't she just listen to me? I was trying to keep her *safe,* and she was dead set against it.

"Brigid!" I yelled. I would figure out the identity of this new woman later; for now, I needed to talk some sense into this woman.

She turned at my voice, her eyes alight. She was happy to see me. But then, as quickly as it had appeared, her eyes and face turned blank, shutting down. I furrowed my brow. What had happened in the course of a night? I got even closer, my boots crunching against the rocks of the shore.

"Caelum," she said, her voice calm and her face still blank. "Is everything okay?"

My blood began to boil again. She had the nerve to ask if everything was okay? After I had just nearly lost my mind at the thought of her missing or in my father's hands? "No, it's bloody well not okay. Why did you leave?"

Her eyes turned to molten flames and narrowed, an eyebrow raising. "I wasn't aware I needed permission from you to go places."

"You do when my father just tried to kidnap you yesterday," I said bluntly. Taking a deep breath, I forced myself to calm down and at least try to approach things rationally. "Now, tell me why you left."

"I went to the others to ask for help," she said. Her tone was so casual, and it irritated me even more.

"I told you not to do that." *Explicitly,* I wanted to add. Out of the corner of my eye, the other girl's lips twitched into a smile as she watched us.

"Did I miss the announcement that I was under your control?" she asked, now seething mad. Her forehead furrowed, and she released the other girl's hands to ball her own into fists.

Shit. That came out wrong. I pushed a hand through my hair, trying to calm down. She was safe, it was fine, there was no need to worry anymore. "No, that's not what I meant."

"Then what did you mean, Caelum?" she asked, arching an eyebrow as her forehead smoothed out. Tension and distrust still radiated from her, though, as if she were afraid I might explode at her again. I didn't like that.

The girl sitting next to her sniffled, reminding me of her presence. Good. The distraction of another person would help me calm down. I turned to the other girl, trying to calm myself. "I'm Caelum. What's your name?"

She also arched an eyebrow at me. "I know who you are. And I'm Sorcha."

"So, you're here to help?" I asked, shocked that any of them had actually agreed to it.

She nodded, her dark eyes full of amusement. "Aye, I am. Now, please continue on with Brigid. I'm sure we'll get to know each other later."

"Aye, thank you, Sorcha," Brigid said, her voice frosty. "Now, what did you mean by that, Caelum?"

I sighed heavily. "I just meant that I thought we had decided that wasn't an option we would be exploring."

"And who is 'we?' Because I certainly wasn't included in

that decision."

"Can we just go back to the house?" I asked. I was doing this all wrong and making her angry when I had truly just been worried. Well, maybe I had been a little angry.

"No, I'm fine here," she said, crossing her arms. "Please, explain why I wasn't allowed to go seek out my family's help."

"Because I knew they would say no," I admitted. I kicked a rock at my feet. "And I didn't like how they had treated you."

Both of her eyebrows shot up. "You didn't like how they had treated me? That's why you didn't want me to ask them for help?"

"Well, yeah. That, and I figured they would say no anyway, and I would have rather spent our energy on solutions that actually had a possibility." I shrugged, not enjoying explaining my reasoning. I wasn't used to explaining myself, but Brigid had me doing it more often than ever. Looking at her, at her narrowed eyes and arched brows, the words just kept spilling out of my lips. "And what if they had kept you? What if they hadn't let you return to me? To us?"

"Caelum, Sorcha is here. She said yes to helping us." Her voice softened as she studied me, and I felt like pulling her into my arms just to reassure myself that she was really here. "And I'm safe. I'm back, and I'm safe, and we're going to save those children and stop your father."

"Aye," I acknowledged. "But that's not your whole family, lass. That's one of, what did you say, eight? That's not exactly going to help us defeat the man."

"No, but it can give us another set of hands and perspective," she said. She looked at her friend. "Sorcha, tell him your idea."

I raised an eyebrow and turned to the younger girl. "Your idea?"

"Don't look so shocked. I do have a brain," she said, smiling. "And aye, my idea. We need information on your father's operations, but obviously, he knows you're looking for it. So, instead of trying to pick it up from the ramblings of drunk fools, I say we go straight to the source."

"That wouldn't work," I replied with a sigh, leaning forward with my elbows on my knees. It had been one of the first ideas we had pitched last night, but my father had likely instructed anyone with any knowledge of his plans to be on the guard for me and my men trying to get to them. "My men would never get anywhere close."

"I'm not a man," she replied, grinning wickedly. Instantly, I understood why she and Brigid were close. "I can go in. They don't know me, they wouldn't suspect me. We grab one of your father's men, preferably one close to him, and we question him. While your father might change plans once he realizes we have one of his men, he can't change them that much. There's only so many places he can take a group of children without being noticed or stopped."

That was…actually brilliant. I was kicking myself for not having thought of it. I simply stared at her. She was young, but she obviously knew something about this kind of business. I wondered what her story was.

"Aye, you'll catch flies if you leave your mouth open," she teased, reaching over to tap the underside of my chin. "Just say thanks, and let's get to work."

I grinned at her. "Aye, little one, let's get to work."

CHAPTER TWENTY-NINE

BRIGID

As we made our way back to the cottage, I was still fuming over how Caelum had burst onto the beach, angry and talking to me like I was disobeying him. Had Caelum even noticed that I was gone last night? Had his anger at the beach been fueled by worry, or was I truly nothing more than another person to watch out for after Maddock's death?

As we entered the cottage, Duncan and Cameron were standing just inside the door. Alan and his men were seated at the kitchen table. All heads snapped our way when we stepped over the threshold.

Cameron's face transformed, his forehead smoothing out and his lips turning up so far it had to hurt his cheeks. He continued to grin widely, looking over my head to Caelum behind me. "You found her."

"I wasn't lost," I grumbled, stepping to the side and allowing Caelum to pass by me. Sorcha came in behind him, moving to stand close to my side.

"Well, we didn't know where you went," Cameron said, not letting my surly mood affect him at all. He looked at Sorcha, curiosity in his blue eyes. "And who's this?"

Before I could introduce Sorcha, Duncan stepped around Cam. Unlike Cameron, his face was still as stoic as ever, his brow furrowed and his arms crossed. "Are you okay? Where did you go off to?"

My eyebrows shot up, mirroring the shock I felt. Quickly, I schooled my features, leaving one brow arched in defiance. Duncan had cared little about my safety after finding out I was a syren, and likely was more concerned over his ridiculous notion I was working with Caelum's father. My voice was steel as I spoke. "I went down to the beach. No nefarious intent, so don't worry your head over it. I promise I wasn't secretly plotting with Caelum's father or any other enemies."

Duncan reeled back as if I had struck him. The shock on his face looked genuine enough that it gave me pause. His voice was softer when he spoke next. "That's not what I meant. We were worried for you, that's all."

I didn't have it in me to have it out with Duncan again. My emotional state, already fragile from yesterday's events, had only been made worse by Caelum's piss-poor attitude. I couldn't deal with the big man's suspicion and anger—or worse, his pretending to care about me. Instead of replying, I turned my focus back to Cameron, physically turning away from Duncan. "This is Sorcha. She's another syren, and she's agreed to help us rescue the children."

"There's more of you?" Alan exclaimed from the table, his voice high.

"Yes," I said, exasperated. Alan was a nice man, but he seemed to have fallen off the rigging a few too many times. "There are eight of us."

"Have your crisis later, Alan," Caelum said with a sigh, stopping whatever reply had been about to come from the other man. "Sorcha is here to help, and she's already got a new plan to find reliable information on my father."

"We're trusting her?" Duncan asked, his voice softer but still harsh.

Anger burned in my veins, and I rolled my eyes. If Duncan wanted to be venomous toward me, that was one thing. But Sorcha would not be the subject of his anger or suspicion. I would not allow it. "She's not in league with his father either. And she's likely the only syren who's never killed someone. So, if you're going to trust any of us, it should be her. Now, get over yourself. Do you want our help or not? Because if not, we'll leave and go stop him on our own while you all sit up all night and talk the issue to death again."

Duncan looked almost…amused? He turned to Caelum. "Was this the fire you had mentioned?"

Caelum grinned, though it didn't quite reach his eyes. "Aye."

I huffed and crossed my arms but didn't respond. I had been slightly nervous around Caelum's men before, but after the events at the house, my mind had other things to worry about. Caelum had made it clear there would be no more future for us, so my focus was on saving the children, then getting them and myself to the contact in Bhodheas, who could help us all start over.

"Let's all eat something, and we can discuss Sorcha's plan," Cameron said, guiding Sorcha over to the table to sit.

I was still upset and hurt by Caelum's indifference, and despite wanting to move on from it, wanting to ignore the knot of pain in the center of my chest, I couldn't. Caelum would likely want me to continue helping to save the children, of course, and I would. But afterwards, I could almost imagine the conversation we would have and him telling me to leave. It didn't sit well with me.

Add to that how upset he had been with me over my going to my family for help, I wasn't exactly keen to speak with him or sit at the table and pretend along with him. Without another word, I turned and went back to the chair I had occupied last night, wrapping myself back in the blanket and sitting to watch the sun continue to rise over the water, painting the blue waves with streaks of red. Sorcha would be able to tell them her plan, her ideas. She was well-spoken and seemed confident sitting there between Cameron and Caelum.

I watched from the chair as they all ate and talked, studying their interactions with my friend. They asked Sorcha about herself, and I was surprised at how comfortable she was, answering their questions as if it were nothing to her. She kept darting glances at me, though, and I saw worry in her eyes. After the third or fourth time, I realized she was not looking to me for comfort, but looking at me as if she were worried about me.

I nodded my head slowly at her, reassuring her that I was okay. She needn't be worried about me. I knew I needed to get up and contribute to the conversation, to ease Sorcha into the new environment, but I couldn't. So, instead, I watched from the chair, focusing on their words and letting them wash over me. If I needed to jump in, I would be ready.

"Brigid, you well?" Caelum asked, coming over to perch on the arm of the chair. He had also been quiet while the others talked to Sorcha. I hadn't heard him approach until he was already upon me.

Looking up at him, I could see the concern shining in his green eyes. I was sure to keep my own expression blank and not betray the swirling emotions I was still sifting through regarding him. Inclining my head slightly, I replied, "Yes. Are you?"

He raised an eyebrow, looking down at me with an unreadable expression. Holding out a hand, he nodded toward the door. "You want to go for a walk with me?"

After a moment of just looking at him, trying and failing to read the emotions on his face, I nodded. I supposed we would eventually have to discuss things, no matter how much I didn't want to. Maybe it would be better to get it over with now. Standing from the chair and ignoring his hand, I turned to him. "Sure. Where do you want to go?"

"Just down the hill, I suppose," he said with a shrug, dropping his hand back down to his side. He tucked them into his pockets, but I could see them balled into fists.

Wordlessly, I stood, offering a nod to Sorcha as she glanced at me walking toward the door. She returned the nod, smiling reassuringly and flicking her eyes to Cameron. He followed. While I felt slightly bad about leaving Sorcha with a room full of strange men, I knew Cameron would protect her if need be.

Sorcha had been laughing and talking with them comfortably when I left, something I was insanely jealous of. I wished that I could have been like that, opening up to them so quickly, with no secrets or fears. Maybe it would have saved us the trouble Caelum and I were in now.

We walked down the winding path, walking through the grass and feeling the wind whip across the knoll. Neither of us said anything as we walked. My body felt as though lightning was passing through it. Every muscle was tensed, waiting for the words to come from Caelum's mouth that would surely break my heart. His shoulders were tight and bunched up around his ears as he walked. Maybe he was building up the nerve. A small part of me hoped it was as agonizing for him to think about as it was for me.

After a moment, he stopped walking. We were at the peak of the hill, looking down at the water a short way below us. Standing side by side, it was a peaceful moment, yet my emotions were still churning inside me, begging to be let out. I had saved Caelum, turned against my own kind for him, and had done so more than once. And he didn't seem to care. Granted, I didn't blame him.

"I'm sorry about Maddock's death," I said quietly, breaking the silence. I needed to get the words off my chest. "I know he was a good friend to you."

His eyes were sad as he turned to look at me. "He was a

good friend. I had known him for years."

I heard the intention beneath his words. *I had known him for years, and I have known you for seconds. You cannot compare to that.* I took a deep breath. "Aye, friendships like that are important."

"His mind was brilliant. He was always analyzing, always looking for a way around things," he said, a fond smile spreading across his face. It dropped suddenly, his eyes sad again. "Maybe if he was still here, we already would have found a way to stop my father."

"You'll find a way," I said immediately. I closed my mouth, swallowing hard, hating how quick I was to reassure him, to comfort him.

Looking up from his boots, he offered me a kind of half-smile that I knew was more polite than anything. "Thank you. I think we will, especially if we can make Sorcha's plan work."

"Aye, she's a smart lass," I agreed, wrapping my arms around my chest. This conversation was painful. The small, polite words that meant absolutely nothing were like knives beneath my skin. *Just tell me,* I wanted to scream at him. I wanted this over with so I could bottle my emotions back up and shove them down behind my indifference.

Caelum didn't reply. He didn't say anything for a long moment, just looking out at the seas beneath the hill. After what felt like a lifetime, he took a deep breath, letting it out harshly and all at once. "I hate that he's dead."

"I'm sorry for your loss," I said, my voice mechanical.

He looked over to me, his brows wrinkling in confusion. "What's wrong, Brigid? You're acting strange."

On instinct, I went to protest, but stopped myself. I hugged myself tighter, as if I could hold myself together and keep from falling apart. "I'm sorry."

"For what?" he asked, stepping over in front of me and holding my arms. I closed my eyes, relishing the heat of his hands against me.

"It's my fault he's dead," I said, my voice barely over a whisper. I was afraid that if I spoke any louder, I wouldn't be able to hold myself back from crying. I hadn't cried in years, and I didn't want this first time to be in front of Caelum and out of pity for myself.

He looked at me, his face void of emotion. For a moment, I thought perhaps he had not heard me. As I was about to speak again, his hands tightened around my arms. "No."

"I know you don't believe that," I muttered, looking down at my feet. My stomach was twisted up in knots over the idea of losing Caelum. Not that I ever really had him in the first place. I had wanted him, though—desperately.

"Believe what?" he asked, his voice exasperated. "What is there to believe or not believe?"

"It was my fault," I explained, still looking down. I could not bring myself to meet his gaze, to see the pain in his eyes over his friend. Did he want me to own up to it? I would if that would make it easier for him. "If your father hadn't been after me and grabbed me, Maddock would still be alive."

Suddenly, one of his hands released my arm and moved to gently cup my cheek. Raising my face, I found his eyes staring intently into my own. "Brigid, that is absolutely not true. The only fault for Maddock's death lies with my father and that giant tree of a man that killed him."

Now I was the one confused. My face scrunched up as I looked at him. For days, he had been angry, avoiding me. What else could have been the reason? "Then why have you been avoiding me? If you didn't blame me for his death…"

He laughed, but there was no humor in it. He squeezed my arm again before moving the hand holding my chin to cup my cheek. His touch was so gentle now, it made me want to cry. "Lass, I wasn't avoiding you. I was blaming myself and mourning the loss of a friend, and I didn't want you around my sore mood."

"Oh." I swallowed, nodding. His explanation made sense, but at the same time, it didn't. There had to be more than that to explain why he had been completely avoiding me and acting as if I was invisible. "I…I don't understand."

"Understand what?"

I took a deep breath, trying to calm myself and form the right words. "I thought you were bringing me out here to tell me you didn't want anything to do with me anymore."

He blinked at me. "What?"

I huffed out a small laugh, pulling myself from his grip and wrapping my arms around my middle once again. As if it would protect me from Caelum breaking my heart. "I would still help you stop your father, obviously, but I was expecting you to tell me that once that's over, you want me to leave."

"No. No, I heard you, *teine*," he said, shaking his head. He blew out a rough breath. "Why would you think that?"

"Maddock's death, you not wanting to share a room, you not speaking to me, you dismissing my ideas and treating me as if I'm invisible..." My words came out too fast, jumbling together. I took a deep breath again. "It all seemed as if you were shutting down, shutting me out, and getting ready to tell me to leave. I thought that was why you wanted to come out here to talk."

"Brigid…I don't blame you for his death," he said, stepping forward. He was so close to me now that only a sliver of air could pass between where our bodies stood.

"But the wreck was," I pointed out. I was screaming at myself to stop talking, to stop giving Caelum reasons to want me to leave, but I couldn't help myself. "You've said that yourself."

He looked at me for a long moment. "You didn't decide to wreck the ship. You didn't decide to kill my men. That was your queen."

"But I still did it."

"Do you want me to hate you, Brigid?" he asked, letting his hand fall away from my face. He took a step back, running his hand over his hair. "Do you want to leave? If you do, just say so."

"I'm being realistic here, Caelum," I said, my voice thankfully steady and not betraying how badly my emotions were swirling.

"No, you're trying to push me away," he said, stepping back up into my space. "You think that you get to tell me what I want and decide what's best for me, but you don't. Only I get to do that."

"Then what's best for you?"

"I don't know, *teine*, but I'd like the chance to find out if it's you." He stepped even closer, our bodies now touching, my chest pressed against his sternum.

Hope rose in my chest where we touched, warming me from the inside out and pulling a smile across my face. He still wanted me. And I still wanted him. Despite all the challenges facing us, maybe we could make this work.

"You really don't blame me for his death?" Despite the optimism fueling my body, I had to be sure.

He raised a hand and gently pushed a loose strand of hair back behind my ear, letting his fingers trail across my cheekbone. "The only person I blame for this is myself."

"But his death wasn't your fault either. You know that, right?"

He smiled at that—a small smile, but it was there. "Aye, I know that, but it doesn't help the feelings, as you well know. I'm sorry, *teine*. And I'm sorry about yelling at you this morning. I was just worried."

"We'll make sure they pay for what they did," I promised, reaching up to place my hand on his face. Our eyes locked, and the promise swirling in his eyes was enough to make my knees weak. Then I registered the rest of his words, and my brows furrowed. "Worried? Why would you be worried?"

"Oh, I don't know, maybe because my father obviously wants something to do with you," he said, his face and tone exasperated as he looked down at me, letting his hand fall from my face to hold me around the waist. "I know you're a big, bad fish lady, but my father is an evil man. I was worried he had found and taken you."

My heart clenched at his worry. While I knew his father

still wanted me for some reason, I hadn't considered that he would have still been searching for me. And more, I hadn't considered it a threat.

"You really have no care for your own safety, do you?"

I grinned viciously at his words, baring my teeth. "Not really, no. I never needed to be concerned after I became a syren. I was one of the most dangerous things in the ocean, and I never ventured onto land often."

"Aye," he said, releasing my face and slinging one arm around my shoulders, pulling me into him. "Well, you're mostly on land for now, so get used to the concern. You need to watch out for yourself more."

His concern touched me, made my heart flutter and my stomach twist. I studied him, seeing the worry etched in the lines on his face. I reached up to put my hand on his cheek, running my thumb over his rough skin and beard, relishing the feel of him beneath my hand. He smiled down at me, something entirely too close to admiration in his eyes.

"Like what you see, Captain?"

"Aye, very much," he replied, his voice gruff. He reached out to tug on a strand of hair before sliding his large hand through the strands to cup the back of my head. He lowered his face down to mine, resting his forehead against mine. Our breath mingled. "You're a very dangerous woman."

"I know," I said, my voice barely over a whisper. I badly wanted to kiss him.

So, I did.

CHAPTER THIRTY
CAELUM

In the next instant, she had risen on her toes and her lips were pressed against mine. Instinctually, my other hand found her bare hip, my fingers digging into the swell of flesh there, pulling her as close as I could until every part of me was touching some part of her. My brain short-circuited as our lips moved together, molding to each other. This was surely what heaven felt like.

Her curvy body was warm against mine, and I could feel my cock pressing firmly against her stomach. I had to strain to keep from rutting against her, though I desperately wanted to. While I doubted she would mind, given the way she was kissing me, I didn't want to scare her off by moving too quickly. I wanted to pull her clothes off and feel her soft body against mine completely. Unfortunately, though, this was not the time or place for that. Knowing that was the only thing that kept me from pushing further and seeing how far she would let me go.

Breathless, we finally pulled away, our chests heaving together and her eyes opening slowly.

We should have been getting back to the cottage and the others, but she was breathtaking, and I had to have her in my arms. I pulled her back to my chest and looked down at her, her own face tilted up to meet my gaze.

"You're beautiful, *teine*," I said, my voice hoarse. My hands encircled her waist, molding her body tightly to mine. I could feel every curve still pressed against me, and my mind was racing, stuck on imagining what those curves would feel like skin to skin.

She tilted her head to the side, staring up at me with attraction in her eyes. It made me feel good that it wasn't just me being affected here. "You're pretty handsome yourself, Captain."

I couldn't take it anymore. The others be damned, I would kiss her again.

With a harsh breath, I bent down and captured her lips with mine, holding onto the generous swell of her hips as I pulled her as tight against me as possible. Our lips moved together, and Brigid's hands found their way over my shoulders and into my hair, pulling it loose from the tie that held it back. As my hair fell around my shoulders, she twined her fingers into it almost painfully and held us closer together.

Panting for breath, I pulled back slightly, my mouth resting against her forehead. Her fingers left my hair, and she trailed them down over my face and neck, making me shiver as her nails scratched at my skin. Coming to rest at my sides, her arms wound around me, and she tucked her face into my chest, squeezing me tightly. I smiled and pressed a kiss to the top of her head. "You keep kissing me like that, I'll never let you leave."

"What are we doing here?" she asked, her voice still muffled by my chest.

I pulled back, looking down at her with my brows furrowed. "What do you mean? What do you want us to be doing here?"

"If I wanted to be with you..." she started, looking up at me. The fierceness and determination in her eyes made me want to kiss her again. "How would that work?"

My heart was racing. While I had only known Brigid personally for a few weeks now, she was already taking up residence in my heart; her personality, her looks, and just her. She had finally begun opening up to me and the others, and I couldn't stop finding an excuse to touch her. Last night had been the hardest night since I had met her; I'd spent it tossing and turning, wanting nothing more than to hold her in my arms and feel her warmth. She had burrowed her way under my skin, and to hear that she felt the same was...mind-bending. But she was right, we had outside factors to contend with.

"Caelum?" Her voice startled me from my thoughts.

I looked down at her, pressing my lips to hers to avoid talking. I didn't want to think about those outside challenges; I just wanted to think about her. I slipped my tongue along her lips, groaning when she opened for me and our tongues met. I kissed her deeply, pouring every emotion I didn't know how to say into the kiss. I wound my hand through her hair and slid the other one down to grip her hip. Without breaking this kiss, I rolled us over so that her back was pressed into the earth and I was above her.

The hand on her hip slid down to her knee over the thin fabric there, and I pulled her leg up around my hip. She moaned into my mouth, her own hands gripping and tugging on my hair. I couldn't help it as my hips ground into hers and I kissed her harder. She was pure fire in my arms, burning up every bit of me.

Panting, we broke apart. I let my fingers slip out of her hair and trace along her cheek. "I told you, you can have whatever you want. And if that's me, well, I'm honored."

She smiled, the expression lighting up her face. I groaned and leaned back down to capture her lips in a scorching kiss.

"We better get going before one of them comes looking for us," I said after kissing her again. We had likely been gone for almost an hour, but I didn't want to stop. Hell, I could easily lay on this grass kissing and holding her for the rest of my life and be content. But we had other commitments we had to uphold, other people relying on us. And at least one man that I needed to kill.

She let out a small sigh, sitting up. "Aye, we better go. I didn't mean to leave Sorcha by herself for this long."

We stood, and I pulled her into my arms again, looking down at her and tucking a finger under her chin to ensure she met my gaze. "But, *teine,* we're not done here. Not by a long shot."

She raised an eyebrow at me, pulling back to nip at my

finger. "We'd better not be, Captain."

With a huge smile on my face, I walked back up to the cottage, Brigid close beside me.

CHAPTER THIRTY-ONE
BRIGID

Unlike when we had returned with Sorcha before, when we stepped through the cottage doors this time, no one paid us any mind. They were all huddled over a map spread across the kitchen table, Sorcha included.

I looked at Caelum questioningly, who just shrugged and walked up to the table. My heart fluttered at his gaze, remembering the feel of those shoulders beneath my nails as I held him while we kissed.

Sorcha and Cam were pointing at something on the map, which I could now see was a hand-drawn map of Brinemoor. They had been busy while we were gone.

Duncan looked up, raising an eyebrow. "Where've you two been?"

"We went for a walk," Caelum replied, peering down at the map on the table. "What's all this?"

Duncan's eyes roved over us both, taking in our appearances. I didn't know if he saw that our lips were swollen or that Caelum's hair was as wild as mine, but Duncan was observant. He could likely guess what we had been doing. He huffed before turning to the map. "Sorcha here thinks we should target higher levels of your father's circle, so we're trying to figure out where they'd likely be staying and going in town."

"That's smart," Caelum said, nodding in agreement. He looked impressed as his eyes flicked up to Sorcha, and he smiled encouragingly. "They'd be more likely to know the finer details that we would need."

I glanced over at Sorcha, who was standing next to Cameron. Her face flushed, and she ducked her head. "Thank you."

"Ah," Cameron said, wrapping his arm around her shoulders and pulling her into his side playfully. "Don't act all shy and humble now that the captain's back."

I was glad Sorcha was already getting along with the men, glad that they weren't holding anything against her for being a syren. Sorcha hadn't played a role in their ship's destruction, and I doubted very much she had a violent bone in her body. Sorcha was a person who cared deeply about others, and it showed. It delighted me that Cameron had already seemed to take her under his wing. No doubt she reminded him of his little sisters.

Sorcha cleared her throat, pulling away from Cam. "Aye, so if we can figure out where your father's men are staying, we'll be able to watch them and see where they go. And from there, we can figure out when would be best to get one of them alone and grab them."

"Aren't they staying at the house?" I asked, leaning over to look at the map as well. There was a large circle around where the house we had infiltrated was.

"Aye, not likely," Cameron said, scratching the back of his neck. "But we figure they've moved on from there since we discovered they were staying there. We expect they're somewhere Caelum wouldn't know about."

I nodded. That made sense, I supposed. A safe house likely wouldn't do much good if everyone knew where it was. "So, how are we going to watch them without being recognized? Caelum's father had a lot of men in that room when they ambushed us, and the ones that got away likely know our faces by now."

Duncan stepped forward, his arms crossed over his chest. "We figure the best plan would be to pair off and rotate watching often. We need to avoid being seen as much as possible, so the fewer of us together at one time, the easier it will be to avoid attracting attention."

"Aye, but some of us are pretty recognizable," Caelum pointed out. He nodded at me. "There won't be a lot of women around with that color hair. And you're kind of hard to miss yourself, Duncan."

"We'll just have to be extra careful, then," Duncan snarked. He looked at me like he was expecting me to argue with Caelum, but I didn't. Caelum made a good point, and if his father was still looking to take me, I'd stand out like a sore thumb.

"I can probably do something to Brigid's hair to make it less noticeable," Cameron said, rubbing his chin thoughtfully as he looked at me.

"Let's figure out a rotation and a pattern first, then we can discuss how we're going to keep from being spotted," Caelum said, rubbing the crinkle between his eyes.

"This is a good plan, Caelum," I said, putting a hand on his shoulder, seeing that he was growing frustrated and upset. I knew they had briefly entertained this idea before and quickly dismissed it, but the way Sorcha had presented it made it sound like a better plan. Maybe Caelum had just needed a new face to suggest something. "We'll find one of your father's top men that we can question."

He turned his head and smiled slightly at me, then turned back to the rest of the group. "We rotate pairings, rotate routes, and if anyone feels like they got recognized, you stop and come back immediately and we'll send someone else out. No one else is going to die because of my father."

Duncan clapped his hands. "Perfect, let's get it together. We can start rotations tomorrow."

"Let's go over some more details first. My father's men are dangerous and cautious," Caelum said, his voice warning. "We need to be smart about this."

Caelum launched into descriptions of his father's top men, describing all he could remember about their appearances and places in Brinemoor they had frequented in the past.

"Do we have any contacts in Brinemoor that would be willing to go against your father and feed us even more information?" I asked, crossing my arms. Despite the butterflies still swarming in my stomach when I looked at Caelum's hands flexing on the table, I knew we needed to focus. And by contributing, I could focus on the plan and not on how I wanted to pull Caelum's clothes off. "What about Galen? Any of the people who reported those children missing in the first place? Would they be willing to help?"

Caelum looked up at me thoughtfully, stroking his beard. "Possibly. Galen is a recluse, but we could ask some of those who reported the children missing. I'm sure we could easily find people who would think my father is a horrible man, but the problem will be convincing them they will be safe if they help us."

"Can we discreetly convince them that if they help us stop your father, they won't have to fear him again?" I asked. If we could get these townspeople on our side, we could learn so much more, so much faster. Caelum was likely right, if the town knew they would not be in danger from Kellan, they would be more likely to help us. But how could we offer protection?

"We can certainly try. While our pairs are in town, we can see who might be open to helping us, even if it's just providing information on where my father and his men are going," Caelum said with a shrug.

"But would any of them tell Kellan that we're asking?" Duncan asked, raising an eyebrow at me. "It's a good plan except for the part where Kellan unofficially rules this town with fear."

"We'll never know unless we ask," I pointed out, returning the expression.

"Okay, simmer down, you two." Caelum sighed. "We need to be very careful about who we approach, and only do so if we think they would absolutely be on our side. We can start with Galen and see who he thinks would help us."

Duncan shrugged. "You're the captain, Cae."

"That's right," Caelum reiterated, raising an eyebrow. I bit down on the inside of my cheeks to keep from smirking. While I was pleased that Caelum was finally telling Duncan off, I knew my amusement would likely not go over well.

Digging my fingernails into my palm to focus myself back on the matter at hand, I refocused my attention. "What do we need to be looking for while we're on patrol?"

"Anything that could be useful," Duncan replied, his tone implying that I was stupid for even asking.

"I'm sorry, I haven't been involved in this plan from the beginning, and neither has Sorcha or Alan and his men. We need more information," I snapped before turning my attention to Caelum. "What information would be helpful? What should we be listening for?"

Caelum's lips twitched up, and from the corner of my eye, I noticed Duncan's expression. If looks could kill, it would have struck me dead on the floor.

"We still need to know where he's really holding the children, where he's taking them, what exactly he's doing with them, and if he is selling them, why and to whom," Caelum explained, ticking off each item on his fingers as he spoke. "If we can figure out their travel patterns or supply routes, that could help us as well."

"When do we start?" Cam asked, a grin spreading across

his face. The others echoed the sentiment with agreeable chuffs and noises.

As Caelum launched into plans for our patrol routes, I stepped back, watching the group gathered around the table. These men, and Sorcha now, were truly willing to do anything to rescue these children from Caelum's father. And now that Maddock had died trying to reach that goal as well, they were all the more involved.

Despite my time with the syrens, who I had thought were my family, I was already more involved and at ease with these men. I still didn't feel like I quite fit in with them, especially with the tension still there between Duncan and me, but I already felt more at home. And that both excited and scared the living daylights out of me. Going back to the others felt wrong now, and so did going south to Bhodheas. But would Caelum want me to stay after this was over? I wasn't sure. The uncertainty of what I would do after this weighed heavily on me.

"Brigid?" Caelum asked, his voice jarring me out of my thoughts.

I snapped my head up to look at him. They were all looking at me expectantly. I had missed something. I cleared my throat, fighting back the feelings of embarrassment. "Sorry, what did you say?"

"Are you okay with teaming up with the other men, if need be?" Duncan asked.

I nodded hastily. "Yeah, that's fine. It's probably better if I'm seen with the others instead of Caelum, Cam, or Duncan, anyway."

The conversation started back up, and Caelum looked at me, a questioning look in his eye. He stepped up closer next to me and brought his lips down to my ear. "You okay?"

"Yeah," I murmured back, eyes still on the others. If I looked him in the eye, I knew my cheeks would burn. I needed to focus, to figure out what my future would be after this. But we needed to get through this mission first. "Just thinking."

"Want to share?" he asked, reaching down to squeeze my fingers.

I looked up at him and smiled, my heart soaring at the genuine concern in his eyes. Our talk earlier had relieved a lot of pressure on my mind, and it appeared to have done the same for him. "Maybe later. We've got planning to do right now."

By the time the rotation and routes were planned out, it was dark outside. Cameron and Finn worked quickly to make dinner, another stew, and placed it on the stove for us all to eat. Bowl in hand, I sat down in the cushioned chair once again. Caelum came over soon and sat down in the one next to me. "So, Sorcha's fitting in well."

I looked over to where she was laughing with Cameron and Finn at the table. I smiled. "Yes, she is. Good for her. She never really belonged as a syren, anyway. She has no violence in her bones."

"Why did she become one, then?" he asked, eating his stew and looking at me curiously.

I shrugged. "She was lost; wanted a family, I suppose. A purpose."

"Well, hopefully she's found one," he said with a smile. "Do you think your queen will come after her?"

My fists clenched involuntarily at my sides at the thought. "No. She won't get anywhere near Sorcha. If she's upset about her deciding to help me, she will punish me, not Sorcha. I won't allow it."

"We'll protect her too," he said softly, pulling at my fingers to unclench my fists. "Now, what were you thinking about earlier? Because I know it wasn't that."

"You," I replied. I waved a hand, realizing how my statement may have sounded. "Us, this—everything, really. I was with the syrens for more than ten years, and I already feel more myself and at home with you than I ever did with them. With them, it was all about…pleasing our queen. I had friendships with the others, of course, but nothing meaningful like you have with your men. Maddock…dying, put it into perspective. And today. I like being here, with you, Caelum, and I'm not sure that I want to give it up."

"Is that a bad thing?" he asked quietly.

"I don't know." I shook my head. This was all too much for me to process right now, and every time I tried, I was quickly overwhelmed. "I feel obligated to return to my queen and the others, but my heart wants to stay here, with you."

He reached over and squeezed my hand, lacing our fingers together tightly. "You do what you think is best for you, *teine;* though I'd prefer if you maybe stopped the whole murder thing. Would make it kind of difficult to make any money on the seas, you know."

"Will you ever tell me what that means?" I asked, the corner of my lip quirking up. "And I don't think I would go back to killing indiscriminately. But I won't promise to never kill again."

"I suppose that's a fair agreement." He released my hand to tug on a strand of my hair. "And you'll figure out what it means eventually, I'm sure of it."

I rolled my eyes, and we fell silent for a moment. I couldn't help myself, so I asked the question I had been dying to know. "Why did you put me in a room alone last night?"

He grinned wickedly, and I knew his answer would also be less than helpful. "Why? Did you miss sleeping next to me?"

I sniffed, raising my chin indignantly. If I admitted that I had missed sleeping next to him, I'd never hear the end of it. "No, of course not. It just didn't make sense to me, that's all."

His grin stayed firmly in place. "So, is this your way of asking if I'll share your room tonight?"

I returned his grin this time. "You lost your chance, Captain. Sorcha is sharing with me tonight. You're with the others again."

"You're a cruel woman, *teine*," he said, still smiling at me.

Maybe this could work after all. Still grinning, I turned back to my dinner.

CHAPTER THIRTY-TWO

BRIGID

Finally, a schedule was set up for the surveillance routine. Two of us would take a turn each day watching the town, walking around and acting like locals while keeping an eye out for Caelum's father or any of his men. We had descriptions of Caelum's father's top men and instructions to keep on the lookout for them. If we saw them, we would just observe, seeing where they went and what they did. At the end of the day, we would head back to the cottage and discuss.

Today, I was on patrol with Cameron and Sorcha. While everyone involved had been hesitant at first, with Kellan still wanting me for reasons unknown, Sorcha and I wanted to help. The argument that had gotten this patrol approved had been Caelum's first true experience with my stubbornness and his first experience with Sorcha's disarming kindness that could get her what she wanted.

So now, Sorcha and I, along with Cameron, were walking along the narrow streets of Brinemoor.

Throughout the day, Cameron ushered us from shop to shop, pretending to browse through various shops and market stalls. It was an exhausting process, but both Sorcha and I knew it was necessary if we wanted to be able to pull off this plan. We needed to not draw attention to ourselves, to blend in with the locals.

As we were turning down an alley to start the journey back to the cottage, Cameron swore quietly, grabbing our arms and pulling us into a nearby shop. He turned and quickly peeked out the window, pushing us back into the corner by the door.

"What's happening, Cam?" I asked, trying to lean around his massive body to see what he was looking at.

"It's Iain, Kellan's first mate," he whispered, looking at us over his shoulder briefly. "He's walking by now."

"Well, see where he goes," I said, pushing Cam so I could peer out the window as well. I saw a taller man walking away from us, but his back was turned. But I trusted Cameron; if he said it was Iain, I believed him.

"Should we follow him?" Sorcha asked, wringing her fingers together.

"We don't need to," Cam said. He pulled back from the window and looked at us with a satisfied grin. "He just went into that bar down there."

"Okay, so we need to see if he goes there again," I said. This was good. If we could find a pattern in Iain's behavior in the town, it would get us valuable information on how best to grab him and interrogate him.

"Aye," Cam replied. "Let's get back to the cottage and tell the others."

For two days now we had watched, taking turns and doing our rotations. We melted into the townspeople, observing anyone and everyone who walked past. While we never found out where Caelum's father and his men were staying, we did discover a crucial pattern. Seeing Iain go into that bar had not been a one-time thing. He was there every night, usually from before the sun set to well after the sun rose the next morning.

As we continued observing over the weeks, he became our target. He would be the one we would capture and question, the one to give us the information we needed to bring Caelum's father down.

Caelum assured us that Iain would have the information we sought, so the decision to go after him was finalized. All that was needed now was a plan to take him and bring him back to the cottage without anyone else noticing.

"How are we going to get him out of the bar?" Caelum asked. We were all sitting around the kitchen table in the cottage, once again trying to come up with a solution to get Iain back here. We'd tried the same thing last night, and it had only devolved into arguing and frustration. I hoped today's conversation would be more productive, but I wasn't entirely optimistic.

"I'm telling you, just knock him out and drag him out the back. We can say he's passed out or something," Alan suggested for the third time. The man enthusiastically wanted to knock Iain out and was telling us this at every chance. It was getting exhausting.

Caelum sighed heavily, pinching the bridge of his nose. I reached down under the table and squeezed his other hand briefly. Looking at Alan, I replied, "If the people at the bar know him, they'll know we aren't friends with him. It has to be something he would do normally and that no one would remember."

"What about a woman?" Cameron suggested. When we all looked over at him, again cooking dinner, he shrugged. "He leaves with women fairly regularly, so what if we got a woman to lure him out and then take him when there's no one else around?"

"He would recognize me, though," I pointed out. Iain had apparently been one of the men standing by Caelum's father in the house when he had tried to take me.

"I can do it," a quiet voice came from the corner by Cam. Sorcha.

Anger and dread formed in the pit of my stomach. As soon as Cameron opened his mouth, I'd known she would volunteer. She had been the one to suggest this plan, and so it made sense she would want to be part of it. But it still filled me with a fear I couldn't push down.

I closed my eyes tightly, scrunching up my nose before relaxing my face and opening my eyes. We all looked over at her. She was sitting in the chair next to the fireplace, watching Cameron cook with her petite body twisted up in the chair and her chin on her knees.

"Absolutely not," I bit out, shaking my head. Sorcha had survived her ordeal of being thrown overboard, but I did not want her to have to experience any more of the evils of man. And these men were the true definition of evil. "It's too dangerous for you, Sorcha. That man wouldn't give a second thought to hurting you."

"Let her do it," Caelum said calmly, looking over at me. His eyes were like steel. "She can do it, Brigid."

CHAPTER THIRTY-THREE
BRIGID

"No, absolutely not," I snapped, my fingernails digging into the wood of the table as I attempted to control my building rage. "We'll find another way."

"Brigid, she's the only one of us my father's men don't know," Caelum tried to explain, leaning toward me.

I didn't care. This mission was dangerous, and we'd be asking Sorcha to get close to a man I knew wouldn't hesitate to kill or capture her if he knew her true intentions. "He didn't see Alan. We don't have to use a woman. Alan can just try to get Iain out to the back."

Duncan snorted but didn't say anything. Probably for the best, as I was spitting mad and ready to take on anyone who spoke.

Unfortunately, Sorcha was the one to speak again. "You just said that wasn't a viable option, Brigid. I can do this. I wanted to help, so let me."

After a pointed glare at Caelum, I turned to the younger girl, anxiety twisting its way up my throat. "This is dangerous, little one."

She rolled her eyes, a habit I knew instantly she had picked up from me. "Obviously, it's dangerous. This whole thing is dangerous. But would you let that stop you?"

I huffed, crossing my arms over my chest while thinking over her point. She was right, of course, I likely wouldn't have let it stop me either. But that didn't mean I was happy about it. "Fine, you can do it. But I want to be there."

"It's too dangerous for *you*, Brigid," Sorcha said softly. "Kellan wants you for some reason. We can't give him the chance to catch you away from the others."

"And what if he just wants a syren in general and we're handing him you on a silver platter?" I returned.

"This is a dangerous mission no matter how we look at it," Caelum said, far more diplomatically than I ever could. "And while it's not ideal to send either of you, if it would make Brigid feel better to be there, I think it's a compromise we can make."

"It's up to you, Caelum," Sorcha said, looking over at him. "You're the captain. And this is your mission."

Caelum looked at her for a long moment as if he were surprised at her easy concession. I figured he was used to dealing with me arguing with him, and Sorcha's agreeableness threw him off. He spoke slowly, "If he doesn't see her face and she doesn't draw attention to herself, I think it'll be fine."

Sorcha turned back to me, determination in her dark eyes. "Fine, deal."

Caelum clapped his hands together, leaning forward excitedly. "All right, that part of the plan is finalized, then. Now, we need to figure out what to do once we get him out of the bar."

"Wait," Duncan said, holding a hand up. "If Brigid is sitting in there alone, even hidden in the corner, it's going to look suspicious. She needs to be with a man."

"Not me," Caelum said, shaking his head. I could have sworn his expression was…disappointed. "He'd recognize me on the spot."

"Let me," Alan suggested. "I wasn't in the house, so he won't think twice about me."

Caelum pondered that and, after a moment, nodded. He looked at me, his green eyes bright with worry and anticipation. "Brigid, you okay with that?"

I nodded, shrugging one shoulder casually. Alan seemed nice enough, and I could handle being alone with him if it meant keeping Sorcha safe. And I would do whatever it took to keep Sorcha safe. "Yes, Captain. That'll do."

"So, you all will be inside the bar. Once Sorcha leads him out, we'll need to have people in the back alley," Caelum explained, running his finger along the map of the town. "We also need people in the front to watch for any other of my father's crew. We should have someone do a search of the bar before Sorcha goes in too."

"Caelum, you and I should be in the back. We're the most

recognizable," Duncan said, leaning in to point at an alley behind the tavern on the map.

Cameron, who had finished cooking, came over and took the seat next to me. He nodded and pointed to the lines on the map detailing the road in front of the bar. "And then Finn and I can position out here along the street to keep an eye on the front entrance."

"When should we do this? Tomorrow night?" I asked. The longer we waited, the more likely it was that Caelum's father would heal enough to continue his plans. I wanted this over with, and soon.

Caelum looked out the kitchen window, where the sun was just beginning to duck down over the rolling hills. He turned back to the rest of us. "Tonight?"

"Aye, tonight," Duncan agreed. "Before anything changes."

Cameron stood, clapping his hands. "All right then, better eat up. We've got a long night ahead."

Finally, our plan was in place, and despite my hesitations about using Sorcha like this, it was a good plan. The others set about talking about supplies and whatnot, and I walked over with Cameron to where Sorcha was still sitting.

"Since we're doing this tonight, you ladies might want to go start getting ready," he said with a smile. He tugged on a lock of Sorcha's dark hair and laughed when she scowled at him. "Let me know when you're done, and I'll do Sorcha's hair up nice and pretty. I'll bring some food in too."

Sorcha and I smiled at him before walking into the room we had been sharing. Wordlessly, we began laying out clothing for the night. While the bar wasn't well-maintained, wearing our casual clothing of borrowed sweaters and knit pants would make us stand out in a way we weren't hoping for. After our shopping trip with Cameron, we each had some pieces that we could use to blend in at the bar, and in Sorcha's case, to stand out and attract the attention of Iain.

I dressed in a similar outfit to one I had worn when recruiting Alan and his men. I pulled on tight, black leather pants that molded to the curves of my hips and legs. Over those, I added knee-high black boots with large silver buckles. On top, I wore a black long-sleeved blouse with lacing detail up the front, along with the same black underbust corset I had worn before. The dark fabric stood out against my pale skin, but it would allow me to go unnoticed in the shadows of the bar.

Sorcha dressed in a much more ostentatious way, pulling on an aesthetically simple but flattering dress. The cream-colored fabric left the attention on her dark hair, and the cinch at her waist emphasized her figure. I had no doubt she would be successful in getting Iain's attention. Sorcha was still young in my eyes despite technically being an adult at her nineteen years. I snarled inwardly at the thought of Iain laying a hand on her. *No one will touch her tonight*, I vowed. Getting Iain's attention was one thing, but he, nor anyone else, would lay a single finger on her. If they did, I would remove that finger. Viciously.

As Sorcha was lacing up her low-heeled shoes under her dress, Cameron walked in, holding two large bowls. He set them down on the dressing table before motioning for us. "You both look lovely. Now, let's get that hair done."

We alternated, Cameron doing Sorcha's hair first while I ate, and then we switched off.

Sorcha ate as she watched us, a thoughtful expression on her face. From the hunch of her shoulders and the tension in her jaw, I knew she was nervous.

"You okay, little one?" I asked. I was unable to turn to look fully at her, but I could see her out of the corner of my eye. If she didn't want to do this, we would find another solution.

She took a deep breath and raised her chin proudly. "I'm fine. I can do this. Just a bit nervous."

"I'll be there the entire time," I said. I wanted to tell her again that she didn't have to do this, but I could see that her mind was made up, and I wouldn't take this away from her if she genuinely wanted it. "We won't let anything happen to you."

Cameron patted my shoulder. "All done."

I stood, immediately bringing a hand up to my hair. Cameron had tamed my mass of waves into a single braid, beginning at the crown of my head and hanging down my back in a thick rope. While my fiery red hair would still be visible, it would now attract a lot less attention than it would if we had left it down and wild.

"You look deadly, Brigid," Sorcha said with a smile.

"We are deadly," I reminded her. "*You* are deadly. Don't forget that, little one."

With a fierce nod, Sorcha stood, taking my seat at Cameron's feet as I took hers at the table and began eating. Instead of a single braid like mine, Cameron began weaving Sorcha's hair into a more intricate pattern, starting at her temples and twining in small strands to keep her long hair back from her face. The braids on either side of her face then met in the back of her head, twisting together and falling down the rest of her hair, which Cameron left loose. It was beautiful and would attract attention just as much as the rest of her would.

I finished my stew and stayed sitting at the table, watching Cameron weave beads into the Sorcha's braids as well. Just as he was finishing up, Caelum walked in, leaning against the door frame. His eyes were molten green fire as he looked at me, scanning my seated body head to toe.

"You got some drool there, Captain," Cameron piped up from the bed, smirking at his friend. He patted Sorcha's shoulders. "You're all done now."

"You do good work, Cam," Caelum said, finally able to speak. He moved to stand next to me and smiled down at me. "You look gorgeous."

"Thanks, Captain," I replied with a grin. I enjoyed being able to distract Caelum. His attraction to me was not disguised, and it made me feel good. Returning the favor, I let my gaze glide over Caelum, taking in his own dark clothing. He was dressed more simply than me, but he still was so handsome that my breath caught in my throat. "But the goal was to look underwhelming."

"You could never look underwhelming to me," he said softly, setting off another storm of butterflies in my stomach.

Sorcha cleared her throat. Caelum and I looked over at her, seeing her smirking along with Cameron. "Are you two finished making eyes at each other? We have things to do tonight, remember?"

Caelum rubbed the back of his neck, the tips of his ears turning pink at Sorcha's words. "Aye, let's get going."

Without any further disruptions or teasing, we all began our trek into town, ready to begin. The bar came into view, and Cameron and Finn murmured goodbyes before splitting off from our group and going along the path in front of the bar, heading down a bit further than the building. There were already townspeople meandering about, heading toward the tavern and pub. Cameron and Finn shouldn't have any issues blending in.

Alan, Caelum, and Duncan escorted Sorcha and I up to the front door of the bar. Hopefully, Iain wouldn't have arrived yet and we would have time to get settled. I reached down to squeeze Caelum's fingers and smiled at him. "Go on, Captain. We'll be fine."

He looked at me for a moment, then after a quick but scorching kiss, he and Duncan left, walking around the side of the building to the alley where they would be waiting for us.

Sorcha grinned at me as we pushed the door open. "He's a good one, huh?"

I rolled my eyes at her. "Be safe, little one. I'll be in the corner watching with Alan."

CHAPTER THIRTY-FOUR
CAELUM

We sat in the alley behind the bar, hiding behind some crates and barrels so we wouldn't be visible, waiting for Sorcha to lead Iain out to us. My leg was bouncing with anxiety. I wanted desperately to be inside, seeing what was going on with my own eyes. I trusted Brigid to keep herself and Sorcha safe, but my heart still thundered in my chest at the thought of them being hurt.

"Relax and sit still," Duncan murmured from my right. "You're driving me crazy."

"Sorry," I muttered, forcing my leg to stop bouncing.

Duncan sighed heavily, keeping his eyes on the door that led to the bar. "She'll be fine. They'll all be fine."

"I know," I replied. "But I still worry. I don't want anyone else getting hurt in this."

"Brigid can handle herself, and she wouldn't let anything happen to Sorcha. You know that."

"Aye, I know. She's deadly, and she'd sooner kill Iain before letting him hurt Sorcha," I acknowledged. "But…"

"No buts, Caelum. You either trust her to take care of this, or you don't."

I snorted, tearing my gaze from the door to look at my friend. "Big words from someone who obviously still doesn't trust Brigid."

"Are we really going to talk about this now?" he asked, not turning to face me. "We're a little busy."

"Might as well," I replied with a shrug. "It'll keep us occupied."

"I just don't understand why you were so quick to forgive her for what happened to the crew. We spent so much time with those men, and it's like you've forgotten them already." His voice was quiet, but I could hear the hurt in his voice.

"I've not forgotten them," I said with a heavy sigh. I now understood his anger and the sadness that lay beneath it. "But Brigid did not kill them, any of them. She saved me, and she's been trying to make up for it ever since she pulled me out of the water."

"But she's killed others before—others like you and like me. How are we supposed to move past that?" he asked, turning to look at me for a moment before turning his attention back to the door.

"You and I have both killed men as well," I pointed out. I didn't want to start an argument with Duncan, not now. But it was important to get this out in the open so that we could move forward as a team. "Do we not deserve kindness or forgiveness any longer?"

"It's different, Caelum, and you know it," he said dryly. "And you should have told us what she was the first time we met her."

"She asked me not to."

"And there's the issue. You sided with a woman you had just met over me, your best friend. Can you not see how that makes me angry?"

I nodded, clarity dawning. "Aye, I understand. And I apologize. I truly do. I thought I was doing the right thing and that once you all knew her, it would be fine. I wanted it to all be fine."

"You should have let us make the decision for ourselves," he said. He rubbed his forehead. "But I understand your decision as well. If we had known then, we likely would not have gone to the cottage or even let you go back."

"I don't want to leave her," I replied, my voice soft. It was the first time I was voicing any of these feelings aloud to anyone. "I enjoy spending time with her. I want her to stay. And I want you two to get along."

Before Duncan could answer, the back door of the bar swung open, banging into the wall. We both slumped down, focus now intently on the door, waiting to see who would exit.

"Now, girly, don't play hard to get," a slurred male voice said. It was Iain.

I narrowed my eyes, watching closely as Iain and Sorcha walked out of the bar into the alley as planned. He wasn't touching her, but it wasn't for a lack of trying. Sorcha continued to push his hands away every time they reached for her. "I told you, sir, I'm not interested."

Sorcha continued walking deeper into the alley, and I saw Brigid and Alan slip out of the still open door.

"I don't care if you're not interested," Iain growled. It appeared he was done playing nice now that he thought they were alone. He grabbed Sorcha's arm, spinning her around and pinning her to his body. His other hand reached around and grabbed her behind roughly. Even from my hiding place, I could see fire and anger build in her eyes.

"Don't touch me," she ground out, the anger palpable as she struggled against him. If she could get free, I had no doubt that we would no longer be able to say Sorcha had never killed a man.

But it wasn't Sorcha I was worried about. Brigid had seen him grab Sorcha as well, and faster than I could blink, she had drawn the dagger at her side and was moving down the alley toward them. In an instant, she tore Iain away from Sorcha and pushed him against the wall with her dagger to his neck.

Quickly, left our hiding place and rushed over to where Brigid had Iain held at knife point. Sorcha was looking on, almost bored, and Alan looked excited. While Brigid was the only one holding him, Iain wasn't squirming. Instead, he just looked almost snootily down at Brigid.

"Give me one reason I shouldn't remove your filthy hands right here," I heard Brigid hiss, pressing the knife deeper into Iain's neck. A thin line of red appeared along the knife's edge. "She's not yours to touch."

I put a hand on her shoulder. "All right, there. Let him go."

"He touched her," she ground out, not moving an inch. "Without her permission."

"Aye, he did," I said, trying to soothe my spitfire's anger. If she killed him now, we'd have a mess on our hands and no answers. I needed her to calm down. "And he'll pay for it. But not here and not now. We need to go."

After a long moment of glaring at Iain, Brigid finally released him, tucking her dagger back into the sheath at her waist. She looked at me for a moment, an unreadable expression on her face, before nodding and moving over to Sorcha. I heard her whispering concerned words to the younger girl.

I turned my attention away from the girls, as I was sure Brigid could handle it. Facing Iain, I looked him over slowly. "So, here we are, Iain."

He spat at my feet, glaring at me while rubbing his hand over the thin pink line left behind by Brigid's knife. "Caelum, you need to control your woman better."

I spared a glance at Brigid, then turned back to him and scoffed. "I don't think so; she's doing just fine. Now, let's go. You're coming with us."

He snorted dismissively. "I think not. I'm not going anywhere but back to your father to tell him what you've done."

"Oh no, Iain," I said, a wicked grin spreading across my face. This would be fun. "It wasn't a suggestion."

At my words, Duncan came up beside him and knocked him over the head with his large fist. Iain crumpled to the ground, hitting with a dull thud. Duncan looked at me with a grin of his own. "We got him."

"Aye, we did," I agreed. I ran a hand over my face and looked around. There was no one else in the alley, but we had to move quickly to avoid being seen. "We've got to get him out of here."

"Alan, go grab Cam and Finn," Duncan instructed. He turned to Sorcha and Brigid. "Lasses, we could use your help over here."

As a team, we were able to get Iain transported back to the cottage without being seen. Once back, we secured him in an outhouse on the property with Finn and another of Alan's men staying out there to guard him. Reassured that our guest wouldn't be leaving any time soon, I walked back to the cottage and went to check on Brigid and Sorcha.

"You ladies okay in here?" I asked, leaning against the door frame. Neither had changed out of their clothes yet, and they were sitting on the bed together, Brigid holding Sorcha's hands. They looked up when I entered.

Brigid smiled at me and stood. "Yes, Captain. How's our guest?"

"Secured," I replied with a smile of my own. I turned my focus to Sorcha. "You sure you're okay, little one?

She rolled her eyes, but still had a smile on her face. "Yes, *Da*. Between the two of you, he was never going to hurt me."

"He shouldn't have even gotten to touch you at all," Brigid grumbled, crossing her arms.

Brigid's protective streak toward Sorcha was adorable and attractive all at the same time. I couldn't help my grin from growing wider, to the point that my cheeks hurt. I nodded my head at Brigid, still looking at Sorcha. "You mind if I borrow our mama bear here?"

"Go ahead," she replied with an equally huge grin.

Brigid scowled at both of us as Sorcha left the room, pulling the door closed behind her. Not wanting to waste a moment, I pulled Brigid into my arms, holding her firmly to my chest. "You know you're insanely attractive with a knife in your hand?"

She rolled her eyes at me, but I didn't miss the grin spread across her face as she tilted her head up to look at me. "I suppose you came in here just to tell me that, eh?"

I shrugged a shoulder, having made up my mind of what I would do. "That, and to do this."

Leaning down, I cupped a hand on the back of her head and pulled her face up to meet me in a scorching kiss. Lips moving together, she consumed all my thoughts. Her small hands moved to grip the front of my shirt, pulling me tighter to her. Her braid bumped into my hand cupping her head, and I grinned wickedly against her soft lips.

She pulled back, breathless. Her eyes were blazing and filled with the same arousal I felt for her. "What is it? Why are you grinning?"

I didn't answer, not with words. Instead, I wrapped that braid around my hand and tugged. Hard. Her answering moan and her eyes sliding shut about made me fall to my knees. I dropped my other hand to her hip, guiding her back until her thighs hit the dressing table. One hand still in her braid, I used it to tug her up until she was sitting on the table. She was stunning, sitting before me with her eyes bright and her chest heaving. I had to kiss her again.

Pushing my way between her thighs, I released her braid and cupped her face in both hands, looking at her before crashing my lips down to hers again. The room fell away, and all my focus came down to the feel of her lips on mine. I let my hands move from her face, wandering down her body and tracing her curves. When they reached the swell of her hips, I pulled her roughly into me, pressing my body against hers. She was all I could think about at the moment, and I wanted nothing more than to peel her clothes off her and have my lips trace the path my hands had just taken.

We pulled back for breath, both of us panting as we rested our foreheads together. I needed this woman like I needed air, and the thought scared the living hell out of me. I could only hope that she felt the same.

"Caelum," she whispered, her eyes burning holes in me down to my very soul. Her voice was breathy and aroused and made my body react even more. I was unbelievably hard.

I had to swallow twice before I trusted my voice to not crack. "Aye?"

"Touch me," she said firmly, despite her breathlessness. She ran a hand through my hair, giving it a brief tug, before trailing her hand down over my shoulders and chest, down my stomach, before hooking a finger in my waistband. She leaned in and ran her nose against mine. "I want you to touch me."

My brain went completely blank. "Say again?"

She laughed quietly before moving her hands to hold my face. She lifted her legs up to wrap around my waist, pulling me hard against her. "I want you to touch me, Caelum. Take my clothes off and touch me."

I nodded almost frantically. I was not expecting her to ask for that, not yet, but I desperately wanted it. "Aye, yes, I can do that."

She leaned her head down to tuck into my neck, pressing soft kisses there. Her hands shook slightly on my chest, and I wondered if she was as nervous as I was. I wanted to please her, to make her understand how much I wanted this. Taking a shuddering breath, I reached around her back and began unlacing the knots of her corset.

As I was unlacing the last knot, she pulled my face back to hers, pressing her lips to mine in a kiss that felt more determined than aroused. I almost pulled back, wanting to remind her that we would take this at her pace, but then her kiss changed, and she melted into me even more. I finally freed the corset from her, pulling it off and throwing it to the ground behind me. I pulled back and looked at her, her chest still heaving and her neck pink.

"Brigid." I swallowed hard. "Are you sure you want to do this? There's no rush."

She opened her mouth to answer, but a thunderous knock at the door had us both jumping apart.

"Captain," Duncan's voice thundered. "Our guest says he'd like to speak to you."

I groaned, letting my forehead fall against Brigid's. I did not want to leave this room. Even if Brigid changed her mind, I wanted to hold her and feel her against me for a bit longer.

She chuckled, patting my chest before unwrapping her legs from my waist. "Let's go. I want to see what he has to say too. And maybe remind him to keep his hands to himself."

I helped her stand, pulling her into my arms once more. I pressed a kiss to her forehead. "You're deadly. But don't think we're done here. I told you earlier, this isn't over."

"Promises, promises," she teased before walking to the door and opening it.

CHAPTER THIRTY-FIVE

BRIGID

After Caelum had taken a moment to calm his body, much to the undisguised amusement of Duncan, we made our way to the outbuilding where Iain was being held. I was grateful for the interruption, despite how much I had wanted to continue. Caelum sparked a fire in me, in my body, that scared me and intrigued me at the same time. I wanted to explore that fire, to explore Caelum, but now wasn't the right time. We had a mission to accomplish, and we needed to stay focused on that and not each other. No matter how much I wanted to lock us in a room and never come out.

Caelum reached down and twined his fingers with mine as we neared the building. He squeezed them reassuringly, smiling at me broadly. How he could still be so upbeat in a situation like this, I would never understand.

We entered the small outbuilding and saw Iain tied to a chair in the center of the room. Finn, Alan, and Cameron were already inside, leaning up against the walls.

Iain's eyes landed on me, and he sneered. I grinned, baring my teeth at him. He was likely just mad that two women had gotten the drop on him.

"You bring your woman to all your fights, Caelum?" he asked, turning his angry gaze to Caelum now. "Can't take on your father on your own?"

"Considering Kellan tried to kidnap her, I'd say this is her fight too," Caelum replied with a shrug.

"You have no idea what his plans are, boy. You should leave this to the adults and go play with the other kiddies," Iain taunted. "And leave your syren at home."

"The syren belongs wherever she chooses to be," I replied coolly, raising an eyebrow at the bound man in front of me. "And you're very lucky that I don't rip your head off your shoulders right this second."

He smirked. "Sure, girly, whatever you say."

I saw Caelum's shoulders tense, and I knew the bastard had struck a nerve, both with what Iain had said to him and to me. I stepped up behind Caelum slightly so he could feel my physical presence. Slowly, his shoulders relaxed, the corded muscles in his neck disappearing once again. When Caelum spoke again, his confidence was back. "Aye, I don't know all of his plans yet. I don't know what he's selling the children for. But that's why you're here."

Iain laughed loudly. "Oh, that's funny, you wee boy. But

I'll not be telling you a thing. I only asked you out here to tell you that you stand no chance."

Caelum shrugged, appearing unaffected by Iain's words. "We'll have to disagree on that, then. Because I think you will be telling us everything we need to know."

He turned to look at Alan and Cameron. Cameron nodded his head once. "We'll watch him, Captain."

Caelum returned the nod, turning back to me and motioning with his chin to follow him outside. We stepped out of the building into the brisk air, and Caelum let out a long sigh. "I shouldn't have wasted the time on him."

I put a hand on his shoulder and squeezed gently. "We needed to hear what he had to say. And now we know we have a difficult time ahead of us to figure out your father's plans."

"I would have rather finished what we started in your room than listen to that daft old man say absolutely nothing."

I raised an eyebrow at him, amused at the source of his frustration. It wasn't that Iain wasn't talking; it was because we had been interrupted. "We'll have time, Caelum. I promise you that."

Duncan walked out of the building, coming up to us. He rubbed the back of his neck. "Sorry, that wasn't as productive as I had thought it would be."

"We need to figure out our plan to work with him," Caelum said, rubbing his face. "I really don't want to torture him unless we absolutely have to."

"I have a feeling we're going to have to, Cae," Duncan said quietly.

Caelum's face pinched, and I could tell he was uncomfortable with the idea of torturing Iain, no matter what he had put him through in the past. I stepped up, putting a hand on his shoulder. "I can do it, Caelum."

Duncan raised an eyebrow. "You?"

"Aye," I said, raising my eyebrow back at him. "I've never tortured anyone before, but I can't imagine it would be too difficult to figure out."

Caelum chuckled, leaning over to press a quick kiss to my temple. "As much as I appreciate the offer, it *is* slightly more complicated than it sounds. I can do it if it comes to that."

"If you're sure," I said, looking into his eyes intently. I could carry this burden for him if he needed me to. I was willing.

"I'm sure, *teine*," he said, smiling. He nodded his head toward the house. "Let me walk you back to the house. You and Sorcha get some rest. I'll join you after I talk to Iain some more."

"You shouldn't be alone," I said.

"He won't be," Duncan said in a surprisingly reassuring tone. "Cam and I will be there too."

Looking at Duncan for a long moment, I nodded. That would be fine. They could keep Caelum from doing anything he wouldn't be able to come back from.

Caelum reached down to squeeze my hand, and we walked back up to the main house. Before we made it to the door, he stopped, pulling me close to him and turning to press me against the cold stone of the house. He brushed his nose along my cheekbone, sighing. "I want to hold you. I know we can't pick up where we left off, there are too many people in this bloody house, but I want to hold you tonight."

"Come find me when you're done, then," I said, pressing my lips to his neck. "I'm sharing a room with Sorcha, but I have a feeling you'll be too tired to do anything but sleep."

He chuffed out a laugh, his breath warming my skin. "Aye, you're probably right."

"Let's get going then, Captain. You've got some questioning to do," I said with a smile as he led us into the cottage. Sorcha was sitting in the chair and looked up when we entered.

"Did he say anything?" she asked, turning her body to face us.

Caelum scowled, the easy smile that had been there a moment ago falling from his face. "No, just wanted to taunt us that he wouldn't be saying anything."

Her face fell slightly. "Oh."

"They'll get him to talk, lass," I reassured quickly. I knew this had been her idea, and I didn't want her to feel like she had failed.

"So, what are you two doing?" she asked, looking around. "Did everyone else stay?"

"We'll be questioning him overnight," Caelum explained. "I was just walking Brigid back to the house."

"And I suppose you'll be wanting to know if you can sneak into our room when you get done with Iain," she said, raising her eyebrow along with her smirk. She was insightful, I would give her that. A smile of my own spread across my face.

"Well, of course," he replied with a grin, not missing a beat. "But it'll be late before I'm done, I imagine."

This man made my heart soar and my stomach clench in ways I never thought I would experience. And no matter what promises I had made to my queen, I knew I couldn't give this up. The revelation made my smile slip slightly, but I pulled it back into place before Caelum could notice.

He pressed another quick kiss to my temple. "You two don't get into too much trouble. Alan will be back in a bit."

Sorcha waved him off, turning back to the fire. He let out a chuckle and squeezed my fingers before turning to leave.

"So, shall we go to bed, then?" I asked, grinning at Sorcha.

"I suppose," she said with a sigh, standing up. She returned the grin, mischief sparkling in her eyes. "But I don't know if we will go to sleep. We have stories to catch up on."

Several hours later, the sun had long set through the window of our room, and I was curled on my side, listening to Sorcha's soft breathing. We had stayed up for hours, talking about all we had missed in each other's absence. It was nice, and needed. Now, as she slept, I studied the moon through the window, trying to stay awake.

The door to our room creaked open, heavy bootsteps sounding.

"You awake still, Brigid?" Caelum's voice was a soft whisper in the darkness.

"Yeah," I said. My voice broke, and I cleared my throat, trying again as I sat up to look at his figure in the dark. "Yes, what is it?"

"Just wanted to see if you were awake," he said, moving over to sit on the bed next to me. "We're stopping for the night."

"Did he tell you anything?" I asked, keeping my voice down to avoid waking Sorcha.

In the moonlight, I saw him shake his head. "No, he didn't.

We'll have to…improve our techniques."

I reached out and squeezed his hand. "Offer still stands, Captain. I can do it for you."

"No, *teine*, I need to be the one to do it," he said, leaning over to kiss my forehead. He tucked a finger under my chin, tilting it up slightly. "But know that I do greatly appreciate the offer."

I pushed up onto my arm to look down at him, my unbound hair spilling over my shoulder and down over my chest, which was covered by Caelum's shirt. "Are you staying the night?"

He nodded again, standing from the bed to remove his boots and shirt, leaving his pants on. "Aye, I need to rest. We have a lot of work ahead of us."

Settling into the bed next to me, he pulled the blanket back over us, pulling me to rest my head on his chest. The silence of the room took over once more, the only sounds our breathing.

"Can I kiss you goodnight?" he asked after a moment.

I pulled back slightly to look up at him, raising an eyebrow. I had little doubt if he kissed me that he would want to stop there. "Is that all you want to do?"

Even in the dim moonlight, I could see his wicked grin. "All I want to do? Not even close. All I will do? Aye, for tonight."

My own wicked grin spread across my lips, and I moved up to press my mouth to his. "Goodnight, Captain."

"Goodnight, *teine*."

Chapter Thirty-Six

CAELUM

Waking up to find Brigid still curled up in my arms was wonderful. I had missed feeling her against me as I slept. Waking up to see Duncan standing in the doorway with his arms crossed and looking down at us disapprovingly, however, was not how I wanted to be woken up. His brow furrowed, and he shook his head at us. It wasn't quite disgust in his eyes, but it was easy enough to tell he did not approve of us spending the night together.

"What?" I asked quietly, trying not to wake Brigid. Sorcha's bed was already empty, the sheets rumpled. "Why do you look so cross?"

"You spent the night?" he asked, raising an eyebrow and looking over at Sorcha's bed.

"Aye. Do you have an issue, or are you just stating facts?"

He raised an eyebrow at me. "We need to get started for the day. One of Alan's men reported seeing more activity with your father's men in town. They're preparing for something."

I sighed, letting my head fall back into the pillow. "Aye, they probably realize we have Iain and are speeding things up."

Duncan nodded, his expression easing up slightly. "Aye, that was my thought as well."

I bent down and pressed my lips to Brigid's hair, shaking her arm gently. She looked up at me sleepily. "Morning. It's time to get up, we've got some more questioning to do."

She nodded and sat up, rubbing her eyes. She saw Duncan standing in the doorway and froze. I hated it. I hated that her body tensed up at the sight of my friend. She cleared her throat. "Morning, Duncan."

He inclined his head at her in greeting before setting his eyes back on me. "I'll let you both get ready. Cam and Sorcha are making breakfast."

Without another word, he turned and left, pulling the door shut behind him. As soon as the door was closed, Brigid let out a huge breath, her body relaxing. I looked over at her, pulling her hand into mine. "You don't have to be nervous around him, *teine*. He won't hurt you."

She shrugged. "He doesn't like me, though. It's hard to relax around someone you know doesn't care for you."

I sighed before filling her in on what Duncan had shared about my father's men.

While it was a struggle, we managed to get dressed without me hauling her back into the bed. Once we were both ready, we walked out to the kitchen, where Cam and Sorcha were serving breakfast. Sitting down to eat, Duncan took the seat next to me.

"So, how are we going to approach this?" he asked in between bites. "Just asking last night didn't seem to work."

I swallowed the food that had suddenly turned to ash in my mouth. "My father's lessons weren't for nothing, I suppose. I know how to torture someone."

"Is there not another way?" Sorcha asked quietly. Her face was pinched, and from what Brigid had told me, she wasn't a proponent of violence, despite being a syren.

Duncan scoffed. "We don't have time for delicate sensibilities. Iain knows where these children are, and we need that information."

Sorcha's face morphed, tensing. She snapped, "I'm aware of that. My point was, won't Iain be prepared for physical pain? I imagine Caelum's father prepared his crew for the possibility of capture."

Hell, she had a good point. I tilted my head, looking at Duncan. "Aye, he likely has."

Duncan let a heavy sigh fall from his lips, turning back to Sorcha. "All right, then, do you have a better idea?"

Sorcha immediately turned to look at Brigid, and the two appeared to have an unspoken conversation before Brigid finally nodded at the younger girl. They both turned back to look at Duncan and me. "We can use our song."

"Absolutely not," Duncan nearly roared, standing abruptly. "We will not be letting you two sing your cursed *song* anywhere near us."

Brigid rolled her eyes, and I knew things were about to get…interesting. Over the last few days, Brigid's apprehension had waned. Her confidence was building in the face of my friend and the other men, and I had a feeling Duncan was about to get firsthand experience with the fire I knew bubbled under her surface.

"Just because you're afraid of it doesn't mean it's not the best course of action. We can keep you and the others from being affected by it," Brigid said, also standing up and facing down Duncan. "But our song induces madness." She hesitated slightly, looking over at me for a moment. "I don't have a song anymore, but Sorcha does, and she can break him."

I looked over at Brigid, trying to catch her gaze, but she was busy staring down Duncan. I was surprised she had admitted that in front of him—to him.

"We can cut off his fingers and he'll talk just the same," Duncan snapped, keeping Brigid's gaze. "And none of us will be subject to falling under your influence."

"For the last time," Brigid said, rolling her eyes, "the song induces madness. We can't control you with it."

Duncan's ears began to turn pink, and I knew that was a sign that his anger was building. Before he could speak again, I stood, interjecting myself. "Okay, we'll do both. If one doesn't work, we'll try the other."

"You'll really trust her to not turn the song on us?" Duncan asked, looking at me like I had lost my mind.

Cameron walked over, standing in between Duncan and me. He put his hands out, palms up. "Let's think this through rationally. Getting upset is only going to help your father."

"Putting wax in your ears and standing outside the building should be enough to keep you from being influenced," Sorcha offered.

Duncan snorted. "Should?"

"We've never actually tried this before, Duncan," Brigid said, her voice icy. "But I have seen sailors on previous ships use the wax and remain unaffected. So, yes, *should.* And you need to watch your tone with her. She's done you no wrong."

"This is going nowhere," I said, stepping in before tempers flared even more. "We need to be working on getting information from Iain, not fighting with each other. Duncan, I know you don't like it, but we're going to try everything we can. Brigid, we're going to try Duncan's way first, and if we get nothing, then you and Sorcha can try your song. Deal?"

They both grumbled, but thankfully there were no other words.

Once we all finished eating in tense silence, Duncan and I stood. I turned to Brigid. "We'll start first. I'll come get you when we're finished."

She shook her head. "I want to come."

"You don't have the stomach for what we'll be doing," Duncan said.

I cut my eyes sharply to him. It was like he was trying to get her to lash out at him. Saying a quick prayer to the gods for patience, I turned back to Brigid. "He won't talk with you there, Brigid."

The look in her eyes made me sure that she was going to argue, but instead, she just nodded shortly. I knew there would be more to this later, but we needed to get started, so I couldn't stop to think about it too long.

Duncan and I walked out to the outbuilding, dismissing Alan and Finn, who had been standing guard. We entered the building and I kicked at Iain's chair. "Wake up."

He grunted, but opened his eyes. His wrists were raw from pulling against the ropes all night, but he appeared otherwise unscathed, if tired. "Oh, goody."

"Let's talk," I said, feigning more nonchalance than I felt. Violence made me sick, especially the kind I was about to inflict on Iain. My own father had done similar to me, and I had once vowed to never do it to another human being. But my convictions had to take a backseat to saving these children. "What's my father planning with the children?"

"I'll tell you nothing," he snarled. "And no pain you inflict will change that."

"Okay," I said with a shrug. I grabbed his left hand, pulling his fingers taut as I brought the pommel of my dagger down onto the bone, breaking his index finger. "What is my father planning?"

"He's planning to kill you," he panted, gritting his teeth.

Stubborn bastard. I clenched my teeth, preparing myself for what I was likely going to have to do next. "Now, now, my father has always been planning to kill me. That's nothing new. What's he doing with the children?"

Only panting breaths filled the room.

"One more chance, Iain," I said, flipping the knife in my hands. "What's he doing with the children?"

He raised his head and spit in my face.

Without another word, I slipped a sharp, curved knife

from the sheath at my side. With no hesitation, I brought it down onto Iain's hand, severing the index finger of his right hand. Bone crunched and blood gushed. My stomach swirled, but I swallowed, keeping my face blank.

"What is my father planning?" I asked, my voice rising to carry over Iain's pained grunts. I had to give him credit, he didn't scream. "What is he doing with the children, Iain? Who's he selling them to?"

Iain brought his eyes up to mine, filled with pain and hatred. "Do what you like. I'm not speaking."

"You're afraid of my father, no?" I asked, letting his head drop and standing up. If I couldn't break him, we would never find out what was happening to the children, and we would have no hope of saving them. I *needed* to get this information. I walked around the chair, moving to stand behind him. I clapped a hand down roughly on his shoulder, relishing the sharp intake of breath he gave at the impact. "You should be. But you should be afraid of me too."

He laughed—the bastard had the nerve to laugh. "Oh, boy, I'm not scared of you a lick. There's nothing you can do to me that I haven't already done to others. Nothing will make me betray your father."

I looked over his head at Duncan, trying to convey that we would be needing Brigid and Sorcha after all. I knew that Iain wouldn't give anything up merely due to physical pain. But that didn't mean I was done. "That's too bad for you, then. My father isn't worth your loyalty."

I grabbed another handful of hair and pulled Iain's head to the side, slicing my knife along his ear, severing it. He roared in pain again, his hands flexing as he tried to staunch the bleeding of his ear. It only made the bleeding in his hand worse.

I walked back around the chair to stand next to Duncan. "Don't let him bleed out. There's bandages in the cabinet over there. We'll try again in a bit."

Chapter Thirty-Seven

CAELUM

I sighed heavily, rubbing the back of my bloodied hand over my forehead to wipe the sweat away. "This isn't working, Dun."

"Aye, I know," he said, with a sigh of his own. We had been trying various methods of physical pain, including cauterizing his wounds and pouring water over a cloth spread over his nose and mouth. We had even severed another finger. Nothing had worked so far.

We walked to a bucket by the side of the cottage and washed the blood from our hands and knives. Drying my hands, I thought of how to broach the subject of having Brigid and Sorcha try.

Duncan surprised me, speaking again. "I guess we should

let the girl try, then."

I raised an eyebrow at him, shocked. "You're going to just let them try? No more fighting?"

"Well, obviously, what we're doing isn't working. And we don't have a lot of time," he snapped. He stopped and sighed heavily. "I just don't trust it. They already ruined our plans once, wrecking the ship. I don't see how you're trusting them so quickly. Did the men we lost mean nothing?"

"Of course, they mean something. I thought we talked about this," I snapped back. "Just because I'm not in the corner crying does not mean I don't feel their loss."

"No, you're just losing your mind over the *creature* that helped kill them."

My anger bubbled up, and I pointed the now clean knife at him. "Watch it, Duncan. My feelings for Brigid are in no way related to what happened with the ship. And now is not the time to be having it out like this. Save it for later. We can mourn when my father is dead."

Duncan shook his head, a disgusted look on his face, but wisely said nothing else. My anger continued to simmer as we walked back into the cottage. Brigid and Sorcha were sitting in the chairs by the fire, talking. They stopped when we walked in.

"Did you get anything from him?" Brigid asked, raising an eyebrow.

I shook my head. "No."

She cocked her head at me, studying me. I had no doubt she could see the anger and frustration on my face, but I couldn't bring myself to elaborate, not after what Duncan had said. Was

I truly forgetting myself for Brigid? I hadn't thought so, but now I wasn't sure. Duncan's anger and sharp words were still shaking around in my brain, and I couldn't help but question myself.

"What do you need to be able to do your song on him?" Duncan asked, crossing his arms and looking at the girls.

Brigid raised an eyebrow and slowly let her gaze move from mine to Duncan's. "Oh, so you're going to let us help now?"

"Aye," he grumbled, repeating what he had told me. "Obviously, what we're doing isn't working. And we're running out of time."

Brigid shared a glance with Sorcha before answering, "Sorcha will need to be in syren form. So, we need to either move him to the water, or we'll need to get a large enough basin to hold her in her syren form."

"We're not untying him," Duncan said immediately. I agreed. If we untied him, even if it was just to move him to the water, we couldn't risk him getting away.

"There's a large enough trough in the back," I said, rubbing my chin. "It'll take us a bit to fill it up from the well, but it should work."

"I know this is asking a lot of you, little one," she said, looking at Sorcha. "We can find another way if you can't do this."

Sorcha took a deep breath. "There is no other way, and you know it, Brigid. You don't have your song anymore. I need to do this."

"Will her song affect you?" Duncan asked, jerking his head at Brigid.

Her eyes twinkled, and one side of her mouth tugged up in a smirk. "Don't know. We'll find out when we find out if it affects you."

Duncan threw his hands up, scoffing before he turned and left the cottage.

I raised my eyebrow at Brigid. Why did they constantly have to antagonize each other? "Did you really have to do that?"

She grinned at me. "Sure did."

Over the next hour, we all pitched in, getting the basin situated in the outbuilding in front of Iain and filling it. He didn't say a word the entire time, just watched us carefully.

The basin finally filled, and now Brigid, Sorcha, Duncan, and I stood outside the building. I looked to Brigid, whose face was apprehensive. If I had to guess, she was worried if the song would affect her as well. I caught her eye and nodded at her. "I'm staying in there with you."

"Absolutely not," Duncan immediately argued. "Even with the wax, you could be affected, Caelum."

"He needs to see that I'm still in control," I pointed out.

"I'm going in with you, then."

"Fine, let's get this started," I replied, not fighting with him. If he wanted to come in, then he could. It would be pointless to argue with him. Sorcha would not hurt us, not intentionally. I trusted that much.

We entered the room, and Iain looked up at us. Even bloodied and obviously in pain, he sneered at us. "Bringing in the women now, are we?"

We ignored him. Sorcha handed wax to Duncan and I, and we promptly put it into our ears, muffling all sound until we were in complete silence. Duncan and I stood behind the basin against the wall, watching as Sorcha and Brigid had another wordless conversation. Brigid moved to stand next to us, and Sorcha began removing her clothes.

Apart from Brigid, the rest of us averted our eyes at Sorcha's nakedness. It felt wrong to look at her, and I was grateful I wouldn't have to cut Iain's eyes from his skull for looking at her. Once Sorcha stepped into the basin and began her transformation, Iain seemed to understand what was happening and began thrashing against his bindings. My father must have warned him of what the syrens could do.

I saw Sorcha's mouth open, and my body involuntarily tensed, but I heard nothing. Iain's body went slack, his mouth falling open and his eyes glazing over. The calm stillness didn't last long, though, and he quickly began flailing, his eyes going frantic as his remaining fingers clawed at the chair.

Sorcha continued singing for a few more minutes, then Iain's mouth began to move. I looked to Brigid, who held a hand out to stop us and spoke to Iain. At his reply, she turned to us and nodded.

I yanked the wax out of my ears. "What is my father planning?"

Iain's head was still thrashing, his body shaking, but he replied, looking at me with panicked eyes. "He's selling the children to a woman. I don't know who, but she only wants boys. She uses them for something."

"Where are they being kept?"

He groaned in pain.

"Speak, or she'll start again," Brigid threatened.

Iain whimpered, actually whimpered. "They're at another house. The woman they're sold to wants them healthy."

"When is he taking them to her?" I asked, trying to keep the franticness out of my voice. We were getting answers, finally.

"Day after tomorrow," he groaned.

"One more question," I conceded, seeing that we were about to lose him. The madness was fading. "How did my father know about the syrens?"

"He's known about them for years. Since I joined him." He panted more, stopping to let out a wheezing chuckle. "I'm surprised you hadn't heard more about them, to be honest. But you never were good at listening."

Iain had been my father's right-hand man since I was a child, which meant my father had known about syrens for much longer than I had feared.

"Where are they leaving from?" I asked, trying to get the last of what I could from him.

Iain groaned but didn't answer. Brigid motioned at me to put the wax back in my ears. Duncan and I both reinserted the wax into our ears, and Sorcha began singing again. Iain thrashed more, and I noticed blood beginning to trickle out of his remaining ear.

Sorcha stopped, and Brigid again motioned to us.

"Where are they leaving from?" I repeated. "Are they leaving from here?"

"Brin...Brinemoor," he panted, his head falling on his chest again. His nose had begun to bleed as well.

"That's all we needed to know," I said, looking at Brigid

and Sorcha. "Thank you, ladies."

"What will we do with him now?" Brigid asked, her face hard. In the basin, I could see that Sorcha had begun to change back to her human form.

I spared a glance at Iain again before reaching to help Sorcha stand and helping her wrap a blanket around her small body. I looked back at Brigid. "He'll die now, don't worry."

She grinned at me, the bloodthirsty side of her coming out to play. "Aye, Captain. Good."

Chapter Thirty-Eight
BRIGID

Dry, human, and clothed once again, Sorcha walked into the kitchen, moving to stand beside me at the counter. We had killed Iain—or rather, Caelum had—and then he and the others had buried the body. Now, we stood, discussing our plans for how to stop Kellan.

"We need to get back to Brinemoor," Cameron said. "They have to be leaving out of the harbor there. We could stop them at the docks."

"There are too many ways for them to escape at the docks," Caelum said, rubbing his hand over his bearded chin. "We need to box them in somehow."

"We still have that ship we borrowed," I pointed out. "We can let them get out into open water and board them there."

Caelum shook his head. "His ship is likely much better armed than *The Voyager* is. We'd never stand a chance. That's why we haven't already targeted it."

"What if Sorcha and I were in syren form and disabled their ship somehow?" I asked. "We'll need to get the children off quickly, away from the violence."

"What if we used two smaller rowboats and Sorcha and Brigid in syren form?" Cameron suggested. "They disable the ship when it's out from the harbor, then we can board, send the children off in the smaller boats. We could sneak in, and it wouldn't be a firefight, at least. They wouldn't be expecting us to come in rowboats."

Caelum nodded. "That could work, but Sorcha and Brigid won't be able to communicate in syren form."

"Yes." I nodded. "I no longer have my song, so I can't speak to her under the water. We'll come up with a solution for that, not to worry."

"We'll need to relocate back to Brinemoor tomorrow," Duncan said. "If they're leaving at first light the following day, we need to be ready and set up before dawn."

"Aye, good idea," Caelum said. "We'll need to get rooms in pairs so we aren't all seen together. Who knows who my father is paying off to inform him? Anyone could be feeding him details."

"We should all get some sleep," Sorcha said softly. I knew what she had done today had affected her, not that she would ever let it show.

"Aye, that's probably a good idea," Caelum agreed. He looked tired, and I knew that today had worn on him too. I had seen the state Iain had been in, and I knew that Caelum would not have let Duncan do any of it for him.

We dispersed, Sorcha going back to our room. I stayed behind, catching Caelum's gaze. He stepped over beside me, and once everyone else had left the kitchen, I pulled him into my arms, tucking my chin into his chest. "You did what you had to."

He sighed, his breath tickling me as he tightened his arms around me. "I know. So did you two."

"We finally have some answers, and we have our plan."

"Aye, we do. Thanks to you," he said. He pulled me back to look at me intensely and leaned down to press a kiss to my lips. "Thanks to you."

"I'm just glad the wax worked," I said with a teasing smile. "Or I'd have never heard the end of it."

He rolled his eyes, but I knew my words had done their job in cheering him up. "Okay, now go get some sleep. We've got a long couple of days coming up."

"You sleep too," I said, poking his chest.

"I'm stealing you tomorrow night. I need you in my arms before we face down my father again," he said with a small smile.

I placed a hand on his cheek, meeting his eyes and hoping he could see the intensity in my gaze. "I like that plan, Captain."

He nudged me toward the bedrooms, nodding his head. "Go on, before I change my mind and drag you off somewhere."

I raised an eyebrow. "And if I wanted you to?"

He swallowed hard, shaking his head. He pointed a finger at me, but the grin on his face told me all I needed to know.

"You're trouble, *teine*. Go to bed."

With a final mischievous grin, I turned and walked into the room I was sharing with Sorcha. When I opened the door, she was sitting on the bed and greeted me with a small smile. I closed the door behind me and moved to sit next to her.

"Do you want to switch rooms again?" she asked.

I shook my head and scooted closer to her. "No, I'm sharing with you tonight. Is that okay?"

She grinned. "Of course. It'll be just like old times."

I answered with a grin of my own. We smiled at each other for a moment before the smile slipped from my face. As much as I wanted to protect Sorcha, I knew she was as fiercely independent as I was and would not be stopped or left behind. "We need to talk about today and the coming days."

She nodded as if she had been expecting it. "Aye, I figured we would. I know you want me out of this, but I want to help."

I sighed heavily. "I know, little one. And I want you to help. But you have to be careful. You promise me that you will be careful."

"I promise, Brigid," she said, taking my hands in hers. "You promise me the same, though."

"I promise," I replied, squeezing her fingers. "Now, are you okay after what you did today?"

"Aye," she replied. She tilted her head slightly, her eyes flitting up. "I won't pretend I enjoyed it, because I didn't. But I understand it was necessary, and I'm fine."

"Good, good." I nodded, swallowing hard. Sorcha deserved more than this violence, than the life of a syren. "What will you do after this? They likely won't take either of us back, you know that, right?"

She sighed. "Aye, I know they won't take us back. I'm not sure what I'll do. Maybe I'll continue to Bhodheas, try to find Owen."

"Does he know you were trying to reach him?" I asked. Maybe if things didn't work out with Caelum, Sorcha and I could travel to Bhodheas together. That would be nice.

"He did. But I have no doubt he's assumed the worst at this point," she said with a shrug. "And maybe he's moved on, but I'd still like to see him and know for myself."

"We'll get you there," I promised. "Once this is over, I'll take you to him myself if I have to."

She smiled widely. "You're a gem, Brigid. And what will you do after?"

"I don't know," I replied, looking down at my hands. "I don't know if Caelum would want any kind of future with me or not. I'll just take it day by day, I suppose. I'll need to find work and a place to live."

"He wants a future," she said, her voice strong with conviction. My heart wanted to believe her, but my mind questioned the reality in front of us. "I see how he looks at you, Brigid."

"I played a role in killing his friends," I said quietly. "And Duncan will never let me, or Caelum, forget it. Maybe we were over before we ever started."

"You don't know that," she said. "You two fit together perfectly. You…balance."

I tilted my head, thinking about her words. We did balance, as she put it. Caelum dimmed some of my fiery anger while still letting me make my own decisions, and I was the serious side to his irrepressible positivity. Maybe we would work after all. "We shall see, I suppose. We have to make it through the next few days first."

"Aye, that we do," she said. She turned in the bed and patted the mattress. "So, let's get to sleep so we can pull our weight. We can't let the boys show us up."

I grinned at her and leaned over to extinguish the lamp before crawling into bed. "Aye, they'll have to rise to meet us."

CHAPTER THIRTY-NINE

BRIGID

Still early in the morning, we made our way into Brinemoor, walking through a thick fog that had built up overnight. It certainly wasn't ominous at all.

We had all arrived separately, in pairs or groups of three. Kellan's men were likely watching, looking for our large party to enter the city, and we wanted to remain as inconspicuous as possible while we prepared. I arrived with Caelum, who, despite protests from the group over our recognizability, insisted on being with me. Not that I minded it. We were facing his father again tomorrow, and after what had happened the last time, I was relishing this time with him.

Before we had left the cottage, it was decided that we would split ourselves between the two inns in Brinemoor, with

Alan acting as a go-between for the groups. We all checked in at different times, under assumed names. Hopefully, it would be enough to keep Caelum's father and his men off our trail, but I had doubts. They knew we had taken Iain, and they knew what most of us looked like now. The plan was for all of us to stay in our rooms as much as possible. At dinnertime, the groups at each inn would meet and go over the plan again for the morning.

We had developed a rough plan before leaving the cottage, but based on any events that happened once we got here, things might have to change.

Now in our room, Caelum and I sat at the small table.

"Do you think tomorrow will go as planned?" he asked quietly. His shoulders were hunched up and his face was scrunched.

"I'm not sure," I admitted softly. Reaching out, I covered his hand with my own and laced our fingers together. "But we'll make it work."

"I can't lose anyone else. And I can't lose these children."

"He won't win, Caelum," I promised, squeezing his fingers with mine. The look of pure desperation on his face broke my heart, and I knew I would do anything in my power to ensure his father was stopped. "You and I will both do whatever it takes."

There was a long silence, then, "Why are you helping me with this?"

My brows furrowed. "What do you mean? Isn't that what you wanted?"

His eyes were fixated on the table in front of him, and he

wouldn't look at me.

"Caelum," I said firmly. He finally raised his eyes to look at me. "What's happening? Why are you asking this?"

"I…" he started. He took a deep breath. "I'm worried you're only helping because you think it's your only choice."

"My only choice?" I asked, raising an eyebrow. "There are children being stolen and sold. Did you really think I would just choose to leave once I found that out?"

"We don't know each other well enough for me to even know that, Brigid," he said. He pulled his fingers away from mine and ran a hand roughly through his hair. "That's the issue. I don't know what you would do."

I leaned back, looking at him. "You think we don't know each other well enough for you to trust that I'm here willingly?"

He nodded, and my heart splintered, filling my stomach like an iron weight. Somehow, this was worse than my belief that he would ask me to leave after Maddock's death.

Despite wanting nothing more than to curl up under the blankets on the bed we were to share, I knew there was more to Caelum's abrupt words than he was letting on. We had only known each other a few weeks, he was right about that, but it felt like it had been a lifetime. More importantly, it felt like it didn't matter how long we had known each other. While I didn't know Caelum's favorite food or what he had done for Yule as a child, I knew what mattered. I knew that he was a good man who cared deeply for others.

"What do you want to know about me, then?" I offered. "Because I know enough about you to know that you would do anything for those in need, you care deeply, and laugh loudly."

"And that's okay with you?" he asked. "You're fine with the fact that you know next to nothing about me apart from that I try to help others?"

I shrugged. "What else do I need to know?"

"I don't know, *anything* else?" he said, his voice turning frantic. He was panicking, and I could see it clearly in his eyes.

I took a deep breath and sat for a moment, working through what I could do. Standing, I bunched up the skirt of the long-sleeved cotton dress I was wearing and moved to straddle Caelum's broad thighs, settling down on them and pulling his face into my hands.

"Brigid," he said, his voice still frantic, but the tone lower. "What are you doing?"

"Look at me," I said, holding his cheeks in my palms. "We could have all the time in the world to get to know each other more once this is over, to learn all the little things about the other that make us unique. But for now, all I need to know about you is if you see a future for us after this. Do you?"

He was silent, his green eyes meeting my own as his hands rested on the creases of my hips. He swallowed hard, his throat bobbing. "Aye, I do. Or I want to, at least. I like you, *teine*, a lot. And I want to see where things can go with us without my father looming over us."

I leaned down, brushing my lips lightly over his forehead. "Yes, me too, Captain. And I want that. I want to spend my days with you, learning things about you. But right now, we have something more pressing that needs our attention. I enjoy being with you, and I want to stay with you, if you'll have me."

"I want that too," he whispered, leaning his forehead down

to rest against my chest. His hands tightened on my hips, and he grew hard, pressing against me between my legs. He lifted his head up to smile wickedly at me. "And there is definitely something else that needs our attention right now."

I raised an eyebrow at him. Oh, he wanted to play? Then play we shall. "Och, I don't know about that, Captain. You seem to keep leaving before the fun starts."

"No one to interrupt us this time," he said, skimming his hands up from my hips and tracing over my sides.

I rolled my hips, grinding down onto the hardness of him before pressing my lips gently to the corner of his mouth. "Then what are you waiting for?"

"Are you sure about this, *teine?*" he asked, his hands flexing on my hips and his face full of desire.

Moving my hands to his shoulders, I leveraged against him as I shifted my weight, lining up his body exactly where I wanted him beneath our clothes. I smiled at the groan that left his lips before leaning down to kiss him lightly. "Aye. I'm sure, Caelum."

Without another word, he turned his head, his lips on mine once again, and my eyes slid shut. One of his hands left my sides to weave into my hair, holding my head in place as he ravaged my mouth. His tongue traced over my lips, and I opened my mouth for him, tangling my tongue with his. My heart was beating absurdly fast in my chest, and my stomach fluttered at the new sensations.

Sliding my hands down from his shoulders as we kissed, I explored his chest and stomach. He was firm everywhere, muscles on top of muscles. My fingers grazed the top of his waistband, and he let out a rumbling noise from his chest that vibrated against my lips.

I pulled back with a smile, confidence and power oozing from my skin. "You like that, Captain?"

He leveled a look at me before moving both of his hands to my hips. He pressed them down as he jutted his hips up to meet me. He leaned in, and his breath tickled my ear, sending shivers down my spine. "Does it feel like I like that?"

"Not sure," I said, suddenly breathless. "Might need to take a closer look."

He shook his head at me, a smile on his face. Then his hands had shifted under my thighs and he was picking me up, standing in a fluid motion. "You're pure trouble."

I grinned at him before leaning in and pressing my lips against his neck, peppering kisses down his suntanned skin. The hair on his chin and neck felt rough beneath my lips, something I had never experienced before. I was used to smooth, supple skin and dainty touches with small hands. Caelum was firm and unyielding and knew exactly what he wanted. He also knew exactly what I wanted, and he was determined to give it to me.

Still holding me with my legs wrapped around his waist, he walked us over to the bed. He put one knee down to hold us before lowering me onto my back. I looked up at him leaning above me, all muscle and arousal, and my mouth went dry. Caelum was a sight, handsome and strong, but what was even more alluring was the kindness I knew was beneath his rugged exterior.

He looked down at me, his eyes unfocused and his mouth

slightly open. I laughed lightly before hooking a leg behind his thigh and pulling him down to me, his hands landing on either side of my head. "You're staring."

"You're worth staring at," he replied, his voice more gruff than usual. His eyes roamed down my body hungrily, and he tugged at the hem of my dress, bunched up near my thighs. "Can I take this off, *teine?*"

My entire body flushed, and I nodded, maybe a little too enthusiastically. I couldn't wait to feel his hands on my skin. "Only if you tell me what that means."

"It means fire," he said softly, his eyes molten green. He didn't waste a moment, leaning back on his heels and grasping the hem of the skirt. Slowly (too slowly, in my opinion), he pulled it up, up, up until the fabric was bunched around my ribs. He bent down, pressing his lips against the soft skin of my stomach. The contrast of the roughness of his hands and beard and the gentleness he touched me with were sending my mind into a spiral. There were so many sensations in my body warring for my focus.

"Still good?" he asked, looking up at me.

I nodded, not trusting myself to be able to speak. My chest was heaving with breathlessness, my mind still racing over his pet name for me. *Fire.* It made my body light up.

He leaned his head back down to my skin, continuing to press open-mouthed kisses to the skin as he pushed the dress further up. The fabric rose over my breasts, and his hand slipped under my back to pull me up to sitting. Our eyes met for a long moment, and my own heat and desire echoed in the swirling green of his eyes. In a motion smoother than I could have ever achieved, Caelum pulled the dress over my arms, leaving my body completely bare to him. My pulse quickened as his eyes skated over my body, darkening with obvious desire.

It made me feel powerful to see how much my body affected him, and I hope he felt the same about me looking at him.

The dress was tossed to the side, and he cupped my cheeks in his hands, pulling my face to him for another kiss. I let my eyes close as our lips moved together, losing myself in the sensations of Caelum touching me.

We pulled apart for breath, but stayed close, our breath mingling. Keeping our gazes locked, I reached down to tug at the collar of his shirt. "Off."

A crooked grin spread across his face, but he shook his head and pressed a kiss to one side of my mouth, then the other. "No, this is about you right now."

I wanted to see him, to touch him the same way he was touching me. I wanted us to feel good together. "Caelum…"

"Don't whine," he said, running his nose up the side of my neck. He caught my earlobe between his teeth and tugged, eliciting a sharp gasp from me. He gently pushed me back onto the bed and traced a hand down my thigh, squeezing it. "You're beautiful, Brigid."

I reached my hand up to rake through his hair, tugging slightly. "You're beautiful too, Caelum."

He smiled at me, and the pure joy on his face made my heart tighten. I had never had someone look at me like that, and now that someone—that *Caelum*—had, I never wanted to lose it.

Before I could think anymore, Caelum bent down and

firmly nudged my legs apart with his shoulders, settling on his stomach between my thighs. He bent his head to my inner thigh and started kissing there, gently at first, but getting firmer and rougher, alternating with nibbling bites that were making my chest heave and wetness gather between my thighs.

"You ever done this, *teine?*" he asked, pausing his kisses with his cheek resting on my inner thigh. He was so close to where I truly wanted him. I could feel his breath against my core.

"Yes, once," I said. My voice was already coming in pants, and he hadn't even started yet.

He raised an eyebrow at me. "Oh, really?"

Despite how aroused I was, I rolled my eyes at him. "I'm not as inexperienced as you seem to think I am."

"When have you had time to be with a man, huh?" he asked, going back to rubbing his cheek against my inner thighs, his beard chafing and scratching.

I raised an eyebrow back at him. "Who said it was a man?"

He stopped abruptly and just looked at me. I could see the wheels turning in his head as he worked through the possibilities. I was a syren, and I had spent the last ten years with the others. While we were all close, yes, we all still had romantic and sexual desires. Some of the others preferred to go to land for a night, while others, like me, found comfort in the familiarity.

"Och. Never thought of that, but it makes sense, I suppose," he said after a moment.

Without a word of warning, Caelum ducked his head between my thighs. His mouth landed on me, chasing all thoughts from my mind.

His tongue worked me over, taking me to heights I had never imagined I could reach. I was glad to be sharing this with him. I wanted it to last forever as he licked, sucked, and nibbled at my flesh.

He took me higher and higher, working his tongue against me. I groaned, my head pushing back into the bed. The sensations were overwhelming, his mouth hot against me, and yet it also wasn't enough. I wanted more.

"More, Caelum, please, more," I begged, reaching down and twisting my fingers through his hair to hold him there.

He obliged and began again with even more enthusiasm, making the coil in my stomach tighten, pressure building. I registered his hand moving against my thigh, but my brain was too far gone to realize what he was doing until his fingers joined his mouth, stroking and teasing.

His tongue slowed down slightly, but the languid intensity was not a reprieve, and I didn't want it to be. Gently, so gently, he eased one finger inside me, sliding it in and out as he continued to work me with his tongue. I was falling apart around him, and it was unlike anything I'd ever felt before. Another finger joined, and he sucked hard on the bundle of nerves at the apex of my thighs, and I was lost, white blinding my vision as I arched from the bed in ecstasy. He continued working me through my climax, bringing my body down from the high as skillfully as he had built it up.

My vision returned, but my breath was still coming in pants, and my body was tingling from head to toe. He pressed a gentle kiss between my thighs and then sat up, grinning at me as he pulled his fingers, still glistening, into his mouth. His eyes closed and he groaned. "You're delicious."

"Come here," I demanded. I hooked a leg around the back of his thigh and pulled him down on top of me, making his lips crash against mine. I could taste myself on his lips and tongue, I could feel the wetness still in his beard rub across my chin. It was delicious.

We pulled back for breath, and I reached for the bottom of his shirt, pulling it up and over his head with ease. I traced my hands over his chest, admiring his body. My hands landed on the waist of his pants, and I tugged.

His hands covered mine and made me stop. "Not tonight, *teine*. This was all for you."

"I want to touch you, Caelum," I breathed out. I wanted it more than I wanted air.

He pulled my hands away and pinned them above my head, moving to hover with his face over mine and a thigh between my legs. "You will. After this is all over. We're taking this slow, Brigid. You've never been with a man, and I'm going to do this right for you."

"I want to do it now."

He grinned, his eyes sparkling. "Oh, you do, do you? Well, that's too bad."

I knew it was childish, but I stuck my tongue out at him. I wanted to touch him and feel him against me and inside me, and he was refusing me because he was being a gentleman. Well, that wasn't the Caelum I wanted tonight.

He moved to hold both of my wrists in one of his large hands. He tapped the tip of my nose with his now free hand.

It still smelled like me, and my stomach fluttered with desire.

"The only thing you're doing now, *teine,* is going to sleep. If we make it through this, I promise you, I'll take you to bed, I'll strip off both our clothes, and I'll ravage you so thoroughly that you won't know your name or my name or which way is up." he nearly growled. "I promise you that."

"Promises, promises," I breathed, insanely turned on. My body wanted more, needed more, and I ground down against his thigh between my legs.

His eyes snapped down to my moving hips before he looked back up at me with another one of his crooked grins. "And what do you think you're doing?"

"Fixing the problem myself," I said with a coy smile. I kept moving my hips, consciously this time, using his thigh to get the pressure and friction I desperately needed.

"Don't let me stop you, then," he said, swallowing hard as he watched me. "But after, we go to sleep."

"We'll see," I said with a grin and began moving with more purpose. He had no idea what he had unleashed with his touch, with his body, with his words. But he would find out soon enough.

CHAPTER FORTY
CAELUM

The sun was just beginning to peek over the horizon as we made our way down to the docks. Not many people were out, and the ones who were paid us no real attention as we walked through the town. The men had their weapons strapped to their bodies, but it wasn't out of place, just as I had told Brigid. No one batted an eye. Once we reached the slip where our small rowboats were moored, we stopped.

"Be careful," I said, pulling Brigid into my arms. I squeezed her tightly, feeling her body against mine and hoping to the gods it wouldn't be the last time. After last night, I needed her more than I had ever needed anything in my entire life. Letting her go reluctantly, I pulled Sorcha in next, giving her a quick squeeze as well. "You both be careful."

Brigid locked eyes with me, her gaze intense. "You be careful as well, Captain."

I nodded, not trusting my voice to not blurt out something that was better said in private. Forcing myself to move, I turned to Duncan and Cameron. "Let's get started."

Near silently, we untied the boats, all of us loading into them. Once the boats were pushed off, Sorcha and Brigid began pulling their clothes off, shoving them into a bag at my feet. While I wanted to watch Brigid reveal her body and relish in seeing her again, I kept my eyes on the horizon. We had to stay focused. *I* had to stay focused.

With a long glance back at me, full of promise, the girls slipped over the side of the boat and into the cold water. Their heads disappeared under the dark surface, but after a moment, they resurfaced, their mouths now full of sharp teeth. Sorcha passed a concerned look to Brigid, who was wincing, and I realized that this was the first time Sorcha had seen Brigid's new transformation.

I let out a harsh breath, pushing back all my emotions as I assessed our situation. "All right, time to go."

Just like we had discussed, we quietly rowed our boats to the mouth of the harbor, where we could sit in wait, fairly out of sight, and see my father's ship when it left. From there, Brigid and Sorcha would disable the ship's rudders so that we could catch up. Thankfully for my nerves, we didn't have to wait much longer. After a while, a ship appeared from the far side of the harbor, slipping out silently into the water. I recognized it instantly, and bad memories of being aboard that ship as a boy threatened to overpower me. Pushing the memories down,

I tried to focus on what was happening now.

I motioned to Duncan in the other boat, letting him know they were coming. It was time to stop my father once and for all. He nodded back at me.

The next few minutes were agonizing as we waited for the ship to get out far enough from the harbor that they could not send for help. Finally, they were out in deep enough water, and we made our move, rowing the boats close to the hull. If anyone cared to look over the railing, they would have seen us. But like my father, his men were overconfident, and it would be their downfall.

In the water, I saw a shimmer flash by, and knew that Brigid and Sorcha were going about disabling the ship from beneath.

The ship slowed, turning unnaturally toward jutting rocks near the mouth of the harbor. Perfect. Sorcha and Brigid's plan had worked. A loud ripping and splintering sounded as Brigid and Sorcha attacked the ship, and we used the noise cover to toss lines and hooks over the side of the ship to secure our row boats to the railing. The crew began shouting, trying to figure out what the noise had been.

Quietly, we climbed the ropes, peering into portholes and gunning hatches as we moved, hoping to find any indication of where the children were. Duncan whistled softly, pointing at a porthole by his shoulder. The children.

I nodded confirmation. We continued climbing, slipping onto the deck quietly and unnoticed. My father's crew was moving about, trying to see what they had run into and how they could fix it. If this had been my crew, I would have reprimanded them for lack of attention until my voice went hoarse. But now, I was grateful for their inattention. Duncan and Cameron were at my back as we moved swiftly across the deck.

It was only a matter of time before we were spotted. As inattentive as my father's crew seemed to be, someone would spot us eventually. I could only hope we could get to the children before that happened.

As usual, my hopes were not reality.

"And where do you think you're going?"

I turned only to see my father standing on the upper deck, looking down at us. At his side was the big man, the one who had killed Maddock. My jaw clenched, and I saw red, furious that the giant oaf had survived after all. "Thought it'd be obvious. We're here to stop you."

In an instant, I whirled around, drawing my sword and blocking the cutlass that had been coming down toward me from behind. Our blades clashed as I backed him up toward the railing. With one final step and a harsh stab, he fell overboard. I couldn't stay to watch, but I saw flashes of scales, and the man disappeared faster than what was natural beneath the waves. The girls had taken him. Good. I grinned.

I turned back to the deck and immediately had to engage with another one of my father's men. Out of the corner of my eye, I noticed the rest of my crew doing the same, fighting against my father's men while the devil himself stood, watching with a grin.

As I continued fighting my father's men, I was trying to make my way to him, my eyes tracking him at his casual position on the upper deck. I needed to end this, and the best way to do that was to end him. In flashes of seeing him between fighting, I could see that the stump where his hand used to be was still heavily bandaged. I hoped that would benefit me in our fight.

The ship began to slant as it started to take on water from Brigid and Sorcha's destruction, and it tilted rapidly to one side. It threw us all off-balance, but I was able to recover quicker than my opponent, and cut him down with a slice to his throat. I kept moving to keep from thinking about what I had done, what I would continue to do.

My father was a skilled swordsman, but it required balance, and I doubted he had time to perfect his swordsmanship with the new adjustments. In a fair fight, he would have beaten me—not easily, but he would have beaten me. But now, adding the tilting of the ship, I had a slight advantage—one that I planned to utilize.

As I fought my way toward the stairs, I saw Cameron and Duncan coming out from below deck, a group of small boys huddled between them. I turned to the rest of our men on the deck and gave a sharp whistle. It was our signal to protect Cam and Duncan as they got the children off the ship.

Without anyone even so much as glancing at each other, we shifted our positions to keep my father's crew away from Cam and Duncan as they moved toward the side of the boat. Painfully slowly, I watched as child after child was lowered down until Duncan and Cameron finally followed. Thirteen children, all around age ten, with disheveled clothes and dirty faces, were in the boat.

I let out a heavy breath. They were safe. We had done it. Even if the rest of us didn't make it off this ship alive, we had done it.

Mission ultimately accomplished, I began fighting my way back to my father once again. Finally, I reached the stairs and rushed up them, only to be blocked by the giant oaf once again. I could hear my heart beating in my ears, rage flooding through my body as I remembered this man's sword swinging down and cutting through Maddock's chest. With a roar I barely heard, I charged him, swinging my sword with all my strength.

It was a stupid move. The giant merely stepped out of my way before moving back with a swing of his own. The metal clashed, and we fought, lunging back and forth.

Where this man was obviously bigger than me, I was faster and much more skilled. After lulling him into a pattern with my strikes, I spun quickly in the other direction, slicing my blade down across his chest, exactly as he had done to Maddock. And for good measure, I followed it up with a backswing of my hilt into the back of his neck.

Before his body even hit the deck, I was moving toward my father, bloodied sword dripping. I raised it to him, surprised that he didn't immediately fight back.

"Congratulations, my son," he said as I held the blade to his throat. "You're officially the pirate you swore you'd never be."

My teeth ground together, my jaw clenching, before lowering the sword and swinging my fist directly into his face. "I'm saving them from the likes of you, father."

He grinned as he righted himself, his teeth bloody. "Still a pirate. Just. Like. Me."

"I'm nothing like you."

"We'll see about that," he replied before pushing me back with his only remaining hand and finally drawing his sword against me. He swung toward me, and I met it, blocking his blow.

"Who are you selling them to?" I asked, our swords clashing together as we fought.

He pushed me back a step, and the grin on his face made my steps falter. "Oh, you mean you still haven't figured that out? Even with that beast of a syren in your midst? I thought you were *smart,* son."

"Who?" I gritted out, tightening my grip on my sword.

"Cliodhna. The syren queen. The goddess who transformed your precious lass into the monster she is," he said. His voice was gleeful.

My stomach dropped into my boots like lead. Brigid's queen was working with my father. Did that mean that she was too? I shook my head. No, I wouldn't go down that path. Brigid was trying to help us. There was no way she was working with him.

As if she knew I was thinking about her, I saw Brigid's head pop up over the waves below. She looked around, eyes violent and frantic. I couldn't help it, I had to know. I took a step backward toward the railing.

"Brigid, did you know?" I shouted at her, keeping an eye on my father.

She swam closer to the ship, looking up at me. She shouted back, "Know what?"

"He's working with your queen." A sick feeling clamped around my stomach. If Kellan had been working with Brigid's queen, did she know about this? Had she known all along? I tried to tamp down the feelings of betrayal—at least until I knew the facts.

Her eyes widened and her mouth fell open, and I knew without a doubt that she had not known either. I could barely hear her voice when she answered, "What?"

"He's working with Cliodhna!" I shouted, in case she truly had not heard me. My heart was racing as I wondered what could be happening in the water. If he was working with Cliodhna, then the other syrens could be on their way to fight against us, and Brigid and Sorcha were alone. My eyes frantically scanned the water, searching for any sign of the others.

Before I could see her response or offer any other information, my father had rushed me again. I turned my attention back to him.

CHAPTER FORTY-ONE
BRIGID

"He's right, you know. Kellan and I are working together."

At her voice behind me, I spun in the water to face my queen. The queen who had apparently been the root of this evil we were working to stop. Her face was bored, but I saw her eyes sparkle with violence. I knew that it truly had been her all along.

"Why?" I asked, twisting and moving through the water to keep away from her.

"Man has forgotten me," she said, bitterness lacing her voice. "And as man forgets, so does the world, and my powers weaken."

"So, you take children to remedy that?" I couldn't believe

what I was hearing. I had trusted Cliodhna, revered her. My heart shattered with betrayal.

She shrugged as if what she was doing was nothing of importance. "Their youth and purity fuels my power. The souls of men are tainted by their violence."

My eyes widened. No, it couldn't be. "You're killing them?"

All those times she spoke of her powers, she was talking about these children. I wanted to vomit. The powers she had given me were from *children*.

The water beneath me changed. We weren't the only ones here; there was someone coming up from below me. I turned to see Maira and the others popping above the water one by one. Cliodhna looked at them. "Stop her and her man. That ship and those boats must all sink, and everyone on them must die."

"My queen?" Kyla asked, her voice confused. She looked at me and then back at Cliodhna. "What's going on?"

"Why are you talking to her?" Maira asked Kyla, her voice angry. "She abandoned us."

I really hoped the others had nothing to do with this horror. Lip snarling, I got in Maira's face. As close as we had been, if any of us had helped Cliodhna or known about it, it would be her. "Did you know about this?"

She bared her teeth at me. "Know what, Brigid?"

"She is the one taking and killing those children I am trying to rescue," I hissed, pointing a clawed finger back at Cliodhna, who was watching us with a look that could only be described as boredom. Turning my back to her was likely a foolish move, but I needed to know the truth of the others' involvement. "We have been serving a queen who sacrifices children to sustain her powers."

Maira's eyes widened slightly for a moment, but she covered it by narrowing them suspiciously."And who told you that?"

"She did." My face was hot with anger, and my claws itched to dig themselves into flesh. I cast a quick glance back to the ship, where I could see Caelum fighting with his father. I wanted badly to help him, but I knew I needed to deal with my own fight first. Caelum was capable and could handle himself.

Maira whipped her gaze to Cliodhna, then to Kyla, then back to me, before landing on our queen once again. Her eyes were suspicious still, but I could see the frantic undertone in them. Perhaps she wasn't involved after all. "Is that true?"

Cliodhna shrugged again, swimming toward us. I turned to face her, and though my back was now to six other syrens, I trusted them more than I trusted our supposed queen. Cliodhna sighed as if we were annoying her. "Yes, yes, Brigid's little tale is true."

"You're using the life force of children?" Kyla asked, her voice quiet but deadly. Her face was pure rage, and I remembered that Kyla had been a mother when she had been changed. "Why?"

"Why not, my child?" Cliodhna laughed. The sound grated on my nerves, and I gritted my teeth, my fangs digging into the gums. "These are the children of men, in case you forgot. And if I remember correctly, that was the same reasoning you gave for not helping Brigid when she first came begging. So, I wonder what has changed."

"We didn't know you were involved in that," Kyla said, her voice faltering slightly. "Or we would have…"

"Would have what?" Cliodhna asked, sneering. She came even closer to us, nearly within my reach now. "What would you have done? Gone against me? Tried to stop me? You all are nothing without the powers I gave you. You were discarded like rubbish until I saved you. You all owe everything to me."

"We owe you nothing," I snarled, fighting the urge to lunge forward and push my claws through her chest. It would likely do nothing but anger her. "All you care about is becoming more powerful."

"You think you can mutiny against me, girl?" Cliodhna curled her lip up and scoffed. "I created you, I gave you purpose, and this is how you repay me? The others will never follow you."

I looked at the others, their eyes flitting between our queen and me, no doubt trying to figure out what was happening and whose side to take.I hoped they believed me and would help me. I doubted that Sorcha and I would be able to fight all six of them and come out alive. "I'm not asking them to follow me. They deserve to know the truth about you and decide for themselves what to do."

"And what's this truth, child?" She rolled her eyes.

"You don't care about us. We're a means to your end."

She laughed loudly, throwing her head back. "Of course you are a means to an end! I created you for a reason—to serve me, not to run about with men and get in my way. It's too bad the men I sent when you first saved that boy failed."

The fishermen…she had been the one to tell them about me? She had sent them to Caelum's cottage? Anger and betrayal burned within my chest.

"We will not help you stop them like you asked," Kyla said

firmly. "Brigid may have left us, but she's never lied to us. And she's certainly never killed a child."

Cliodhna rolled her eyes again, and my fingers twitched beneath the water, itching to pluck the eyes from her skull. "I truly don't understand what is so important about these children. They are nothing to you, and their sacrifices allowed me to create you, to save you."

"Then I would have rather died." Kyla looked at me, determination clear in her eyes and the set of her jaw. "What do you need from us, Brigid?"

Cliodhna whirled at me, rage in her eyes. "You see what you've done? You've destroyed this family."

I met her gaze with anger of my own. "No, you did that on your own. I merely opened their eyes to the monster you are."

She growled and lunged for me, her talons out. I was ready for her, though. Moving swiftly, I avoided her strike.

She growled in frustration, moving toward me once again. We danced in the water, both above the waves and below, swiping at each other and dodging. She was fast, but I was fueled by anger so palpable I could feel it radiating through the water. I couldn't let her live. She was a monster. Urging my body to move faster, I pushed harder, trying to get closer. My claws reached out, swiping at her side. They glanced off her side, scraping slightly, but I knew it wasn't enough to do any damage.

If anything, it just seemed to irritate her. She paused in her movements, tilting her head as she studied me. "You are so insignificant. This bores me."

With a wave of her hand, magic pushed through the water,

driving me back until I could no longer make out the features of the others. Sorcha looked back to me before moving to take my place in the fight.

Recovering from the blast of waves, I hurried back toward Cliodhna to help Sorcha. But I was too late. Sorcha tried to dodge a swipe of claws, but she must have moved the wrong way. I could only watch in horror as Cliodhna's claws dug into her chest. My friend went still, and the water began to turn red around her.

No. *No.*

I surged forward, pulling Sorcha away from Cliodhna and into my arms. *No!*

Cliodhna pulled away with a frustrated scream. "Insolent girl! Now look at what you've done."

I pulled Sorcha more into my arms, holding her to me. My eyes blurred and my throat burned. "No…no, Sorcha."

"What have you done?" Maira hissed at Cliodhna, moving forward toward us. "Sorcha was innocent."

"She sided with the traitor, that is not innocent," the icy goddess replied, watching us intently. She seemed disinterested yet again, not caring that she had just killed one of her own. Her icy eyes flashed back to me, retribution burning in them like blue fire. "This is your fault."

I heard the words, but they echoed in my ears as I held the body of my friend in my arms. Blood spread in the water around us, and tears ran down my cheeks, landing on her face. My vision was blurry as I looked down at her.

Sorcha blinked slowly, looking up at me. "Bri…Brigid?"

"Yes, Sorcha, what is it?" I sobbed. "What do you need?"

"Find Owen," she said. "Tell him...tell him what happened."

I nodded furiously as my tears continued to fall. "I will. I'll find him, and I'll tell him everything. I'll find him, I promise."

"Love you," she whispered, closing her eyes.

"No, no," I sobbed. I shifted her so I could tap my palm against her cheek. "Open your eyes, stay with me."

A hand touched my shoulder, and I jumped. I whirled, ready to fight whoever had touched me, but it was Kyla. There were unshed tears in her dark eyes. "She's gone, Brigid. She's gone."

With a snarl, I let Sorcha's body fall from my arms into the water, and I lunged at Cliodhna, my claws out. She wasn't ready for me this time. Swiping at her face, satisfaction flooded me when my talons ripped at her flesh.. She cried out in pain as blood began to pour from the wounds, staining her white hair pink. Her hand clapped against her face, staunching the blood flow slightly.

Her eyes were like daggers as she glared at me. "You will regret that."

"I highly doubt that," I bit back. Moving toward her again, I vowed to kill her for what she had done. Sorcha had been innocent. She'd done nothing to Cliodhna. The queen's lack of caring would be her downfall. *I* would be her downfall.

Before I could reach Cliodhna, she dipped beneath the waves and shot off toward the open sea. She would not escape my wrath. I moved to dive beneath the water to follow.

"Brigid." Kyla's soft voice stopped me in my tracks before my head dipped below the surface.

Looking after where Cliodhna had disappeared for a moment, I eventually turned back to the others. Kyla's eyes were shining with tears as she held Sorcha's body in her arms. The rich color of Kyla's skin made Sorcha's body look all the more pale.

"Why didn't you help her?" I asked, my voice cracking. "You were all *right there.*"

"We need to put her to rest," she said quietly. She ignored my statement and pleas.

Hurt washed through me. My revenge and anger could wait; Sorcha deserved better than this. I nodded, looking down at my hands beneath the waves. My hair fell down into my face. I didn't move to push it away. "Yes, of course."

"What will we do?" Maira asked, her own voice uncharacteristically quiet. "Sea or land?"

My head snapped up at her words. "I don't want her in the sea. Cliodhna will find some way to taint that."

"Then we'll bury her on land," Kyla promised, her voice stern. She looked over her shoulder. Cam was moving in an empty rowboat toward us. "Let's get her on the boat."

Chapter Forty-Two

CAELUM

I don't know what pushed me to look over the railing. Looking back, I think Brigid's sorrow and anger had traveled through the water and had become palpable. Whatever the case, my eyes managed to catch the moment she clung to a small body as she flung her head back and screamed. It was a sound I would never forget. I watched as she swam toward the rowboat in the distance, unable to process what I was seeing. Sorcha was dead.

From the deck, I couldn't hear what was said, but Cam must have convinced her to give Sorcha to him; he took the small girl from Brigid's arms and pulled her up into the rowboat with him and Finn, who had turned the children away.

"Och, such a young one," my father said, smacking his lips.

I turned back to him, my anger and energy suddenly revived. "This is your fault."

"Actually, no," he said, and lunged at me with his sword. I blocked it with my own, and our fight had begun anew.

I shoved him back with my sword before I thrust at him. He blocked me, pushing me out to the side and exposing my midsection, which he quickly took advantage of, trying for a thrust of his own. But I was faster and stepped out of the way. We circled each other, taking any opening the other left, metal clanging together as we fought.

A quick sidestep and a slash down, and I had landed the first hit—barely. My blade nicked the side of his cheek at the top of my arc, but he stepped back far enough to avoid the blow. He countered with a step forward and another thrust, but his balance was off, and the sword angled down toward my thighs instead. I dropped the tip of my blade and countered, knocking his out to the side. I followed it up by bringing my arm down, slamming the pommel into his wrist.

The sword fell from his hands, landing at his feet, and he looked at me, anger and desperation written across his face. He narrowed his eyes. "You've not won yet."

Like the desperate fool he was, he charged at me. Without a sword, he was defenseless, and I could have easily killed him. Perhaps I should have, but he was still my father, and the moment of hesitation I had was enough to change my mind. I blocked his punches with my forearms rather than my blade before sweeping my leg out and catching his ankle, sending him crashing to the deck.

Lip curled in a snarl, I kicked the sword away, the metal

clattering across the wooden deck. Finally. I pointed my sword down at my father. "Yield, and I'll not kill you."

"You're weak, son," he said, the cut on his face weeping blood. He wiped at it, smearing crimson across his only remaining hand. "I would never give you this mercy."

"I told you, I'm nothing like you," I gritted out. I didn't want to kill him, but I would if I needed to.

"Well, I'll not yield," he said. In an instant, he drew a dagger from his belt and swiped at me.

I jumped back but wasn't fast enough. The metal sliced into the skin of my lower leg, cutting deep. The pain jolted through my body, but I gritted my teeth and tensed the muscles. Despite my earlier words, I knew I couldn't let him live at this point. I knew he would just continue the fight, and I needed to end this. Any sentimentality between us had been lost long ago. Now, he was just trying to kill me.

With a kick, I knocked the dagger from his hand, and without hesitation, plunged my sword through his chest. His body tensed before going limp, blood trickling slowly out of his lips. His eyes stared up at me for a moment before looking off into nothingness. I stepped back and turned away without looking, my stomach heaving at what I had just done.

I had just killed my father. Gods, I had killed him.

I staggered over to the railing, taking gulping breaths of sea air, attempting to stop the bile turning sour in my throat. He had deserved it, but that didn't make the pain and confusion any less real.

I saw Brigid in the water, still at the rowboat, gently stroking Sorcha's hair while Cam spoke softly to her. I continued taking breaths, watching her as I tried to calm my racing heart and churning stomach. She calmed me, even from a distance. Brigid was my solace, and after this, I was never going to let her go. I just needed to tell her that and hope she would feel the same.

I tried to avoid looking at Sorcha's small body as they held her in the boat. I looked at the other syrens, studying them as they huddled together away from the boat, watching the scene before them. My gaze kept flitting about, doing anything to keep from looking back at my father behind me, lying on the deck with my sword still in his chest.

I watched Brigid nod shakily and pull back from the boat, and Cam turned it back toward the harbor. I could see the silver shining in her eyes and the wetness on her cheeks. She floated in the water, her tail swishing beneath her, as she wiped furiously at her eyes. I wanted to reassure her, to hold her, but we weren't finished here yet.

The other syrens came up beside her, but she pushed them away, directing them to follow the boat, which they did. I only hoped that meant they were on our side now. I doubted she would have pointed them toward Cam and the children if they weren't.

Behind her, the water swirled, and a white figure swam through the water, a silvery tail following—Cliodhna. I straightened up, leaning over the railing as much as I could.

"Brigid, look out!" I shouted, seeing the white-haired syren shoot down into the water before surging up from beneath Brigid.

Before she could react, the queen had Brigid in her grasp

and was pulling her down into the depths until I could no longer see her beneath the dark waves. The look of terror on Brigid's face as she was pulled down was haunting, and I could do nothing to save her from my place on the ship.

My heart stopped. This feeling was nothing like I had felt before, nothing like I had experienced moments ago with my father's death, or even with Maddock's. No, this was much different.

She was gone. Brigid had been taken.

THE STORY ISN'T OVER YET...

Caelum has a lot to do after that ending.

Download the extended epilogue from his POV here:

FŌLLŌW JESSICA S. TAYLŌR

Stay connected with Jessica:

SUBSCRIBE TO THE NEWSLETTER:
https://www.subscribepage.io/jessicastaylor

BOOKBUB:
make sure you enable New Release Alerts to get emails about sales and releases
https://www.bookbub.com/authors/jessica-s-taylor

WEBSITE:
https://authorjessicastaylor.com

INSTAGRAM:
https://instagram.com/authorjessicastaylor

FACEBOOK:
https://facebook.com/authorjessicastaylor

FACEBOOK GROUP:
https://facebook.com/groups/syrenscove

TIKTOK:
https://tiktok.com/@authorjessicastaylor

OTHER WORKS BY
JESSICA S. TAYLOR

Seas of Caladhan Duology:

The Syren's Mutiny (Book 1)
The Captain's Revenge (Book 2)

Standalones:

Hollowed: A Sleepy Hollow Reimagining

Acknowledgements

I first want to say that this would not have been possible in the slightest without the encouragement and support from my friends. Gabbie, Leah, Leez, you ladies are my best friends, and I am so grateful for all you've done for me to support me and encourage me and lift me up in this process.

I'd also be amiss if I didn't thank my husband for support this crazy adventure and feeding me goldfish and pizza rolls as I write. You're the best, tater. Thank you.

To my family, namely my twin, who always supports me no matter what, my grandma, who got me into reading (and smut) in the first place, and my parents, for never batting an eye when I told them I wanted to be a writer, both when I was 13, and again at 24.

I always have to thank the most wonderful ladies I've ever had the pleasure of knowing through Bookstagram. Leah, Ashley, Bethany, Laura, Reva, and the rest of the Cult, you guys light up my day whenever I see messages from you.

To Scarlett, thank you for believing in me and pushing me to do better.

Finally, to anyone reading this. Thank you. From the bottom of my heart, thank you.

ABOUT THE AUTHOR

Jessica S. Taylor was born and raised in Kentucky, but has been moving with the waves and is currently residing in southern Maine with her husband and cat, Nebula.

Jessica's love of reading and writing began at a young age with the help of her grandmother and her local library, and she hasn't looked back since. Similarly, her love for pirates, mermaids, and all things fantasy have only grown more intense with time.

Subscribe to her newsletter and connect with her on all the platforms over on her website at www.authorjessicastaylor.com

PRAISE FOR
THE SYREN'S MUTINY

"Taylor's deftly told fantasy romance will draw readers in from
the first page to the last."
- PUBLISHERS WEEKLY BOOKLIFE REVIEW

"Jessica S. Taylor introduces us to a vivid and beautifully
detailed new world full of vengeful syrens, quick-witted
pirates!"
- WHITNEY DEAN, author of The Four Kingdoms series

"Pirates and sirens and bad guys, oh my! Jessica S. Taylor has
blessed us with a fresh and enticing spin on pirates and sirens."
- MORGAN GAUTHIER, author of A Song of Shadows &
Starlight

"The Syren's Mutiny gave a fresh take on syrens, pirates, and
rivalries that drive the story forward. A magnificent read."
- LAURA H. @elitereading

"A memorable debut with beautiful world-building, flawed
yet loveable characters, and a delicious, slow burn romance."
- JENNY HICKMAN, author of A Cursed Kiss